A

Murder of

Convenience

Hannah Blank

A

Murder of

Convenience

HIGHTREES
BOOKS

HIGHTREES BOOKS
Imprint of Prism Corporation
New York

Published by Hightrees Books,
   an Imprint of Prism Corporation
   P.O.Box 20775, Cherokee Station
   New York, New York 10021-0075

All characters and incidents in this book are fictional; no references to
actual persons are intended. The background regarding treatment of
Jews in France during World War II is consistent with history.

Library of Congress Catalog Card Number 99-90046

Blank, Hannah
A Murder of Convenience /
Hannah Blank

p.cm.

ISBN 0-9652778-1-X

Printed in the United States of America

10 9 8 7 6 5 4 3 2 1

For my husband and best friend Leonard

HISTORICAL NOTE

France and Great Britain entered the war against Hitler and the Axis in 1939, after German tanks rolled into Poland. Hitler, pursuing no less than world domination by the "pure" German "Aryan" race, invaded and quickly subjugated one European country after another: Austria, Czechoslovakia, Poland.

In May 1940, German tanks rolled across the frontiers of Belgium, Holland and Luxembourg, and invaded France. French and British military forces could not stop the Germans, who greatly outnumbered them in tanks, planes and men. British air squadrons lost more than half the total aircraft of the Royal Air Force in one night of fighting.

France fell in one month. She might have held on longer, but the French military command was thoroughly disheartened. The French Prime Minister resigned and Marshal Pétain formed a new French government to beg Hitler for an armistice. In England, A French Resistance movement in exile was led by a then-obscure French general, Charles deGaulle. A fierce and courageous underground Resistance movement in France could not overcome the Germans.

In Winston Churchill's words, "Millions of (French) civilians and demobilized soldiers, trudging past the wreckage and rubble of defeat, returned home to a life of hunger and privation while the German army of occupation lived on the fat of their land...

"The (French) admirals might have fled to British ports to keep the Navy fighting but they preferred to obey orders from the Pétain government, even when this meant fighting the British, their allies of only a week before." In the separate peace France made with Hitler, more than half of France was occupied by the Germans.

The unoccupied portion, which included Paris, was administered by the so-called Vichy government, composed of Frenchmen whose antisemitic zeal sometimes exceeded even that of the Germans. The Vichy government enacted a series of laws identifying and restricting Jews before shipping them to their deaths.

French citizens who were Jewish, (even veterans who had fought for France in the previous war), and Jews from conquered countries who had escaped to France, were identified, rounded up, and deported to Nazi death-camps with the cooperation and collaboration of many of the French people.

More than 75,000 Jews, including some 11,400 infants and children, were deported from France by the Germans, often with the complicity of the French. Of the nearly 76,000 Jews shipped from France to the death-camps, less than 2,300 survived.

Heroic efforts in England had been going forth since the 1930's to rescue refugee children from Germany and other places of risk. When the British government learned that Jews were to be deported from Vichy France, the British War Cabinet authorized admission of 500 children; but the Vichy government refused them exit permits.

The French role in helping the Germans dispose of Jewish countrymen was not well-known abroad until many years later, and is still not fully acknowledged in France.

World War II ended in Europe in 1944, but even a decade later, poverty and deprivation still existed widely in France. In the 1950's, the time period of this novel, young Americans who came to Paris on the G.I.Bill or Fulbright scholarships or parental generosity found that their dollars went very far. But they sometimes encountered animosity and envy.

PART

ONE

1

With only one boarder, and he a taciturn individual who seemed indifferent to improving his minimal French, breakfast had concluded quickly: Madame Fleuris and Monsieur Fleuris, the only other two at table, rarely spoke to each other. Germaine was now shuffling between dining-room and kitchen clearing the table.

Madame Fleuris sat rigidly on her habitual perch in the salon, a small once-gilded salon chair, staring through the chink in the gauze curtains down into the courtyard below, looking out for her newest paying guest. Mademoiselle Kugel had left a month's payment in advance the previous Friday; she was supposed to be moving in today after fetching her trunks from storage at the train station where she had checked them while she gallivanted around France for a couple of weeks. Those young Americans! It was obscene the money they had. And the number of Jews! It was disgusting.

A steady rain was falling, forming puddles in the dimples of the gray cobblestones. A patch of dismal gray sky was visible over the dismal gray walls. Her prison. Her lifelong prison thanks to that fool of a husband of hers. He had long ago dissipated the *dot* she had brought with her as a young bride more than forty years before, and then he had lost in vapid extravagances and stupid investments whatever of his own holdings had remained after raging inflations and devaluations of the franc had ravaged them.

When her parents and his had first arranged this marriage of convenience it never occurred to her or to her family that in her married life she would be anything but well-off. They could not have foreseen that in her old age she would be reduced to catering to crass young Americans; even to *Jews!*

Yet here she was, waiting for one now. And relieved enough to get her, a giggling young American girl who was pleased by everything and clearly was very rich. It galled Madame Fleuris to be serving a Jew, and although about to benefit from it, she envied and begrudged the young girl's wealth. But it was already mid-September, the August vacations were well over, and she was worried that she still had two rooms vacant, the two small *chambres de bonne.* formerly maids rooms, on the attic floor. Even with the numbers of foreign students growing each year since the war there were fewer who could afford decent accommodations than there were impoverished old ladies with cavernous apartments to provide them. Cheap. Except for the Americans the students only seemed to want cheap. Not necessarily good.

She was praying that the *Liberté* would disgorge someone who would apply for one of her rooms. The docking of the *Liberté* might be her last chance to fill her *pension* to full capacity for the school year.

A week before the *Liberté* was due to dock at LeHavre, Madame Fleuris had taken the precaution of calling upon the clerk at the students housing bureau to check that her listing for the *pension* Fleuris was still in place, and was accurate. With a modest tip discreetly passed to the clerk she encouraged the girl to give prominence to her listing to any suitable applicants, by which she particularly meant Americans.

Of the five large apartments in the building, one to a floor, the Fleuris apartment on the fourth floor was the only one that had been turned into a *pension.* The widow Poivriere had lived alone in her large place on the fifth floor ever since Monsieur Poivriere elder had died and the son Pierre had married and moved to Lille.

Madame Poivriere did not need to rent out rooms or serve strangers. She had an income of her own, and she had been left a good income by her husband. That was the difference.

Madame Fleuris had offered a choice to Mademoiselle Kugel between the two available bedrooms in the apartment itself. (The other two were occupied, one by the guest who had moved in earliest, the taciturn Monsieur Branford Duane Lee the Third, the other by Madame and Monsieur Fleuris.) The two *chambres de bonne* under the eaves were not in question, obviously too modest for this particular customer.

The rooms Madame Fleuris showed Mademoiselle Kugel were similar to each other in furnishings and size, and in fact comprised what had been intended to be the master suite, with one chamber for the master and one for madame, connected by a common door which could be locked.

Each room was large and of elegant proportions, and Mademoiselle Kugel had bubbled enthusiastically over both of them. She had enthused over the proximity of the apartment on Rue des Ecoles to the Sorbonne where she would be taking *la cours de la civilisation française pour les étrangers*, she had raved over the charming *vrai* French salon in the apartment where Madame Fleuris had indicated that they would all be taking coffee Sunday afternoons speaking French, together with the Fleuris' married daughter Lucille, son-in-law Philippe and grandson Jean-Francois.

(Madame Fleuris thanked *le bon dieu* every day for her son-in-law Philippe Jumelle, a decent well-situated man who had been willing to take their daughter despite the very modest *dot* they could provide her. The fact that he had an older brother who was a stain on the Jumelle escutcheon was of no importance to her, it was indeed the reason Philippe had been willing to take Lucille. And she thanked God that the couple had borne a son rather than a daughter so that his future match would be the other family's expense.)

Mademoiselle Fleuris quoted Mademoiselle Kugel the monthly rate. It included breakfast every day, midday dinners Monday through Saturday, afternoon coffee on Sunday, bedlinens changed every two weeks, and one bath per week. After only the briefest reflection, noting the connecting door between the two rooms, Mademoiselle Kugel opted to take not one but both rooms: one for herself and one for her clothes.

She agreed without question to paying for two rooms double the rate for one room, even though food for only one person would be provided. Madame Fleuris was grateful for the windfall; but the young girl's *insouciance* at the overcharge aroused her envy and scorn.

Madame Fleuris graciously granted her new boarder a second bath per week free. Other *pensionnaires* would be charged one hundred fifty francs for a second bath. (Nobody could have more than two baths per week whatever they might be willing to pay, for fear the gas water heater couldn't handle a larger load.)

Mademoiselle Kugel also requested that her bedlinens be changed weekly rather than every other week. While viewing this as typical Jewish aggressive bargaining, Madame Fleuris, still well ahead on the deal, reluctantly assented.

Mademoiselle Kugel paid in cash in advance for one month, withdrawn from an immense wad of thousand- and five-thousand franc notes), and arranged to move in the coming Monday. She would have to fetch her trunks from the storage facility at the Gare du Nord where she had deposited them upon arriving on the boat-train from LeHavre.

To Madame Fleuris it was painfully ironic that after the French had done their best to rid themselves of the Jews, handing more than seventy-five thousand of them over to the Germans to be shipped to the camps in the east, now, a mere dozen years later, Jews were pouring into France in greater and greater numbers along with all the other Americans, flaunting their dollars and their crass tastes.

There was even talk that the stupid French populace might actually once again elect a Jew as its president – Mendes-France! Madame Fleuris had not yet fully forgiven her compatriots for electing as Premier the Socialist and Jew Leon Blum, years before. At least he had gotten his comeuppance: he had been arrested and put on trial for causing the French defeat in 1940, after he left office, amd he had been incarcerated in Buchenwald.

Madame though sitting very still was struggling inwardly with anger and anxiety resulting from a trip earlier that morning to the rooms under the eaves on the sixth floor.

She had learned from her maid Germaine who had heard it from Madame Poivriere's maid Gabrielle that Madame Poivriere had given a listing to the student housing bureau for her vacant attic room, with no apartment privileges, at a very cheap rate.

Madame Fleuris was concerned that Madame Poivriere's would compete with her own *chambres de bonne,* which of course were priced more dearly because any occupants would be *pensionnaires,* provided with breakfasts, dinners, a bath per week, bedsheet changes every other week, and the use of the W.C. in the apartment. If a student came with both listings in hand, Madame Fleuris wanted to be prepared to point out in detail all the shortcomings of choosing the Poivriere room.

But one inadvertent glance at the padlocked door at the far end of the hall near the sink had careened her mind back to a hot and humid day in July of 1942 when she and Madame Poule the concierge had made repeated trips up five flights of stairs and down, between the apartment on the first floor and the maids' rooms under the eaves on the sixth floor. On each climb up they were laden with clothing, silver-framed photographs, boxes of trinkets, from the apartment on the first floor. They left the furniture, and the Turkish carpets. They were going to rent out the apartment, furnished, to foreigners who would pay more dearly than any French.

The two women dumped each load willy-nilly in the small unfurnished room upstairs, then went back for more. Later they would sift through the piles for booty, but at that moment it was urgent to empty the apartment of anything per-

sonal. That done Madame Fleuris had Germaine clean the
apartment thoroughly, scrub down the kitchen, polish the
ponderous mahogany furniture and the parquet floors.

Madame Fleuris now made a shaky way down the two
flights of stairs to her own apartment without having inspected
Madame Poivriere's vacant room.

As Madame Fleuris stared down at the courtyard an eerie figure glided into view, a figure in a hooded ankle-length
black coat. The face was hidden in the folds of the voluminous hood.

Moments later the doorbell sounded and Germaine was
ushering in the hooded figure, who when she removed the
monklike coat proved to be a young girl with thick dark hair
pinned together at her nape, a sallow complexion and large
solemn brown eyes. Germaine took the girl's coat, which was
glistening with raindrops. She introduced the girl as Mademoiselle Miriam Winter, a student seeking a *pension.* The girl's
voluptuous figure was clad in a black turtleneck sweater and a
sweeping black wool skirt, a typical uniform, Madame thought
scornfully, of Left Bank Communist intellectuals.

A chill had passed through Madame Fleuris at the sight
of this girl. Her solemn dark eyes, her unblinking gaze, something frighteningly familiar about that face reminded Madame
of the Maisel child whose family had been taken away on that
day in July 1942. She would now be about the age of this
young woman before her, and might look like her. "You're a
student, Mademoiselle?"

"Yes."

She had not responded, "Yes, Madame."

"You"ll be going to the Sorbonne?"

"No. The Ecole des Beaux Arts."

"You are an American?" The girl's accent was not unmis-
takably American but her rude manners were!

"Yes."

"You were born in America?"

"*Qu'importe?*"

What did it matter? It mattered a great deal to Madame Fleuris! But she ignored the rudeness. She needed two more boarders. "You'll feel *chez vous* here, we already have two Americans." If the girl decided to move in, Madame Fleuris would check her passport for birthplace.

"I would like to see the room."

"Of course, of course. The two rooms I have remaining are *chambres de bonne*, upstairs."

She led Mademoiselle Winter up the two flights. This time she was careful to avert her eyes from the padlocked room at the left end of the hall.

She had barely removed a large old-fashioned key from her apron pocket to unlock the first of her rooms, which were the middle one and the room on the far right, when Germaine came up the steps her carpet-slippers flapping to inform her that a young man had just arrived who was seeking a room, a very handsome well-dressed young man, American, *tres propre*, who said he was a friend of Monsieur Tobey Peters. Should she bring him right up here?

Madame Fleuris assented. She was gratified. If both Americans decided to stay, her *pension* would be complete before dinner! She would have to dispatch Germaine to the market for another rabbit for the stew.

The new arrival, Monsieur James Giardini, was in his mid-twenties, tall, slender and elegant in a British raincoat, and with a handsome friendly face.

Monsieur Giardini and Mademoiselle Winter exchanged little smiles. The smile looked odd on the visage of the young woman whom Madame Fleuris had already decided was strange, if not sinister. And as for Monsieur Giardini, if he were a friend of Monsieur Peters, the odds were good that this young man was also a pederast, though if anything like his friend, well-mannered and discreet. To Madame Fleuris if appearances were acceptable then behavior could be overlooked.

The two young people inspected each of the rooms Madame Fleuris had unlocked, pronounced either of them acceptable and in fact there was nothing to distinguish one from the other. Each was very small, with a white tile floor, crowded with a narrow bed on which was a straw mattress. An armoire was shoved up against the window. It would have to be moved if one wanted to open or close the swinging window or the shutters. Completing the furnishings leaving no space unfilled were a small stuffed armchair, an alcohol-burning stove (the sole heat source for each room) and a small table-lamp on a commode. Extra bottles of alcohol sat on top of the armoire.

The commode, Madame mentioned, contained a chamber-pot. Of course her *pensionnaires* were welcome to use the W.C. in the apartment but perhaps it might be inconvenient during the night to go down and up the two flights. Germaine would be emptying the chamber pots in the mornings when she did the rooms. Madame showed them where the *minutière* button was on the wall. The hall-light would remain lit for one minute after pressing the button.

The monthly price for attic room, breakfast and dinner was thirty thousand francs per month, or about seventy-five dollars at current black market rates.

Each of the Americans expressed an interest in taking one of the rooms. Mademoiselle Winter as the earlier arrival was given first choice. She spoke for the room at the far right, leaving Monsieur Giardini the room in the middle.

Monsieur Giardini asked who occupied the other rooms. Madame was calm as she remarked on the first room by the sink, the one that was padlocked, that it was "dead storage". The next, to the left of the room which would now be Monsieur Giardini's, was vacant. It was the property of Madame Poivriere, who had purchased it from another resident in the days when she kept two live-in servants. Madame Fleuris did not trouble to mention that the room was available for rent. The room to the right of Monsieur Guardini's and between him and that chosen by Mademoiselle Winter was also owned by Madame Poivriere; it was occupied by her maid Gabrielle.

Madame Fleuris led her two new *pensionnaires* from the

sixth floor down the wide oak staircase to the Fleuris' fourth floor apartment, where Madame Fleuris would make sure to collect a month's payment in advance and to make very clear the rules of the house.

Before sitting down to business Madame showed the two young people around the apartment: a huge old-fashioned kitchen, where Germaine, flour up to her elbows, was rolling out a large pastry round; a formal salon furnished with straight-backed gilt salon chairs, a forbidding dark satin damask sofa, and various antique desks and occasional tables where they would take coffee with the family on Sunday afternoons; a bathroom with its gas-heater suspended right over the tub, where one bath per week was allowed; and in a separate closet, the W.C.

Monsieur Giardini excused himself for a moment to make use of the latter, as Madame Fleuris led Mademoiselle Winter into the large dining room. They sat down at the ponderous mahogany table. When Monsieur Giardini joined them a few moments later he grinned at his compatriot and said in English, "Miriam, you've just got to go in to the W.C., pretend you have to if you don't, you'll see what I mean." The girl looked relieved to be told to go to the W.C. as if she had wanted to but had been too embarassed to ask.

They sat around the dining-room table, its polished mahogany gleaming through an ecru lace cloth, as Madame Fleuris elucidated the house rules.

No visitors of opposite sex in the rooms ever.

No visitors of same sex in the rooms after five p.m.

No cooking in the rooms.

No washing laundry in the landing-sink or in the apartment-bathroom. Madame Germaine did washing by tghe piece.

Nothing was to be fastened to the walls.

No electrical appliances were to be used in the room, not even little coils for boiling water in a cup. No additional lamps could be brought in.

Only French was to be spoken at meals. If a *pensionnaire* did not know how to express a word or phrase in French it was permitted to say "*Comment dit-on en français...*" followed by the English word or phrase. This privilege was not to be abused by preceding an entire monologue in English with the "*comment dit-on*" phrase.

During this litany Germaine shuffled in to inform Madame that three blue-overalled workmen and a taxi-driver were staggering up the stairs with one of Mademoiselle Kugel's steamer trunks, a monstrously huge thing. Germaine opened the apartment-door wide, a double door. But the trunk was so huge the four men could not fit it through the opening. They dropped it on the landing with a thud that made Madame shudder and went back downstairs for *another* trunk! Just then Mademoiselle Kugel herself came bounding in, thrilled that her trunks had arrived.

She was unfazed by the problem that they wouldn't fit through the door, declaring that she would unpack the trunks in the hall and then "someone" could take the trunks downstairs to store them somewhere. Madame Fleuris acknowledged that there was probably space in the basement where the central heating system was housed, but that it would cost Mademoiselle Kugel something per month for storage. Mademoiselle Kugel waved away this as of no consequence, and Madame Fleuris regretted not naming a higher figure.

Germaine volunteered to assist Mademoiselle Kugel in carrying her belongings piece by piece from her trunks in the hall into her rooms, but Madame Fleuris needed Germaine to begin preparing dinner for six after running to the market for another rabbit for the stew.

2

Jamie and Miri kibbitzed as Judy unpacked. Miri sat primly in the center of the threadbare damask satin chaise longue, observing her new fellow *pensionnaires* with mixed feelings. Jamie was handsome enough, tall and slim with straight black hair and dark eyes, and a nice smile. But he seemed rather flip. Judy was short and plump, and bounded around like a happy little puppy. Miri did not like puppies.

Jamie was lounging gracefully against a huge carved mahogany armoire, counting out loud as Judy skipped back and forth with loads from the trunks in the hall to her rooms. He counted up to nineteen by the time she had brought in all the cashmere twin-sets.

"What on earth do you need thirty-eight sweaters for?" Miri asked querulously, at the same time entranced by the spectrum of colors of the sweaters, a whole variety of reds, purples, blues, whites, beiges, browns. Forty, actually, as Judy was wearing yet another cashmere twin-set, this in a sunny yellow, bringing out the thin yellow line woven through her dark Scottish tartan pleated skirt. On her feet were white bobby-socks and black-and-white saddle shoes, which made her feet look too big for her short plump legs.

"My mother thinks the drycleaners here in France will ruin my clothes so she wants me to wear things just until they get almost raunchy, then put them away to take home for cleaning, and wear other, clean stuff."

Jamie said cheerfully, "Your mother sounds like a paragon of common sense. But with that strategy, are you sure you'll have *enough?*"

Listening to these inanities Miri knew she should stop wasting time here, should go to fetch her suitcase and check out of her hotel, but began to wonder if she wouldn't be better off after all in a room at the Cité Universitaire. She had decided on a *pension* on the Left Bank to be near the schools, museums and the legendary cafes.

The student housing bureau had provided her with several room-for-rent listings within walking distance of the Ecole des Beaux Arts, which Miri planned to attend. From these listings she had chosen the *pension* Fleuris because it was cheap, and because the particular room she had been shown was a real garret under a real roof of Paris and reminded her of Van Gogh's painting of his room at Arles except that in van Gogh's painting there were paintings – his own – askew on the walls and these walls were bare. She could imagine hanging her own paintings here, once she had painted them.

Finding herself with two shallow people who would be wasting time day after day, she wondered if she wasn't in the wrong place?

It wasn't as though she hadn't met anyone more interesting yet. She had already met one intellectual and one artist right on the *Liberté*, even before arriving in Paris. (On the ship she had also met one tall good-looking Frenchman who was a terrific dancer, but he was a banker so that didn't count.)

Renee Rubin was brilliant, an unmitigated intellectual, a Fullbright in philosophy. From the moment they met, in the tiny inner third class cabin they were to share with two other girls for six days, Miri had felt intimidated by her.

Renee was short, pear-shaped and walked like a duck, but that detracted not a whit from her self-assurance. She immediately screened each of her new room-mates for intellectual acumen and serious purpose, quickly dismissing the other two – a boy-crazy blonde who made it clear she would only come back to the cabin to change from one tight sweater into another and replenish thick gobs of mascara and lipstick at the tiny mirror over their tiny sink; and a wretched creature who moaned in the bunk from seasickness, and threw up even before they set sail, leaving a sour smell hanging in the airless cabin which threatened to last for the whole voyage.

But Renee seemed satisfied with Miri's response to her quizzing, that she would be studying painting at the Ecole des Beaux Arts. She especiallyapproved that Miri had taken courses in existentialism at Columbia's School of General Studies. "An artist informed by philosophy! We'll have some good conversations!" She thrust her right hand forward to shake, saying they may as well get used to the French way. "I just graduated from Radcliffe magna cum laude," she announced, "and now I'm on a Fulbright in philosophy. I did my honors thesis comparing the aesthetics of Sartre, Kierkegaard and Heidegger, and my original plan for my Paris research was to probe the thinking of today's French intellectuals and then write a book about it.

"But two things intervened in rapid succession which redirected my thinking. One was that in my preliminary reading I became more aware of the distinct anti-American pro-Communist biases in the positions of many of them, and frankly, I would find it repugnant to dwell in depth on these themes, however much they might be justified philosophically.

"The second thing that happened was that someone told my father a tragically ironic story of a European relative, something that had happened during the war.

"This man had escaped from the Nazis in 1939 and by paying an exorbitant bribe got passage on a ship that became infamous in American history, the St Louis, because of the refusal of President Roosevelt and our government to aid the refugees on board. This ship set sail from Hamburg for Cuba carrying over nine hundred Jewish passengers, most of whom had been issued visas for Cuba. Until Cuba tried to extort

additional payments from the philanthropic organizations trying to aid refugees. This was refused for fear it would start a
spiral of extortions from the other South American countries
granting visas to Jews. The Cubans were able to get additional bribes for only twenty-two of the passengers, so they
nullified the other visas. Nevertheless the shipping officials
allowed the St Louis to set sail from Hamburg. When it arrived in Cuban waters, however, the ship was refused permission to dock. And the Cuban government allowed only the
twenty-two passengers with visas to go ashore.

"Here's what happened to the rest of the passengers. The
captain dropped anchor in waters off Florida, while many
people and organizations tried to negotiate saving these refugees, but despite widespread publicity and moral pressure,
Roosevelt refused to let the ship dock in the United States,
refused to take ashore any of the passengers, and the ship had
to turn around and head back to Europe, with its human cargo
likely destined for death.

"Belgium, France and the Netherlands each agreed to take
some of the passengers, and about two-thirds of them were
divvied up and taken by these countries. You'll notice that
one of these good Samaritan countries was France. That is
where my father's acquaintance's relative ended up; France.
That was in 1939.

"He managed to get work, despite many restrictions
placed on Jews from 1940 on, when the Germans took over
France. But in 1942 there were massive round-ups of Jews,
aided and abetted by ordinary French citizens, and they were
shipped to the death-camps. This relative was one of the ones
rounded up, and he died in Auschwitz, handed over to the
Nazi murderers by the same country that had saved him from
that fate three years before. Isn't that horrible?"

Miri murmured her assent.

"That's when I decided to change my project theme. Here
I was, going to France just as I heard that story from the past.
It seemed like a call to do something useful. Help set the record

straight. So I'm going to do research on French Jews under the Vichy government and the Occupation and how ordinary citizens were involved with what happened. Well, what do you think?"

Miri who had no idea what to think but didn't like saying so murmured, "Sounds hard."

Renee puffed up duck-like. "For someone who has tackled Sartre, Kierkegaard and Heidegger it is feasible."

"Oh I'm sure!"

Have you read Kierkegaard yet?"

Miri had not, and knew that she would have to before this friendship could go anywhere. She would also have to read up on Vichy France, which she had never heard of. But she wasn't interested in French Jews, or any Jews, for that matter.

Although she had been born Jewish she had no intention of "being" Jewish, and she did not like Jews. Her own father, though a devout Jew externally, going to *shul* on major holidays and even fasting on *Yom Kippur*, nevertheless let his wife hit Miri, and once push her down a flight of stairs. Miri's stepmother also was "observant": every Friday night she placed a napkin on her head, lit candles and prayed over them. But she had stolen Miri's stamp-book in which she had been saving babysitting money to buy a war bond.

"You're Jewish, aren't you?" asked Renee, disconcertingly reading her mind.

"I was born Jewish but I'm an atheist."

"Well you're still Jewish. If they come to get us they won't ask whether we're believers or not."

"That's all over and done with," Miri said, wondering as she said it whether she believed that was true.

"You couldn't be more wrong! It never is over and done with. Antisemitism is a Hydra of a thousand thousand heads. That's why my baby brother Victor who was the valedictorian of his high school class in 1947 and could have gone to Harvard or anywhere went straight to Israel to fight. He's still there too. Thank God he survived the war. Now he's an officer in the Israeli army. Look." Renee removed her wallet from a brown leather handbag and flipped through plastic-encased snapshots to a picture of Victor. A burly bearded hulk in a uniform frowned at the camera. Miri was fascinated; she was glad somehow he wasn't there in the cabin with them.

"I read French perfectly, of course, but I need to work on my spoken French, quickly, so I can start interviewing people in connection with my research. How is your spoken French?"

"Fluent."

"Really! How did you manage that?"

"I listened a lot."

"To what?"

"Linguaphone records from the library, then going to the International Club at Columbia where guys of every nationality are only too happy to talk your ear off, and going to *"Les Enfants du Paradis"* over and over and not looking at the titles. Also reading Colette and Camus. And looking up every word."

"I'm impressed. I had three years of French at Radcliffe and I still can hardly speak a word even though I read it fluently of course. I've read all of *"L'Etre et Le Néant"* in the original. I'm going to have to go to the crash course at the Alliance Française until classes at the Sorbonne start. Will you help me practice my spoken French while we're on the ship?"

"If I can." Miri would have been more flattered at the request if she had not feared that she might have to talk about Kierkegaard.

As it turned out, she didn't have to talk about Kierkegaard or even Sartre on board, and she didn't even have to help Renee practice her French. Renee quickly found a small group of Frenchmen returning from apprenticeships at a big bank in the States and appeared to be practicing on them. She wasn't listening as much as she was talking a lot, so that probably explained why she couldn't understand others so well.

Miri did a lot of eating and dancing. One of the Frenchmen, Paul Something de Something or Other, was a good dancer, but as he was a banker her interest did not extend beyond his moves on the dance-floor.

The other interesting person Miri had met on the *Liberté* was Vanessa Tate, an artist. It was on the last evening before the ship docked at Le Havre. Vanessa said that she had been seasick up in second class for the whole trip until this last day and now was wending her way around third class where she thought people might be more interesting. Miri was one of the people whom Vanessa Tate thought looked interesting.

At first the compliment was not returned. Vanessa was one of those tall, slender, long-legged patrician blondes who looked like just the sort of person Miri would usually avoid, on the assumption that she was a shallow snob of mediocre intelligence. But it had turned out that Vanessa wanted to be an artist too, and was also going to be studying at the Ecole des Beaux Arts. They looked forward to seeing each other there, but Vanessa wanted Miri to look her up before classes started in a month. Vanessa was going to be living at Reid Hall, the American Women's University Center. Miri didn't know where she would be staying so it was up to her to look up Vanessa. Miri planned on doing so as soon as she had done at least one really good painting. (She had also promised Renee to get in touch but knew she would not until she had read up on Vichy France, and had read Kierkegaard's "Either/Or" and these were not her number-one priorities.)

Judy Kugel was shaking out a fur coat from the second trunk and flung it onto the chaise Miri had just vacated. A brown velvety beaver. Then she took a second fur coat from the same trunk and shook that out too, a black Persian lamb.

"*Fur* coats? *Two* fur coats? What on earth for? You're going to look like somebody's mother!"

Judy chuckled. "My mother has four. Plus a silver fox stole."

Jamie held up the beaver appraisingly. "Do you have a slinky gown to go beneath this? You could go to the opera and pass for royalty." He then flung the luxurious coat around his own shoulders and paraded regally across the room, to Judy's giggles and Miri's disgust.

She had to make better use of her time than this! For over a year she had worked three jobs instead of her usual two, to save up for passage and at least six months in Paris. And by September 1953 when she was twenty, she was able to sail third class on the *Liberté* to France.

She was not seeking adventure, or fun, or romance. In fact she was scornful of those who were. She was going to Paris partly to study art, but mostly to save money. Tuition for the whole school year at the Sorbonne or the Ecole des Beaux Arts was only about fifteen dollars, versus the fifteen dollars per point she had been paying at Columbia as a part-time student, plus more than that for a class at the Art Students League. And living in Paris would be cheaper than in New York. The French government subsidized students' food, museum admissions, theater tickets. And everything was cheap with American dollars.

"The French opera is terrible," Miri said. "The voices are terrible. And who wants to hear *"Manon"*?"

"But the staircase is magnificent!" Jamie grinned. "For ascents and descents with pomp and circumstance. Now that I think of it wouldn't it be fun to dress up and go to the opera on some gala night?"

Judy said yes politely; Miri determinedly declined. "Dressing up" was not something she wanted to do. It was what her stepmother did, constantly. And anyway, she had no dressy clothes.

Jamie shrugged. "Well I still insist that you see the magnificent staircase."

At that moment Germaine knocked gently on the door to tell Judy that she had a phone-call. From America!

Judy bounded off. Jamie and Miri smiled at each other shyly, relieved when Judy bounded back in to announce, "That was my Mommy, calling from Great Neck, just making sure that the phone here works. If it didn't I think she would make me move! She's going to call me every Sunday evening."

"What for?"

Judy ignored this scowling query, already chuckling over something else she wanted to share with them. "You've got to see the note in the W.C.!" she chortled.

"I already have," Miri scowled. "I can't stand that holier-than-thou kind of attitude!"

"You read the handwritten sign over the so-called toilet-paper, only it isn't real toilet-paper, it's torn-up old phone-books on a hook? *'Ici c'est une maison chrétienne. Ne prenez pas le dernier morceau de papier même si vous en avais le besoin.'*"

"'This is a Christian household,'" Miri translated. "'Don't take the last piece of paper even if you need it.'"

Judy giggled. "Well I don't have to worry. I'm not Christian! So if I need it I'm going to take it!"

Jamie nodded and smiled.

Miri said, "I'm going to carry my own paper. I'm going to take some at my old hotel when I go back to check out and bring back my things."

"I'll go with you to help you carry your bags," Jamie said.

Miri tried not to show how moved she was by this kindness. She wasn't used to people being kind to her, and it bothered her to be affected by it.

Déjeuner was to be served every day at one o'clock. On this their first day all the new *pensionnaires* were on time. Already at the table, but rising to greet them in a courtly way, and shake hands with each, was Monsieur Fleuris, an old bushy-bearded gentleman with twinkling eyes. He seemed bewitched by the two young girls, whom he invited to sit on either side of him, to the scowls of his wife.

Just at one o'clock their fellow American, Branford Duane Lee the Third who had moved in at the beginning of the month, arrived and nodded coldly at the newcomers. He was a tall lanky long-nosed Southerner in khakis, a white tee shirt and a Harris tweed sports-jacket with suede patches on its elbows.

Over the soup Judy tried to get acquainted with him. He answered her patient questions in monosyllables and did not offer a single statement or show any interest in anyone. Undeterred by his coldness Judy gleaned from him that he was studying in Paris on the G.I. Bill, possibly doing doctoral research, possibly in history. He did reveal that he was an avid horseman, but as nobody else there knew a thing about horses Bran once more subsided into silence.

By the time the soup was slurped and cleared, Miri realized that Madame and Monsieur hated each other. Monsieur would mumble something into his beard, his eyes twinkling, Madame would glare at him angrily, and he would grin merrily back as if he were enjoying making her very very angry.

He pronounced Miri's command of French *merveilleuse.* Madame grudgingly agreed that it was very good – for an American.

"You *are* an American, aren't you, Mademoiselle Winter?" Madame Fleuris squinted at her suspiciously.

"I am."

"Born in America?"

"You saw my passport when I moved in."

At that moment Germaine her felt slippers flapping carried in an enormous porcelain serving bowl steaming and aromatic, and placed it before Madame Fleuris.

After Madame Fleuris had dished up and passed to each person at the table a portion of the stew, larger portions for the male guests than for the female, she attempted to encourage her guests to speak in French with one another. This was the educational portion of their residency at the *pension* Fleuris, of which Madame was quite proud.

"Since you are all new to one another, you might each relate your reasons for coming to Paris, and what you are studying. Mademoiselle Kugel, won't you begin?"

Judy was happy to say that she was happy to be in Paris,

where she hoped to learn French and meet lots of people whom she would be able to keep in touch with once back in the States. Judy's French was halting, and her accent was *épouvantable*, but she made the most of the few words she knew. Monsieur seemed enchanted with her effervescence.

Jamie Giardini said he was in Paris to learn not only French but other languages – he was taking private tutoring lessons in Russian with a Russian countess, an *émigrée*. He was already fluent in Italian. He wanted to work for NATO.

Miri said she was there to study painting and see the great paintings at the great museums.

Bran said he was there to use the Bibliotheque Nationale.

Madame returned to a question she had put to Miri earlier. Was she born in America?

"Yes."

"You don't look American, Mademoiselle."

"Everyone looks American, Madame," Branford said haughtily. "There is no set of homogenous characteristics as in countries which have been inbred through countless generations."

Miri stared at him. Maybe he was intelligent. Madame continued interrogating Miri. Did she have brothers and sisters?

"No."

"Not that she knows of," Jamie laughed.

Were her parents living? What did her father do?

"*Qu'importe?*" Miri demanded. It was none of Madame Fleuris' business.

For shock value Miri briefly considered announcing that until she graduated from high school three years before she had lived in a garden-apartment lunatic asylum in Queens where a crazy stepmother beat her up daily for imaginary transgressions and a father so terrorized by the madwoman that he always said Miri must have deserved it.

Miri's mother had died some years before. Miri was not sure she had been sane either, but at least she hadn't beaten up people. Her worst actions had been to try to prevent Miriam when little from engaging in death-defying activities such as roller-skating and bike-riding. Also, she did to try to forcefeed her the cream which she skimmed off the top of the Walker Gordon milk that was left in glass bottles outside their door each morning.

But she ended by saying nothing. Madame, with a sarcastic remark about the *épouvantable* manners of most Americans, began interrogating Judy.

Unlike Miri, Judy Kugel was quite happy to respond to the grilling, having only felicitous information to report of her hard-working money-making strict but kindly father, her loving mother, and an older brother Ellis who though a pain in the butt had brought into her life lots of good-looking college friends as prosperous as the Kugels were. Ellis, recently married, had a smaller house in walking distance, their father's wedding gift.

Madame Fleuris listened lips pressed together.

After the meal Judy invited her fellow *pensionnaires* to a local cafe, to compare first impressions. Bran declined and slouched off, but Jamie and Miri accepted.

"What do you think of our landlady?" Jamie asked. "Isn't she a bitch?"

"She glares all the time as if she's angry," Judy said. "I think her girdle is too tight."

"She real was curious about you, Miri," Jamie grinned. "Suspicious, in fact. As if you're not who you say you are."

"Well I am." Miri sipped the hot chocolate Judy had insisted on treating them to, even while resolving not to spend much more time like this. As neither Jamie nor Judy was an artist or a philosopher, Miri was not particularly interested in either of them. Jamie was good-looking and nice but so far he hadn't said one brilliant thing. And Judy was a harebrained clothes-horse. Miri didn't like Bran, either, even though he might be intelligent and she knew nothing about him except that he was a Southerner, a horsey Southerner.

Miri was eager to meet some real artists, and also some authentic existentialists.

She knew she really ought to look up Vanessa Tate, who might be a real artist. But first she wanted to get some really good paintings done, to show that she was a real artist too.

And she'd look up Renee Rubin one of these days too, once she had read Kierkegaard's "Either/Or".

3

Pétit dejeuner at the *pension* Fleuris was very *petit*; hardly more than bread and water with a small pitcher of boiled milk on the side. The choice was ersatz coffee, pale tea, or watery cocoa. But the bread was delicious. Crisp baguettes collected warm from the oven at the neighborhood bakery by the big-footed square-jawed *bonne*, Germaine, at the start of her fourteen-hour workday at the *pension*.

A thin measured curl of butter and a dollop of jam completed the allotted repast. No seconds.

As the days and weeks passed it was clear that Monsieur Fleuris delighted in all four of his American pensionnaires. He would beam at them from behind his bushy white beard, enchanted with Judy's exuberance, Jamie's antics, Branford's courtly manners, and Miri's bosom.

Madame Fleuris, on the other hand, hated all of them. She would glare at them with naked hatred. It was probably nothing personal. She made it clear that she hated all Americans. She hated them for their wealth, whether they had it or not. (Miri certainly didn't. By American standards she was poor, but in Paris she was well off thanks to the exchange rate—three-hundred-fifty francs on the dollar at American Express, four hundred over tea in a glass in a cafe near Chatelet.) She hated them for their obsession with plumbing, their fast food, their crass ignorance of French art and literature, their barbaric preference over wine for beer or Coca-Cola (or milk! heaven forfend), their *épouvantable* French accents, and the fact that Fate had failed to deal her the hand she felt she deserved, that of wealth and a husband who did not visit his mistress of forty-three years every afternoon at three except Sundays.

The *pensionnaires* heard the lament of Monsieur Fleuris' infidelity at least once at each *déjeuner*. The litany of his fecklessness was invariably followed by a recital of the goodnesses of her son-in-law Philippe Jumelle, and concluded with a fervent thanks to the *bon dieu* for such a paragon.

As soon as Monsieur Fleuris excused himself from each meal his wife would rant that he was off to see his mistress and that he had betrayed her from the beginning of their marriage as well as squandering her *dot*, thereby reducing them to keeping a *pension* and preventing them from providing Lucille with the kind of *dot* which would have enabled her to make a more lofty match.

Madame Fleuris' situation compared unfavorably with that of Madame Poivriere, the widow on the fifth floor. Monsieur Poivriere had not only conveniently ceased to incommode his wife by considerately dying, but had left her well-fixed. And the *dot* the Poivrieres had been able to provide for their own daughter Michelle had won her an industrialist from Lyons – to say nothing of the fact that Madame Poivriere did not spend her days overseeing the cooking and cleaning and laundering for four strangers but had her privacy and could spend her time as she pleased.

Fire would rage in Madame Fleuris' eyes as she spoke. In forty-three years she had never forgiven her husband, never resigned herself, never left him. She had been faithful but a martyr and kept picking at the scab to keep it raw. It was an amazing example of tenacity.

It frightened Miri to think of it because she valued tenacity. Suppose she too was crazy, and didn't know it? People who were crazy were always sure that they were sane. In fact

Miri's one hope that she was sane was that she was worried
that she might be crazy. She considered asking Branford Duane
Lee the Third what he thought, since he would probably be
objective, since he didn't care anything about her, or any of
them, but since she didn't know if he was sane or not himself,
she couldn't be sure he would know whether she was.

Miri's plan to avoid her fellow *pensionnaires* didn't en-
tirely work out. Avoiding Branford Duane Lee the Third was
easy: he avoided them. At meals he remained glacially aloof,
unresponsive to Judy's incessant chatter and Madame Fleuris'
inquisitions, and would quietly slide out after meals day after
day once again having revealed nothing new about himself,
to the intense annoyance of both Judy and Madame Fleuris.

Germaine reported to the girls that Monsieur Duane Lee
kept his books in a locked suitcase under his bed. She knew
they were books from the heavy weight of the suitcase when
she dragged it out to clean under the bed. Madame Fleuris
had been tempted to force it open at one point on the grounds
that if it was pornography Monsieur Duane Lee would be
breaking the law. On the other hand if it was not pornography she would not be able to justify the snooping. She left it
alone.

Madame Fleuris had once tested the waters in Jamie's
hearing to learn if Bran was antisemitic, by making sugges-
tive remarks and seeking his concurrence. But she had been
met by stony silence as had any of her other overtures.

Jamie reported this with glee to Judy and Miri, who now
had further reason to loathe their landlady.

It did make Miri somewhat anxious. Jamie sensed this,
and reassured her: "Don't worry, she won't put poison in your
soup, you're a source of income!"

Judy Kugel was impossible to avoid. She was like an enthusiastic puppy who won't take no for an answer in its demands for attention, especially from people who dislike dogs.
She would wait for Miri after breakfast so that they could walk

part of the way to school together, she would insist on treating Miri to hot chocolate at the corner cafe. When Miri tried to escape to her room Judy would climb the two extra flights to follow her upstairs, trying to inveigle Miri into some party or other or to make a fourth on a double date. Judy's obsessive sociability annoyed Miri. It wasted time she should have been spending on her work. She was angry with herself whenever she didn't resist.

As for Jamie, it turned out that Miri liked him. They would go together to the Saturday afternoon tea-dances at the American Club for Students and Artists on Boulevard Raspail.

But these weren't real dates.

They had quickly discovered that they were both existentialists and both loved to dance. They would do the Lindy together, and Miri would dance other dances with other boys unless they were rude or Egyptian while Jamie played ping-pong in another room. If someone put on a Charleston record Jamie would enter the *salon*. He liked to do the Charleston, at which he was a veritable Astaire, his long thin arms and legs jiggling and flailing like a marionette, while everyone, having cleared the dance-floor to watch him, stood around clapping in rhythm and chanting, "Charleston! Charleston!" with nostalgia for an era they had not experienced and understood nothing about.

Miri sometimes wondered if anything would come of it with Jamie Giardini. They went around a lot together, they shared a passion for art, he always did the Lindy with her, he was very nice to her. But he had never tried to kiss her.

On one of these Saturdays at the American Club, a tall blonde good-looking German named Gerhardt whirled Miri around in a Viennese waltz. She only learned that he was German when he told her so. His English – with an American accent – was perfect. Miri loved the Viennese waltz. Gerhardt's was exhilarating. When the Strauss record ended Gerhardt saw her to a seat and actually bowed from the waist; she had only seen such bows in the movies.

Jamie came over just then, flush from winning at ping-pong. He told Miri with a laugh that he had defeated a Fulbright scholar in philosophy. A moment later the defeated player came up behind him. It was Renee Rubin, Miri's shipboard cabin-mate.

Renee was purple with rage. Not only had she had lost at ping-pong, her specialty, but Miriam had never looked her up, and now here she was, dancing with a Nazi!.

"Gerhardt's not a Nazi, and neither were his parents. He's more Americanized than I am, he likes Coca-Cola, Chevies, and wants to make money and get ahead."

Gerhardt was too young to have been in the Hitler Youth, he said. All the Germans in Paris were too old or too young to have been Nazis, and none of them had lived close enough to a concentration-camp to have smelled anything peculiar and therefore suspect that something horrifying was going on there, or even near enough to know of its existence. He felt deep guilt for what his parents' generation (but not his own parents, they had lived far out in the countryside and didn't know what was going on) had done to the Jews. He was very attracted to Jewish girls, he said. He might marry one. American, of course. There weren't any German ones left.

"And he proposed to you?" Renee asked sarcastically.

"No, we just do the Viennese waltz together." Miri was startled at the idea of marrying Gerhardt. He was much too bourgeois and shallow for her. After all you couldn't be waltzing all the time.

"You should have called me before this. You know I didn't know where you would be staying," Renee scolded. "Where did you finally move to?"

"A *pension* near the schools."

"How old is the concierge there?"

"The concierge? How old? I have no idea. Why?"

"Old," Jamie inserted.

"Good. I'll want to interview her for my research. You can translate for me."

Jamie asked, "What are your researches?"

"My topic is an inquiry into the treatment of French Jews during Vichy France and the Occupation. I want to question anyone mature who was living in Paris during the Occupation, but especially French persons. I want to find out what they were doing while the Germans were occupying their City of Light! I've been doing a literature search and it's horrifying what you find the more you dig. The laws that the French government made against some of their own citizens, Jewish citizens who paid taxes, fought for France in its wars... They passed a law that only a tiny percentage of those entering colleges and professional schools could be Jewish."

"Big deal," Miri said sullenly. "Do you think Princeton or Yale let in any old number of Jews?"

"But that's bigotry, not the law of the land! Don't you see the colossal difference? I went to Radcliffe. If I hadn't gotten in there, there would have been plenty of other good schools to go to, like Columbia."

"They hate Jews there too," said Miri.

"I really don't care who hates who," said Renee gruffly, "it's what they do about their hate that matters. Do you know that the incarcerating of Jews for shipping off to German camps was the French government's idea? The Germans didn't even have to tell them to do it! I'm looking into this. I want to find people who did this to try to understand why."

"And if they collaborated," Jamie put in, "you think they're going to volunteer that information to you?"

"Of course not, dummy. At least not right off. But if I persist I might find out things. I want to find out what went on with the Jews, their own Jews, French Jews. Where did you say your *pension* is? I'll come and visit you and you can introduce me to the old-timers."

Miri was mortified at the thought of Renee turning up and barking her interrogations at Madame Poule the concierge, but Jamie for some reason was sympathetic to Renee's objective, and gave her their address.

"How come you're so interested?" Miri asked him. "You're not even Jewish."

"The Nazis murdered a lot of Jews," he said with a cryptic smile, "but they didn't murder only Jews."

Renee threatened to show up soon, and she reminded Miri that she would require her assistance as a translator. Miri was horrified at the thought of putting embarassing questions to Madame Poule, or maybe even to Monsieur or Madame Fleuris. Now she would have to be on the lookout for Renee to be sure to disappear if Renee did turn up.

By now it was November. On the following Monday, Miri started at the Ecole des Beaux Arts. One day there and Miri knew the Beaux Arts was a disappointment. Her instructor, a strutting little man with a black goatee, liked to be called *maître* and went around from easel to easel patting girls' bottoms; but he didn't say one useful thing about the drawings she had been doing. The cavernous room was freezing, colder than outside, with just one wood stove which failed as a heater but filled the room with acrid smoke which was being blotted up by Miri's hair and clothes. And the model was a pathetic shivering scrawny thing who looked cold and hungry.

When classes let out for the day Miri ran into Vanessa Tate in the milling crowd. They laughed over the encounter, both saying they had been sure they were going to meet here. They went to a café together to compare their initial reactions to the art school. They found that these were similar. But as Vanessa pointed out, the real thing about being in Paris wasn't what you could learn at the Ecole des Beaux Arts from some pathetic losers, it was – being in Paris! Time enough to get back to technique with real artists at the Art Students League when the year here was up. She had heard too that a new wave of powerful artists was developing in New York, who hung out at the Cedar Bar in the Village, and she was anxious to start hanging out at the Cedar Bar too, and hopefully get invited up to some studios to see what they were doing. But first she was going to make the most of her year in Paris. Miri felt lightened by Vanessa's optimistic outlook.

Then they compared their living quarters. Vanessa was physically comfortable at Reid Hall but disliked the fact that just about every resident was an American. Many of them were together in a group from a Southern college doing their third year abroad; they travelled in a pack everywhere, in their little white gloves, speaking French to one another in embarassingly Southern American accents. They would make a special point to *tutoyer* one another, that is, say *tu* and *toi*, the intimate form used for addressing intimates, children, servant and dogs.

Vanessa thought Miri's *pension* sounded much more authentically French, but she wasn't about to give up unlimited baths, big American breakfasts with orange juice and eggs or cereal and unlimited real coffee. Her room was large enough in which to set up an easel and paint, and it had a balcony overlooking Reid Hall's walled garden.

Although the original building had been the hunting-lodge of the Duc de Chevreuse in some previous century, it gave the impression of a convent. Once those heavy outer doors clanged behind you at one end, joining the U-shaped building, with the stone wall completing the enclosure, you were shut in and the world shut out as if you had taken the vows and the veil.

Miri pondered wistfully the unlimited baths and American breakfasts and the room large enough in which to set up an easel. But she dismissed the thought of moving: it was probably too expensive for her, and even if she could afford it, they were probably full.

On neither point did she think to ask.

They compared notes on people that they had met. Vanessa was seeing two young men, a funnily romantic Spanish lawyer and a wacky Swede who was a terrific painter but was not often sober enough to paint anything. Miri was envious. She could only talk about her fellow *pensionnaires* and

Renee Rubin. Neither Jamie Giardini nor Branford Duane
Lee the Third aroused much interest on Vanessa's part. She
did think Gerhardt sounded like he might have possibilities,
at least for a fling. She hadn't been to the American Club for
Students and Artists on Boulevard Raspail yet, but when she
got around to it she would be sure to look him over.

4

The Thursday following their encounter at the American Club Renee walked in on them during *déjeuner*. Germaine showed her into the salon, then announced her to Madame Fleuris and the two *pensionnaires* whom Mademoiselle Rubin was visiting, Mademoiselle Miri and Monsieur Jamie. Jamie excused himself from the table immediately to greet their guest; Miri felt coerced into doing the same.

Judy was curious. "Who's Renee Rubin?"

Jamie signalled her to come along with them to the salon. "She's a brilliant humorless intellectual who hates losing at ping-pong. She's doing her dissertation on how the French Jews were treated by the French government and regular French citizens during World War Two. She wants to interview old-timers who were around then, like our concierge, and landlady and so on. I met her at the American Club. She was a cabin-mate of Miri's on the *Liberté* coming over. She's really into this. I think we should help her."

"Absolutely! I'm all for it!" declared Judy enthusiastically. "What can I do?"

"She'll tell you soon enough," Miri said sullenly.

The three of them entered the salon, where Renee sat stiff-backed on a little gilt salon chair, reading a book she had obviously brought along. She jumped up, shook hands with Miri, Jamie, and Judy when she was introduced.

"They told me what you're doing," Judy said ebulliently. "I think it's great!"

Renee eyed her skeptically. "What are you doing in Paris?"

Judy explained that she was going to the *cours de la civilisation française pour les étrangers.*

"Oh," said Renee, dismissively.

Judy ignored the snub. She bubbled, "I want to help so here's what I can do. I'm inviting you to *déjeuner* with us, I'll pay Madame Fleuris for the extra meal, otherwise she probably wouldn't even let you sit down at the table! Then you can interview Madame Fleuris and Old Bushy Beard while we're eating. They are certainly old-timers!"

Jamie congratulated Judy on her generosity. Renee thanked her brusquely. But Miri was unhappy at the idea. She only hoped that Renee's French had improved enough by now to put embarassing questions to Monsieur and Madame Fleuris herself and not expect Miri to do it for her as she had originally demanded.

The plan could not be implemented at once. Madame Fleuris was agreeable to having an extra – paying – guest at *déjeuner,* but not at this *déjeuner.* She had not provided enough food for an extra person. They settled on the following Thursday, the first day all of them, as well as Madame Fleuris, would find it convenient.

Judy, Jamie and Miri went to cafés together more often than Miri really approved of. But somehow she kept going, sucked in by their obsessive affability. They would rehash the same questions again and again: whether the chicken stew had really been rabbit, whether the beef stew had been horse; whether Madame Fleuris would ever murder her husband for his lifelong fecklessness; whether Monsieur Fleuris would ever murder his wife for her incessant nagging; whether the golden-boy son-in-law Philippe Jumelle was going to be beatified, maybe even sanctified; whether the French really hated to bathe or just envied the Americans for being able to afford bathtubs; why Madame Fleuris was still so skeptical of Miri's true origins that she had even set Germaine to snooping and asking her questions.

These were not edifying discussions and Miri hated herself for indulging in them again and again.

Almost always the threesome went to one of the legendary Left Bank cafés popular with Americans for their past glory days of Hemingway, Fitzgerald, Simone de Bouvoir and Sartre and other Olympians of culture.

But on Wednesday afternoon the threesome went to the scorned Café de la Paix, near the Opera, a tourist-trap, at the behest of Judy, who was to keep a rendez-vous there with a young man whom her mother had arranged to meet her.

Seymour Levin was the elder son of an old high school friend of Judy's mother whom she had run into at a Hadassah luncheon. The Levins were not as well off as the Kugels were but the son was a Harvard graduate and well worth trying out on her daughter. He was currently in the U.S. Army, stationed in Garmisch, and now he was coming to Paris on a few days leave.

It was the beginning of December. Despite the damp chill Judy persuaded Miri and Jamie to sit huddled with her at an outdoor table.

Jamie was wrapped in a splendid tweed Sherlock Holmes coat, with a shoulder-cape; he sipped a hot toddy. Judy was swathed in her beaver and sipped hot chocolate. Miri blanketed in her monklike black coat was also drinking hot chocolate.

The three of them congratulated one another smugly at their ability to endure such discomfort with a smile.

As the three of them were staring out at the passersby watching for the American who might be Judy's appointment, all three simultaneously were electrified to see Madame Fleuris, their own old landlady, in a black coat and feather-trimmed black hat and little veil, walking calmly on the arm of a squarely-built extremely handsome saturnine young man in a camels-hair coat.

"Tobey Peters!" Jamie exclaimed.

"A gigolo?" Judy giggled. "Madame Fleuris?"

Jamie leapt from his chair and dashed off after the pair. Judy and Miri saw him speaking and smiling with the two, then the young man withdrew something from his inner jacket pocket which he handed to Jamie, shook hands, Madame offered hers to Jamie, then the odd couple continued their stroll and Jamie returned to their table at the cafe.

Judy giggled, "That must be the *amant* Old Bushy Beard was teasing Madame Fleuris about at *déjeuner.*"

Earlier that day, as fruit and cheese were being served, Madame Fleuris urged the rest of them to relax and enjoy the rest of the meal, but she had to excuse herself for an appointment.

"She has a rendez-vous with her *amant!*" twinkled Monsieur Fleuris.

His wife scowled at him.

After the meal the two girls had adjourned to Judy's rooms. Judy stretched out on her chaise longue and Miri sank into a luxuriously stuffed armchair. Then Judy leapt up, remembering her stash of Toblerone chocolate. "Old Bushy Beard is so cute," she giggled, unwrapping a roll of chocolate, "saying his wife was off to meet her *amant,* when he's the one who goes off every day to his ancient girlfriend."

"Well I can't stand her but in all fairness she did deserve better treatment from her own husband than she got," said Miri.

Now they saw who the so-called "*amant*" was.

Back at the café table, Jamie informed them excitedly, "Tobey Peters is a good friend of mine. He's just arrived back in Paris from a trip to Spain. Actually I'm surprised he hadn't gotten in touch with me yet. But I think he just got back. He's taking Madame Fleuris to tea at Rumpelmayers to repay her for a kindness she's done him. He lived at the pension last year, that's how I heard about the pension – from Tobey."

"Kindness?" Judy screeched. "Madame Fleuris? Are you kidding?"

"Well it must have been something significant," Miri said, "taking Madame Fleuris to tea can only be a penance."

"I know what it's about," Jamie grinned. "Tobey gets huge allowances from his mother and grandmother but he's supposed to toe the line and live the way they think he should live, study music with Nadia Boulanger, look for the right kind of debutante to settle down with, preferably a French daughter of the nobility, that sort of thing. Not carouse and carry on in unacceptable ways. So he writes them pure fiction about his doings, while he travels around doing the unacceptable, and Madame Fleuris posts the letters from Paris. For this he not only pays her, but takes her to Rumpelmayer's from time to time when he's in town so that she'll feel that they are friends, not just doing business. Anyhow, listen."

He withdrew from his coat-pocket what Tobey Peters had just handed him, white cardboards which proved to be engraved invitations to an art-opening to be held in a fashionable gallery and sponsored by Baroness Alexandra, the middle-European wife of a wealthy American industrialist.

He had urged Jamie to attend the *vernissage,* and to bring some glamorous young girls with him if possible.

"So I'm inviting you two and you must dress as glamorously as possible as the affair will be very toney, replete with champagne and caviar, and princes. In fact the artist whose work is to be displayed is himself a prince. The baroness is *très* rich and goes all out."

"Dress glamorously?" Miri said. "Then I'm not going. I don't have any glamorous clothes. And I wouldn't waste a franc on buying any, not even at the Marché aux Puces!"

"Oh come on," Judy pleaded. "I'll lend you whatever you need. It sounds like fun. And," she added slyly, "it is art."

This debate was interrupted by the arrival of a tall young man in a too-large gray tweed coat who peered intently at

Miri with deep dark brown eyes. "Judy Kugel, I hope?" He had a nice face but his ears stuck out and Miri took an instant dislike to him. She shook her head no and pointed at Judy who had broken out a broad grin.

"Oh well, right church, wrong pew," he smiled. "Hi. I'm Seymour Levin." Then he pulled up a chair to their table. He was carrying a string bag, the sort Frenchwomen used for carrying their groceries, but it contained a number of books. Miri eyed the bag curiously.

"I couldn't resist picking up a little light reading at the English bookstore nearby, not available at the PX." He displayed the titles: "Lady Chatterley's Lover" and three titles of Henry Miller.

"Dirty books!" laughed Judy. "All the new male arrivals make a beeline for them."

"It's dumb that you can't buy them in America," Miri grumbled, "not that I ever would of course, but you should be able to. And you should be able to see 'Citizen Kane'. Once I got to Paris I went to see it at the Cine Club and I can't understand why it's banned in America anyway."

"Hear! hear!" said Seymour Levin smiling at her appreciatively. But Miri had said all she was going to say. Seymour unsuccessfully attempted to make small talk with Miri, switched to Judy, who had been won over by his geniality, then invited all of them to join him at dinner that evening. "Nothing fancy, I'm not rich, but I won a big pot at poker just before coming to Paris."

"We had our big meal at mid-day," Miri said.

But she was not backed up by Jamie or Judy, both of whom thanked the newcomer for his invitation and agreed to accompany him to the restaurant he mentioned, a place none of them had visited, although all had heard of it.

"Tourist-trap," pronounced Miri.

"I like tourist-traps," Seymour laughed. "They usually have fewer cockroaches than your typical quaint neighborhood hangout."

Seymour departed for his hotel, swinging his string-bag of books, and the other three returned to the pension.

Jamie and Judy had only the nicest words to say about Seymour.

Back at the pension the two girls ensconced themselves in Judy's room at the latter's suggestion. She admonished Miri to be nicer to Seymour. "He did not take his eyes off you once, and with your horrible family and impoverished circumstances and weird attitudes you aren't going to meet a Harvard graduate that easily, and nice looking too, who is going to get serious with you."

But Miri had hardened her heart against Seymour Levin, G.I., who would be going back to Garmisch in only three or four days and whose ears stuck out.

At dinner, however, where he and she sat side by side on a banquette while Jamie and Judy sat opposite them in chairs, she was unusually vivacious, not at all hostile, and pretended not to notice when he put his arm around her waist.

While Judy and Jamie were in a deep discussion with the sommelier, getting an important lesson on wine they could take back home, Seymour Levin began telling Miri all about himself although she had not asked. He had graduated Harvard college, where he had majored in business, and almost immediately he was drafted. The really great thing was that the Korean War had just ended almost that minute, the truce was signed less than a month before he was sent to Fort Dix for basic training. They wanted to send him to officers' training but he refused because it would have meant staying in the army a year longer than as an enlisted man.

There was a lot of angling for good transfers once Basic was over, but he didn't bother trying because he had noticed that when men finished Basic they were shipped out to places they hadn't asked for unless they had connections. He had no connections.

They next sent him to school to learn how to run automatic accounting machines that gobbled up cards which had been punched with numbers by clerks and did accounting much faster than bookkeepers.

He was the only one in his group who did not ask for Europe, or anywhere particular, because he thought it was the kind of plum assignment they only gave to soldiers who could pull strings. But then they shipped him to Garmisch, assigned to work at FOUSAG, Finance Office United States Army Garmisch.

At Garmisch he worked in a basement. His job was overseeing keypunch operators punching cards and printer-operators running the printers that made reports out of the cards. He had to solve problems when there were errors, or machinery malfunctions, and he had to look at all the reports. That part was the captain's responsibility but the captain expected Seymour to catch all the problems for him.

This was the most boring thing Miri had ever heard in her life. "This is the most boring thing I have ever heard in my life," she said.

Seymour remained cheerful. "That's okay. I'm not boring. You'll see." He already had his arm around her waist; now he squeezed tight.

He hoped to transfer to Paris at some point in time. It was a possibility. FOUSAP, Finance Office U.S. Army Paris, was a bigger operation than FOUSAG. Paris consolidated the accounting reports from FOUSA's all over Europe to send to Washington. So if he did a great job in Garmisch he might get bumped up. He knew he would like being in Paris, especially the great jazz you could hear there, but he wasn't wild about the French. They were parasites. Everything wonderful about Paris had been built in the past. The French weren't doing anything new or vital in the present. Their future looked bleak, unless the United States kept giving them money. They still owed America their war debt from World War One, and owed mountains of money for World War Two. His opinion was that they would never pay it back, and the U.S. politicians wouldn't make them. He asked Miri how she liked Paris.

"I like some things, the overall beauty of the place, the ancient buildings and bridges and parks, and the quaint costumes religious types wear, and the workmen in their caps and overalls, and I love going to the museums and sitting around in cafés. But it's cold and gray. And the French are mean. They write 'U.S. Go Home' on the walls. And the only intellectuals I've met so far are Americans."

"Tell me about yourself. Your family."

"No thanks!"

"Jukes and Kallikaks, huh?"

That made Miri laugh. "They're not retarded, they're worse. My stepmother is a sadist and my father is spineless and never stopped her from beating me up."

"They sound awful. So awful that you don't have to feel guilty about having nothing to do with them, the way some kids do because their parents are only borderline mean and neurotic." He grinned. "The man who marries you will get a bonus. He wouldn't have to bother with any in-laws!"

Despite these auspicious inroads, she refused to go out with him during his next three days in Paris. But she was secretly pleased when she got a letter from him soon after his return to Garmisch.

He made only a brief reference to their meeting, saying she was very pretty and funny, and then he moved on to more impersonal topics, describing a typical day on his job in the army running some sort of punch-card center, which sounded unbelievably boring and which she barely read, and mentioning that he had won another big pot at poker which he was saving for when she came to visit him in Garmisch (fat chance) and discussing the latest book he had read and liked, Dostoyevsky's "Crime and Punishment". This was certainly acceptable. She would read it too, so she would have something to write back about.

She spent several hours analyzing his handwriting with the aid of a French book on graphology she had bought along the quais for fifty francs, from which she concluded that his handwriting bore out the impression of the text, that he was intelligent, serious, kind and reliable, with a sense of humor. But what the handwriting didn't say was that his ears stuck out, and he made her nervous.

Besides, there was Jamie, who was always around, and the possibility of seeing Jamie's handsome friend Tobey Peters again.

Even as she had said no to attending the *vernissage* Miri was thinking that if she did go she would see that friend of Jamie's again. Nevertheless she held out until the very day of the *vernissage,* not sure right up to the last minute whether she would go, despite Judy's coaxing. She did attend the fashion show in Judy's room as Jamie gave his considered opinion of what she should wear. She sat with hands folded in her lap on Judy's chaise while Judy brought out one dress or suit after another for Jamie's inspection. Many met with his approval; he was able to leave the choice to Judy herself. He retrieved her beaver coat from the closet. "Wear this and it won't matter which dress you choose."

"I was thinking of wearing my Persian lamb."

"*Très chic.* Then maybe Miri could wear the beaver?"

"Of course she can."

"Oh no!" Miri protested. "No no no."

"Why not? I think it would be fun if we both wore furs."

"I don't want to wear anyone else's clothes."

"This isn't clothes, this is a fur coat."

"Go on, Miri," Jamie urged. "The beaver is you."

"Now I'll find a dress for you," Judy declared.

But there Miri drew the line. She didn't want to wear someone else's clothes, and ran upstairs to slip into a dress she thought would pass their inspection, a long-sleeved princess navy wool jersey she had found in a thrift shop on Third Avenue which would have fit her as if it had been made for her if she had weighed about fifteen pounds less. The fact that it had once been "someone else's clothes" didn't bother her once she paid three dollars and made it her own.

"It's not bad," said Jamie looking at her appraisingly, when she had presented herself back in Judy's rooms, "but it would look dressier without the white collar and cuffs. It's not a sexy design but as it's too tight that will do!"

"You can wear my pearls with it," Judy said. "I'm wearing my charms."

Judy Kugel had not only a gold charm bracelet like that of every other nouveau riche suburban American girl, in addition her doting daddy had had a necklace made for her of solid gold charms all around a long gold neck chain. They included a tiny bicycle with tiny moving wheels, a tiny sewing machine with moving treadle, and a bird that swung back and forth pecking at a piece of tree-trunk, all in eighteen karat gold.

Judy in the other room had wriggled into a black sheath and emerged like a little round black sausage, with the gold charms all around her neck. She held out the pearls for Miri. "Twenty-one. My daddy started it with eighteen on my eighteenth birthday and adds one on each birthday."

"Do you have any bitchy shoes?" Jamie asked Miri.

"I don't know what you consider 'bitchy' but all I have is these Capezio ballets and a pair of French clumpers with thick gum soles."

"Wear the ballets then," Jamie sighed. "And don't forget to wear lipstick."

He himself had dressed meticulously in an Italian-cut dark suit, white shirt with historic-looking collar, and silk Italian tie. His Sherlock Holmes coat around his shoulders, and the two girls in furs, the three set off and found a taxi at the nearby stand. Jamie took a jump-seat and they were off, in a light mood.

There was a packed crowd in the gallery already, in a din of chatter, most holding champagne glasses and some cigarette-holders. Jamie dashed off to get the girls champagne, leaving Judy and Miri to survey the crowd.

"Notice anything peculiar about this crowd?" Judy asked.

She had noticed a glamorous middle-aged woman in a gold lamé gown surrounded by young men, who might have been their hostess, but she couldn't see any other women in the room besides themselves.

"Don't you think that's weird?"

"Well I don't know if it's weird, but it should make you happy. Didn't you say it might be a good opportunity to meet men?"

Judy made a disgusted sound, pulled her Persian lamb closed and announced, "I'm leaving!" Before Miri could ask why, Judy was gone.

She was standing there alone, waiting for Jamie with the champagne, and trying to spot Jamie's good-looking friend in the crowd, when a large box-shaped woman, heavily made up and garishly dressed, sidled up to Miri. She put a gloved hand heavily overlaid with flashy cocktail rings on Miri's arm and said to her in a husky voice, "You and I want the same thing from him, don't we dear?"

"We do? Who?"

The woman sneered, her pancake makeup cracking, "You'll see who wins, and it won't be innocence and naivete, it will be devilish cleverness and a willingness to do whatever is wanted."

Just then Jamie arrived with three glasses of champagne, the woman snatched one of them from him, quaffed it in a gulp, winked at Jamie and swayed off.

Before Miri could ask Jamie about this garish woman he led her through the crowd to the woman in the gold lamé gown, still surrounded by young men. He pushed right through, and said in a sweet tone, "Baroness, may I present Miri Winter, also an aspiring artist?"

The baroness glared from Miri to Jamie, and turned to talk with one of other companions. Miri noticed the garish woman standing nearby, studying the baroness intently.

"I think I'll look at the paintings," Miri said. She left Jamie in the little crowd around the baroness, and pushed her way to the outer edges of the room where she could scan the paintings on the walls.

She had no competition for this. She moved slowly from one painting to another, with the dawning realization that these paintings were not only not art, they were an inept stupid waste of good paint. She left.

Judy was in her room writing letters. She had changed into an emerald green tweed skirt and matching cashmere sweater set, and saddle shoes. Miri returned the fur coat with thanks. It really had been toasty warm. "Why did you leave so early?"

"You didn't stay so long yourself!" Judy giggled.

And that was all that was said that day about the *vernissage*.

5

Madame Fleuris had been agreeable enough when accepting five hundred francs from Judy Kugel for a meal for her guest Renee Rubin, and had behaved with perfect correctness when Mademoiselle Rubin was introduced. But once they were all assembled at the big mahogany table, with Renee seated between Miri and Judy, Renee wasted no time in beginning her assault. As soon as the soup had been ladled up and a bowl passed to each person at table, Renee posed her first question to Madame. In adequate French, having rehearsed it beforehand, she asked: "Madame, were you acquainted with any Jews living in Paris before or during World War Two?"

Miri, blushed deeply and felt very uncomfortable. "She said, looking at Madame Fleuris, "Renee Rubin is doing her graduate studies about France during the war."

Madame stared grimly at her new guest. "A Jewish family did live in this very building. But I cannot tell you anything about them. We were not personally acquainted."

Renee in a hoarse whisper asked Miri to translate this reply for her.

"Your French sounded good," Miri whispered back.

"I rehearsed all the questions I could think of to ask, but now I can't understand the answers."

Miri translated for her.

Monsieur Fleuris, with his usual weakness for young girls, even girls who were shaped like a pear, smiled at Renee as he told Miri he knew a little more about that Jewish family. She could tell their visitor that the Jewish family had been arrested by the French police one day in July 1942 when many Jews were rounded up and taken away, and had never been seen again. "A regrettable and ignominious day for an otherwise glorious nation," he sighed.

Madame scowled at her husband.

Miri translated these remarks into English for Renee, who muttered that to Madame it hadn't seemed all that regrettable! She nodded an acknowledgment to Monsieur Fleuris, who smiled at her benignly.

Renee remarked in English that of course the police would know that this family was Jewish. From her reading she had learned that all the Jews had previously been required to register so the police knew where they all were. In fact by that time they were required to wear yellow patches in the form of a star of David sewn conspiciously on their clothing.

"And they went along with this?" Judy shrieked. "Why didn't they protest?" She turned to Miri. "Can you imagine if the major of New York City said we had to do that? Wouldn't he be mobbed, torn to shreds? My daddy wouldn't stand for it."

"Rebellion obviously wasn't in their gut," Branford said. "They were law-abiding citizens." He sneered ironically. "And that was the law."

"What was the Jewish family's name?" Renee asked in French.

"Maisel," said Monsieur Fleuris.

"Didn't anyone look for them?"

Miri repeated her question in French.

Monsieur shrugged. Madame cast an angry look at Renee. Germaine, who was at that moment bringing in a large platter of mixed root vegetables, stood still for a moment gazing at Miri, who had translated Renee's question.

"Who was in the family?"

Again Monsieur Fleuris supplied a reply. "Monsieur Maisel, a man in his forties who had an optical shop on the the courtyard; his wife, a quiet woman who tended her home and her two children; a boy about ten; a girl about twelve."

"The children were arrested too?" Judy was horrified.

There was silence. Madame sat with her lips pressed tightly together, her back straight, a grim far-away look on her face. She was as usual tightly corseted, and dressed in black; a Grim Reaper.

Renee kept going. "What happened to their apartment?"

Madame Fleuris calmly answered this. "When it became apparent that the Maisels were not returning, the apartment was rented to another family."

"But what about their stuff? Their furniture? Their clothing?"

In a dismissive tone, Madame said that that was enough of such grim talk, it was time for dessert and pleasant conversation. She asked Jamie in falsely cheerful tones if he had seen any amusing films lately. He looked at her as if she were crazy.

Germaine brought in a bowl of oranges.

Renee pocketed her orange, urging Miri to do the same and said, "Come on."

Miri who had been discomfited by the whole situation was happy to leave, and looked at Judy who was also pocketing her orange, although Renee had not invited her along. Miri thought that was rather rude, since Judy had paid for her *déjeuner.*

The three girls adjourned to Judy's rooms, where Judy stretched out on her chaise longue and the other two sunk into fat upholstered armchairs. Then Judy leapt up, remembering that she had a stash of Toblerone chocolate, which she passed around.

Renee looked around her at the luxuriously furnished room and through the doorway to the second room. "Some setup," she said.

"Judy is rich," Miri said with a laugh.

Judy bubbled. "It's true. And I like it!"

"*Noblesse oblige,*" Renee said sententiously. "What are you going to do with your life?"

"Get married, I hope. And have happy kids."

Renee ignored this. "I want to talk to the concierge too. Don't they always know everything that goes on?"

"This one sure does!" Judy giggled. "I don't think she ever sleeps, you can't sneak in in the morning without some sly remark from her."

"And she was here during the Occupation, right?"

Judy shrugged. "She's old enough, that's for sure."

Renee retrieved her black chesterfield from the hall armoire, while Judy donned her beaver coat and tossed a thick brown quilted jacket at Miri so that she wouldn't have to climb upstairs for her coat. Then the three descended the stairs to the ground floor. Renee turned to Judy. "It would be better if only I and Miri approach Madame Poule so that she won't feel as ganged up upon." She insisted that Miri translate.

Judy looked disappointed but did not insist. Miri was outraged on Judy's behalf that Renee seemed to feel no gratitude to Judy, who had after all invited her here – Miri would not have done so! – and had paid for her meal.

Madame Poule nodded to them through the window to her loge. Miri was uncomfortable at what Renee had asked her to do, but plunged into it. She explained to the concierge that her friend was doing research about the war for her studies and could Madame Poule spare them a few minutes to share her recollections?

Madame Poule had more than a few minutes to spare as she did very little besides watch anyone coming or going in the building. She was glad of the company. Pushing aside a small vase of artificial flowers, she placed a little plate of biscuits in the center of the round table around which she invited them to sit.

Madame Poule did have something to add about the Maisels and their apartment. She remembered them. They had seemed like good people; quiet, minded their own business. Their daughter Berthe was a bit of a hellion, unlike her parents and brother who were on the quiet side. She was a pretty thing, too, with brown hair and big brown eyes that could bore right into you.

Madame Poule remembered very well the morning the police had come for the Maisels. She had been looking out of her loge. One of the police told her where they were going. They already knew that the Maisels lived on the first floor and went straight up, coming down a short time later gripping all four of the Maisels who looked disheveled and confused, but not making a fuss.

Suddenly in the courtyard Berthe broke free from her captor and started kicking him and screaming that she didn't want to go with him and he should let her family alone. The parents cringed at this, the mother pleaded with Berthe to quiet down and the father gave her a brusque order to do so, but Berthe kept kicking and screaming at the police, who were getting impatient and annoyed.

Madame Poule stepped out of her loge, took Berthe by the hand and offered to the police to bring the girl later. She didn't ask where to, and they didn't say, but they seemed grateful and left peacefully with the two adults and the little boy. By this time Berthe was sobbing and Madame Poule tried to comfort her, all the while wondering what to do with her. She had a shrewd idea that the Jews were being shipped to internment camps, and from there to even worse fates. Did she really want to be part of that?

She fed Berthe some hot chocolate into which she had spooned paregoric to quiet her down, and gave her bread and a bit of precious jam she had been hoarding. After her hysterics, and the hot chocolate laced with the narcotic, Berthe became very subdued. Madame Poule explained to her that to be safe she would have to go away. Madame Poule couldn't send her directly to her mother and father, as she didn't know where they were right now, but she would send her to a place in the country where she would be safe. She would have to do exactly as Madame Poule instructed her: she was to forget her name, forget everything, including what had happened to cause her to forget. If anyone asked for her identification card, she should say she had lost it. If anyone asked where her parents were she should say she didn't know, because she couldn't remember who they were. If anyone asked where she was going, she should say "Dieppe". If they asked why, she should say she didn't know. In other words, she was to act as if she had lost her memory or was retarded.

Madame Poule took the now quiet girl to the train-station, bought her a third-class ticket for Dieppe, and entrusted her to the conductor, explaining that the poor child was addled, that he was to see her safely to Dieppe, where she would be met. Then she dashed off before, hopefully, the conductor could imprint a clear recollection of her on his brain.

"Who was to meet Berthe Maisel in Dieppe?"

"I had no idea. I just thought it was a good place to send her. It was by the sea, and a harbor. If the Resistance was operating to get people out, it was a logical place for it. I had to trust to *le bon dieu* because I didn't know what else to do."

"So you don't know what happened to Berthe Maisel?"

Madame Poule cast her eyes down, and shook her head.

"And what happened to the Maisel apartment?"

Madame Poule hesitated before replying. "After awhile it seemed that the Maisels would not be returning, so it was rented to others."

"What about the Maisels' things?"

Madame Poule shrugged. "It was a long time ago, Mademoiselle."

Renee brusquely thanked Madame Poule for speaking with them.

Miri huskily thanked her too. Madame Poule's recital had made her feel deeply sad. She felt an echo of how she had felt when her mother died. Alone. In an empty gray place.

Renee asked Miri to go with her for coffee. She had a plan for getting more information out of the Fleuris, with Miri's help, which she wanted to expound. But Miri was feeling sick to her stomach, and declined. She was going to go back up to her room for awhile and then go to class.

In the courtyard Judy was waiting for them. "Well? How did it go?"

Renee indicated her satisfaction. Miri said nothing. She was feeling ill and just wanted to get back to her room for awhile. This did not deter Renee, who simply marched up the six flights of stairs behind her. Judy followed.

Germaine was rattling around on the sixth floor when the girls arrived. She greeted them deferentially, indicating to Miri that she had left her clean laundry on the bed. Miri thanked her, wondering why Germaine would bother to mention that since she would see it in a moment. And it wasn't time to pay.

"Ask Germaine whether she lived here during the war," Renee demanded.

"I know she did," said Miri, noticing that Germaine, who did not speak English, nevertheless had picked up on Renee's mention of her name. "But Madame Fleuris will be angry if we interrupt Germaine in her work. She puts in a fourteen-hour day as it is."

"Oh go on and ask her, it won't take but a minute."

Judy withdrew a hundred-franc note from her coat pocket and proferred it to Germaine. "Germaine, *pour vous.*"

Germaine looked puzzled, but accepted the note with a nod of thanks.

Judy said, "Germaine, our friend here is studying the war. If you have any recollections she would like to hear them. Especially about Jewish people in the neighborhood. What happened to them if anybody knew."

Germaine hesitated.

But she eventually said, "In the dining-room I heard

Mademoiseelle Miri asking about the Maisel family. I can tell you something about them. After the Maisels were taken away Madame Poule and Madame Fleuris cleared away a lot of personal things from their apartment and stored it upstairs in the *chambre de bonne* belonging to the Maisels, the room at the end near the sink. Madame Fleuris had not asked me to help. I think she didn't want me to know much about it. But when she saw that I had seen what they were doing she told me to clean the Maisel apartment thoroughly, scrub down the kitchen, polish the furniture and the floors, and brush out the Turkish carpets. Some time after that a group of Finnish businessmen moved in. They couldn't speak a word of French except *bon jour*. They had a Finnish cook and a Danish maid who lived right in the apartment with them, not upstairs. They couldn't speak a word of French either. I guess at the food markets they just pointed."

When Miri translated this for Renee she became very agitated. "We've got to get into that attic room!"

Judy also bubbled with excitement at the idea, and suggested that they enlist Jamie, who would surely want to be in on it, and might be helpful at how they should go about it.

Miri felt tense and anxious at the mere thought of breaking into the room, but said nothing. She excused herself and went into her room to lie down. She had the impression that Renee and Judy were continuing the discussion about breaking into the padlocked room as they left together, but tried to concentrate on "*L'Etre et Le Néant*" as that book usually put her into a somnolent state.

But Judy soon roused her with loud rapping at her door. She was breathless, eager to help Renee. Miri excused herself: she had to get to class.

She did make it to the afternoon session at the Beaux Arts. A couple of French art students spoke to her in a friendly way, but she wasn't in the mood for light talk. She was dreading the possibility that Jamie and Judy would collaborate with Renee to do the break-in and would inveigle her too.

6

Renee was going to stay in Paris during the holidays, continuing her researches. Miri therefore planned to disappear over the Christmas holidays to avoid being coerced into helping Renee.

Judy wanted her to go to London with her, to look up some American friends who were studying at Oxford. But Miri didn't want to go anywhere with Judy. Nor did she want to accept Judy's Christmas present, a dazzling multicolored silk scarf.

But Judy insisted. "I didn't buy it especially for you, it's just one of my old things that doesn't go with anything I have."

"It's beautiful. But I don't have a gift for you."

"That's fine. I get everything I want. And some things I don't even want! Please take it."

Miri's prolific correspondent Seymour Levin, writing frequently from Garmisch, wanted her to come there although he did warn her that his workload would be especially heavy the last couple of weeks of the year, because they were processing all the year-end reports. He had won another big pot at poker and offered to pay her train fare round-trip between Paris and Garmisch, but that sounded too much like being treated as a kept woman and she certainly wouldn't have accepted, even if she were going, which she was not.

Vanessa Tate was going with a group of girls from Reid Hall to Austria skiing, and would have been happy to have Miri join them, but the mere thought of skiing made Miri feel faint.

What she really wanted was to go to Italy, and she wanted Jamie to go with her. Jamie had already travelled all over Italy, knew a lot about it, and spoke fluent Italian.

But he had other plans.

He did, however, help Miri plan her trip to Italy, mapping out the most important museums and churches and piazzas, and within them the most significant works to see. After looking up what was on at LaScala, he recommended that she make Milan her last stop. So she would be going to Rome first, then Florence, then Milan. On Christmas Eve, just hours before her train left for the twenty-four-hour ride to Rome, he took her to midnight mass at a Franciscan monastery in Montparnasse where little soprano choirboys dressed in brown robes like miniature monks sang as their procession wound down the side aisles of the church and up the center.

She adored Italy, especially Florence. The narrow winding cobblestone streets arriving suddenly upon a dazzling piazza, the delicious food in tiny cheap restaurants, the peddlars on the Ponte Vecchio, but most of all the art. She thought of leaving Paris and moving there until her money ran out, but the men pinched too much. They kept pinching her on the street, and rubbing up against her, and it made her nervous.

Then in Milan, her last stop before returning to Paris, a strange thing happened.

On her last night she attended "*Il Trovatore*". The singers were tremendous, there was some young soprano named Maria Meneghini Callas as Leonora who was fabulous, but Miri had to leave before the end of the last act in order to catch her train to Paris. She had her small valise with her at the theatre.

A man who had spoken to her during the intermission followed her out of the theatre as she slipped out while the lights were down and the performance was still going on, (so he had obviously been watching her) to go directly to the train back to Paris. He ran after her as she signalled a taxi, jumped into it beside her and rode with her to the train, all the while telling her how *bellissima* she was and how he had fallen in love with her! All this in French with an Italian accent! His name was Luigi something-or-other and when she wouldn't tell him her name he kept calling her "*bellissima* Beatrice". He was balding but had a young face, with watery gray eyes.

He actually got onto the train as she did, and riding as far as the border, all the while babbling in Italian, having exhausted his eloquence in French. When the conductor came for their tickets, he was obliged to buy one on the spot. At the border however his outpouring of passion came to an abrupt end. He had no passport. So when they got to the border he had to get off the train and take another train back to Milan. It would have been immensely flattering except that she couldn't help suspecting that he was utterly *non compos mentis.*

She related this incident at the first *déjeuner* after the holidays, when they were all reassembled at the *pension.* Madame Fleuris had introduced the topic, "How I spent my Christmas holidays," to get all them to practice their French, which had been neglected for the duration of the holidays.

After listening without interrupting, Madame Fleuris made a derogatory comment about Italians, Judy sighed that Luigi sounded wonderfully romantic, Jamie and Monsieur Fleuris merely smiled, but it was Branford Duane Lee the Third who surprised them by voicing an opinion. Also, there was something odd about Bran: he was suntanned.

"It didn't happen," he pronounced. "It was a dream. A perfect Freudian dream."

"Of course it did. I just told you."

"You only think it did, because it was so vivid. But you dreamed it. The symbolism is all there. The balding man is your father. He's importuning you, in a reversal of the Oedipal situation, and you say you don't understand but it's evident that you do, perfectly. Your leaving before the end of the last act is a potent symbol too but I'll leave that aside for the nonce. As Nietsche asked, 'How much truth can you take?' The fact that he was stopped at the border – Incredible! He couldn't pass over the line, in effect, of what society would allow."

All of this had been spoken in intelligible French which however did not endow it with more sense than English would have.

After responding monosyllabically to Madame Fleuris' insistent question about what he had done over the holidays – "skiing" – Bran slid away. Judy and Madame Fleuris began speculating on whether he was studying psychoanalysis or was just *fou.*

Although Miri was too busy trying to be an artist to waste much time on small-talk, and therefore tried very hard –without always succeeding – to keep her conversations with her fellow Americans, except for Jamie, to a minimum, she would speak with Germaine and Gabrielle, Madame Poivriere's maid, whenever she happened to meet one of them on the stairs or the landing, to practice her French. Gabrielle, a pert young country girl, for her part was very chatty, pleased that a "*demoiselle*" would give her the respect of saying "*vous*" to her and of listening to what she had to say. Her mistress, Madame Poivriere, of course, *tutoyer'*ed her as the French did all servants, children, dogs and cats. (The condescension presumably extended only to domestic animals. Miri couldn't imagine anyone *tutoyer'*ing a tiger.)

At one of these chance encounters shortly after her return from Italy Gabrielle told Miri that Madame Poivriere's second *chambre de bonne* had been let. Gabrielle's principal interest in it was that it meant more work for her.

Gabrielle's duties, besides cooking, serving, cleaning the big Poivriere apartment on the *cinquième* and scrubbing laundry for Madame Poivriere, now included cleaning the tenant's room and emptying her chamber-pot. The widow Poivriere did not allow her new tenant to use the W.C. or the bathroom within her apartment on the *cinquième*, nor did she provide food as did the *pension* Fleuris where Miri was staying. The tenant had to eat all her meals out.

According to Gabrielle, Madame Poivriere had only rented out the *chambre de bonne* because she felt guilty living alone in such a spacious apartment while there was a housing shortage in Paris. Despite offering it for rent through the student housing bureau at the start of the school year, the extra room had remained vacant ever since Miri had arrived in September. In fact she had thought about asking Gabrielle to ask Madame Poivriere if she could rent it to use as a studio, but never got around to it, and then over the Christmas holidays, while she was away in Italy, the new tenant moved into it.

A day or two after Gabrielle's report Miri herself met the new tenant. She was a year or two older than Miri, of the same height and coloring, but much slimmer and *très chic.*

There was something strange about their first encounter, which took place on the stairs between the *cinquième* and the *sixième.* They stared at each other out of uncannily similar dark solemn eyes, in mutual surprise at their resemblance to each other.

The newcomer smiled. "This is as close as we're ever going to get to our *doppelgängers.*"

Miri agreed. She could have been looking in a mirror, not an ordinary mirror but a fun-house mirror that made one's reflection fatter or thinner; she was the fatter, her neighbor the thinner.

Her name was Emilie Werner, she sold handbags at the Galeries Lafayette and she had a lover. This Miri learned after Emilie invited Miri into her room for a cup of instant coffee. Her landlady, Madame Poivriere, did not permit cooking in the room, nor did Miri's landlady, Madame Fleuris, but the small electric coil stuck in a china cup boiled water very quickly and was easily hidden.

Emilie invited Miri to take the one small armchair in the room. She herself perched on the narrow bed. A gray velvety cat curled in a ball in her lap, and Emilie petted it absently as they spoke. She asked Miri about herself, what she was doing in Paris ("studying art" – "nice to have money enough to do useless things"), whether she had a lover ("no" – *"dommage"*) and then reported with a happy smile that she herself had a lover. He was married, unfortunately, but was very kind. She had met him when he came by to purchase a gift at the handbags counter at Galeries Lafayette.

While they were talking Emilie removed her suit-jacket, under which she was wearing a short-sleeved white silk shirt. Her arms were extremely thin and boney. Miri gaped at a bluish tattoo on Emilie's right arm.

Emilie noticed Miri staring. "That's right," she sighed, pushing her arm forward so that Miri could see the numbers, "I was in Auschwitz. I was still a child when they seized me, but I grew up fast." She shook her head. "I can't talk about it any more now."

Miri had not asked her to. Miri was too horrified to have wanted to hear a word. She thanked Emilie for the coffee and left abruptly. She was feeling poorly anyway, sneezing and slightly stuffed as if a cold were coming on.

Afterwards she felt remorseful at being so abrupt with Emilie, and wanted to make amends somehow. The multicolored silk scarf Judy Kugel had foisted on her – she hadn't even wanted it, and she certainly didn't want any gifts from Judy – seemed like a good way to make amends.

She didn't seek out Emilie, but waited until the second time they met on the stairs again, about a week after the first encounter.

Miri told Emilie, "I have something for you."

Emilie looked as if she needed some kind of a lift. Whereas at their first meeting she had been serene, and when speaking of her lover even happy, now she looked very very sad. She might even have been crying recently. Miri reached into her room and snatched the scarf from her night-table where she had been keeping it in wait, then proferred it wordlessly. She knew she was being gauche, but Emilie nodded her thanks. Emilie seemed to understand what this was about, for she asked Miri, "Are you Jewish too?"

This was not the time to go into a long philosophical explanation and saying "no" without qualifications would have been a lie, so she merely nodded. Emilie thanked her for the scarf and they went their ways.

Miri thought Renee Rubin would want to hear about Emilie Werner, but she didn't call her.

A couple of days later, however, a Wednesday, Renee telephoned Miri at *déjeuner*. She had two reasons for calling: one, she wanted to inform Miri that there was to be a gathering of existentialists at a *cave* near Saint Germain dès Près on Sunday evening, only six hundred francs for food and wine, and it was likely that Sartre would be there. She urged Miri to attend. Miri, genuinely interested, said she would be there.

Secondly, Renee wanted to plan the break-in of the padded room and wanted to have a meeting as soon as possible, perhaps that evening, with Miri herself, and "*la vâche qui rit* and *l'eau qui fait pshssst*" to plan it.

Miri had no idea what she was talking about. Renee had to explain that Judy was "*la vâche*" and Jamie "*l'eau*" and was annoyed that her witticism hadn't been appreciated. How could Miri have failed to notice the advertisements posted everywhere, one of a laughing cow, *la vâche qui rit*, advertising a packaged cheese of that name; and the other a green bottle of Perrier, the water that goes pshssst! Explained to her, Miri thought these epithets were only mildly funny, as Judy did laugh a lot but was not like a cow. And there was more to Jamie than carbonated water. To change the subject from the break-in she blurted out, "There's a new tenant in our building who was in Auschwitz."

"Interesting. What's her name?"

"Emilie Werner."

"Now about that meeting to plan the break-in..."

Defeated, Miri said, "I'll put Judy on the phone and you two can make the arrangements."

Judy came back from the phone in the kitchen in high spirits. "That Renee is really gung-ho! I've invited her to *diner* with us at the brasserie for tomorrow night. My treat," she told Miri and Jamie. "We can have *choucroute.*"

Over coffee at a nearby café, Judy brought Jamie up-to-date. Renee wanted them to help break into the padlocked room on the *sixième*, the room which had been the Maisel family's *chambre de bonne*, where some of their belongings had been stashed after they were arrested during the war .

Renee thought there might be something in there that could help her in a search for members of the Maisel family!

Jamie immediately agreed. Miri said nothing.

But the supper-meeting did not take place. Renee had pushed too hard. When Judy called her from the café to tell her the time and place of their supper-meeting, Renee stated that she was coming early so that she could drop in on Emilie Werner first. Judy told her that Madame Fleuris did not allow outside guests after five o'clock in the rooms either in the apartment or upstairs.

"But she's not a tenant of Madame Fleuris!"

"Well you can't just come in off the street to drop in on someone you don't know, without having someone to introduce you."

"I don't see why not."

"Look, do what you want, but my invitation to supper is hereby cancelled."

Judy came back from the phone red in the face, uncharacteristically angry. She told Jamie and Miri that she had un-invited Renee. "I'm having second thoughts about getting involved in an illicit project with someone that pig-headed. But I have to admit I would like to see what's in that room. Maybe we could break in ourselves, without Renee."

Jamie was agreeable. Miri said nothing.

7

Miri did not go to the tea-dance that Saturday. She was anxious to start rereading *"L'Etre et Le Néant"* to prepare for meeting Sartre on Sunday. This time she wouldn't skip as many pages.

Miri read late into the night.

She wouldn't have admitted that she was nervous at the thought that Sartre might be there, but while changing into a navy wool turtleneck and voluminous skirt sufficiently serious for a gathering of existentialists, she tipped over the small alcohol stove which provided the only heat to her little room, spilling the whole reservoir of alcohol and spreading its fire.

The alcohol ran along the tile floor, flames leaped from the stove to the alcohol, and as the alcohol flowed along the uneven tile floor, the blue flame snaked under the bed igniting the *paillaisse.*

She flipped the straw mattress onto the floor, dumped icy water from the washing pitcher onto the flames, stomped on it all and somehow put the fire out.

The damage was conspicuous. Pieces of straw were falling out of the gaping hole, jaggedly edged in black, in the mattress-casing. The linen sheet had been singed brown by the flames.

Madame Fleuris would be livid when she learned of the damage. She would no doubt charge Miri for a new *paillaisse*, to say nothing of new sheets, although the ones on her bed probably predated the first world war, possibly had been part of Madame's *trousseau* in prehistoric times.

Germaine would discover the damage when she changed the sheets, but that wouldn't be for more than a week. So Miri had time to figure out what to do.

One possibility was to replace the damaged mattress casing and linen sheet. She could buy secondhand linens at the Marché aux Puces. She had already bought old sheets there once before to use as paint-rags, getting a big basketful for a hundred francs, or twenty-five cents. They were cotton, though, not linen, like the ones on her bed, and did have a few rips in them. If she could find secondhand sheets in linen to replace the ones she had damaged then she could use the burnt ones as paint-rags and it wouldn't be a total waste of money.

By the time she put the fire out it was too late to go the *vrai cave* to possibly meet Sartre, and to Miri's surprise she felt, rather than regret, relief that she wouldn't have to spend four hundred francs especially since she had kept falling asleep over *"L'Etre et Le Néant"* and couldn't remember much significant about what it was about.

Renee would be annoyed with her, of course, but it couldn't be helped.

She decided to go to the movies. The Cluny theater was showing Louis Jouvet films week after week. Any one of them would do. She had seen *"Volpone"* twice already but wouldn't mind seeing it again.

Nobody was around on the sixth floor. Jamie didn't answer her knock on his door, and no sounds were coming from any of the other rooms.

Sometime during the night or early morning she awoke choking and sneezing and shivering uncontrollably in spite of the extra blanket that Germaine or Madame Fleuris had left on her bed the night before.

Her bladder was near bursting. She huddled into herself, hugging her knees and rubbing her icy feet together, appalled at the thought of getting out of bed in that damp chill air to make the long trip down two long winding flights of stairs, then having to unlock the apartment door without awakening anyone and finding her way to the bathroom in the dark.

But the alternative was the chamber pot, and in four months she still hadn't gotten used to using it. She didn't like not being able to instantly flush the unpleasantness away instead of leaving the odorous contents for the *bonne* to collect hours later. So there she huddled shivering and choking, refusing to recognize the inexorability of having to go to the bathroom, that it wouldn't go away by willing it, until the ache of doing nothing became worse than the nuisance of doing something and she relented and reached for the chamber pot.

But she would not leave it in the commode for hours, for Germaine to collect when she cleaned the room. So pulling on her old pink chenille robe and slipping her frozen feet into felt slippers like those the *bonnes* wore she decided to carry the chamber-pot down to the end of the hall to dump it. Besides the covered pail there was a sink there with a single faucet of cold nonpotable water used for cleaning the rooms on the floor.

At first she intended to carry out her mission in the dark, afraid that if she pressed the *minutière* button on the wall, the light, shining through the chinks in their doors, might awaken one of the others on the floor. But the fear of spilling the chamber pot was stronger, so she pressed the *minutière* button and began padding down the hall, wishing she had not selected the room farthest from the sink.

She passed Gabrielle's room, then Jamie's, then just before the padlocked room beside the sink, was Emilie Werner's. She managed to reach the pail without spilling the contents of the chamber-pot until she could dump it, trying to ignore her revulsion, rinsed it and turned to go back to her room. She felt a cold draft of air on her feet. It was coming from the space under Emilie's door between the door and the jamb, as if her window were wide open. It was so cold in the *chambres de bonne* these January days that it seemed incredible anyone would want the window open. Just then the *minutière* went out. Standing there in the dark, the cold draft blowing from beneath the door, Miri was startled and frightened by a shrill yowl, maybe Emilie's cat, and froze in place in the dark.

She decided to wake up Jamie.

In the dark she tiptoed to Jamie's door and knocked softly. There was no answer. She knocked harder. This time, although Jamie still did not respond, Gabrielle did. She stuck her head out her door. Light from her room streamed into the hall.

"Oh it's you, Mademoiselle Miri! Is there a fire?"

Miri laughed crazily, thinking of her alcohol fire earlier in the evening. "No, no, Gabrielle, it's–" What could she say? She couldn't say "it's nothing" because it might be something. She said, "I'm sorry I disturbed you, Gabrielle."

"Not at all, Mademoiselle Miri, it's almost a quarter to six, I would have to get up in fifteen minutes anyway."

Miri was relieved that it was morning. "You rise at six?"

"Of course. I have to bring coals to the kitchen-stove, start the fire going, make Madame's coffee – she likes it very early before she takes her little dog Lili for a long walk."

Miri went back to her room, crawled back into bed and pulled the blankets up to her nose, shivering more than ever, but had to sit up almost immediately as she was again attacked by choking and sneezing.

Her supply of clean handkerchiefs was diminishing and the price of Kleenexes was outrageous, so she tried willing herself to stop sneezing, but it didn't work. She tore up some unused paint-rags.

At seven she prepared to go down to *petit déjeuner* in the apartment, with Madame and Monsieur Fleuris and the other *pensionnaires*. She pulled on the same navy turtleneck and skirt she had worn the evening before, then opened the shutters and pulled the little stuffed chair near the window to sit with a blanket over her legs where she could gaze down into the cobblestone courtyard and watch anyone arriving or departing from the building, as nosey as any concierge! She was watching for Jamie. She assumed he had been out all night, or he would have heard the racket she made at his door, especially after Gabrielle opened hers.

Although the sun had not yet risen, there was enough light from the windows of the workshop on the ground floor to make out shapes. Eventually she saw someone crossing the courtyard, not from the outside, where she was watching for Jamie, but from the building toward the outside doors. It was a man in a beret and long black coat, shuffling slowly. He was carrying four large metal boxes, two tied together in each hand. He stopped for a moment, placing the boxes on the ground, apparently to adjust one of the cords. When he stood up again he glanced around for a moment and Miri saw enough of his face – or rather, his bushy white beard – to recognize that it was old Monsieur Fleuris. She wondered what he could be carrying in those metal boxes, and where he was going with them so early in the morning.

A few minutes later Jamie entered the courtyard from the outside, giving a friendly wave to the concierge as he passed her loge. He must have spent the night with somebody else. She felt a pang. Jamie seemed so right for her. Besides being an existentialist he loved art and he always knew the good things to do.

He had shown her the Place des Vosges by moonlight.

He had insisted that she climb the narrow stone steps spiraling up inside a tower of Notre Dame.

He had invited her to a *vernissage*. He couldn't help it that the paintings were awful.

He had helped her plan her Christmas trip to Italy, and had taken her to midnight mass at a Franciscan monastery on Christmas Eve.

He knew the restaurant that had the best chocolate cake in Paris and it wasn't even expensive, *chez* Henriette.

But he obviously had someone else.

She went downstairs to breakfast.

8

"That's some cold you've got there, Miri," Jamie said, as she sneezed into her table napkin.

Jamie had slid into his seat for *petit déjeuner* seconds after Miri had arrived. Branford Duane Lee the Third and Judy were already there.

"You do look horrible," Judy said cheerfully.

"You need a room with central heating," Jamie said. "That alcohol stove is not enough."

"That's all *you* have," Miri reminded him.

"Jamie spends less time in his own bed than you do in yours," Judy giggled.

After last night Miri had to admit to herself that Judy's observation was probably true. But how had she divined that, since her room was here on the fourth floor?

"*En français, mesdemoiselles, s'il vous plaît!*" cried Madame Fleuris.

"*Jamie dit que Miri a besoin d'une chambre avec chauffage centrale,*" Judy laughed.

The rule that they had to speak French at table was wearing thin. Their French was improving as they lived their daily lives.

"*Du chauffage centrale,*" said Madame, ever vigilant of the partitive and still triumphant that the Academie had forced an American corporation to employ it on their billboards in France, "*Buvez du Coca-Cola*" instead of the more pithy "*Buvez Coca-Cola*".

And, Madame Fleuris continued indignantly, she herself had put an extra blanket on Miri's bed last night.

Since Madame had made no mention of the damage to the *paillaisse* and sheets, she obviously had not yet discovered it.

Miri sniffled all through breakfast, though not as badly as earlier that morning. It looked as if she was going to have to splurge on Kleenexes. If Madame Fleuris hadn't been such a miser she could have used toilet-paper to blow her nose. But Madame Fleuris' idea of toilet-paper was torn-up pieces of telephone-book, pierced through and hung from a nail.

They were chewing the last of the baguettes and draining the last drops of ersatz coffee and muttering that it was time to get going, when Germaine, her felt carpet-slippers flapping, suddenly came scuttling into the dining-room to whisper excitedly in Madame Fleuris' ear.

A lead weight sunk in Miri's belly. She was sure that Germaine having gone upstairs to make the beds had discovered the damage to her *paillasse* and sheets and was now reporting it to Madame. She waited in dread.

But at Germaine's whispered words, Madame arose from her seat without so much as a glance at Miri, or at any of them, and swiftly stalked through the swinging door into the kitchen, followed close on her heels by Germaine.

As soon as his wife left the room Monsieur Fleuris stood up and shuffled from one to the other of everyone at table to shake hands and say *bon jour* before leaving the apartment. They heard the outer door slam behind him.

Judy put a finger to her lips, then pointed toward the swinging door to the kitchen, through which Madame and Germaine had passed. She tiptoed over, waving the others to join her. Bran declined with a curt shake of his head, though he did not yet depart for wherever it was he went every morning. He remained in place as usual as silent and as stiff as a stick.

Jamie and Miri tiptoed over to join Judy at the swinging door. Bran remained alone at his place at the table, sipping the dregs of his coffee.

The threesome would normally have dashed off by now for a second breakfast together before dispersing to their various classes.

It had started with Judy and Miri going for hot chocolates, then Jamie introduced them to a bar near Cluny where hardboiled eggs in a bowl on the counter cost fifty francs each. There they would each peel and eat an egg and sip a cafe filtre, a thick black bitter liquid, while they grinned at each other to be amongst *vrai* French workmen in blue overalls tossing back Calvados with their coffees.

Judy quietly edged open the swinging door a few inches; they could hear muted conversation within the kitchen.

At first they couldn't make out the words, heard only murmurs, until a voice cried shrilly, "But Madame the *pauvre petite* has been strangled!"

"Tell me, Gabrielle," Madame Fleuris demanded, her own voice growing louder and shriller than usual, "how can you be sure she was strangled?"

"Madame!" shrieked Gabrielle, "I saw it with my own eyes! I had gone to Mademoiselle Werner's room to clean it. I knocked on the door. There was no response. I tried the door. It was not locked, and it opened with ease. There she was! She was lying on the bed with the scarf wound tight around her poor neck!"

"The *pauvre petite*!" said Madame Fleuris.

Miri was aghast. Emilie Werner! Her heart began thumping wildly at the thought that the killer might have been lurking in the shadows even as she had been standing in the dark wondering about the cold draft from under Emilie's door.

Judy had gripped Miri's arm and was squeezing it like a tourniquet.

"You're giving me gangrene," Miri said.

Judy let go.

"I ran downstairs," Gabrielle sobbed, "to seek Madame Poivriere but she had gone out with Lili the dog and so I ran back up to find Germaine and ask her what I should do."

"Now quiet down, Gabrielle. I will tell you what to do. And you too, Germaine." Madame's tone was harsh. "You are not to speak of this matter to anyone at all until the police come to pose their questions." She herself would contact the commissaire of the quartier. She ordered Germaine to go up to the sixth floor, stand guard at Mademoiselle Werner's room allowing no one to enter, and to speak to no one. Madame would keep Gabrielle with her until the police should arrive. As Gabrielle was the one who had found the body she would be an important witness. In the meantime perhaps Gabrielle would be good enough to make herself useful and prepare more coffee for the Americans, since they would have to be questioned by the police before they could be allowed to depart for the day.

The Americans could hear Germaine's felt slippers flapping as she left the kitchen by the service-door, while some-one, no doubt Madame, dialed the telephone.

The one telephone in the apartment was in the kitchen. None of the *pensionnaires* was allowed to make a call without Madame's knowledge. She preferred that they make outgoing calls from a pay-phone at one of the cafés. She even kept a supply of *jetons* on hand to sell to them at a slight surcharge, even though they could be gotten at any café, and for incoming calls she charged the recipient a service-fee.

Judy was the one most affected by this rule. Her parents called her from Great Neck every Sunday night; boys were always calling her for dates; girls called to invite her to parties, and friends of her mother who were newly arrived in Paris called at Mrs Kugel's request to check up on her darling daughter, to find out if she was any closer to her goal of finding a nice Jewish American boy to marry, preferably one who was going to be a doctor or lawyer, although a dentist or certified public accountant would be acceptable in a pinch.

Madame Fleuris' voice was much louder and shriller than usual. They could hear her perfectly as she spoke on the telephone. "M'sieur le Commissaire? This is Madame Fleuris of 10 *bis* Rue des Ecoles, *quatrième arrondissement.* I wish to report a suspicious death. A young woman by the name of Emilie Werner who is the tenant in the *chambre de bonne* of a neighbor of mine, a Madame Poivriere on the fifth floor who is not in at this moment, appears to have been strangled. In any case, she is dead. The *bonne* of Madame Poivriere, Gabrielle, found Mademoiselle Werner dead, perhaps strangled, when she entered Mademoiselle Werner's room to clean it. I have posted my own *bonne* at the door so that nothing should be disturbed.... No, Monsieur le Commissaire, I have not seen the corpse myself." She said she had thought it more *convenable* to avoid the site until the police should investigate. A few polite phrases more, then Madame Fleuris hung up and was dialing someone else.

"Philippe? *C'est toi?*"

Philippe, the inimitable son-in-law.

Madame expressed concern that since Lucille and Philippe did not have a telephone in their apartment, Lucille might learn of the murder on Rue des Ecoles by word-of-mouth and might worry that her mother was in danger. Madame Fleuris ordered Philippe to leave his bureau directly and go reassure Lucille that all was well and that the death on Rue des Ecoles had nothing to do with the family Fleuris, that the victim was a tenant of a neighbor of theirs, Madame Poivriere. Their only connection was that Madame Poivriere's *bonne* had discovered the body and rushed to tell their own Germaine who had come to her mistress with the news. Madame Fleuris informed Philippe that she had already called the commissaire of police in the quartier, and all was in hand.

Judy and Jamie and Miri had tiptoed back to their seats around the dining-room table, had given Branford, who feigned indifference, a hasty summary when Madame Fleuris came through the swinging door. Hearing them conversing in English, she said with false brightness, "*En français, mes enfants, en français, s'il vous plaît!*" Just referring to her *pensionnaires,* two of whom she couldn't stand, as "*enfants*" instead of the usual "*mesdemoiselles, messieurs*" was an amiable departure for Madame Fleuris.

She resumed her seat at the head of the table, her back straight, a strained smile on her thin lips. She informed her guests that an unfortunate incident had occurred and that they were to remain where they were to be interviewed by the police before they left for their morning activities. She told them that she had ordered Madame Poivriere's *bonne,* Gabrielle, who was helping out for the moment, to prepare more coffee. She would be bringing it out shortly. Madame Fleuris requested that they remain to partake of it. They all murmured assent. How could anyone refuse the offer of seconds on coffee, especially when a murder had been discovered on the premises?

Madame Fleuris' lips trembled as she told them that the *pauvre petite* Mademoiselle Werner upstairs, a new tenant of Madame Poivriere's, had just been found dead, perhaps strangled!

They all responded with appropriate shock and dismay, although their eavesdropping had forewarned them.

"The Police Judiciare will no doubt be investigating," said Madame Fleuris, shaken. "I have already informed the quartier's commissaire. He and his assistants are no doubt already on their way." She requested that all of them wait for the police to arrive to question them and avoid a second visit. She was sure their questions would be brief and would not incommode them much.

Judy whispered to Miri, "But Bushy-Beard isn't here, so they'll still have to come back!"

Miri recalled Monsieur Fleuris' mysterious excursion that morning with the metal boxes but couldn't think of any way in which it might have been connected with Emilie Werner's death.

The police would ask each of them what they had observed. As an artist Miri felt she should have seen things others would have missed, but she had missed out on the biggest opportunity of all by not opening Emilie's door and looking in when she felt the cold draft.

Miri tried to recall possibly useful facts from her two conversations with Emilie Werner. There was the married lover, and the job at Galeries Lafayette. And the concentration-camp tattoo of course, but the police would see the tattoo for themselves. And that weird *doppelgängers* thing; but Miri was not about to call their attention to *that.*

When she thought about it she was terrified. A murderer had lurked on the very floor where she slept. She realized she would have to move —- as soon as possible.

The apple-cheeked Gabrielle in her maid's black and white uniform now brought in a large tray with individual pots of steaming aromatic coffee and a plate of croissants which was handed round! Miri felt as if Gabrielle were staring at her questioningly, as if wondering if her nocturnal walk had anything to do with Emilie Werner's death.

Madame Fleuris stared hard at the plate of croissants. "Where did you get these croissants, Gabrielle?" she demanded.

"I saw there were none so I ran to the bakery down on the corner," Gabrielle said cheerfully. "I charged them to Madame Poivriere's account."

This mollified Madame Fleuris, though she continued glancing anxiously toward the door. When the bell did sound she seemed to tense her already rigid back even more.

It was not yet the police. The stout self-important son-in-law Philippe Jumelle, more red in the face than ever, strutted in, going up to his mother-in-law and kissing her on the cheek.

The Americans had seen him many times. Philippe with his pale wife Lucille and their pale skinny pimply son came to the Fleuris apartment every Sunday for *déjeuner.* Whichever of the *pensionnaires* happened to be around (*déjeuner* was not served the *pensionnaires* on Sundays) were invited to join the family party for after-dinner coffee on these occasions.

Philippe Jumelle now reassured his mother-in-law that he had alerted Lucille, assuring her that her parents were safe. As for Lucille, Philippe reported that she was as well as could be expected. Meaning, given her hypochondria. Now he had come to be of whatever assistance he could to his mother-in-law.

Philippe made the rounds, going around the table from one to the other, shaking hands and repeating "*bon jour, mademoiselle*" or "*monsieur*" as required until each person at the table had received his or her own personal handshake and *bon jour*. Madame Fleuris meanwhile was expressing her pleasure that her son-in-law had shown her the respect of coming to be of assistance to her.

"Not that she needs his assistance," Judy whispered to Miri across the table, "she's got everything under control."

"And how much use can he be?" Miri whispered back. "He's more upset than Madame Fleuris is. I think he's angry that he had to leave a desk full of work for nothing."

Judy whispered back, "Maybe he's worried about his spotless reputation as a proper bourgeois and *functionnaire* being tarnished by being married to the daughter of someone who lives in a place where a lurid crime took place."

Moments later, the first of the police arrived.

PART

TWO

9

Dantan had barely hung his threadbare overcoat in the armoire in the clerks' room when the youth who ran errands stuck his grinning face around the open door and hollered, "Quick, Monsieur Dantan! Chief Inspector Goulette wants to see you at once!" Then the grin was gone, off to summon another subordinate, or transport files, or fetch beer and sandwiches for the chief from the corner bar.

Doggedly scratching at reports at their desks the men on either side of Dantan lifted their heads and looked at each other quizzically. A need for Dantan had not been noticeable in the year since he had joined the P.J. as an interpreter. "Dead men don't speak English," his fellow clerks had guffawed more times than he could find funny.

Dantan, a young veteran of the French war in Indochina, where he had been grievously wounded, had only been offered the post as interpreter thanks to the kind and persistent efforts of a fellow soldier, Jean-Jacques Pilieu, who had lain in the cot beside him in the military hospital ward. Pilieu had been a policeman in the Latin Quarter prior to his military service. After his discharge he was able to join the P.J. and eventually become an inspector.

When Alphonse Dantan was discharged some months after that, Pilieu began his campaign to persuade Chief Inspector Goulette that his comrade at arms Alphonse Dantan would be a big help in the Division. Pilieu played on his chief's known distaste for the bureaucrats of the Sixth Section, which concerned itself with aliens in France. In the past they had taken over in serious crime cases where Goulette was convinced he and his crack inspectors should have had jurisdiction. Pilieu pointed out that his friend Dantan spoke, read and wrote English expertly. Pilieu left his clever chief to deduce the rest; namely, that such a presence in the Police Judiciaire would give Goulette a measure of independence from the Sixth Section. Goulette took the bait, and Dantan joined the unit as an interpreter in which his friend was an inspector.

When Alphonse Dantan was nine years old, in 1939, his father went to war, and less than a year later was dead, killed fighting in the Argonne.

The elder Dantan had been a teacher at a boys' school. After his death his widow could not afford life in Paris with a growing boy for whom she could never get enough food. And she was lonely. She longed to go back to Dieppe where she had been born, and where she had spent her childhood. Her parents were long gone, her only brother had been killed in the war, and years before her sister had married a man who moved her to Persia where he worked for a big company. But there was an old-maid aunt, her mother's sister, still in Dieppe. Madame Dantan wrote to her aunt, asking if she and her son might move in with her. She emphasized what a hard worker she was, that she could help her aunt keep up her house and kitchen-garden, and also mentioned her small pension. Her aunt responded immediately with an invitation for the widow Dantan and her small son.

The widow Dantan fully intended to help her aunt keep up the big near-empty house, and to contribute most of her widow's pension, but it didn't work out that way. The cold damp weather and the cold damp house were not kind to Alphonse's mother. She fell ill, possibly with pneumonia (the doctor was never called), and died. Now the old aunt not only did not receive any monetary contribution or help with the house, but she was stuck with a little boy who was incessantly in motion and always hungry and only wanted to play on the rocky beach.

Alphonse's great-aunt was a devout woman. She went frequently to confession, pouring out to the *curé* remorse for her anger at her grand-nephew. The *curé* came up with a solution. He knew of a small clandestine group who were smuggling Jews to England, a few at a time. He would try to get young Alphonse included in one of their shipments.

So it came to pass that one chilly moonlit night, when fishing boats dotted the waters, a burlap sack wrapped in fishing nets, containing Alphonse, was carried down to the dock and tossed into a small boat along with other bundles similarly wrapped, then huddled under tarps as the fishermen set out. At a point distant from the French shore, a motorcraft puttered out from the murkiness, the fishing-nets were removed for reuse, and the burlap bags were handed over the side to seamen on the motorcraft which sped to the English coast while the fishing boat returned to the waters of France to catch some fish before returning home.

In English waters the burlap bags were opened, and the men and the few children who clambered out were wrapped in coarse wool blankets and given drinks of hot beef broth. Near dawn the boat docked, they were met on shore, British soil, by an immigration official and a health inspector, organized by one of the charitable agencies struggling to rescue children. The men took off to previously determined destinations. The children were stashed in a hay-wagon and delivered to a farm in the English countryside.

A group of Englishwomen which included one nurse, several schoolteachers, a farm-worker, and the elderly owner of the farm, were harboring children, Londoners' children sent to the countryside to save them from the Blitz, orphans of war, Jewish refugees, children scavenged from England, France and all around wartorn Europe.

As foster families were found to take in one or more of the children, they were sent there. The ones, like Alphonse, for whom there were no takers, remained at the farm, their first haven.

The Englishwomen firmly but kindly supervised and taught the children. They were given farm chores, taught English vocabulary and grammar, penmanship, arithmetic and the Our Father. They were fed milk from the cows they helped to milk, and eggs they hunted out in the coops, and home-grown vegetables which everyone helped grow. Alphonse grew strong and wiry, and tolerated life among the motley brood.

It was only much later that Alphonse understood that the same year his father fell on the battlefield, leaders of France made an ignominious truce with the Nazis while their besieged allies fought on.

By the time Alphonse was repatriated, at the age of sixteen, France had been liberated and General deGaulle had made his triumphant return to France, thanks to the graciousness of General Eisenhower, who understood the need for the French to restore their bruised self-esteem. By that time the old *curé* who had helped him get to England had died, and so had the maiden great-aunt. She had bequeathed her house in Dieppe to him. Dantan could realize only very little from the sale of this house but for whatever he could get he sold it and moved to Paris to study for his *bacho* and begin his life as a man.

During his six years in England he had become fluent in English, and somewhat literate as well. He had read the essays of Elia, many of Sir Walter Scott's adventures and had even struggled with several works of Shakespeare.

Alphonse contemplated a future as a don. His father had been a teacher. He had an idea of the pros and cons of the job. He would study the literature of France and of England and become an expert in comparative literature and eventually become a professor either at Oxford or the Sorbonne.

That was his early dream.

He began studying at the Sorbonne, shivering in the cold cavernous halls with fellow students from all over, many of them even poorer, and debating with them at the cafés.

But when he was twenty he was conscripted into the French army. With alarming dispatch he was uniformed, trained, equipped, and shipped out with many other troops to join the French Expeditionary Force fighting the Vietminh in Indochina.

Dantan was not swept up with enthusiasm for killing. His goal in the army was to conduct himself honorably but not necessarily heroically, and to survive.

He was in an infantry battalion, at first assigned to one of the small garrisons in the mountainous jungles between two rivers. They maintained a defensive position and waited out the long rainy season with skirmishes with Vietminh guerrillas in the dense jungle and defensive reaction to scattered mortar fire. He was then transferred to another post in the region at Nghia Lo, which was strategically important because the village was the capital of a tribe fervently friendly to the French, the T'ai. Nghia Lo was less than one hundred miles from Hanoi. The year before Dantan had been shipped in, it had been the target of a fierce but unsuccessful attack by the Communist General, Vo Nguyen Giap. The French had responded quickly by dropping in parachute battalions which with foresight had been stationed nearby, and they saved the garrison from the Communists – then. The following year, at the end of the monsoon season, Giap attacked Ngia Lo again with his infantry producing such heavy mortar fire that in less than an hour more than seven hundred Frenchmen were killed, and uncounted Vietnamese, and the remaining soldiers had to flee with paratroop cover to forts further back from the strategic ridge. It was in this battle that Dantan was severely wounded, rescued and carried back by his comrades, and eventually transported to complete his recovery in a military hospital in France.

His war experience killed that part of Dantan's spirit which could find intellectual fascination in the imaginings of dead artists. He could no longer think of imparting enthusiasm and insights to callow youth. What was the use? They would in their turn become cannon fodder, as he had been, and his father before him.

Until the morning of January 18, 1954, when he was hurriedly summoned to the chief inspector's office, Dantan's work at the P.J. had largely consisted of translating or verifying others' translations of documents from English to French of individuals who had come to the notice of the French police, not usually to their advantage. It was not interesting work nor was it well-paid. He knew he was drifting, living moment to moment, but couldn't muster enough psychic energy to do anything about it.

Sometimes he daydreamed about marrying a good girl with a *dot*, but he didn't know any, didn't have any particularly good ideas on how he could find one, thought it unlikely he could persuade her to marry him if he did, since he had poor prospects, and even if she became enamored of him for his physical charms, her father would undoubtedly be less complacent.

Besides his trivial chores on the job at the P.J. Dantan served as Pileu's interpreter in the latter's moves on charming rosy-cheeked English girls, giggling Americans or, more scarce but the most bewitching, Scandinavians.

Though he couldn't speak more than a few words of anything but French, Pilieu was a connoisseur of foreign girls. The Swedes were the most abandoned and fun, but scarce; the English, charming and soft but difficult to get into the sack; Americans varied from intensely inhibited to aggressively determined to do it all, and could be difficult as they liked to be told that one was in love with them; and the few Spanish girls he had managed to encounter were hot but also hot-headed and could fly into a rage over nothing.

Pilieu was a gourmand rather than gourmet: he enjoyed them all!

Dantan's attempts to teach English to his friend so that he could make his own pick-ups without an assistant came to naught. Dantan's few wry remarks to the target in impeccable British English were usually sufficient to get Pilieu going with her, and after that words were unnecessary. The two friends would have a beer outdoors at a cafe and look around until Pilieu noticed someone for whom he was struck with an urgent need to meet immediately. Pilieu, a crooked smile on his pleasantly ugly visage, watched as Dantan approached her table and said a few words . Dantan made light of his friend's predicament until she tittered behind her hand, at which point Pilieu strode to her table and sat down grinning happily. Tall for a Frenchman, broad shoulders and slightly crooked Roman nose, large hands and feet, he had no trouble making contact without Dantan's help with girls who spoke French, but he was more intrigued with foreigners. Plump, thin, tall, short, shy, bold, blonde, brunette, he managed to find something to charm him in all of them.

The two comrades had come out of their battle experience and medical recovery quite differently. Whereas Dantan went through the motions of daily life with little or no enjoyment or any other feeling, Pilieu savored life more than ever after almost losing it. He was continually climbing into hotel beds with foreign girls he successfully picked up, he enjoyed rich meals with gusto, he guzzled wine by the liter.

Pilieu had retained the faith of his childhood and made good use of the confessional. After all, if one got one's hands dirty one washed them, and if one got one's soul dirty, one did the same. Those indolent priests who lived comfortably, supported by others, should earn their keep once in awhile!

Dantan had no difficulties in trolling for girls in his own right. Though lacking the easy outgoing manner of his friend, he had penetrating dark eyes and swarthy good looks, and exuded sexuality.

But as he had a *petite amie* who satisfied his immediate physical needs, he rarely bothered to roam. This was not out of fidelity, but inertia. He felt a sincere affection for his little friend but it was no grand passion – on either side. They would go on as they were until one or the other was struck by a *coup de foudre* and went off with someone else, or had the opportunity to marry someone rich.

Sometimes Alphonse felt a faint temporary desire for something more: challenging work; passion in his life. But the feeling would pass before he had done anything about it. Pilieu try as he might could not impart his *joie de vivre* to his friend.

It was only a few minutes past eight but already the air of Chief Inspector Goulette's small office was dense with acrid smoke, and a fresh Gauloise was dangling loosely from his lower lip. Pilieu was leaning against the wall, and an older inspector whom Dantan knew only by sight, Vouray, a shrunken man in baggy clothes which may have fit him before the war, when there had been more food. Vouray slouched in one of the two straightbacked chairs flanking Goulette's desk. The chief inspector waved Dantan into the other.

"Sit down, Dantan," he growled. "Your services as an interpreter are required. A victim of murder has just been found at 10 *bis* Rue des Ecoles." This was a stone's throw from the Sorbonne. "The quartier police are there and forensics are on their way. There are several Americans living in the house who may have material information regarding this case. One may even be a suspect. Thus your services as an interpreter are wanted."

Chief Inspector Goulette was respected by the other inspectors. He was grim and reserved. He solved most of his cases. He was old enough to have seen it all, young enough to still feel something. Dantan was electrified to be included by him on a murder case.

A real assignment, not make-work out of pity!

After a giving his team a quick briefing, Chief Inspector Goulette, with Inspectors Vouray and Pilieu, and the interpreter Alphonse Dantan, retrieved and pulled on their coats and berets, clattered noisily down the wooden stairs and out the portals of the P.J. where they hailed a taxi.

It was only a short distance from Quai des Orfevres to 10 *bis* Rue des Ecoles, practically around the corner, down Boul' Mich' a bit and then there you were. The younger men could have traversed it in minutes on foot but Goulette loathed walking if he could ride, especially in the presence of those younger and fitter and faster. And Vouray, who forced himself to walk when he was on his own time, for exercise, suffered from rheumatism and appreciated the luxury of a ride when he would have to keep up a pace. The two older men followed by Pilieu piled into the back seat, then Dantan as the junior person present flipped down one of the jump-seats for himself, his whole being, heart, breathing, mind, quickened by the prospect of real work; a meaningful challenge.

10

As they rode along Boul' Mich', crowded at this hour with students, Goulette imparted the few facts he had learned on the phone with the quartier's prefecture. The victim, Emilie Werner, was a young woman about twenty-three years old, a salesgirl at Galeries Lafayette, where she had worked for more than two years.

She had been found in her attic room at around half past seven that morning by a maid who had come to empty the chamber pot. Mademoiselle Werner was renting the room from the widow Poivriere who owned and resided alone in the apartment on the fifth floor. Mademoiselle Werner had occupied the attic room at Rue des Ecoles for only the past four weeks. Leclerq in Records was going through the residency cards to identify her previous domicile.

The maid, Gabrielle, who had found the body also lived in a room on the sixth floor; she was employed by Madame Poivriere. But after her discovery she had run screaming to the maid at the *pension* Fleuris, Germaine, because her own mistress was not at home. In fact it was Madame Fleuris who had called the prefecture.

Two of the other *chambres de bonne* on the sixth floor were occupied by Americans who were *pensionnaires* in the *pension* Fleuris on the fourth floor. Along with Gabrielle, they should be among the first to be questioned, hence the need for Dantan. And not just for what they might have seen the night before.

Madame Fleuris had informed the prefecture that on Sunday evening she had gone to the sixth floor to bring an additional blanket for one of her *pensionnaires*, Mademoiselle Miri Winter, and reported that she was just emerging into the darkened hallway before turning on the *minutière* when she saw Monsieur Giardini stealthily leaving Mademoiselle Werner's room. At the time Madame thought it must be a lover's tryst and though she disapproved said nothing, nor did she make her presence known.

In view of the murder, however, Madame Fleuris wondered whether the visit had not had a more sinister motivation.

The two Americans whose rooms were on the sixth floor were Monsieur James Giardini, age twenty-four, a language student. Mademoiselle Miriam Winter, twenty, was an art student at the Ecole des Beaux Arts.

At that bit of information Pilieu dug an elbow into Dantan's ribs. Dantan gave Pilieu a sardonic glance.

Pilieu, Goulette declared, was to interrogate the maids Gabrielle and Germaine, and Madame Poivriere, particularly for background information on Mademoiselle Werner, and the building concierge for comings and goings she might have observed. Goulette himself would question Madame Fleuris, since she had reported seeing Monsieur Giardini at the crime scene at a sensitive time. And with Dantan interpreting, he would question the two Americans residing on the sixth floor.

The inspectors would also try to extract pertinent information from the other two Americans who resided at the *pension* Fleuris, in rooms in the main apartment on the fourth floor, Monsieur Branford Duane Lee, age twenty-seven, and Mademoiselle Judith Kugel, age twenty-one, student in the *cours de la civilisation française pour les étrangers* at the Sorbonne.

Another dig in the ribs from Pilieu.

Vouray would question occupants of the apartments on the first, second and third floors, as well as the shopkeepers on the ground level with entries on the courtyard.

"Should one of the Americans become a serious suspect, we will be obliged to liaise with the Sixth Section, which as we know concerns itself with aliens in France. But I will pursue my investigation in the meanwhile."

Vouray muttered deprecations about the Sixth Section under his breath.

Chief Inspector Goulette fell silent, filling the taxi with acrid smoke from his Gauloise cigarette.

The thought of the Sixth Section gave Dantan some anxiety. They would have interpreters of their own. Suppose they tried to dispossess him from this assignment? This was the first thing the chief had asked him to do that was not an act of charity, to justify his meagre pay. It was imperative that he accomplish something worthwhile if not remarkable in this case as soon as possible.

Pilieu and Dantan spoke in low tones. "You're a lucky fellow to be interviewing the two young American girls!" Pilieu told him. Pilieu tried to commit Dantan to arranging a meeting for him too. Dantan, his enthusiasm in his job aroused for once, would promise nothing that might jeopardize it. Pilieu reminded him in a whisper that all the Americans who dallied in the schools and cafés of Paris seemed to be rich, compared to themselves, and if they were pretty besides—!

Dantan was glad when his friend ceased his banter. He wanted to focus professionally on the case, no side action with women who might be involved in the case as sources of information.

The case had elements that might complicate matters. The young woman had only resided at her present address for the past four weeks. Could she in that time have formed such empassioned entanglements that they could lead to murder? Surely the driving force for her death had come out of her past? Of course she could have known one or more of the residents of Rue des Ecoles before moving there. Or was it a spontaneous unpremeditated killing, arising from a fatal moment of conflict and unbalance?

His musings were interrupted as their taxi pulled up along-side the entrance to the weathered stone building with the large carved wooden door. Goulette paid, and the four of them got out quickly.

A uniformed policeman from the quarter met the three inspectors and the interpreter at the concierge's loge. He informed the chief inspector who was where: A uniformed policeman was on guard at the scene of the crime on the sixth floor, as was an evidence technician, the police photographer. and the medical examiner. The latter had arrived just a few minutes before. Another officer was in the Fleuris apartment on the fourth floor with Madame Fleuris, her four *pensionnaires*, her son-in-law Philippe Jumelle who had just arrived, the Fleuris maid Germaine, and the Poivriere maid who had found the body, Gabrielle. Madame Poivriere, who owned the *chambre de bonne* which had been rented to the victim, was not at home. Gabrielle thought she might be out walking her little dog Lili. Another uniformed officer waited at her door.

The pack of four clattered up the stairs to the sixth floor first, to inspect the scene. The tiny attic room could not accommodate all at once who had business there. The police photographer had already set up his tripod and flash and heavy equipment and had taken his photographs and removed himself and his equipment to the hallway, awaiting any further instructions from Chief Inspector Goulette. The evidence specialist was gathering bits and pieces of whatever he considered relevant. The medical examiner, a stoop-shouldered scrawny man with a gray complexion and sad eyes, had examined the victim, who was sprawled on a narrow bed, a brilliant multicolored scarf wrapped tightly around her neck, her long pink lounge-robe hanging parted so that her legs were displayed.

Inspector Goulette could only survey the scene from the doorway; the other three could barely see over his shoulders.

The M.E. seemed prepared for Goulette's insistence upon an estimate of time of death before he could get to do tests,

and with a sigh and evident reluctance put time of death –
with many qualifications – as possibly at midnight, plus or
minus two hours, perhaps three. He promised possibly a closer
estimate after the post mortem.

Vouray, armed with that small item of possible information, left the others and clattered back down the stairs to begin canvassing neighbors who may have seen persons coming and going at 10 *bis* in that time period.

Then Goulette, Pilieu and Dantan clattered down two
flights to the Fleuris apartment, where a pert country girl in a
clean white apron ushered them in to a large formal dining-
room. There around the long mahogany table, in carved-back
walnut chairs, were an elderly straight-backed woman in a
black dress, a portly middle-aged man, two young men, and
two young women, wide-eyed, sitting on the edge of their
chairs. One girl was a sensual type of generous proportions,
dark-haired with deepset dark eyes and a wide mouth; the
other also generously built had light brown curls and green
eyes. Dantan could sense Pilieu staring at them both with
hearty appetite, and he himself found both quite pleasing.

"Mesdames, messieurs, I am Chief Inspector Goulette,"
the chief growled. "I am in charge of this investigation. I beg
your patience and cooperation. I would like to ask each of
you a few questions."

Madame Fleuris moved forward, provided introductions,
but when she began commenting on events he waved her off
impatiently. "Where is the person who found the body?"

"That was Gabrielle, the *bonne* who admitted you," said
Madame Fleuris stiffly, at the same moment tinkling the little
silver bell near her place at the table.

The rosy-cheeked Gabrielle popped her head out of the
swinging door to the kitchen.

"Come here, *ma petite*," said the Inspector *tutoyer*'ing her
in a kindly voice.

Gabrielle bounced happily into the room, smiling
broadly, like a star taking a curtain-call. She had been reported

to be shaken by her discovery – was reported to have run to the older bonne at Fleuris, Germaine, because her own mistress was out – but had clearly bounced back from the shock and looked as if she would enjoy a little limelight.

"You are the one who discovered Mademoiselle Werner... in her present state?" he asked delicately.

"*Oui M'sieur l'Inspecteur.*"

"Then Inspector Pilieu here–" he nodded at the young inspector who gave her a boyish smile –"will speak with you, *ma petite.*" Pilieu led her into the kitchen, Gabrielle swishing her bottom proudly behind the inspector as he ushered her through the swinging door to the kitchen.

Pilieu had expected they could speak there in private, but Germaine, the older maid was there, the Fleuris' maid. Germaine was busy making coffee. Her presence didn't really bother Pilieu. He proceeded with the interview, as Gabrielle had already poured out to Germaine whatever had occurred to her after discovering the murdered young woman, and he saw no harm in Germaine hearing her repetition of it. It might even help, as a corrective to Gabrielle if she attempted to embellish her story to make it more interesting. He would interview Germaine next.

Chief Inspector Goulette turned to Madame Fleuris. "This gentleman is Monsieur Dantan, the interpreter. He will aid me in questioning the Americans."

"My *pensionnaires* speak French very well," said Madame Fleuris. "We speak only French at meals."

The inspector ignored this information. "First I will speak with you, Madame, and then–" turning to Philippe Jumelle, "then you, Monsieur."

"With all respect, M'sieur l'Inspecteur," said Madame Fleuris in a conciliatory tone, "my son-in-law Philippe Jumelle, who is a manager with the *Societé Nationale des Chemins de Fer Français*, has nothing to do with this investigation. He is here merely because I telephoned to him to so that he would inform my daughter of the events – they have no telephone at home – and he merely came here to be of service to me after the body of the *pauvre petite* had been discovered and reported to me by my *bonne* and that of Madame Poivriere. He should be permitted to go about his business now."

"In any case I will speak with Monsieur Jumelle shortly," said the inspecteur curtly, with a stern glance at the portly red-faced son-in-law. He murmured a few words of instruction to Dantan before going through the double glass-paned door to the salon with Madame Fleuris, leaving the son-in-law and the four *pensionnaires* under Dantan's cool gaze.

Dantan asked each in turn around the table their names, ages and occupations, as Goulette had asked him to do, speaking French to the portly son-in-law Philippe Jumelle, and English to the others.

Philippe Jumelle, in a pompous and self-important tone, announced that his presence, his decision-making and oversight were all very much needed at his bureau, and he couldn't sit around very much longer, now that he had ascertained that his mother-in-law was all right.

When Dantan spoke to the green-eyed American girl, Mademoiselle Judith Kugel, she asked flirtatiously where he had learned his "English English". Her twinkling green eyes and curly light brown hair gave her a pixie charm.

"In England," he smiled. She seemed a merry little thing, not ruffled by a sudden violent death in their midst.

He turned next to the sultry brunette. "And your occupation, Mademoiselle Winter?" He already knew the answer perfectly well: art student at the Ecole des Beaux Arts. But Goulette wanted a statement from each person.

"I prefer to be called Miri," she said tartly. Her voice was an anomaly, childishly high-pitched. "You know, like Colette. Nobody even *knows* her last name!"

"Willy," Dantan said calmly. "Sidonie Germaine Colette...Willy." He was pleased when she seemed impressed.

Branford Duane Lee the Third was gangling and thin, like a rangy cowboy from an American Wild West film. He was affecting a bored expression.

The fourth American, James Giardini, a slim dark elegant young man, could not conceal his anxiety. Understandable if he had indeed murdered the poor young woman! Or even, while innocent, knew that he was under suspicion by his landlady. Dantan couldn't read anything from either of the young men's expressions. The bored one could be a criminal with no conscience, hence no anxious feelings flitting across his visage, the nervous one could be as innocent as a babe, and feeling almost as helpless.

Madame Fleuris and the chief inspector returned to the dining room at that moment, Madame said that she would tell Germaine to make more coffee, and pushed her way through the swinging door into the kitchen.

Jamie said wryly, "Too bad it wasn't a double homocide, she might have sprung for a couple of fried eggs."

Judy smothered a giggle, but Miri suddenly announced in perfect French, with an ironic glance at Dantan, "I need to go to my room for a fresh handkerchief. I have a cold." She snuffled to demonstrate her need. Miri's eyes were indeed tearing, but whether because she was unhappy or from a cold, Dantan could not tell.

"Not now, *ma petite*," said the chief inspector in a kindly tone. "We'll ask Germaine to fetch it for you. Monsieur Dantan and I will be needing to question each of you in turn."

"Don't bother," Judy said, bolting out of her chair. "I have Kleenexes in my room, I'll get some." She darted off to her room before she could be stopped, returning with a fistful of tissues which she dumped in front of Miri.

Chief Inspector Goulette signalled to Philippe Jumelle. "Monsieur Jumelle, we'll dispense with you first so that you can return to your bureau."

"I'll pay you for them," Miri told Judy, snuffling into one of them, "I know they cost a fortune in Paris."

"You don't owe me anything," said Judy. "I've got mountains of them in my room. My mother uses them as stuffing in the goodie-boxes she's always sending me, and the customs don't charge me duty on them because they think they're just stuffing."

"I have a Russian lesson with Madame de Regeczy," Jamie said petulantly. "I am leaving!"

"Please don't, James," said Branford, to the evident surprise of the other Americans. "We Americans have to stick together." He leaned across the table inviting the three other *pensionnaires* to huddle. He said quietly, but perfectly audible and intelligible to Dantan, "I'm going to refuse to be questioned unless at least one of you is present. I want an American witness to what the French police later say was said by me. Their anti-American sentiment may color their interpretation, perhaps even unconsciously."

"Me too," Judy whispered. "That's a good idea."

Miri nodded, looking frightened, as if at the thought that she had not anticipated such a danger herself.

James looked unhappy. But he too concurred.

The son-in-law and the chief inspector returned from the salon just as Germaine was bringing in a fresh pot of coffee and a new pitcher of hot milk. Gabrielle followed, with a second big platter of croissants.

Philippe, instead of rushing off to his bureau where he was very much needed, rejoined them at table and gratefully accepted a cup of coffee from his mother-in-law. He reached for a croissant, and Madame Fleuris pushed the platter close to his place.

Chief Inspector Goulette signalled Dantan and Monsieur Giardini with a nod toward the salon, but before the latter had risen from his chair Monsieur Branford Lee spoke up and announced that the four Americans wanted to be questioned in the presence of one another.

The chief inspector shrugged and nodded to Dantan that they would do so, at least at first. He then asked Madame Fleuris' permission to use her telephone and was shown into the kitchen. He took Monsieur Dantan with him, explaining that for diplomatic reasons they could not put much pressure on the Americans yet. If they were not going to cooperate voluntarily he would, though reluctant, have to call in the Sixth Section.

In the kitchen Goulette made a phone-call to an official at the Sixth Section whom he strongly suspected would not be in yet. He was right. He left word that Chief Inspector Goulette was investigating a homocide of a French national, but wished to alert the director that several Americans lived in the same building as the victim. So far all was under control but if he should need the assistance of the Sixth Section he would be in touch.

"With God's help," Goulette said fervently to Dantan, "we will have solved this case before anyone with initiative gets my message." Before they returned to the dining-room he briefly summarized for Dantan the results of his interview with Madame Fleuris. She held fast to having witnessed Monsieur Giardini leaving Mademoiselle Werner's room around nine the night before. She herself was not observed by him as the hall-light had not been turned on by either of them, and when she saw how stealthily he moved, she thought it prudent to remain behind until he had gone into his own room and closed the door.

Based on that statement Goulette judged it prudent to interrogate Monsieur Giardini in depth, at the Police Judiciare.

11

Miri was feeling sick at the thought that the murderer might have been in Emilie's room as she had walked past it. While the chief inspector and the handsome interpreter were in the kitchen, Judy looked as if she were bursting to talk. But for once she didn't. Branford was unchanged from his usual self, dour, aloof and silent. Jamie, too, had sunk into a quiet slump.

Madame Fleuris and Philippe whispered together, darting occasional worried glances toward the salon, the kitchen or the door. Munching more and more croissants Philippe kept repeating how *épouvantable* it all was.

"I should like to get back to my office," he grumbled. "Naturally I have nothing to contribute to this investigation." (Or to anything else, Miri thought.) Though he and Lucille and Jean-Louis had visited on the previous afternoon, as they always did on Sunday, he had naturally, he repeated again and again, had no occasion to mount to the sixth floor and therefore had no useful information to impart. But the chief inspector had asked him to remain for possible additional questions after the Americans had been questioned.

"Naturally," Madame Fleuris sighed, looking at her son-in-law with solicitude. "But you know how the police are!"

Miri was surprised. She would have thought Madame Fleuris would have been an ardent admirer of the police.

Judy could contain herself no longer. She began babbling hysterically.

Who could have done such a thing?

Who was – or had been – this Emilie Werner anyway?

Why had she moved to 10 *bis* Rue des Ecoles?

Why couldn't she have just stayed where she was? And where was that?

Where had she come from anyway?

Why did she have to rent that rat-hole anyway? Judy herself could have used it in a month or two to store the spring and summer clothes her mother was going to send her from Great Neck.

Who had followed Emilie here to kill her?

And where was he now for goodness' sake?

Branford Duane Lee the Third, who rarely spoke, and even more rarely offered compliments, nodded approvingly. "Very good, Judy, you have just stated all the essentials of the police investigation. Once they find the answers to all your percipient questions their case will be solved!"

"I just know that if my parents hear about this they will make me come home," Judy wailed.

"That's ridiculous," Miri said. "They might want you move out of this place. I could see doing that myself. But go all the way back to the States?"

"You don't know my mother."

Miri had no desire to.

Moving out, however, suddenly seemed like a great idea! She wouldn't have to worry about a killer stalking the corridor outside her room, and she wouldn't have to face Madame's wrath over the burned *paillaisse.*

"Just don't tell her," Miri said.

"Oh I won't. Not on purpose. But I'm so afraid it will slip out when I'm talking with my parents on the phone."

The Kugels telephoned from Great Neck every Sunday night. They had just called the night before. "You have a whole week to rehearse not telling them," Miri pointed out.

When they had finished all the coffee and all the croissants the Americans looked from one to the other with sighs.
The chief inspector and the interpreter were still in the kitchen.

"We don't have to wait around," Branford pointed out.
"We can tell them that we have things to do and that we agree
to meet with them later."

"They're going to have to come back anyway if they want
to talk to everybody in this building," Judy said, with a meaningful look at Monsieur Fleuris' empty chair. "What about
old Bushy Beard anyway?" Judy whispered with a sidelong
glance at their landlady. "He's sort of mysterious sometimes
himself."

"You don't know the half of it!" Miri whispered. The other
three Americans huddled closer as Miri told then about seeing Monsieur Fleuris leaving very early in the morning carrying four big metal boxes.

Jamie looked at them dully. He had other things on his
mind.

Bran dismissed Monsieur Fleuris' movements as irrelevant
to the murder. "It's not as though the body is missing," he
said sardonically, "and Monsieur Fleuris was carrying it out
in parts."

"Eeeeek!" Judy shrieked.

Just what Miri had been thinking!

"I still think it's worth looking into," Judy said. She announced her plan to get up very early the next morning and
keep a look out for Monsieur Fleuris in case there was a repeat performance with the boxes.

Then she gave a little shiver. "Miri, how about if you stay
in my rooms tonight and watch with me tomorrow morning?
You could sleep on the sofa in my dressing-room, it has to be
more comfortable than that freezing hole upstairs anyway."

The warmth of Judy's room was tempting but Miri was
offended by Judy's characterization of Miri's own room as a
"freezing hole" even though that was exactly what it was, so
she refused. "If Monsieur Fleuris *is* somehow involved in this

crime, and he finds out I'm staying in your rooms, he might suspect that we're suspicious, and if he's a murderer I don't want him worrying about what I might know."

"Very prudent," Bran remarked. "You girls should stay out of the investigation. It's the job of the police, let them do it."

Judy said, "Well I'm going to spy on old Bushy Beard even if Miri won't stay with me. I'm curious."

Inspector Goulette and Monsieur Dantan returned to the dining-room. The Inspector informed them that it was possible that a liaison from the Sixth Section of another directorate, the section concerned with aliens in France, would be joining the investigation. He did not say when.

Inspector Goulette indicated that he wished to interview Monsieur Lee next.

"As I told you before, I would like my American colleagues to be present as witnesses. Otherwise I request that any questioning be postponed until a representative of the American Embassy can be present."

"Me too," said Judy.

Miri also mumbled agreement.

Dantan translated all this for the chief inspector, who then mumbled something to Dantan, who then said genially, "My dear ladies and gentlemen. The chief inspector wants you to understand that we are not inquisitors. We merely seek such information as you may be able to provide in order to assist us in our investigation into this crime. Look here, we will sit among you at table and pose our questions to each of you in the presence of all of the others. Is that satisfactory, Mister Lee?"

"Yes sir, that will be just fine."

Monsieur Dantan told Inspector Goulette that Monsieur Lee agreed to the arrangement, obvious from his nod.

Goulette turned to Madame Fleuris. "Madame, if it will not incommode you to leave the room, I could conduct my interviews with all the Americans at once, with the aid of Monsieur Dantan of course, right in this room."

"Of course, Chief Inspector," said Madame Fleuris with a sour smile. She had clearly intended to listen in on the Americans' discussion. Had the chief inspector let Madame remain Miri wouldn't have been able to tell him about seeing Monsieur Fleuris very early that morning carrying out big boxes. Now she had the choice of whether or not to mention it.

Madame Fleuris left and the questioning began, with the Inspector stating the question in French, which they all more or less understood, then Dantan repeating it in English. He then translated their responses into French for the Inspector.

It made for slow going and gave Miri a chance to study the interpreter to decide what she thought of his looks. She was favorably disposed to like him because for one thing he knew Colette's last name, and for another he spoke perfect English, even though it sounded snobby with that silly British accent, but then, he couldn't help it if he had happened to learn English from people who talked that way, and for another he was really handsome. He actually looked more Spanish, with his swarthy skin and black hair, than French. She decided he and she would make a striking couple.

Of course she was very fond of Jamie too, but there was nothing stopping her from liking both of them until she decided to go to bed with one of them, she wasn't sure just yet which.

The question began with the kind of bureaucratic detail the French were enamored of, and much of which Monsieur Dantan had already asked them – surname, Christian name even if one were not Christian, mother's maiden name, date of entry into France, passport number, purpose and projected length of stay in France and all the sort of thing which they no doubt already had in dossiers somewhere in their records as they always collected passports and had you filling out forms whenever you turned around.

Then he asked questions pertinent to the crime. "Were you acquainted with the deceased, Mademoiselle Emilie Werner?"

Branford said, "No I don't think I have ever seen her, or if I have, I didn't know who she was."

"Your own room is located where?"

"Right in this apartment." He waved a sketch in the air of its approximate location.

"Did you mount to the sixth floor at any time on Sunday? That is to say, yesterday?"

"No."

"Would you be kind enough to describe your movements yesterday from about six in the evening onward to midnight?"

"I went out around four to the American Club on Boulevard Raspail, where I exercised, swam in the pool, and showered before going out to dine at the home of some friends in the banlieu."

"And then, Mister Lee?"

"And then I returned around midnight."

"Thank you, Mister Lee." Monsieur Dantan translated the exchange for the inspector.

As for Jamie, he said he had seen a new young woman on the sixth floor a few times in the past week or so. He didn't know if that was Mademoiselle Werner. They had never spoken.

As he had asked Branford, Monsieur Dantan now asked Jamie, "Monsieur Giardini, would you be kind enough to describe your movements yesterday from about six in the evening onward to midnight?"

Jamie, surprisingly, turned red. But he was calm as he replied. "I went out, I don't know exactly what time it was. Eightish. I met a friend for aperitifs and then we went for dinner."

"Where did you go for aperitifs?"

Again Jamie reddened, but he did respond. "Café Montparnasse."

The chief inspector told Dantan to ask Monsieur Giardini the name of the person he met.

Jamie, whose French was excellent, didn't wait for Dantan to translate the question. By now he was purple. He shook his head slowly.

Miri wondered if he were having an affair with a married woman! That would explain why he had never tried to kiss Miri herself.

She was surprised that the chief inspector did not press the point.

"When was the last time you saw Mademoiselle Werner?"

"A few days ago. Before the weekend. If the woman I saw was in fact Emilie Werner. Thursday or Friday."

"What if I were to tell you, Monsieur Giardini, that you were seen going into Mademoiselle Werner's room on the sixth floor on Sunday evening."

"Whoever said that is utterly mistaken. I was not acquainted with Mademoiselle Werner and I certainly have never entered her room."

Monsieur Dantan again repeated in French the conversation for the benefit of Inspector Goulette. The latter this time did not merely nod, but told Dantan to ask Monsieur Giardini again for the name and address of his friend.

Again without waiting for Dantan to repeat the questions, Jamie, his expression grim, said, "I decline to provide further detail at this time."

"Merci, Monsieur Giardini," said the chief inspector coldly, then turned to Judy. Dantan smiled at her.

She smirked at him, twisting a strand of her light brown hair around a well-manicured finger, jangling the solid gold charm bracelet dangling at her wrist. A teeny gold Eiffel Tower, a teeny gold Arche de Triomphe, a teeny gold gargoyle added to those she had brought from home were supposed to show that she was a Paris-lover.

"I've never met Emilie Werner. I haven't been upstairs since before Christmas. I only go there to gossip with Miri."

Dantan muttered to the inspector, with a glance at Miri, "*la voisine.*" The neighbor.

"And now Mademoiselle Winter please." She was sure he was leering at her. She could feel a blush creep up her neck. She had to blow her nose before replying, not a very glamorous gesture. Judy passed her another wad of tissues.

"I met Emilie Werner twice. The first time she told me that she had just moved in, was renting the room from Madame Poivriere, that she worked at Galeries Lafayette, in handbags, and that she had met her lover there."

"Did she tell you the name of her lover?"

"No".

"When did you last see Mademoiselle Werner?"

"I think it was this past Friday." Miri did not mention seeing Emilie's concentration-camp tattoo. They would surely see it for themselves when they examined the body. "One thing more. I don't know if it means anything or not." Reluctantly, because she didn't want to have to explain what she was doing there, but he didn't ask her to, she told him of her early morning venture down the hall to the sink and the cold blast of air coming from under Emilie's door as if a window were wide open.

"Was that when you rapped on Monsieur Giardini's door?"

"Yes." So Gabrielle had told him of seeing her. She was glad she had decided to mention it.

"I don't suppose you looked in?"

Miri shook her head. She felt like an idiot, not to have done so. She should have realized that the window wide open, and the door ajar, was strange on so cold a night.

She decided to say nothing to the detectives of having observed Monsieur Fleuris leaving the building with his boxes. She could think of nothing that tied it to the murder. "I assume you want to know my movements on Sunday." Miri volunteered that she had gone to the American Club.

"And did you see Mister Lee there?"

"No, but I only went there to take a shower. I went straight to the women's locker room, so I wouldn't have seen him in the club. Right after my shower I left. Then I came back to my room to change my clothes because I had been invited to a gathering of existentialists."

"So you went out again? What time?"

"Well, I got sidetracked and never did go to the gathering of existentialists. I did go out, but much later than I had originally planned. I think it was around nine by that time. I went to the movies. At the Cluny. To see *'Volpone'* for the third time."

"When you returned was it so late that you had to ring the bell for the concierge to let you in the front door?"

"Yes, that's right. She scowled at me as usual. I bet she doesn't scowl when the guys come in that late!"

"When you returned to your room did you encounter anyone on the sixth floor?"

"No, nobody. I got undressed and put on my flannel pajamas and crawled into bed and read Delacroix' journals – in French, of course – until I fell asleep. Until I woke up sneezing and coughing.Then I went down the hall to the sink to dump something"--she was grateful that he did not ask her what--"and that's when I noticed the cold air blowing from under Emilie Werner's door. I went to wake up Jamie but he didn't answer, Gabrielle woke up from the knocking and stuck her head out the door and told me it was about a quarter to six in the morning."

Miri felt from the way he was looking at her that if this were not a murder investigation Monsieur Dantan would have asked her for a date right then.

Monsieur Dantan again translated for Inspector Goulette. Inspector Goulette had questions for another of the Americans. Vouray, who had by now slipped into the dining-room and was standing behind the table, asked the chief inspector whether it would not be advisable to wait for the Sixth Section liaison before pressing the Americans too hard.

The Inspector disagreed. "I must get the facts in this case. I am not conducting diplomatic negotiations." He looked hard at Vouray. "You sound like a member of the Sixth Section yourself, old man." His voice sounded a little contemptuous.

"I beg your pardon, Chief Inspector," Vouray said humbly.

"Never mind, old man, I'm sure you had my best interests at heart. But I'll tell you something. The P.J. does real work that is a service to France. The Sixth Section consists of a pack of functionaries who act officious, and obstruct the doing of real work."

Dantan was eyeing the two inspectors intently. Goulette clapped his arm around Dantan's shoulder. "So don't you even think of transferring over there."

"I never had such a thought, sir."

"Good."

The chief inspector smiled smugly, "I like not having to depend upon them for translations and such." He added, "I do have additional questions for the Americans."

Branford said calmly, "I decline to respond until you have demonstrated to my satisfaction that further information is necessary to your investigation at this time and that you have a legal right to demand it of me. Good day, gentlemen." He gave them a slight bow, and walked slowly and in dignified fashion from the room, with no protest voiced from anyone.

Miri was impressed. She had thought of Branford as an odd but boring stick. He was odd, and he was boring, but he was also brave.

Inspector Goulette with a nod toward Jamie mumbled something to Monsieur Dantan.

Jamie said angrily, "I already told you that I spent the evening and night with a friend."

"And the name of this friend?"

"As Mister Lee said to you, I'll provide that when and if I'm convinced it is necessary to your investigation." He rose clumsily, tipping his chair backward with a crash.

Madame Fleuris came scurrying stiffly into the room to see what had happened.

The inspector did not press the point. He murmured, "We shall revisit this question if need be."

At that point Miri thought they were done. But Inspector Goulette offhandedly said to Jamie, in English, "One moment please, Monsieur Giardini. A small point." He nodded toward the salon. Jamie looked unhappy but followed docilely enough, with Dantan on his heels. Judy and Miri waited tensely, and Madame Fleuris sat straight-backed and expressionless. They emerged just a few minutes later. Inspector Goulette then indicated that the interviews were concluded, and thanked them all. Madame was unusually cordial, also thanking the Americans for their cooperation, as if it were *her* investigation! Jamie pulled his dufflecoat and beret from a peg in the foyer, Miri retrieved her long black coat and they left together to go to their usual café to talk over events.

Judy pleaded with them to wait for her, then made them wait interminably while she changed her clothes and put on fresh makeup. She came out wearing the velvety brown beaver coat.

Miri had felt strange and attractive the time Judy had lent it to her to wear to the *vernissage*. But a fur coat was not something Miri wanted. She didn't care for ostentation. And besides, she couldn't afford it. And even if she could she didn't think she would ever want anything her stepmother liked, which included fur coats.

The outside air was cold and raw but Miri's sneezing and choking abated soon after they stepped out the door. She could breathe better too. The Will had triumphed! She explained to Judy that as an existentialist she believed that she made her own destiny, and that by willing it she had actually cured her cold!

"Sounds like Christian Science," Judy laughed. "A girl I went to high school with nearly died because when her appendix burst her parents who were Christian Scientists just kept praying for quite awhile until her father got really upset and worried and rushed her to a hospital. It was a near miss. After she recovered they all became Presbyterians. Or Methodists. Something like that."

"It's not the same thing. In my case I wasn't praying, which is futile, I was exercising my Will." Miri remembered the tissues. "Listen, Judy, I want to pay you for the Kleenexes. I know they're horribly expensive over here."

"Oh no, you don't owe me anything, I didn't buy them in Paris. My mother keeps sending me packages of stuff and she wraps everything in wads of Kleenex. I have tons of them."

As they strolled down the block to their café, Judy asked Jamie what Inspector Goulette's aside had been all about. He laughed it off. "A big nothing!"

They decided to sit at an outside table, where another hardy group were huddled around a table. They didn't look American; they were dark-complected with intense almost desperate expressions, and were puffing away at Gauloises Bleues whose acrid smoke was blowing their way.

There were times, actually, when all of Paris smelled of Gauloises Bleues. Miri had tried them, and had choked. American cigarettes were much too expensive for her here. She did try High Lifes for a short time, the French idea of an American cigarette (they pronounced it "hee leef"), but they were expensive too and also tasted awful. Finally to save money she just stopped smoking.

Judy was eyeing the dark men warily. "I think they're Algerians," she whispered. "All the Algerians in Paris are plotting to bomb something," she said. She had heard this from her one of her multitudinous expert friends.

"What about Camus?" Jamie said. "Even during the war he didn't bomb anything, he just wrote."

"Camus who?" said Judy.

Jamie and Miri looked at each other and smirked.

But Jamie's smile faded. "Inspector Goulette acted as if he thought one of us had done it," he said unhappily.

"I didn't think so," said Judy. "It was just normal sorts of things he asked. What you would expect in a murder investigation?"

"But asking us to account for every second of our movements since yesterday at coffee? Names, places..."

"That's what they do in murder investigations. Anybody who reads mysteries knows that!"

"Why us? I don't like it."

"But Goulette didn't make an issue of it when you and Bran wouldn't give him details," Judy pointed out.

"Well I'll be damned if I'm going to tell the police who I was with. It's none of their goddamn business." He picked up his books and took off for his Russian lesson.

12

Miri would have left as soon as Jamie did but Judy pleaded with her to stay behind and talk with her some more. The fears stirred in Miri by the murder made her want to get away by herself and think whereas Judy reacted with an urgent need for companionship.

"Who do you think did it?" Judy asked anxiously.

"I have no idea. And I really don't care who killed Emilie Werner, as long as I'm nowheres near them."

"Jamie certainly seemed upset, didn't he? Not at all his lighthearted fun self. Almost," she persisted, when Miri didn't reply, "as if he did have something to hide!"

She had inadvertently hit on a point that was worrying Miri too. She too had noticed Jamie's uneasiness. It occurred to her that Jamie might be having an affair he wanted to keep secret, maybe with a married woman. And that would explain why he had never tried to get anywhere with Miri. She thought she had better get over Jamie.

Besides, Miri thought Monsieur Dantan had looked her over as if he were interested in her. But of course while the investigation was in progress he wouldn't ask her out. It wouldn't be professional. She hoped that the case would be solved quickly so she could see if anything would come of it.

"I wonder if anyone else is in danger," Judy said still in that anxious tone.

Miri wondered the same thing but would not admit it. "Maybe they'll catch the killer right away."

"It must have been committed by someone Emilie Werner had known before she moved here, don't you think?" Judy asked hopefully. "Probably a *crime passionelle*. If so it wouldn't affect us. And I've never even met her, in fact I never even heard of her until she got murdered. It's a terrible thing, of course, but it doesn't get to me. As long as my parents don't find out about it and want to drag me home. In fact," she said with awe, "it's kind of thrilling, a murder right on our doorstep. That Monsieur Dantan, wasn't he good-looking?"

"I didn't notice."

"You didn't notice his terrific sex appeal? Miri, how could you not notice? I wonder if he's married."

"He wasn't wearing a ring."

"Oh good, you noticed. I wanted to look but I was afraid of being obvious. You know, Miri," Judy giggled, "this murder is going to do wonders for our popularity."

"What are you talking about?"

"Once any guy finds out we live in the same building where it occurred, and that we were even questioned by the police, he'll want to know more about it and it will be just another thing to talk about when you're getting acquainted!"

Miri had always suspected that Judy was a pragmatist – and they were the worst, no principles – but this was appalling. "Well I have no intention of talking about the murder in order to improve my popularity."

"You know, Miri, you could be a lot more popular if you would just fix yourself up a little. Stop wearing navy blue and black for one thing. You've got a lush sexy figure but you don't make the most of it, you cover it up with baggy stuff! You look like an Orthodox babushka!"

Miri was upset by her comparison, as she thought of religion as the opiate of the masses, and Orthodox Jewry the absolutely worst tyranny of women. "If this conversation has degenerated into a fashion-tips session I'm leaving."

"Don't you like boys? Don't you want to get married?"

"Of course I like boys, but as for marriage I've never seen a single marriage that was happy so why should I assume mine would be the first? I want to be an artist. If I fall in love I'll have to see what happens."

"But what about sex?"

"What about it?"

"Don't you feel attracted to anyone?"

"If I fall in love I'll have to see what happens."

"Are you kidding? Haven't you ever felt attracted to a man you weren't in love with?"

"Have you?"

"All the time!" she said merrily.

"Boy, that really must interfere with getting things done."

"Other things, yes!"

Something was certainly interfering with Miri getting things done. She just wasn't painting much since she came to Paris. She kept thinking it was because she needed to work alone, not in a studio surrounded by dolts, but she hadn't done what she could to get her own studio or a room big enough to set up an easel in. She could have asked Madame Poivriere to rent her the room Emilie Werner finally rented, but in three months she hadn't. And now that Emilie was dead, and the room would be vacant again as soon as the police got through with it, she knew she wasn't going to again.

"I wonder what old Bushy Beard was doing when '*la pauvre petite*' was getting herself murdered," Judy mused. "It's just really strange that you should spot him leaving with those mysterious boxes just when she was getting murdered."

"It was not just when she was getting murdered, or I would have seen the murderer. I really don't think Monsieur Fleuris had anything to do with it."

"Who knows?" Judy said. "He's an old letch, he's always leering down our bosoms. Maybe he went upstairs and made a pass at Emilie, she told him off or even laughed at him, enraging his French male ego and he killed her."

"If Bushy-Beard were going to kill anyone, he would have done in that hag of a wife long ago."

"I'm not saying I suspect him, I'm only saying he could be a suspect. After all, anyone in the building could have gone up to the sixth floor Sunday evening and done it. There was nobody home up there except Emilie Werner once you went out for the evening, Jamie went out for the evening, and Gabrielle must have been at work in Madame Poivriere's apartment at least through dinner and cleaning up afterwards. So Emilie Werner was up there alone, and anyone could have joined her without being seen. Once Lucille and Philippe and that creep Jean-Louis had left, Monsieur Fleuris would have left, presumably to visit his mistress as he always did. But who was to know if he went up to the sixth floor first to make a pass at Emilie Werner – after all his mistress must be an old lady by now – and then after she laughed at him and he killed her he went on to his mistress' place."

"I don't think Bushy-Beard could do such a thing. But I do agree with you that it would have been easier for somebody who was in the building legitimately, or the concierge would have seen him and told the police." This thought made Miri very uneasy because it meant that the killer might still be close by.

"We don't know that she didn't," Judy pointed out. "The concierge is probably the first one the police questioned when they got here and we have no idea what they've learned. We should try to find out. And anyway, it could have been anyone else in the building who was around Sunday night. There's the photographer and his family on the *deuxième*, maybe he was doing pornographic photographs and Emilie was modelling for him and she somehow was threatening his public respectability. Or that huge family on the *troisième*, or most likely, now that I think of it, is Madame Poivriere herself, since she was Emilie Werner's landlady. Madame Poivriere is probably as proud of her respectability as Madame Fleuris is. Maybe she has a secret life not so respectable, Emilie discovered it, and was trying to blackmail her so Madame Poivriere decided to put a quick end to it. It's a fact that Madame Poivriere made sure to stay out in the freezing cold with that little spoiled dogbrat of hers long enough to miss out on the first round of interrogations by Inspector Goulette and his sidekicks."

"But Emilie only moved here a few weeks ago, over the Christmas holidays. How could she even have gotten to know any of Madame Poivriere's shameful secrets? Madame Poivriere's *bonne* Gabrielle told me that Emilie Werner wasn't even allowed into the apartment, not even to use the W.C. If anybody was going to know anything racy about Madame Poivriere it would be Gabrielle, not Emilie Werner."

"Well I was only giving that as an example, I didn't say I believed it. But you know, Miri, that's a good idea. We should talk to Gabrielle, find out what she knows, what she told the police. We may even find out stuff from her the police didn't. You're always talking to the maids so they like you, and I've got the money for the bribes. That's two advantages the police didn't have!"

Miri ignored the suggestion. She had no desire to play detective. She just wanted to get as far from the killer as possible, and also as far as possible from a shallow time-waster like Judy Kugel.

Judy took off for her classes at the Sorbonne. Miri started walking, without attending to where. She knew she should haul herself over to the Ecole des Beaux Arts, but she just didn't feel like painting.

Despite her desire to get away from the murder she couldn't help worrying about it.

On the one hand Judy's theory of a *crime passionelle* was the most comfortable, since it meant the killer wouldn't be after anyone else, unless they had evidence on him and he found out that they did, but on the other hand how did he get in and out without being seen by the concierge if it wasn't someone who lived in the building or who visited often enough to be familiar?

Miri chided herself that an artist should be able to dig her hands into her psyche for the images and memories and dreams and nightmares and mold and pummel and carve and combine the stuff however gruesome into art. But she couldn't. She was upset and scared over the murder, and angry at herself for being upset and scared, and somehow the nervous energy, far from driving the engine to create, was churning in her gut and giving her nausea rather than creative images.

As Miri walked along lost in thought she nearly crashed into three nuns in flowing black habits with huge white headdresses like Tenniel's off-with-their-heads Duchess in Alice in Wonderland scuttling past her whose quick little dodging steps prevented the collision. Miri was fascinated with their outfits, and changed direction to stay on their heels until she had managed to memorize their wide headdresses and flowing black robes and their scuttling. She wondered why on earth they were always in such a hurry when they thought they had all Eternity?

Before this encounter she had already started collecting pieces in her head for a painting of religious figures; not a spiritual composition, rather a bitterly satiric procession like Ensor. These nuns were added to a priest riding a bicycle, on his head a black widebrimmed hat with a round crown; and the choirboys in little brown Franciscan robes and sandals. In the background she would paint a high thick impenetrable gray stone wall on which was splashed in white paint, "U.S. Go Home".

She had been walking without seeing where she was. Now she saw that she was across the street from Saint-Sulpice. She stared up at the domineering towers. She still hadn't gotten around to coming to hear duPres, the world-famous organist, playing the world-famous organ, which Jamie had told her she ought to do.

If she turned in one direction she would get to school. But the cavernous studio was always cold and filled with acrid woodsmoke. And she didn't feel like working. If she walked in the opposite direction she could cut through the Luxembourg Gardens, flat and serene, the trees bare and brown, and somewhere if she could find it was Reid Hall, on Rue de Chevreuse. She could look at their rooms. And leave a note for Vanessa Tate.

As Miri frequently got lost in her peregrinations of Paris she always carried in her pocket her little red "*Plan de Paris Arrondissement par Arrondissement.*" From this she now eventually determined that Rue de Chevreuse was a short street making a small triangle with Boulevard Montparnasse and rue Notre-Dame-des-Champs. She was within steps of it.

She passed a long stone wall partially covered with pasted-up posters. In an exposed area on the stone was written in large white chalk letters "U.S. Go Home". Someone was writing that everywhere. Monsieur Fleuris had assured the Americans when the subject came up at dinner one day that it didn't mean them − students, or even tourists − it meant NATO or something like that. Still, Miri didn't like it.

The heavy carved-oak outside doors to Reid Hall were open. The henna-headed concierge in her loge was quick to ask Miri's name and whom she was visiting. She spoke English with a Russian accent.

Miri asked for Vanessa Tate.

"She awaits you?"

"No."

The concierge sighed, and consulted a board with rows of hooks from some of which large hotel-like keys were hanging. "Eh no, Mademoiselle Tate is not in at this moment." She thrust a pencil and small sheet of paper toward Miri. "Would you care to leave message?"

Miri shook her head. "Could I have a look around?"

"You want reside here?"

What Miri wanted was just to have a look around, but she said yes to avoid further discussion.

"You American university woman?" To Miri's blank look she added, "You attend American university in states?"

If two afternoon courses at Columbia's stepchild, School of General Studies, qualified her then the answer was "Yes."

The concierge made a call at her switchboard and a few minutes later an old woman in a pair of thick eyeglasses, a tweed suit and oxfords with cuban heels, her gray hair pleasantly disheveled, as if she had been running her veiny fingers through it in thought, came bustling up to take charge of the visitor.

Miss Bancroft combined a rapid tour of Reid Hall with an inquisition. Pointing out the row of small salons on the ground floor where friends could be entertained she noted that these rooms, and the center garden, of course, when the weather was fine, were the only areas where men were allowed. Did Miss Winter understand? Sure?

Here was the dining-room, unfortunately closed at the moment. You could get an egg at breakfast, dinner was in the evening as it should be and not plunk in the middle of the day when you were trying to get things done. At dinner one well-bred young Frenchwoman on a meal scholarship was seated at each of the tables, to ensure that the girls were exposed to French culture and given an opportunity to practice their French. Where had Miss Winter gone to school in the States? Columbia? Ah. What was she doing in Paris? The Beaux Arts? Hmmm. What had brought her to Reid Hall? Oh you're acquainted with Vanessa Tate? A lovely young woman from a lovely family.

There was something reassuring about the place. The building itself was hundreds of years old, a two-story U-shaped ochre-colored stone structure surrounding a garden. The fourth side of the garden was enclosed by a high stone wall. It was a snug enclosure that might have looked like a convent to Miri except that she had never seen a convent, except in the movies. The building had started out as a hunting-lodge of the duc de Chevreuse. Montparnasse must have been all wooded! With wild animals to hunt! Since then the place had been updated with central heating, bathrooms with real toilets and big bathtubs. "The girls share the bathrooms but nobody seems to complain about not being able to get a bath."

The furniture Miri saw when Miss Bancroft showed her a room was large enough for twentieth-century bodies. The small individual sitting-rooms on the ground floor where residents could entertain guests in private were furnished with small overstuffed sofas and chairs covered in floral chintz. "The maids serve *té complet* in the afternoons. There's an extra charge for that."

Most of the residents were students in Paris for the year. But a few were alumnae of various ages who dropped in for shorter stays, so there was sometimes a room available. "We do have one at present, as a matter of fact, though I should warn you that as it is on the corner it is a trifle drafty. Here is what would be your room." The room was more than large enough to set up an easel in, and it was warm. Miri didn't feel a draft at all.

She looked out the French window at the balcony, and the garden below waiting for spring, its iron benches empty and dead leaves blowing around the browned lawn and dried dead flowers in the beds. "This room must cost a lot," she sighed.

"It's a hundred ten dollars a month," said Miss Bancroft, "including breakfast and dinner."

Even Miri could afford that! It was more than Madame Fleuris charged, but not that much more. And there would be bigger breakfasts and unlimited baths.

Miri, feeling as if she had passed a test, was escorted back to Miss Bancroft's office to hand over eleven ten-dollar travelers checks for the ensuing month, to begin the next day, before she was even sure that she wanted to move in there. It sounded too little-white-glove-ish for her but it was too late now, and she had wanted to get away from Rue des Ecoles and a murderer, so maybe her unconscious had taken over. A rather frightening thought. She wondered what else it might do without her conscious permission.

Miri left to wander the short distance to Boulevard Montparnasse when someone came up behind her.

"Is that you, Miriam Winter?"

Miri whirled around. It was Vanessa Tate. They both broke out laughing.

"I've been meaning to send you a *pneu*," Vanessa said. "I haven't been to the Beaux Arts lately."

"Now you don't have to. I was just at Reid Hall looking for you, and I'm moving in there tomorrow. There was a murder in my building, right on the same floor as my room. I wanted out fast."

"A murder! Do you have time to talk now? Come back with me and I'll make some coffee in my room. If you don't mind warm water from the tap and milk from a tube?"

They walked back to Reid Hall, Vanessa breathlessly questioning Miri about the victim and the other occupants of 10 *bis* Rue des Ecoles. The henna-headed concierge greeted each of them by name as she handed Vanessa her key and gave Miri a familiar nod. She was already recognized as an in-person.

"I hope it won't be too little-white-glove-ish for me," Miri said as they climbed the stairs to the residence floor.

"Oh there are all sorts of girls here. There is one large little-white-gloves crowd, all from the same dinky little college in the South, doing their junior year here. They're very social, but mostly with one another, and they talk endlessly about American boys and Italian clothes and French wine and *Fleurs des Rocailles* perfume. But there are some others who are interesting."

She unlocked her room and invited Miri in. It was very similar to the room Miri had been assigned but had taken on the personality of its occupant. An interesting unfinished painting rested on the easel near the window. Other canvases, face inward, were leaned against whatever wall-space was not taken by furniture. The room smelled of turpentine and stale cigarette smoke. "Sit anywhere."

Of the chair at the desk, two upholstered chairs by a coffee table, or the bed, Miri chose an upholstered chair. Vanessa sank gracefully to the floor into a cross-legged position. She lit up an American cigarette. It smelled wonderful but Miri refused her offer, as she couldn't afford to resume the habit. "Are you getting to the Beaux Arts much?" Vanessa asked.

"Sometimes."

"I know," she laughed. "Same here. It's so darn dreary. Not what I expected. But Paris is marvelous! I'm doing a lot of work but mostly in my room. When I do go to class I find myself snooping around to look at other people's work."

Miri shuddered at that. Other students' paintings usually made her nauseous. "I haven't been able to work in my old room, it's too small. But the one they gave me here in Reid Hall is nice and big. Tell me about the more interesting girls here."

"Well there's a soprano and a contralto on Fulbrights who are studying musicology with Nadia Boulanger who is some kind of a legend in music apparently. They do everything together and they fight constantly. One has a fierce temper – the contralto – probably comes of playing Carmen too much – and the other is cheerful and sweet and stubborn and sings *exultate jubilate* like an angel. There's one Negro here – the southerners in the groupie-group are rattled by that but there's nothing they can do but make snide remarks as nobody else gives a darn – she's an acting student shooting for the Comedie Française – wants to do Racine. Bethel Washton. She did a reading from *"Phèdre"* for us one night. Fantastic! But I don't know if the French'll ever let her into their national theatre, they're so provincial. Her French seems perfect though, at least to me. And they did love Josephine Baker. Then there's a girl from Montana studying at the Cordon Bleu who is engaged to an agronomy student back home and having a torrid affair with a South American diplomat here."

This all sounded much more interesting than the *pension* Fleuris. Miri had already told Vanessa about her fellow *pensionnaires,* "Branford Duane Lee the Third from a horse farm in Kentucky who's sort of a stick doing doctoral research on some unknown subject on the G.I. Bill, another fellow, Jamie Giardini very aesthetic and an existentialist like me, Judy Kugel from Great Neck whose goal is to find a husband."

Vanessa hadn't been impressed the first time, and she wasn't now. "I'm never going to get married," she declared. She had risen and was making instant coffee from the tap at the little sink. "It would interfere with my work. I'm going to have affairs. There was a guy at school, a sculptor, I could have seen myself married to but he wasn't interested in me."

"You don't think you would ever want to have children? Even after you had gotten somewhere with your work?"

"Definitely not children! Do you have any idea how much work they are? I do. I'm second oldest of six, and the oldest girl, so I had to help with the younger ones, and they don't leave you any time or psychic energy for anything else. My mother has been a martyr to us. I don't want to be a martyr. I want to be an artist. In fact I'm thinking of getting a hysterectomy so I can enjoy sex without having to worry about a slip-up with my diaphragm."

Miri was awed by her guts.

"But it's not so easy. Doctors don't like to take out healthy organs. I'm thinking of going to England to see if they'll do it there. I know a girl who got an abortion there, but she said she had to throw screaming fits and tell all sorts of lies hysterically to try to demonstrate that she was psychologically unbalanced and would go completely over the edge if she had to go through with the pregnancy and birth. And getting abortions everywhere else is really scary. You could die. A girl I went to high school with did die. She went to a real doctor who did abortions, but something went wrong and she bled to death because he wouldn't take her to the hospital because he didn't want to be found out. He hid her body in some sort of a storm drain but somebody's Labrador retriever found it, and the whole story finally came out."

"A girl I went to high school committed suicide while her parents were in Florida over Christmas and the rumor was that she had been pregnant."

"You see? It's easier to just avoid the whole situation. Diaphragms don't always work. I have one, but I don't trust it."

Miri didn't even have one. She hadn't given any thought to this particular potential disaster! And she was supposed to be intelligent.

She was stunned and impressed by Vanessa's decisiveness. Much as she wanted to be an artist she could not bring herself to make such an irreversible decision. Even though she wasn't a husband-hunter like Judy Kugel somehow vaguely she felt that someday with the right person it might be nice to be married. She wondered if this meant she wasn't a true artist deep down.

Vanessa handed her a mug of the lukewarm coffee-like liquid, placed her own on the floor, then sank back down to her cross-legged position and lit up another cigarette. "Tell me more about the murder."

"I don't know much about it. The body was discovered this morning. The victim was my neighbor on the sixth floor, that's where all the *chambres de bonne* are. It might have happened during the night." She told Vanessa how in the very early morning she had gone down the hall to the sink near Emilie Werner's room and and had felt the cold gusts from under her door.

"Too bad you didn't take a peek."

Miri shuddered. She had been terrified on that cold landing.

"I would have!" Vanessa gave a little breathy laugh. "Did you know the victim well?"

"Hardly at all. She had only moved into the building a few weeks ago, over the Christmas holidays while all of us were away. A mystery figure, in a way, because nobody had gotten to know her. She had rented her *chambre de bonne* from an apartment-owner on the fifth floor. I also have a *chambre de bonne* and we met on the stairs. But all I know about her is that she had a lover – I never saw him – who was married – and she worked at Galeries Lafayette. In handbags. That was where she met him, when he came in to buy a gift. There was one sort of spooky thing. She and I looked a lot alike. When we first met we just stared at each other. She said something about never getting closer to our *doppelgängers* than that. It was really eerie. Of course I'm heavier than she was, she was boney thin actually, but that was the main difference. She had been in a concentration camp."

"A concentration camp! You mean during the war?"

"That's right. She was a child when they took her."

"How horrible! To think that after surviving all that here she is murdered. How horrible. Any suspects?"

"So far they haven't arrested anyone."

"It's thrilling! A real murder mystery!"

Miri was somewhat dismayed that Vanessa Tate's reaction was so similar to Judy Kugel's, whom she had already written off as a featherbrain, whereas Vanessa, she thought, was more serious.

"I hope they catch him quickly. My room is on the same floor as Emilie's, it could have been me. But of course I'll be moving in here very soon."

Vanessa frowned. "Why would that be, unless he were choosing a victim randomly? There's no connection between you and the victim. Other than the coincidence of having rooms on the same floor."

Intellectually this was persuasive, but Miri still felt sick in her gut. She hated herself for being such a coward, and was determined not to let it show.

Vanessa said with relish, "This is like a good mystery story. I love murder mysteries. When Miss Bancroft took you around did she show you our library?"

She had not. Vanessa suggested that they look at it now. She led Miri to a dimly-lit room with high ceilings and the walls lined with books. There was a large library table surrounded by chairs in the center of the room, and a small round reading-table with two easy chairs and a floor-lamp with a big tulip-shaped silk shade. The wood floor creaked as they clumped on it. Vanessa was wearing the same kind of clumpy thick-soled French shoes that Miri wore.

"This place is kind of creepy, isn't it?" Vanessa said. "If there are any ghosts in this building this is definitely the room where they would walk."

Ghosts were not something Miri thought about much.

"Whenever I come in here for a mystery I feel as if I'm going to see something spooky," Vanessa added in a breathy voice, "perhaps the ghost of the duc de Chevreuse!"

She sounded as if she was serious. But if she had talent as an artist Miri might still want to be friends with her so she held back a laugh and instead made a serious suggestion.

"Maybe you should bring a camera along and see if you can get a shot of him."

"Oh no, I think that would scare him off. If I were a ghost I would definitely not put in an appearance if I thought someone were going to capture me on film."

"How do you even know that a ghost would know that you were bringing your camera? If the ghost is the duc de Chevreuse then they didn't even have cameras in his day so he wouldn't know what it was. Unless of course ghosts can keep up. What a thought! Suppose you could keep learning even after you're dead! That would solve the problem of not having enough time to read everything. Except that I don't believe it."

"I'm not sure," Vanessa said thoughtfully.

"Well I'm sure."

"How can you be?"

"The reason I'm so positive that ghosts do not exist is that if they did exist my mother would have definitely figured out how to show up as one in order to haunt me. She always hovered over me when she was alive."

"Not necessarily," Vanessa said thoughtfully. "Not all dead

people show up as ghosts. Your mother may be in heaven, not tortured with some unfinished business on earth. I've always had the impression that ghosts are the souls of persons who left earth in troubled circumstances, violence and all that, and they wander as wraiths seeking peace."

"Well I'm sure it would have troubled my mother to leave a ten-year-old daughter, especially if she could see whose hands I fell into. That would be an incentive for her to come back if she could have! No, there's no such thing as ghosts, or souls, or God. This is all there is. I'm sure of that."

Vanessa shuddered.

One of the tables held stacks of well-worn books, all of them apparently mysteries.

"Take one," Vanessa said encouragingly. "You can return it after you move in."

"I never waste my time reading anything that isn't great literature."

"That's like saying you never eat pretty candy! Here's one I liked..." She took up a tattered volume from the table.

In spite of herself Miri reached for it. She wanted Vanessa to like her. She wanted a friend who was a dedicated artist. The book was "The Murder of Roger Ackroyd" by Agatha Christie.

"You'll never guess who done it," she said with a little laugh.

"You're right, because I'm not going to try."

Vanessa laughed. "Rather solve the real-life murder?"

"On the contrary I want to get as far away from it as I can."

13

Déjeuner was already in progress when Miri slid into her seat at the massive table. For once she wasn't hungry, but she decided to eat anyway so that she wouldn't have to spend money on a meal in the evening. She would be glad when she could eat suppers at Reid Hall. The soup had already been served, slurped and cleared, Germaine had placed a bowl of stew before Madame, who was in the process of apportioning it onto individual plates as Miri arrived.

The seat diagonally opposite Miri, Jamie's, was vacant.

Madame was very strict about starting on time. Miri apologized to Madame for her lateness.

"Well at least you haven't been arrested too!" squealed Judy. "Jamie's been arrested!"

"What?"

"We don't know that, Judy," Bran said calmly. But he looked worried. "He is being interrogated by the *juge d'instruction*. It seems that a witness saw Jamie leaving Emilie Werner's room last night around the time that the medical examiner has now estimated her death took place."

"Who could have seen him?" Miri demanded indignantly. "I don't believe it for a second! Somebody's lying!'"

Madame Fleuris glared at her.

"Or," said Bran quietly, "merely mistaken."

"They came for him just as we were starting the soup!" Judy cried.

Madame Fleuris was not enforcing the speak-only-French-at-table rule.

"Jamie wouldn't hurt a fly!" Miri simply could not believe he had been involved in a murder, regardless of who had said they had seen what. "He's a civilized person. He showed me the Place des Vosges by moonlight. He took me to the tiniest church in Paris, Saint-Julien-le-Pauvre. He showed me the lifesize statue of Voltaire with the mischievous eyes in the lobby of the Comédie Française. He took me to Christmas Eve midnight mass at the little Franciscan church with the monks and little choir boys in brown robes. He got me to eat a snail. He is not a murderer."

"All very cogent arguments," Bran sneered.

"Who says they saw him?" Miri demanded.

Silence.

She looked from one face to another. Madame Fleuris was as stonefaced as usual, Monsieur Fleuris the twinkle gone from his eyes looked uncharacteristically grave, Judy was subdued and Branford more remote than ever.

The witness could only have been Gabrielle, Germaine or Madame Fleuris.

Gabrielle lived on the *sixième*, Germaine went there daily to clean Miri's and Jamie's rooms, and Madame, of course, snooped everywhere. She would sometimes let herself into their rooms for the ostensible purpose of making sure that Germaine had cleaned properly, but actually to poke her nose into their things. Judy joked about writing herself a really gross letter signed with some imaginary name, to shock Madame, but hadn't gotten around to it.

It wasn't likely to have been Germaine who saw someone coming out of Emilie's room. On Sundays she only worked in the morning, preparing and serving *petit déjeuner* before heading to church for the rest of the day.

It could have been Gabrielle, who wouldn't have thought anything of it at the time, she would have assumed he was Emilie's lover. Miri would corner Gabrielle and ask her.

But if it wasn't Gabrielle or Germaine then it had to be Madame Fleuris. Possible. Madame had been on the *sixième* to put an extra blanket on Miri's bed some time after Miri had left for the movies on Sunday.

"I hope that our young friend will return to us soon," sighed Bushy-Beard.

"If he's a murderer," Madame Fleuris snapped, "I don't want him in my house!"

"Jamie is not a murderer," Miri said.

Madame Fleuris scowled.

They finished the rest of the meal in silence, then Miri followed Judy to her room to discuss the situation. Bran surprised them by coming too.

Judy sprawled on her bed; Bran sat at the desk. Miri perched on a stuffed armchair. "Well?" Judy said. "What do we do now?"

"I can't believe Jamie could have had anything to do with the murder," Miri said.

"Same here," Judy said.

But Bran was not so sure. "What do we really know about one another? Nothing essential. For all we know Emilie Werner and Jamie knew each other before Emilie moved into this building, and that was why she did move in. Then something went wrong..."

Miri looked at him incredulous. "You honestly think that Jamie is a murderer?"

"No, I'm merely advancing it as one of a myriad of possibilities. My personal opinion is valueless since it is not based on facts. Neither is yours."

"I'm sure he didn't do it," Miri repeated.

"I'm going to send a telegram to my father and ask for money, in case Jamie needs to hire a lawyer."

"What about the American Embassy?" Miri said. "Bran, would you go there and see what they can do?"

Branford looked uncomfortable at the request; he said nothing. He didn't agree, he didn't refuse.

"Bran?"

Bran glanced down.

"I'd like to know who said they saw Jamie leaving Emilie Werner's room," Judy said. "They had to have been mistaken or lying."

"Jamie could have been leaving Emilie's room and still not have killed her," Bran pointed out reasonably. "He might have had a thing going with her. It was convenient, both of them on the sixth floor. No concierge to observe their comings and goings."

That would have been true for Jamie and Miri too, she thought ruefully, but nothing, absolutely nothing, had ever happened between them.

"I think we should try to find out who the so-called witness was and what they actually thought they saw."

Bran said, "Judy, you're free of course to do whatever you want but my advice is to stay clear of the investigation. It won't help, and you could get hurt."

"Well how can we help Jamie?" Judy wailed.

Bran volunteered, "I'll try to find out if he has actually been accused, or is merely being interrogated. The French justice system is different than ours. When we suspect an individual of a crime, the police and district attorney investigate. If they find what they think is sufficient evidence it is brought to a grand jury which decides whether to indict, and if it so decides, then and only then is the individual brought to trial. Here in France they investigate *after* the suspect is arrested."

"What!" Both girls shrieked.

Judy wanted to dash right off to the Herald Tribune and get a reporter to write an exposé. Bran advised waiting to see how the French police had in fact dealt with Jamie.

Miri hadn't wanted to get involved, but she was uneasy that Jamie might not be treated fairly. She had to do what she could. He was her friend. Judy had no qualms whatever about plunging in and helping. That shamed Miri.

After Bran left, Judy brought out some chocolate, a cardboard tube of Toblerone. "What do you think we should do now?" she demanded, munching chocolate and passing the tube to Miri.

"We could start by finding out who said they saw Jamie coming out of Emilie's room. That's fishy." Miri explained why it was possible to have been Gabrielle or Madame Fleuris, but almost certainly was not Germaine, and was probably not Gabrielle. "I'll talk to Gabrielle."

"I'll come too."

"You don't have to. Gabrielle is used to talking to me."

"But this isn't just talk, this is business."

"What are you talking about?"

"Not only do you want Gabrielle to tell the truth about whether or not she was the witness – and it may not be to her advantage unless we make it to her advantage – she might have other information besides. That she would only part with if paid for." Judy reached for her big brown leather handbag and burrowed until she came up with an exquisite French wallet in burgundy calf, which had compartments for each denomination of French currency. She pulled out a note and waved it around. "This is our secret weapon."

"You want to *pay* Gabrielle to talk to us?"

"Not just to talk to us, to tell us something useful. Maybe even something she didn't tell the police. But we can't just go to the Poivriere apartment cold, in case Madame Poivriere herself answers the door. She wouldn't want us to disrupt Gabrielle at her work. So let's ask Germaine to speak to Gabrielle, and tell her we want to talk to her."

They found Germaine working in Bran's room, brushing the furniture, her brooms and brushes and pail stacked in a corner. Judy looked around inquisitively as if a glimpse of Branford Duane Lee's room might offer a clue about what he was up to in Paris, but there was nothing to see, the room had no personal belongings in sight. It looked like a hotel room awaiting a new guest.

Germaine was unperturbed that they wanted to talk with her. Whatever occurred she seemed to accept it. She was a plain square woman with big hands and feet, and she had been sweeping and scrubbing and serving all her life. Miri wondered if she had ever thought she could accomplish any more than that.

"Germaine, we want to talk with Gabrielle," Miri said. "I was hoping you could tell her so and arrange it as we didn't want to bother Madame Poivriere directly."

"Very well, Mademoiselle Miri. I'll speak with Gabrielle sometime today and I'll tell you this evening."

Judy slipped Germaine some money. "Do it now, Germaine." Judy spoke commandingly, *tutoyer*'ing Germaine, who was more than twice her age. Miri was embarassed for her.

Germaine pocketed the note without expression, put down her brush, wiped her hands on her apron, and left, her felt slippers flapping.

"We'll be in my room, Germaine," Judy said. She smiled at Miri. "That's the way to get things done."

"You don't think Germaine might have felt insulted?"

"The French are never insulted when you offer them money. As long as it's enough."

Once they were settled in Judy's room Judy brought out the Toblerone.

Germaine returned shortly. "Mesdemoiselles. Gabrielle will be pleased to speak with you but she cannot do so until tomorrow morning before she starts work at six. Madame Poivriere is having some friends in to dine."

Judy and Miri looked at each other. "We're lucky we're not Gabrielle or Germaine, or people even worse off or someone we couldn't stand, like Madame Fleuris or my stepmother," Miri said. She would have to remember that the next time she got really fed up with herself.

Judy made a face.

To Germaine Judy said, "Tell Gabrielle we'll come see her in her room tomorrow morning at six."

Germaine nodded and started to withdraw.

"Wait!" Judy called. "Germaine, are you the witness who told the police they saw Monsieur Giardini leaving Mademoiselle Werner's room last night?"

"No, Mademoiselle." Germaine scurried out of Judy's room in haste.

"Germaine's so great," Judy sighed. "I wish I could take her back to the States with me. For when I get married I mean. We have a great maid, Ruby, in my mother's house, she's been with us since before I was born. Germaine would be even better. She works like a dog and never complains. Ruby complains all the time, it's as much of a reflex as breathing. My Daddy says it's part of her charm. Of course, she's getting old, Germaine, I mean, I don't know how much longer she could keep up like that."

"Then take Gabrielle," Miri said sarcastically, "she's got a lot more years left in her!"

"Oh no! She's too pretty and probably an awful flirt. I wouldn't want her around my husband."

"If you had one."

"Oh I'll have one one of these days."

This was precisely why Miri had tried to avoid Judy Kugel, the sort of person who would plan the maid she wanted when she got married before she even had the fiancé. She hauled herself out of the comfortable easy-chair.

"You're going already?"

"I have something to do."

Judy pressed a thick wad of tissues into her hand. "Here. Just in case your sneezes come back."

Miri accepted them guiltily. She didn't want to talk to Judy as much as Judy wanted.

As Miri climbed the wide winding stairs to her room she couldn't help but try to imagine what stealthy figure had made its way silently up these stairs last night.

She didn't trust the police to bother looking for the actual murderer if they had evidence that seemed to implicate

Jamie. Most people were lazy and did the minimum it took to get by instead of trying to do things right. And in this case, where they could pin it on one of *'ces americains!'* they would be only too happy to do so. Unless of course they were worried about diplomatic repercussions, as that Monsieur Dantan seemed to imply. But he didn't have any say-so, that was obvious, he was just the interpreter. So if she really cared about what happened she was going to have to look into it herself, even though the thought scared her.

Another unpleasant chore awaited her, to break the news to Madame Fleuris of her departure. She stood awhile on the sixth-floor landing rehearsing in her head how she would tell her. It was not even the middle of the month yet and she was paid up at the *pension* until the end of the month. Miri knew that Madame Fleuris wouldn't give her a refund for the balance of the month. She would be lucky if she didn't make a fuss about not getting enough notice. And of course Miri hoped Madame hadn't heard from Germaine yet about the holes burned in the straw mattress and the sheets when the alcohol stove overturned.

Miri turned around and went back down the stairs to the fourth floor to tell Madame Fleuris about her departure. She looked in the kitchen first. Germaine was scrubbing laundry on a washboard at the big double laundry sink. She told Miri that Madame Fleuris was having tea alone in the salon. Germaine said she would bring Miri some too. Madame was sitting stiffly on a straightbacked chair and waved to Miri to do the same. She was a disagreeable old bitch but at that moment she seemed pathetic and lonely.

Nevertheless Miri did what she had come to do. "Madame Fleuris, I'm leaving here at the end of the month," she said bluntly. Actually she planned on moving out immediately, but didn't want her to tell Germaine to strip the sheets from the bed until she had moved all her stuff to Reid Hall.

Madame glared at her angrily. "That will leave me with two vacancies on short notice!"

"Two?"

"I certainly cannot allow a criminal suspect to remain under my roof! I have instructed Germaine to pack up Monsieur Giardini's belongings, strip the beds and prepare the room for some other *pensionnaire*."

So as soon as Jamie was released from the police, he would find that he had no place to sleep. Great. "Have you heard from him?"

"No, nor do I have a need to do so."

"Suppose the *juge d'instruction* decides Jamie didn't do anything wrong, that someone else murdered Emilie Werner. You're still going to throw him out on the street? And even if he is a suspect, that doesn't mean he's guilty. In America, which you think is so barbaric, a person is innocent until proven guilty. Proven. Not suspected. Proven. I thought you represented yourself as a Christian. Is that Christian behavior? And what about throwing the first stone?"

Madame Fleuris closed her eyes. A tear rolled down her wrinkled cheek. She opened her eyes and looked at Miri without the usual hateful glare, "You are right, mademoiselle. I apologize. I shall allow him to remain."

Miri was stunned by the effectiveness of her outburst; a little frightened at her ability to move someone so seemingly intractable.

She hurried out of the apartment and raced up the winding stairs to the sixth floor, and her room. She took down her one valise from the top of the mahogany armoire and began throwing things into it. She was sneezing again, and was out of handkerchiefs. There were the tissues Judy had pressed on her, but she was saving them for use in public. She tore a piece from the old linen bedsheets she had bought at the Marché aux Puces to use as painting rags. She would have to use Kleenexes though if this kept up. Her painting rags were too valuable to use for her nose. She could use and then wash later the hand-embroidered borders she had cut off the old sheets to use sometime in a blouse or something, an intricate almost sculptural floral design worked completely in white satin threads.

It didn't take long to throw everything together. All she had was the one valise, her paintbox and easel folded together, a small straw case she had found at the Marche aux Puces in which she kept junk, a few books, the small pile of *livres jaunes* she had found along the quais for a few francs–"*Les Enfants Terribles*" by Jean Cocteau, "*Mitsou*" by Colette, "*L'Education Sentimentale*" by Flaubert and also his "*Trois Contes*" with a magnificent blackbearded head on a tray on the back cover and "*Le Noeud de Vipères*" by Francois Mauriac. They had been published in the Thirties and all had wonderful quaint woodcuts, the real reason she had bought them. She hadn't read any of them although she meant to sometime or other. Browsing the bookstalls along the quais was one of the things she liked best about Paris.

The thought of moving worried her. She hoped she was not like the dog in La Fontaine's fable, "The Dog and The Wolf". The dog lived in a warm doghouse and was given good food, but he was on a chain. The wolf had no home and had to forage for food, but he was free. When the wolf longed for the food and shelter that the dog had and the dog offered to trade places, the wolf refused, because his freedom was too precious to trade it for security and comfort.

To reassure herself that she was still an intellectual even though she was moving to a place that was warm and allowed unlimited baths she began reading one of the *livres jaunes*, "*Mitsou*" by Colette.

Right at the subtitle she got stuck for meaning: "*Comment l'Esprit vient aux Filles*". How the spirit comes to girls? What did that mean? Oh well. It was obviously about a dancer. A woodcut above the start of Chapter I showed her in a tutu, stepping down a spiral staircase, holding the banister, head slightly down as if watching her feet, a crown of roses around her head, and a sort of lance trimmed with roses in her other hand. Long eyelashes like a Shirley Temple doll. There was a dot in the middle of one breast, it almost looked like the breast was a cut-out from the sleeveless top. Yes, she was the star. Make-up on her dressing-table, face-powder made of rice, old-fashioned stuff. Chit-chat with other dancers with funny names, like "Little-Thing" (*Petite-Chose*).

This was not Miri's kind of book, but Colette was an artist, and at least there seemed to be two officers, named by the color of their uniforms, Blue and Khaki, and then another man, the Important Man (*l'Homme Bien*), who kissed Mitsou's hand and mumbled a lot of stuff Miri didn't bother to look up in her dictionary. She started skipping more and more. The second chapter woodcut was of a very old man with pince-nez and a beard, French cuffs—his cufflinks represented by a dot, no doubt *l'Homme Bien*. So she was probably a kept woman, Miri skipped too much of the text to be sure. Much of it was written like a play, all talk, which should have made it easier to read, but still she skipped.

She stopped at the page where Mitsou was spelled out in capital letters and periods, "M.I.T.S.O.U." and read that part. Mitsou was explaining to Little-Thing how she got the name "Mitsou". The letters M.I.T.S.O.U. stood for the two companies her boyfriend Pierre was the administrator of, *Minoteries Italo-Tarbaises et Scieries Orleanaises Unifieés*.

A knock at the door startled her.

She opened the door a crack. It was Jamie. He looked exhausted; haunted; with dark shadows under his eyes. But he managed a wan smile. "I've had it." He came into Miri's room and dropped into the little stuffed chair, then noticed the valise on the bed. "You going somewhere?"

"I was thinking of moving to Reid Hall."

"Just thinking about it and you've packed already?"

"Never mind about that. Tell me what happened to you."

"I'm too tired to talk right now. I'm all talked out. I've got to get some sleep."

"Why did they keep you so long?"

"Because they think I killed Emilie Werner. Ha!"

"Where did they get that idea?"

"They have a witness who claims to have seen me leaving Emilie's room last evening around the time their police doctor says she was killed. I never went near that girl. And I left here at least three quarters of an hour before they say I did. I was out the rest of the evening and night too."

"Who said they saw you in Emilie's room?"

He shook his head. "They wouldn't tell me."

"How did they treat you?"

"They didn't torture me if that's what you're worrying about." He gave a weak laugh. "But it's no fun getting pummeled with questions for hours, the same ones repeated over and over, sometimes one tough guy, then another, that oily interpreter monotonously and patiently translating their same questions and my same answers over and over. They kept bringing in fatty ham sandwiches and coffee." He gave a little laugh. "I almost told them I would confess if they would only switch to Camembert! But seriously, I'm tired. That's all. Very tired. There was nothing to tell them. I knew nothing of Emilie Werner. Nothing. I don't even know what she looked like. I can't imagine why someone said they saw me coming out of her room. Maybe I have a *doppelgänger*."

The word startled Miri – Emilie had said the two of them were *doppelgängers*.

"Germaine denied seeing you coming out of Emilie's room. Judy and I asked her."

"My guess is that it was Gabrielle. She probably did see some man, maybe the one who actually did kill Emilie, and mistook him for me."

"Well can't the police check that out, you know, with a lineup or something?"

Jamie shrugged and hauled himself to his feet. "I've got to get some sleep."

"You said you left here before they say someone said they saw you leaving Emilie's room. What about where you went? Can't someone there provide you with an alibi?"

Jamie gave her an odd look and slumped back into the chair. "When is an alibi not an alibi?" he mumbled.

"What? What's that supposed to mean?"

"It means I can't tell them whom I was with or where I was."

"Why not?"

"Because."

"Because why?"

"Never mind that."

"What do you mean, 'never mind that'? Your life is at stake."

Jamie gave a mirthless laugh; almost a cough. "Our lives are always at stake, we just don't usually think about it."

Miri couldn't figure out if he had just said something profound which she couldn't figure out, or if it was just sophistry. She didn't want to ask him whom he had been with, as it was seeming more and more likely that he had some other girlfriend, probably married, since he wouldn't talk about her. But it seemed awfully Victorian to refuse to reveal who she was even though had he done so he could probably have rid the police of their suspicions of him.

"You mean because it would hurt your friend?" If she really loved him she would be willing to come forward to save him from standing accused. But of course if she didn't love him but was just playing around then she might even lie and say she hadn't seen him.

He shook his head. "It would ruin my chances for the kind of career I want."

"This is either very fascinating and provocative and must be explained, or it's gross hyperbole!"

"Miri, I've got to get some sleep." He shuffled out, and a moment later she heard his door close.

Miri wanted to know who had said they had seen Jamie leaving Emilie's room, but she was too frightened of coming to the attention of the murderer to do anything about it on her own. Then she hated herself for her cowardice.

14

Pilieu and Dantan sat in a corner of the "Café des Flics", as the café nearest the P.J. had been affectionately dubbed by neighboring tradesmen. Their small table was laden with two steaming cafe filtres, a platter of fried sandwiches of ham and cheese on ficelles, and two small glasses of potent Calvados, which the waiter refilled as soon as they were quaffed.

They had made up to meet at seven on Tuesday morning, an hour before the meeting called by the chief inspector of the investigators involved in the Werner case. They would compare notes of their findings of the day before, hear Doctor Fogelberg's post mortem report and forensic findings to date, and brainstorm how to proceed.

Monday had been a busy day for them all. From the victim's identity card, found in her handbag, the photography lab had enlarged and printed her face, with copies for each of the detectives who were questioning neighbors, concierges, shopkeepers, not only in the vicinity of Rue des Ecoles, but up in the Pigalle area, where Emilie Werner had lived for two years in a small unsavory hotel. It was a hotel that rented rooms by the hour; she was one of a very few residents who paid by the week. They would have to look into whether she was a girl of the streets. That could significantly broaden the investigation.

Dantan noted every detail, every word. In the one day of assisting in the questioning Dantan had formed an ambitious goal: he wanted to solve the case! He wanted to find the definitive clue, or extract the definitive confession, which would nail Mademoiselle Werner's killer, and propel Dantan out of the clerks' room into the ranks of investigators.

To Pilieu, whom he had confided this at breakfast, this was a breathtakingly unrealistic goal. Nevertheless he was enthusiastic for his friend, glad to see a glimmer of ambition after months of depression and anomie. He promised to give his all to helping Dantan achieve this.

He made a specific offer. He would take Dantan along to any future interviews or surveillance to which he, Pilieu might be assigned. He would impart to Dantan any evidence uncovered which did not come out in common discussions in which Dantan took part. The price was that Pilieu wanted Dantan to arrange a meeting for him with one of the American girls at the *pension*, the taller dark one. Pilieu had merely glimpsed her in the Fleuris apartment before taking off on his own assignment, but he knew he urgently wanted to meet her.

"This is very irregular, Jean-Jacques. You know that. Wait until the case is closed."

Pilieu groaned. "One must seize the day, Alphonse. She might go back to America before the case is closed. Or meet another man. Anything could happen. I know you want to remain very professional, and I do too. We can keep the meeting within the framework of the investigation. What we can do is think up some brilliant questions to ask her, then follow up, and report the results to the chief inspector afterwards. I'll take the blame for pursuing it without consulting with him first, and say I dragged you along for interpreting."

"Very well. I'll agree once you have produced the so-called brilliant questions."

Pilieu gulped his coffee, and looked pensive. "Tell me what transpired in the interviews with the Americans, then I may be able to think of something."

"You'll hear it all at Goulette's meeting. Let's get going."

The room in which they were to meet was small and windowless, and smelled of scorch and stale cigarette smoke. It had once been a file-room crammed with old oak file-cabinets stuffed with crumbling old records some dating back to the previous century. A clerk seeking something in the room had been smoking, a burning ash landed on a receptive piece of paper, and the room quickly went up in flames.

The clerk had been pulled from the fire injured but alive. All the records were destroyed.

Goulette shrugged off the loss of the files. He had the room shoveled out and scrubbed, had schoolroom chalkboards mounted on two adjacent walls, and an old table and a few rickety chairs moved in. The walls were still streaked in black. They had not been repainted. Goulette preferred the smell of smoke to that of paint. He sometimes went there to think, and he sometimes held small meetings there.

Pilieu and Dantan were the first to arrive, but soon were followed by the chief inspector, then Vouray, and Doctor Fogelberg, the chief of the forensic technicians.

Goulette stepped up to the front chalkboard, then asked Doctor Fogelberg to present his findings to date. A Gauloise Bleue between his lips, Goulette set up columns on the chalkboard: "Time", "Item", "Source", "Probability", "Investigator"; "Follow-Up". On the side chalkboard he wrote similar headings, substituting the word "Individual" for "Item".

Dantan had equipped himself for the meeting with a notebook and pencil. Whatever Goulette wrote on the chalkboard he copied down, together with any relevant thoughts of his own. Emotionally he was suddenly back in the schoolroom, where the English ladies made very sure the pupils were not slacking off and where the boy Alphonse had actually enjoyed school and was not a problem.

Referring from time to time to pages in a blue folder, Doctor Fogelberg began with time and cause of death. As he spoke Goulette scrawled brief notes on the chalkboard. He began with time of death.

Death had occurred between eight and eleven p.m. based on the contents of the stomach. The owner of the neighboring brasserie had informed Vouray that the victim had dined there early, at seven. The waiter remembered that she had eaten a sausage, sauerkraut, and boiled potato and had drunk a beer, then left without loitering. The stomach also contained chocolate.

Vouray interjected that in his canvassing of the neighborhood, when he described the victim the owner remembered her. She had eaten at the brasserie several times before, always alone. "'A completely genteel young lady,'" Vouray said that the brasserie-owner had said.

The inspectors knew from previous meetings of this sort that interruptions from anyone, if pertinent, were always welcome. Formal presentations were merely the skeleton on which to hang ideas and facts from no matter whom, to fill out their image of the case.

Goulette wrote under Item, "time of death"; under Time "8-11 p.m" and next to Source, "(1) contents of stomach; (2) brasserie-owner, brasserie waiter." Probability was noted as 90-95% Investigators were listed as (1) Doctor Fogelberg, (2) Vouray. On the other chart he entered "Werner" as Individual, time as "from 7 p.m. to 8 p.m." and Source as "brasserie-owner, waiter."

Goulette himself noted that Madame Fleuris said that she had mounted to the sixth floor around nine p.m. to provide one of the *pensionnaires* with an extra blanket. At that time she had observed someone emerging from Mademoiselle Werner's room. He entered a brief note on this and said he would have more to tell them about this later.

The blood contained a powerful sedative. Impossible to determine the time it had been ingested. Goulette noted the next item "sedative in blood" and Investigator as Doctor Fogelberg, with question-marks in each of the other columns. Under Follow-Up he wrote "Fogelberg-identify, Vouray-search room, Poivriere apartment, question Mme Poivriere."

A chamber-pot containing urine was found in the commode. Chemical analysis corroborated the presence of the sedative. This was briefly noted on the chalkboard.

Rigor mortis had set in quickly. The room was very cold; the temperature was four degrees Celsius, only two degrees greater than the outside temperature, which was unseasonably cold. The window and shutters had been found open, and may have been so for hours. Based on lividity the body had not been moved from where the victim met death.

Goulette asked if anyone had any ideas concerning the open window.

Vouray remarked that since it was freezing outside it was unlikely that Mademoiselle Werner had opened it while she was alive. Perhaps the killer had done so to speed up rigor mortis to confuse the time of death.

Nobody else volunteered any ideas. Dantan wished fervently that he could think of something clever to offer, but he could not. All he could volunteer was that the American *pensionnaire* Mademoiselle Winter had said that when she walked down the hallway on the sixth floor at around twenty to six Monday morning she felt a cold draft from under Mademoiselle Werner's door. Goulette gave him a brief nod.

The chief inspector seemed concerned enough about the open window to note it as a separate item, with question-marks in all the other columns.

Death had been caused by garroting. The silk scarf had not caused the strangulation, it seemed to be purely decorative; it covered the cord actually used. The origin of the cord had not yet been identified.

Numerous fingerprints were lifted from around the room. They had yet to ask anyone at 10 *bis* to provide their own prints, for comparison. It took considerable time to go through the dog-eared card-files in Records, comparing a print in question card by card with each print on file, should they find that some prints in the victim's room did not match any of the known persons in the vicinity.

They had not found any human hairs other than those of the victim, but they did find a profusion of cat-hairs.

Pilieu provided the explanation, obtained from his interviews with Gabrielle and with Madame Poivriere. Mademoiselle Werner had owned a cat. Upon her death Madame Poivriere, who had a dog and did not want the cat in her apartment gave permission to Gabrielle to keep it.

Chief Inspector Goulette did not bother to make a note, as this seemed irrelevant to the murder. He thanked the doctor, his hand outstretched for the blue folder, when Doctor Fogelberg said, "Just one more thing, gentlemen. On the victim's right arm was an Auschwitz tattoo."

The hush that followed was if each man were holding his breath.

The doctor handed the blue folder to the chief and took his leave.

"What does anyone make of that?" Goulette grumbled.

"An enemy from the past?"

"She seems to have survived her enemies of the past!"

"The name Werner... It isn't Jewish."

"Not only Jews were incarcerated."

"It isn't French either."

"A forged identity?"

"Enough!" Goulette barked. "We should make every effort to solve this case without going down that uncharted path!"

They proceeded with a discussion of the evidence.

Contents of the room were unexceptionable. All seemed logically to belong to the deceased. And seemed undisturbed. On a small desk stood a handbag of fine black calf, with a golden snap closure. In the handbag the items they found were also unexceptionable: an unadorned linen handkerchief touched lightly with scent; one key, which fit the door of her *chambre de bonne*; one well-used lipstick; and a worn leather wallet. The wallet contained four hundred francs in paper money (some coins were loose in the bottom of the bag), a bus carnet with a few strips left, a second-class Metro carnet with two tickets left, the victim's identity card, and a pneumatique addressed to "*Ma chère* Mitsou" and signed "Pierre" requesting a rendez-vous at a certain restaurant near Pigalle.

"Madame Poivriere's son is called Pierre," Dantan observed.

Goulette shrugged. "So are hundreds of thousands of other Frenchmen. But naturally we'll start with him. After all his mother did rent the room to Mademoiselle Werner. Perhaps it was at his behest."

A copy of the identity-card photograph had made it into *"Aujourdi"*, which published a brief but lurid story on page one. The chief inspector had informed importuning reporters only the identity of the young woman (potentially useful to have published, in the event someone from her so-far unknown private life came forward with information), probable cause of death and the fact they were looking into the crime but as yet had not identified any suspects.

This was true only to the extent that Goulette was still not persuaded of Madame Fleuris' accuracy of observation.

Goulette related the salient facts of his questioning of Madame Fleuris.

She had learned of the crime when her maid Germaine came to her to tell her that Gabrielle in entering Mademoiselle Werner's room to clean had found her body and had run off, first to her mistress, who was not home, then to Germaine. Madame Fleuris had then telephoned to the commissaire of the *quartier* – who then had called Goulette.

Madame Fleuris said that she had reason to believe that one of her *pensionnaires*, Monsieur James Giardini, had committed the heinous deed!

Madame had gone up the sixth floor on Sunday night to bring an extra blanket to Mademoiselle Winter's room. The young lady was not in, and Madame simply left the blanket on the bed. As she was leaving the girl's room, a young man hurried out of Mademoiselle Werner's room, seemingly stealthily, as he was on tiptoe and scurrying like a frightened rat. The *minutière* had gone off, and he did not press it back on – another proof of his guilty behavior –but it was her *pensionnaire*, Monsieur Giardini, of that she was sure! Naturally she had no idea at the time that a crime had been committed, she assumed that Monsieur Giardini had been having an assignation with the young woman.

Disgusted as she was at his immorality, she was not totally surprised as she knew a thing or two about the nature of the male animal, her own husband having betrayed her throughout the years.

The next morning, when her maid told her of the poor young woman found dead upstairs, Madame Fleuris immediately recalled seeing her *pensionnaire* steal away from that room.

She could not say exactly what time it had been. She regretted this very much but she simply could not say.

"What does Monsieur Giardini have to say about this?" asked Pilieu.

"He denies categorically ever visiting Mademoiselle Werner's room. He denies even being acquainted with her. He acknowledges seeing a new face on the sixth floor in the past couple of weeks but they never spoke. He says he knows nothing about her. We'll go into his interview a little more. He went out on Sunday evening, he says at a little after seven."

"The concierge was chagrined to say that she never saw Monsieur Giardini go out. She likes to claim that she misses nothing. We know that is not humanly possible, if only because of calls of nature. She did see him return – early Monday morning, around six.

"And neither of the maids saw him Sunday evening," said Goulette. "As for Mademoiselle Miri, she herself went out late that evening – "

"According to the concierge, around nine," interjected Poilieu.

"And did not see him Monday morning when she tried to rouse him that morning about a quarter to six."

"So according to the time-table so far," Vouray said laboriously, "he could have murdered the girl, then gone out and stayed out all night for all anyone knows."

"Where did he say he went Sunday evening?"

"He didn't," Goulette said.

Dantan knew that the young man had refused to say, and they had not pressed him, yet.

"We'll have to interrogate him further." Goulette turned to Dantan. "You and I. After this meeting. At the P.J."

Goulette asked Vouray to report next. Vouray had interviewed the concierge at 10 *bis*, occupants of the apartments on the third and fourth floors, as well as the optician whose shop was on the ground floor facing the courtyard. He had also interviewed concierges of the adjacent buildings, shopkeepers around the corner – fishmonger, baker, pork-butcher and tobacconist, as well as personnel at the brasserie and at the Cluny movie theater.

The net result was that only the brasserie-owner and waiter responded to the photograph of Mademoiselle Werner. The concierge at 10 *bis* had noticed her leaving the building around ten minutes before seven, confirming the time set by the men at the brasserie. The concierge also remembered the time the young woman had returned. It was eight-thirty. She was unaccompanied. No, she did not have any callers and it was unlikely that anyone could have slipped by her loge that night, she was very vigilant. Pilieu also had the concierge's comments on other residents of 10 *bis* but Goulette asked him to hold that until they got to the other individuals.

The tobacconist vaguely thought the photograph looked familiar but she could not recall when she had seen the young woman last; certainly not Sunday evening, as her shop was closed.

Pilieu had questioned the Poivriere *bonne* Gabrielle and the Fleuris *bonne* Germaine, and Madame Poivriere herself, eventually, once she had returned from a lengthy morning excursion. The findings were as follows:

Gabrielle had worked late in Madame Poivriere's apartment on Sunday evening, as there were guests to dinner. After serving all the courses at dinner she had to wash up the dishes and pots, and scrub the kitchen floor and cabinets. Then she put away the good silver in its flannel pockets, the good china in its cabinet, and then she ate her own dinner. All that done, she went up to her room to bed.

She saw none of her neighbors on the sixth floor until early the next morning, about a quarter to six, when she heard noises, opened her door, and saw Mademoiselle Miri pounding on Monsieur Giardini's door. They spoke briefly, Mademoiselle Miri, who was always very gentle with her, and always said *vous* to her, apologized for waking her up, she said she had to get up anyway. No, Monsieur Giardini did not open his door.

She then got dressed and went down to Madame Poivriere's apartment to start the coal-fire in the kitchen and prepare breakfast. She assumed that Madame Poivriere was still asleep when she went upstairs to clean her room and that of Mademoiselle Werner's. That was when she found the body. She rushed downstairs to the fifth floor, but Madame Poivriere had apparently gone out, so she rushed down to the fourth floor and got ahold of Germaine to tell her what she had found and asked what she should do. Germaine had taken over, kept her busy helping with the breakfast for the *pensionnaires* while Germaine and her mistress took care of calling the police and keeping everyone around until the police came.

Goulette made a few entries on his chart asking for discussion to estimate at what time Gabrielle might have gone upstairs, as she did not know. She said she had been very tired and just did not look. Dinner had been served at eight. Ten persons were present, Madame Poivriere and her son Pierre Poivriere who had come to Paris on business on Thursday or Friday, then came to visit his mother on Saturday and had stayed over Saturday night but was going back home to his wife Sunday night; four couples, friends of Madame

Poivriere. There were numerous courses, soup, fish, meat, vegetables, fruit, cheese, sweet, and then coffee in the salon. It must have taken no less than two hours, perhaps as much as three. That put it between ten and eleven. Then Gabrielle's cleaning-up had to have taken a good hour, therefore she could not have gone upstairs much before eleven, and probably somewhat later. Past Doctor Fogelberg's outside time of death. Probably.

Germaine had little to contribute. She had not been on the sixth floor since Saturday until Gabrielle hysterically sought her out Monday morning around eight, and after informing Madame Fleuris of Gabrielle's hysterical report she had gone upstairs to guard the crime-scene until the police should arrive. She was asked questions about each member of the family and each of the Americans. She had only good words, a few good words, she was not a garrulous woman, to say about any of them. She did confide that she liked Mademoiselle Miri the best, as she was calm, spoke excellent French and was kind to the maids. Germaine thought she might be an aristocrat in disguise, as she had exquisite hand-embroidered handkerchiefs which had each cost a pretty penny, and she dressed extremely conservatively.

Madame Poivriere was very forthcoming once Pilieu finally was able to speak with her. She invited him into the dining-room for the interview and told him to take as long as he liked to question her. She was a very chic slim lady of perhaps sixty-something who must have been a beauty once.

She could tell him very little about her tenant. The young woman had only been renting the room since a few days after Christmas.

Madame Poivriere had originally listed the room with the student housing bureau at the Sorbonne in the fall at the beginning of the school year but it had not been taken. Several students had viewed it in the autumn but when they learned that they would not be permitted to use the W.C. in her apartment but would be confined to using a chamber-pot that seemed to deter all the potential tenants. Madame didn't care, she didn't need the money, she only had listed the room out of conscience because of a housing shortage in Paris, particularly cheap rooms for students. But she didn't want anyone coming and going in her private apartment, so when it wasn't rented at the beginning the school year she forgot about it. In fact she was quite surprised when Mademoiselle Werner turned up right after Christmas with a room-for-rent notice from the student housing bureau. By then Madame Poivriere hadn't thought about the room in months.

Mademoiselle Werner explained that she was no longer a student, she worked at the Galeries Lafayette, but she needed an inexpensive room. She agreed to all the conditions.

Madame Poivriere knew nothing further about the young woman, perhaps she should have been more cautious and asked questions, but she saw no need to. Before the young woman moved in, Madame's son Pierre looked into the information Mademoiselle Werner had told them about herself, and he verified that the young woman was indeed employed at the department-store and had worked there for over two years with no untoward incidents. A perfectly *propre* young lady.

(Just how the brasserie-owner had described her.)

As for the timetable connected with Madame Poivriere's Sunday-evening dinner-party, dinner had indeed been served promptly at eight for ten persons, and all but her son and one couple, who left early, had adjourned to the salon for coffee and brandy at about twenty to eleven.

She had not noticed what time Gabrielle finished cleaning up and gone upstairs to her own room, she was preoccupied with her guests, most of whom stayed until midnight.

No, Gabrielle did not cook dinner for Madame Poivriere. A cook came in to do important meals. The cook had dished up, Gabrielle had served, and the cook left for home around ten. She woulld be back on Wednesday. Poireau took the cook's name and address.

Goulette noted on his chart that the cook had left the Poivriere apartment within the time of death of Mademoiselle Werner and asked Poilieu to try to verify what time the cook had arrived home Sunday night. He didn't really think the cook was a suspect but he liked to dot all the i's and cross all the t's. (One of the clerks who worked beside Dantan, and was frequently importuned to recopy something all over because of miniscule corrections, said that the chief inspector liked to cross his i's and dot his t's. He was the same wit who had originated, "Dead men don't speak English.")

Chief Inspector Goulette then briefly summarized his questioning of the son-in-law Philippe Jumelle. He knew nothing. He had come summoned by his mother-in-law to offer moral support and to reassure his wife that her mother was safe.

The potentially important individual to interview, Pierre Poivriere, lived and worked at some distance from Paris. One of the inspectors would have to make a day of it if they were to question him.

As for the four Americans, the chief inspector asked Dantan to summarize for Pilieu and Vouray what had been learned.

"First of all each of the four of them insisted on being questioned in the presence of all of the others. Chief Inspector Goulette agreed to this. They don't trust us."

Vouray mumbled that they had some reason, given the despicable performance of the French government in capitulating to the Germans only a month after France was invaded.

There was a moment of silence; perhaps embarassed silence. It was well-known at the P.J. that Vouray had played an active and dangerous part in the French Resistance. Even those who had collaborated at the time now admired and even envied him for his past.

"But these Americans were just children during the war," said Pilieu. "Surely that war can't be on their minds."

"We were children then too," said Dantan. "And I still

feel certain things keenly. My father fell in the Argonne. I was ten. And I was shipped out of France to England, where I was raised by English ladies taking care of orphaned children displaced by the war from all over Europe."

"All right, men, to work," said Goulette gruffly.

Dantan took up his account again, embarassed by his digression. He would dispense first with the two *pensionnaires* who occupied rooms within the apartment on the fourth floor and had no reason to go to the sixth floor, unless of course, invited by one of the others.

Monsieur Lee had been very close-lipped about his own whereabouts on Sunday evening, or any other time, for that matter, but the concierge had seen him leaving around seven-thirty and returning after the doors were locked. He had rung the bell to be admitted at around midnight. It was a busy hour, as many of Madame Poivriere's guests were leaving at around that time too. Despite his secretiveness Monsieur Lee seemed to be exonerated fully.

Mademoiselle Kugel also had gone out, around seven, confirmed by the concierge, returning around eleven. This was borderline for the hour of the victim's death, but Mademoiselle Kugel was heard by Madame Fleuris returning to the apartment, and staying in, from about eleven on. Furthermore Mademoiselle Kugel represented that she had never met the victim, did not know her even by sight.

"Now for the two *pensionnaires* who reside on the sixth floor," Dantan went on. "Beyond what you've heard already we learned nothing from Monsieur Giardini. He flatly denies the events described by Madame Fleuris. He says he never spoke with the victim, certainly never entered her room, and left the house Sunday evening at eight, which would be an hour or more before the murder.

"Monsieur Giardini refused to say where he went. He apparently stayed out all night. Mademoiselle Winter knocked on his door at twenty to six on Monday morning without response, and the concierge reports seeing him return to the building around six that morning. As for Mademoiselle Winter, she reported two brief conversations previously held with Mademoiselle Werner, in the course of which she learned that the latter had a lover, a man she had met when he made a purchase at her counter at the Galeries Lafayette. Mademoiselle Winter went out at around nine, according to her own account and that of the concierge."

"Where did she go?" asked Pilieu.

"She said she went to the Cluny movie-theatre to see '*Volpone*' for the third time."

Pilieu smiled at this. Dantan knew Pilieu enjoyed a good laugh at the films of Louis Jouvet, though he suspected that something like "*Carnival à Flandres*" was more to his simple taste than "*Volpone*".

Vouray grumbled that much of this was a waste of time. "The answer will be found in the victim's life before her move to 10 *bis* Rue des Ecoles. Someone made his way past that officious concierge – who is not as alert as she makes herself out to be – after all, she missed seeing Monsieur Giardini going out, and it's obvious he did," he said sarcastically, "or he couldn't have been seen coming back!"

Goulet said, "There's merit in what you say, Vouray. We need to get to work investigating her known contacts at her previous residence, as well as associates at her place of work. I want you to get right on it."

Vouray nodded assent.

"And you too, Pilieu. Split up the interviews between the two of you."

Pilieu acknowledged this by moving closer to Vouray and exchanging a few whispered words.

"Dantan!" the chief inspector smiled. "I see you have been taking copious notes. Perhaps you would be good enough to write them up precisely and clearly, and ask one of the clerks to type them with three carbons so that each of you good men can have a copy."

Dantan was delighted at the request, delighted that the

chief inspector viewed him as somewhat useful, and delighted that the chief inspector had allowed for a copy for him.

Writing up his notes would give him a chance to study them as he went. Nothing had leaped out at him at the recitals. He was determined to make the most of this opportunity of escaping the trap of treading water as an interpreter in domestic spats, translator of documents of pathetic aliens who had gotten themselves in petty trouble.

"You and I, Dantan," said the chief inspector, "are going to collect Monsier Giardini and bring him to the P.J. for a more intensive interrogation than he experienced before. I want to get to the bottom of where he was that evening, in order to get some corroboration or not of the time he departed 10 *bis* Rue des Ecoles."

Pilieu made a hasty gesture to Dantan of quaffing a drink and said only to Dantan, "Later?"

Dantan nodded.

15

Tuesday was Miri's bath night at the *pension* Fleuris. She would have preferred later in the week, but Jamie had Thursdays, Branford Duane Lee the Third Fridays, Judy Wednesdays and Saturdays (she got two because she was paying for two rooms). Madame reserved Sundays and Mondays for whomever was willing to pay the two hundred francs surcharge for an extra bath. But it didn't matter anymore. Starting tomorrow she could have as many baths as she wanted at no extra charge.

She undressed and put on her pink flannel nightgown, red quilted robe, and French felt concierge slippers to go down to the apartment, bringing soap, towel and a change of underwear. She managed to slip past Judy's rooms without being caught for a conversation. She wouldn't have wanted to let slip that Jamie was back, as Judy would have persisted until she got the details and out of curiosity might even have barged in on him upstairs.

Turning on the hot-water tap the gas-heater on the wall beside the tub emitted its familiar pop, then its hum, and Miri could glimpse the blue flame through a slit in the heater. She was always vaguely apprehensive that the gas would explode, but it never did.

It was a relief not to have to wash her hair that night. She would be able to do so in Reid Hall the next day—and every day after that if she wanted to! She could never get her hair clean *chez* Fleuris. It was long and thick and there was never enough hot water to rinse out the soap. Jamie had suggested she get it cut short, to make it easier to wash. But she had no intention of wasting time at hairdressers, or putting her hair up in pincurls the way Judy did.

Even though she usually felt best on bath-night, that night she couldn't fall asleep. Despite the blanket Madame had added she felt a chill. Her cold seemed to have come back. She was sneezing again, and her eyes were itchy. She decided to see how Jamie was holding up.

She had to tap several times at his door before he responded with a mumble.

"Jamie? Are you awake? It's me, Miri."

He opened the door. The room was dark. "I was asleep. What's up?"

"I couldn't sleep."

"Come on in."

"You were asleep? I thought you'd be up worrying."

"I was, earlier. Then I got sleepy. Come in before you catch cold."

Miri was shivering. He had pulled on a blue silk robe, lit the lamp, then reached for something from the upper shelf of the armoire, a bottle, and poured some into two small glasses from the same place. "Here. Calvados. Swallow it fast."

It burned going down, wracking her with an immense shudder.

Jamie tossed off his drink, then climbed back into his bed, still wearing his blue silk robe over his pajamas. Miri climbed in next to him. He wriggled away from her closer to the wall. She was still wearing her red quilted robe over her flannel nightgown. There were therefore four layers between their skins. But she thought maybe this was the time that something would happen.

Nothing did. He left the lamp on and as they lay there in their sleep-clothes and robes he told Miri more of his ordeal with the detectives. There was some kind of internecine ping-pong going on at the Police Judiciare, it seemed, and he was the ball. The regular detectives wanted to arrest him and sic the *juge d'instruction* on him, while the interpreter kept urging them to hold out until they could collect more corroborating evidence to avoid meddling by the American Embassy.

Then he offered Miri another Calvados "for the road". But she didn't want to hit the road. Instead she burrowed deeper under the covers, laughing. The bed was very narrow, the straw mattress squeaking. She tried to reach under his robe to touch him but before she could get past the flannel pajamas he pushed her hand away.

"I would like to but I can't," he whispered.

"It won't take long..."

"You don't understand. I don't want to try. I don't like it."

Miri wasn't wild about it herself, but she had never heard of a man who didn't.

He went on, "Miri, it's hard to believe that you didn't know this already, but since you seem ignorant, I'll tell you. I prefer men."

At first she didn't get it. She had to take it apart word by word and then put it together again slowly before she understood what he meant. Then she felt sick.

"You're upset," he said glumly.

Miri nodded.

"You never suspected?"

She shook her head.

"Not even after we went to the prince's *vernissage* last November?"

"No." There had been some strange and unpleasant aspects to that afternoon which she hadn't understood, that was all.

"I'm amazed. That was partly why I invited you to the *vernissage* so you'd understand about me."

"Well I didn't. What was the other 'partly'?"

Jamie gave a cynical little laugh. "Oh that was Tobey Peters' idea. He said it would get under Lady Alexandra's skin, if we brought two fresh young girls, rosy and nubile, would make the old bag horribly jealous. She's so vain, can't bear the thought that she was once beautiful and isn't, anymore. Tobey thought it would be fun to torture her."

"And you too? You thought it would be fun?"

"Not really. But I humor Tobey. He's a horrible bitch if you don't."

"Isn't Tobey Peters the fellow you and I saw strolling with Madame Fleuris one day?"

"That's right. And you met him at the *vernissage*. I saw the two of you deep in conversation. He was in drag. Didn't you and Judy ever talk about it afterwards? I'm sure Judy caught on!"

She realized now that it must have been that woman with the heavy makeup who had come over to talk to her.

Besides Judy and Miri, and the hostess Lady Alexandra of course, she hadn't noticed any other women among the guests. So Tobey Peters must have been that repulsive person she had assumed was a woman. "Judy and I never did talk about it. She left the *vernissage* almost immediately after we arrived, while you were getting us champagne. Remember she wasn't there when you came back with the champagne, and you gave one glass to that repulsive woman who was haranguing me?"

Miri had been standing alone, waiting for Jamie and the champagne and Judy had taken off already, when a large squarely built woman, heavily made up and garishly dressed, pushed her way through the mob and sidled up to her. She put a gloved hand heavy overlaid with big flashy rings on Miri's arm and said in a husky voice, "You and I both want the same thing from Jamie, don't we, dear?"

The woman was so repulsive Miri couldn't very well consider her a rival; she didn't answer and the garish woman sneered, "You'll see who wins, and it won't be innocence and naivete, it will be devilish cleverness and a willingness to do whatever is wanted."

Just then Jamie arrived, the woman took one of the glasses of champagne, quaffed it in one gulp, winked at Jamie and swayed off.

"You don't know who that was?"

"She didn't mention her name."

"That was Tobey Peters."

Miri found it hard to believe that the handsome man they had seen walking with Madame Fleuris was the same person presenting as a woman, however coarse and over-made-up.

"Tobey likes to dress up like a woman sometimes. That's why he had such heavy makeup on at the vernissage. To cover his beard. Now do you get it?"

Miri nodded.

"So I thought you already knew about me," Jamie sighed.

"Maybe you could get to like it, sex with girls, I mean. You know, like spinach. I always hated spinach until I got to France where they make it better. And call it *épinard* which sounds better. A developed taste."

Jamie laughed, "Sex is not like spinach!"

She said suddenly, "Let's get married."

"What!"

"Married."

"I just told you. I do it with men."

"Well we're so compatible sex doesn't matter."

Jamie laughed very hard at that. "Sex is the *only* thing that matters!"

He got out of bed and poured himself another Calvados.

"I thought it was the other stuff you liked me for," Miri said. "We're both existentialists and love Italian Renaissance art and so forth."

"That's right. I like you very much. As a friend. You're funny – sometimes funnier than you know – and you're intelligent, and you don't manipulate people. But I don't want to go to bed with you. I don't mean like this. This is just a pajama party, it's fun. I mean the way adults go to bed."

"You didn't say anything when I got into your bed."

"You were cold, is all. You know, Miri, you ought to look for another place to stay. Or get Judy to give up one of her rooms so you can have central heating. Although with a murderer on the loose you'd be better off just moving."

"I told you. I *am* going to move. I've already paid a month in advance at Reid Hall and I can move in any time as soon as I get my stuff over there."

"I'm glad for you. I'll help you move."

He was still being so nice she just couldn't believe he didn't love her.

Something occurred to her. "Is that why you won't tell who your alibi is?"

"That's right. I was with a man Sunday evening and all night, a close friend of mine. He's an officer in the U.S. Army, working in Paris at NATO. He has an apartment on the Right Bank. We get together every Sunday, just the two of us, sometimes more often but without fail on Sundays. I left Rue des Ecoles about a quarter past seven, not eight o'clock the way the police seem to think I did, and went straight to Joe's apartment. I was in his place long before eight o'clock. Nobody else came in or out, and I don't think his concierge saw me as I usually make a point of trying to evade her notice when I go in or out there. That's to keep Joe from getting into trouble with the Army. Not that our friends don't know about us, but there are unpleasant investigations going on in the States so it's a precaution.

"This morning after you and I had gone to the cafe, I was still feeling uneasy at the hard line the police seemed to be taking with all of us, so I phoned Joe at his office to tell him about the murder and how the police had questioned everyone at the pension and how I had felt uneasy at Inspector Goulette's questioning."

Tears welled up in Jamie's eyes. "After the police released me this evening, before I came back here I went straight to Joe's place, intending to tell him that I needed his testimony, that the police suspected me. His concierge told me that he had gone somewhere with a valise but that if I were Monsieur Giardini he had left a note for me. She handed me an envelope Joe had left with her in case I came by. The note said that he had asked for leave to visit a sick relative, which was granted, and he would be in touch. He didn't say when. He obviously doesn't want to get involved. He's scared."

"You could show this note to the police so they would at least hold off until he comes back."

"I wouldn't do that to him."

"But look what he did to you! Deserted you when you needed him!"

"He isn't trying to hurt me, he's simply saving his own skin. You can't fault a person for engaging in self-preservation."

"It's not right."

"It's what it is."

"But what if they arrest you? Put you on trial!"

"How can it come to that? They can't possibly have any evidence to connect me to the crime. I didn't do it. I didn't know Emilie Werner. I was certainly never in her room. The French are civilized people, they are not going to indict a person on one person's say-so, with no back-up. And if they did against all odds go forward with this, then I think Joe would come forward."

"But by that time they might not believe him. It might be too late. They might think that he was making it up just to save your neck."

"There's nothing to prevent them from thinking that even now, if he were to come forward."

"Maybe you should hire a private eye to find out who really did it! Judy said she was going to wire her father for money to help you hire a lawyer if you needed one. Hire a private investigator too."

Jamie shook his head. "I can't think about any of that now. I'm too tired."

Miri took the hint, finally, clambered out of his narrow bed and went slowly to her room.

She felt hurt, rejected and disappointed, but most of all she was angry. She kept ruminating over how she had been fooled. Not that Jamie had done so deliberately. But she still felt like a fool. She was glad that she was moving out of the *pension* Fleuris. She could make a new start somewhere else where they didn't know she was stupid.

16

Some kind of vague hope which she hadn't put into words but which had been sustaining her was gone. She knew she wouldn't be able to sleep, so to keep warm she unpacked her valise and put on all her clothes, layer by layer, the navy princess dress first because it was the tightest, then put the quilted robe over her lap, took up the book by Colette she had started reading and stuffed herself into the little upholstered chair, which she had pulled as close as possible to the little lamp on the commode.

But she couldn't get back into the book. This made her feel guilty, to be bored by Literature, but still she put it aside and retrieved the mystery Vanessa had suggested, and began reading that instead. She was going to have to, anyway, as Vanessa would probably ask her at some point how she had liked it.

It was soothing to enter the encapsulated little world of the stuffy doctor-narrator and his gossipy old mah-jong-playing sister... She read and read and at some point dropped off to sleep right in the chair and slept that way all night.

She was suddenly awakened by a loud rapping on her door. It was already the next morning. Judy, had come to collect her so that they could question Gabrielle before she started her day's work at six a.m.

Judy burst out laughing when she saw Miri. "What on earth are you wearing? Everything?"

"That's exactly right," Miri said coldly. "I was cold."

"Well are you going to go anywhere like that? I mean, we said we would talk to Gabrielle this morning, remember?"

"I remember." Miri began peeling off sweaters, removed the skirt from over the slacks from over the dress. But she couldn't very well wear the navy princess dress for everyday so she had to wriggle out of that, then put a skirt and sweater back on.

Judy was bubbling. "I made a really tremendous discovery!" She didn't wait to be asked what it was. "I found out where Bushy-Beard keeps his boxes!"

She had set her little travel alarm-clock for five, had gotten out of bed and dressed, and then parked herself by a crack in her door until she heard sounds in the hallway and saw old Monsieur Fleuris shuffling down the dim hallway from his bedroom. She stealthily followed him and for a moment thought he was going to exit the apartment without putting on a coat, for he had reached the foyer, with Judy clinging to the wall hoping she was in shadow. But he did not go out the front door. Instead, he unlocked the padlock on a door which the *pensionnaires*, if they had thought about it all, had assumed was a closet. He went into this closet, or room, stayed quite awhile, as Judy became more and more tense that Madame Fleuris, or even Germaine, might appear and find her hanging around there. Eventually he emerged—with four metal boxes!

Judy dashed back to her rooms and from the window in her clothing-room watched him cross the cobblestone courtyard and out the big doors to the street. He was carrying the boxes.

"I want to break into that room and see what's what!" she declared.

Miri was horrified at the thought. This was worse than trying to break into the padlocked *chambre de bonne* on the sixth floor, as this room was in the main apartment, where anyone could come along at any time. "Count me out."

"Don't worry, not now. Now we have to talk with Gabrielle."

Judy rapped on Gabrielle's door.

"Who's there?"

"*Les americaines,*" Judy sang out.

Gabrielle opened the door wide and invited them in. Her room was a riot of color and prints, a Matisse gone mad, an Indian paisley on the little bed, garish floral curtains, an old chenille bedspread dyed purple thrown over an upholstered easychair.

Gabrielle herself, whom they usually saw in a black and white maid's uniform, was wrapped in a brilliant green silk kimono embroidered with a pattern of dragons in red and yellow and white and black. Miri immediately felt she would like to paint the fantastic garment, though not on Gabrielle, whose country roundness was bland where what was needed was someone exotic and powerful who would not be over-shadowed by the colorful brilliance of the robe. Miri made an immediate decision to borrow the robe from Gabrielle once she could find the right person to sit for the painting.

Gabrielle noticed Miri staring at her kimono. She gave a little laugh and smoothed it down on her legs. "An *ami* brought me this from Indochina." She waved them onto the small bed. She herself sat on the one chair.

"He was a tourist in China?" Miri asked awed by what that must have cost.

"He was a soldier!" Gabrielle looked at Miri scornfully. "He stole this from the knapsack of a dead comrade who would have no further use for it. Then he himself was wounded, and sent home, and managed to keep it from being stolen from him in turn."

"It's fabulous!" Judy breathed.

"Did he recover?" Miri asked. "Your *ami?*"

"Yes, mademoiselle, he had a full recovery. And now he is preparing to marry someone else."

"Oh. How mean."

Gabrielle sighed. "I understand it. The young girl has a *dot*, I have nothing. With her *dot* they will be able to start a business, have a livelihood and independence."

Miri was outraged not only that a young man would give up the girl he loved so as to get the wherewithall to start a business but that the jilted girl would acquiesce in the philosophy.

"How much money did she have?" Judy inquired with interest.

"Four hundred thousand francs, mademoiselle."

Judy murmured to Miri in English, "That's only a thousand dollars if you change it on the black market. Can you imagine marrying for money when it's only a thousand dollars?"

"I can't imagine marrying for money whatever the amount," Miri said with a sarcasm lost on Judy.

Judy had turned to Gabrielle and was staring covetously at the robe. "Where do you think I could buy a kimono like yours?"

Gabrielle looked at her slyly. "Perhaps right here, depending on the price."

This was a wonderful omen for what they had come to accomplish! And furthermore, if Judy did buy it from her, Miri would have a better chance of borrowing it for her painting.

"But surely mesdemoiselles you did not come here to purchase a kimono?"

"That's right, Gabrielle," said Judy in a surprisingly businesslike tone. "We came to buy something more valuable. Information."

"Information?"

"The inspecteur seems to suspect the American, Jamie Giardini, of murdering Mademoiselle Werner," Miri explained. "We're trying to find out all we can about Emilie Werner and about what happened Sunday night, to come up with other possibilities."

"The Inspecteur Goulette has already questioned me."

"To begin we want to know what you told him," Judy said. "Did you tell them that you had seen Monsieur Giardini leaving Mademoiselle Werner's room on Sunday evening?"

"No, Mademoiselle, but I happen to know that Madame Fleuris did so."

Judy leaned forward. "How do you know that?"

"Germaine told me. It was when Madame Fleuris was bringing a blanket up to your room, Mademoiselle Miri, that she saw him."

"I did find an extra blanket on my bed when I came back late Sunday night."

"That old hag, she's probably blind as a bat," Judy murmured to Miri in English. "It could have been Jack the Ripper for all she could have seen." To Gabrielle she said, "As I told you, Gabrielle, we want to know not only what you told the inspector, but perhaps facts that would help that you didn't tell them. And we're prepared to pay for that information."

Gabrielle cocked her head at Judy. "How much?"

"That depends on what it is worth. You will have to trust me to be fair."

"You mean I have to tell you this information first, and then you will decide what it is worth? Suppose I tell you everything and then you say it is worth nothing?"

"I promise I won't do that. I'll set a minimum of, say, five hundred francs even if it is worthless to us."

"One thousand."

"No. But I'll make it six hundred. But remember, more money if the information is worth it. Nothing, if you do not agree right now."

"Very well. Let's start."

Judy placed a five-hundred franc note and a one-hundred franc piece on the little commode beside Gabrielle's bed, and said, "First tell us what hours you yourself were on the sixth floor on Sunday night, and everyone you saw during that night."

"As I told the police, I served dinner in the apartment on the fifth floor to Madame Poivriere, her son, and eight guests, then I washed up, had my own dinner, then scrubbed the kitchen floor, then mounted to my room up here on the sixth. That must have been around ten. I saw no one at that time. As I remained in my room for the night after that I saw no one who might have mounted after that hour." She gave us a sly smile. "Except for my visitor."

"And who was that?"

Gabrielle shook her head. "I didn't tell the police about him and I'm not going to tell you two young ladies. He has had nothing to do with the poor Werner's murder."

"How can you be sure?" Miri demanded.

"Never mind that, Gabrielle," Judy said soothingly. "Let me explain that your visitor might be important because of whom he might have seen when he was leaving."

"I don't want to get him into trouble," Gabrielle said. "I don't mean with the law, but what would be much worse, with his wife."

"A married man."

Gabrielle nodded.

"We won't tell his wife," Judy said softly, as she ostentatiously removed a five-thousand-franc note from her red leather wallet and dangled it in front of Gabrielle. Gabrielle hesitated only an instant before reaching for the note and then laughing, "It was Pierre Poivriere!"

Pierre Poivriere, it turned out, had been her lover ever since she came to work for Madame Poivriere when she was fifteen years old. Then Pierre got married, the year before, and moved away. They saw each other much much less. He came to visit his mother about once a month unaccompanied by his wife, when he had business in Paris. On those occasions he would stay the weekend at his mother's, and usually managed to pay at least one visit upstairs to Gabrielle's little bed.

"You didn't tell the police this?" Judy said.

"No. There was no reason. Pierre certainly did not kill the poor Emilie Werner, so why involve him?"

"He might have seen someone up here."

"There was no one, I assure you, mademoiselle, at the hour when Pierre was here. When he left my room I watched him from the doorway, pressing the *minutière* for him. Had he seen anyone I would have seen the same."

"I suppose Pierre Poivriere is a handsome young man?" Judy asked.

"Exceedingly," Gabrielle grinned smugly, and then obligingly produced from under a pile on her little vanity a photograph of a smiling young man in white shirt and dark trousers. The picture appeared to have been torn from what must have been a group photograph.

Judy gushed over his good looks, bringing a happy smile to Gabrielle's face. What Miri noticed immediately was that Pierre Poivriere was of a similar build, slim and wiry, to Jamie Giardini, and also had dark curly hair. Stepping into a dark hallway Madame Fleuris could easily have mistaken him for Jamie!

"Did he come up soon after you did?" Miri asked Gabrielle.

"Oh he was up here already, waiting for me," Gabrielle laughed. "He had said goodnight to his mother as soon as dinner was over, then came up here instead of leaving, whereas I had all the cleaning up to do, and I hadn't eaten yet."

So except for Emilie there had been a period when Pierre Poivriere was alone on the sixth floor!

That would have given him plenty of time to kill Emilie – for whatever reason – they would have to probe for that – and then relax as if he had been in Gabrielle's room all that time. He knew she wouldn't come upstairs right away, she had work to do. This was a definite clue!

"Did Emilie Werner ever tell you anything about herself?" Judy asked.

"Did you know she had a lover?" Miri added.

"Oh yes, I heard about him, Mademoiselle. A married man."

"Did she mention his name?"

"Never, unfortunately."

"You told the police about him?"

Gabrielle frowned, trying to remember. "There was very little to tell. I knew nothing about him."

"You say he was a married man. Did you tell the inspecteur that?"

"I may have. I don't remember."

"But that could be important!"

Gabrielle shrugged. "I told him what I told him. That's all."

"You must have been terrified when you opened Emilie's door and saw her body lying there," Judy said sympathetically.

"Oh yes indeed, Mademoiselle, I was shocked. Her face – it was contorted and purple, her arms and legs flung at awkward angles like a marionette. Her eyes were open and staring. And her beautiful Italian silk scarf, it was wound around her neck. It was so very cold in the room –"Gabrielle shuddered as if reexperiencing the cold – "as cold as the grave itself. The shutters were opened wide as was the window."

At that moment an odd braying sound outside Gabrielle's closed shutters caused her to leap up from the bed and swing open the shutters. Into the room from the window-sill leaped a gray cat like the one Miri had seen in Emilie Werner's room. Gabrielle snatched up the cat. It dangled limply over her hands like a ragdoll, staring at them from glittering green eyes.

"My *chou-chou!*" Gabrielle said, looking pleased. "Isn't he charming? He belonged to poor Emilie. I've given him a new home with me. Madame Poivriere said I might." She nuzzled the cat, who licked her nose. "Mitsou, Mitsou," she said softly, then placed the cat on the floor. It silently slithered across the floor toward Miri, rubbing its body sensuously against her legs. She was not comfortable by that, she didn't like animals up close. She had nothing against them as long as they stayed in Africa or at the zoo, but she didn't want close contact with them. She was afraid to push it away for fear it would scratch her, and just stayed very still until it finally, braying, slowly wended its way over to Judy, who reached out to pet it but it slid away, disappearing under the bed. Within seconds Miri was sneezing.

"I thought I had gotten rid of that cold," Miri said, embarassed because she didn't have a handkerchief.

"Maybe you're allergic to the cat," Judy said.

"Allergic to a cat? I never heard of such a thing."

Judy assured her that allergy to cat-dander was not uncommon.

Gabrielle tried to coax the cat out from under the bed, calling, first, "Mitsou, Mitsou," then "mish-mish-mish," to no avail.

"That's funny," Miri said. "Colette wrote a book called 'Mitsou' and I was just reading it. I bought an old edition along the quais."

"It's possible that the cat was named after the book," said Gabrielle. "Emilie adored Colette's books. She talked to me about Colette, in fact she lent me a book to read that she thought I would like, '*La Chatte*'. Is 'Mitsou' about a cat too?"

"I don't think so, at least not so far. I've only read a part of it. I bought it for the woodcuts. So far it's about a dancer and her various boyfriends."

"Emilie loved cats. '*La Chatte*' is about a young man who loves his pet cat more than he loves his new bride, and she is so jealous she kills the cat."

Judy said, "Sounds sick."

"I think it sounds interesting," Miri said. It certainly sounded better than "Mitsou" anyway.

Gabrielle offered to sell it to Miri. "I have read it." She rummaged around on her little vanity where clothing, cosmetics and magazines were in a jumble, coming up with the book from under a pile of lacy underwear.

Miri didn't have any money with her, but Judy had brought a big supply, for bribes, and offered to lend Miri the price of the book. After looking inside the front cover to see what Emilie had paid for it used, she offered Gabrielle fifty francs for the book; this was accepted gladly.

As Miri flipped idly through the pages, looking at words randomly to see if she would be able to read this book without a dictionary, a piece of paper fluttered from between the pages to the floor. She felt a sudden rush of excitement as she snatched it up. Suppose this were a clue!

Judy had the same thought, for she immediately said, "If it's anything valuable it's mine, I paid for the book."

But it was only a "*chambre à louer*" form, a room-referral handwritten on the kind of form they used at the student housing bureau. It simply said, "Room for rent, *chambre de bonne*, very close to the schools. Apply to Madame Poivriere, 5*ème*, 10 *bis* Rue des Ecoles..."

It was utterly familiar to Miri. She had gone through dozens of similar forms when she first arrived in Paris and went to the student housing bureau for help in finding a place to stay. Even the handwriting looked familiar.

"She rented the room through the student housing bureau," Judy said. "How come a student didn't rent the room?"

"Oh Madame had listed the room with the student housing bureau at the start of the school year," Gabrielle said, "but no one took it at that time, perhaps because Madame was unwilling to provide board or even to allow access to the apartment for the W.C. or the bath. Madame disliked the idea of having strangers at her table, or even in the apartment, and had no need for the money. She had only made the room available to let because she was aware of the housing shortage in Paris. I think she was relieved when no one rented it in the autumn, and had forgotten all about doing so when Mademoiselle Werner came along."

"Did Emilie tell you anything about her family, Gabrielle?"

"She never spoke of them, Mademoiselle. She spoke of cats, and of her lover, and of Colette's writing, and of her job at Galeries Lafayette, where she sold handbags, and where she had met her lover when he came to purchase a gift."

"Did you see her last Thursday or Friday, when she seemed so sad?" Miri asked.

"No, I don't think so. She was content whenever I saw her."

"Thank you very much, Gabrielle," said Judy, adding another hundred francs to the bills and coin she had already placed on the commode. "You have been very gracious as well as helpful and we appreciate it."

At the landing Judy suddenly mumbled "*esprit d'escalier*", ran back to Gabrielle's room, stuck her head in the door and exchanged some words with the girl.

They rattled down the stairs to the fourth floor to confer in Judy's rooms, Miri clutching the copy of '*La Chatte*'.

"Well that was worth five thousand seven hundred fifty francs! Let's see what that is in real money... Fourteen dollars and forty cents. And we've really got something for the police!" Judy glowed. "Wait till they hear that Pierre Poivriere was on the sixth floor that night – before Gabrielle came upstairs. And that he looks like Jamie. And according to Gabrielle, Emilie's lover was a married man. And Pierre Poivriere is a married man. This is great stuff!"

"Let's go right after breakfast to see Inspector Goulette."

Judy looked down to pluck a speck from her skirt. "You don't have to go too. I can tell the inspector everything we found out. After all, I'm the one who bribed Gabrielle. And you're so busy with your painting."

This was the first time Judy hadn't tried to trail along after her. She should have been relieved, but she felt hurt that Judy wanted to exclude her just when she wanted to see Monsieur Dantan again. He had seemed to be interested in her, and she wanted to see him again to see if she could get interested in him.

But Miri was too proud to get into an argument with Judy, and she certainly was not going to tell her the reason she wanted to help bring the information to the police, in case nothing came of it with Monsieur Dantan, so she said nothing. But at that moment she made up her mind to look for other clues that she could bring to Monsieur Dantan's attention by herself.

Besides, Jamie was still her friend despite the fact that now she knew nothing was going to come of it, so she should have been just as concerned about getting police suspicion removed from him as she would have been if he hadn't revealed what he did. But she wasn't. But she was going to act as though she was. She didn't want it to show that it mattered to her.

"Now remember," Judy urged, "not a word of this at breakfast! Not even to Jamie!"

"You're the big-mouth, not me," Miri grumbled.

Jamie tried to play his old self at breakfast, trading Miri his butter for her jam with a good imitation of his own mischievous grin. But the sparkle had gone from his eyes. He looked resigned and dejected, ready to accept martyrdom. He could not afford a lawyer and wasn't going to try to get one. He refused Judy's offers of financial help. He shrugged off all suggestions. "What will be, will be."

Miri was angry that he wouldn't take action on his own behalf. For the first time since they had become acquainted she saw him as just a little person after all, not so smart after all, and in one way – when she thought of him kissing and fondling another man – disgusting.

Judy was chattering non-stop as usual, with one impractical suggestion after another on what Jamie should do, from leaving town to hiding out at the Embassy. But she managed to avoid letting anything slip of what they had learned from Gabrielle.

Even Bran was more talkative than usual. He thought it

imperative that Jamie's rights under French law be clearly
identified, and that he obtain an American lawyer conversant
with French criminal law as soon as possible. Whatever action an American lawyer could take on his behalf should be
taken. Bran did not treat lightly the threat that Jamie might
be incarcerated without what the Americans would consider
adequate evidence.

Neither Bran nor Judy knew about "Joe" or they would
surely have pressed Jamie to reveal his name to the police,
who might track him down. Wherever he had gone, if he were
at a hotel, he would have had to present his passport and fill
out an identification form which was sent to the police.

None of them confronted Madame Fleuris over her
misidentification of Jamie to the inspector, as if it would be
bad manners to do so! Madame for her part was as stiff-backed,
disapproving and self-righteous as ever.

All pretense of speaking French at table was tossed out,
with Madame Fleuris silent at the infractions. Madame Fleuris
had worse offenses to criticize that morning. For Monsieur
Fleuris had brought a newspaper to breakfast, "*Aujourd'*", which
had photographs all over the front page.

Madame Fleuris was furious at the introduction of this
sordid material to polite discourse, but the tide of interest in it
overwhelmed her objections.

The centerpiece of the front page was a faintly smiling
Emilie Werner, apparently a replica of her *carte d'identité*
photo. Another picture showed an older woman in a feath-
ered hat and a dark fur coat just outside the heavy doors of 10
bis Rue des Ecoles. This was Madame Poivriere, according to
Monsieur Fleuris. Another shot had been taken from the courtyard up at the shuttered windows under the eaves. And then
there was a photograph of the Americans! They had snapped
Jamie, Judy and Miri as they were strolling down the Rue des
Ecoles together!

Miri couldn't take her eyes off her own image. She looked
much better than she thought she did. She almost didn't rec-

ognize herself. She had been caught in profile, her hair pulled tight over her ears and fastened at the nape with a barrette. She looked dignified and austere! But her voluminous navy skirt looked dowdy rather than serious.

Monsieur Fleuris kept murmuring into his beard, "*Quel dommage, quel dommage!*"

Judy said, "It's so stupid the way they always print a picture of murder victims grinning as if they were happy to be murdered."

"It's better than showing them dead," said Bran.

Miri recalled Gabrielle's description of Emilie's body, flung down like a marionette. The contempt sickened her.

"*En français, mesdemoiselles, monsieurs, s'il vous plaît!*" cried Madame Fleuris.

"*Comment se dit-il en français* 'ugh'?" Miri asked.

"'The victim appeared first to have been drugged,'" Monsieur Fleuris intoned, reading from the article. "'Then she was garroted.'"

"*Dégoutant!*" muttered Madame Fleuris. "Disgusting. Not a proper subject for discourse at breakfast."

"'A silk scarf,'" Monsieur Fleuris went on, "'was found wound around the victim's neck but is not construed by the investigators to have been the instrument of death.'"

"What was?" Judy asked.

Monsieur Fleuris shook his head sadly. He continued reading from the newspaper. The death was estimated to have occurred between the hours of seven and eleven in the evening of Sunday the seventeenth of January.

That was eight or nine hours or so before Miri had stood outside Emilie's room and felt the cold air on her feet.

Jamie asked to see the newspaper, which he perused rapidly. "Listen to this. Inspecteur Goulette is quoted as saying that they are close to solving the case."

"They always say that," Judy said. "It doesn't mean a thing. – Did they mention Monsieur Dantan in the article?"

"No. And they don't seem to mention at all that any

Americans were questioned. That's a good sign."

"Not necessarily," said Bran. "They're being diplomatic, that's all," said Branford. "They don't want to bite the hand that feeds them unnecessarily, not that they won't do it if it suits them..."

"It also says her arm bore the tattoo of a concentration-camp inmate."

Nobody said anything. But Judy cast an anguished look at Miri, who looked away.

Monsieur Fleuris sighed, "She was so young." He was gazing at the photograph of Emilie on page one as Jamie held up the newspaper to read an inner page.

"Not so young that she hadn't known how to get herself into trouble!" Madame snapped.

"You don't know that, my dear," said her husband mildly.

"If she hadn't been engaged in immoral activities she wouldn't have gotten killed," Madame declared definitively.

"Not necessarily," Judy said in English. "Suppose she had left her lover for someone else and the jilted guy didn't want her to be happy if he couldn't have her? Maybe that's why she moved here in the first place, to get away from the first lover."

"That can't be right," Miri said, recalling her conversation with Emilie Werner. "She said she had met her lover while she was at work at the Galeries Lafayette. And she was smiling over the thought. If she had left him she wouldn't have spoken of him so happily."

"That could have been the *second* lover," Judy said.

"The replacement for the one who then killed her."

"That would fit with her looking sad the second time I saw her, if the first one had shown up and she had had to face him and so forth."

"I wish you two girls were the detectives on the case instead of that Inspecteur Goulette," Jamie said wryly. "I like your theories better than his."

"Everyone who knows you knows you couldn't have done

it," Miri said. "They'll find out the truth."

Branford raised an eyebrow.

"I wouldn't be surprised if Miri and I solved this case," Judy giggled.

"You two," said Branford, "should stay completely out of it. Let the police do their job. Don't interfere, don't get in the way, don't put yourselves at risk." He rolled up his napkin, stuffed it into its ring, and excused himself from the table.

"Quite right, Monsieur Branford," said Madame Fleuris. "Leave the investigations in the capable hands of the Inspector Goulette, and let us not discuss this sordid unfortunate event at table."

Monsieur Fleuris was the next to leave. He went round the table shaking hands with each one there, wishing them each "*bon jour*" and pecking his wife on the cheek despite her stonefaced expression.

The moment he was gone Madame Fleuris burst forth with an angry tirade on the subject of Monsieur Fleuris' infidelity, treachery, insouciance with money and with the feelings of others as if they had never heard it before. She was more hysterical than ever.

She glared at Jamie as if he were the culprit. "What do you think, Monsieur Giardini? Do you think your sex has the right to go here and there at your own pleasure, while your wife remains faithful and performs her duties?"

"It is regrettable, Madame," said Jamie carefully, "when individuals of either sex do not do what is right."

Madame Fleuris did not seem overwhelmingly satisfied with this response, but at least she ceased her tirade. She summoned Germaine to clear.

Miri was amazed that Madame Fleuris seemed to have so little conscience about having pointed the finger at Jamie, erroneously of course, that she could confront him like that.

Jamie announced that he did not want to sit around talking about the case. "I'm trusting to the fact that I'm innocent and that eventually the truth will out. I'm going to go to my

Russian lesson with the Countess de Regeczy."

Judy was in haste to leave too.

Miri went upstairs to repack the clothing she had piled onto herself during the night. The mystery novel she had been reading was on the seat of the little stuffed chair. She picked it up idly, intending only to find her place, but ended up slumping into the chair to read a few pages.

It was engrossing. She kept on reading awhile.

17

The next morning, Wednesday, Dantan applied himself to expanding and typing up the notes he had taken at the previous morning's meeting. Pilieu and Vouray were off to Pigalle to learn what they could of Emilie Werner's life before she moved to Rue des Ecoles.

Pilieu had again insisted to Dantan that he think of a reason to bring him and Miri Winter together, but after the intensive interrogation of James Giardini the day before, at which Dantan had assisted as interpreter, though Giardini's French was very good, he had no taste for going outside Goulette's plans and tactics. He was reluctant to do anything that would anger Goulette, but more than that, he was concerned that purely social moves, whether in the guise of professional actions or not, might disrupt progress toward solving the case.

While he was writing, later that morning, he received a surprise visitor. The grinning errand-boy popped into the clerks' room to inform Dantan that a young lady, an American, wished to see Monsieur Dantan in connection with the Werner case. He had written her name on a slip of paper: Judy Kugel.

Dantan said he would meet with her in the file-room, as they still referred to the scorched hole-in-the-wall.

Once again he found her cute and whimsical and sexy. He helped her out of an expensive camel's hair coat and placed it on a chair, as there was no place to hang it. She was wearing a tight fuzzy pink sweater he thought was very fetching. He could not help but notice that even as she spoke seriously of having important information for the inspectors, her body movements were flirtatious. She jangled her bracelet as she talked. Its dangling baubles looked solid gold. She might be rich. But then, all Americans in Paris seemed rich compared to everyday Parisians.

He offered her the least rickety of the chairs and sat down opposite her.

"Miri and I got Madame Poivriere's maid Gabrielle to talk to us," she smirked. "She told us stuff she didn't tell you guys. Relevant stuff."

Dantan smiled at her. He would have been happy to cuddle her right then and there and had the distinct impression it would not have been unwelcome, but he decidedly wanted to hear the "relevant stuff". "And that was?"

"There was another man on the sixth floor on Sunday night!" She tossed her head teasingly.

"Who was it?"

"Pierre Poivriere! Madame Poivriere's son. Her *married* son! He sleeps with Gabrielle sometimes when he visits his mother without his wife. They had a thing going before he got married and moved away, and he stays in touch so to speak ha ha ha!"

Two things immediately occurred to Dantan. He thought of the *pneu* found in the victim's handbag signed "Pierre". And secondly, he recalled that Gabrielle had worked in the fifth floor apartment until at least ten on Sunday night. "Did she tell you what time he came upstairs?"

Judy's greenish eyes gleamed. "Better than that! she told me that he was upstairs in her room waiting for her when she finished up work and came to her room. He had left his mother's party earlier, pretending that he wanted to get an earlyish start on the drive home, when he actually went up to Gabrielle's room to wait for her. He could have been the man

Madame Fleuris saw whom she thought was Jamie Giardini! They're similar height and build."

"You've met Monsieur Pierre Poivriere?"

"No, but Gabrielle showed us a picture of him. It had been ripped off a group photo."

"That's interesting," Dantan said carefully.

"There's more!" Judy said gleefully.

"Indeed!"

"Yes! Gabrielle told us that Emilie Werner told her that she had a lover, and he was a married man too."

"Did you get the impression that Gabrielle had ever met Emilie Werner's lover?"

"I'm pretty sure she had not. I'm sure she would have said so if she had."

Dantan said, knowing he was being indiscreet, "The victim's wallet held a note signed by someone named Pierre."

"Wow! What if he were rolling in the hay with both of them!" She giggled. "Maybe that's why Emilie moved there! To make it easier for him to call." She added, more somberly, "and then something happened between them, jealousy, maybe, and threats..."

"It's something to think about, surely," said Dantan, "but it would be best if you said nothing further about this."

"Oh I wouldn't breathe a word!"

"Good. Now think – Judy." He called her by her first name consciously but she didn't seem to notice. These Americans were always informal! "Think. Did Gabrielle say anything else about Mademoiselle Werner's lover?"

"That's it." Judy spread her hands out. The charming little bracelet jangled on her wrist flirtatiously. "Oh wait. She did say that she met him for the first time when he came to purchase a gift at her counter, handbags, at the Galeries Lafayette."

"Did she say when that meeting took place?"

Judy shook her curls charmingly.

Dantan longed to prolong the interview but decided it would be imprudent. He stood up to shake hands with his visitor and thank her, but she was not ready to take her leave.

"Let's go have a hot chocolate," she giggled. "Or you can have a beer of course, or whatever you police types drink. Brandy? Personally I'm addicted to hot chocolate. Where's a good place around here?"

He consulted his pocket-watch. "It's nearly time for dinner. May I offer you a meal? I know a place with Spanish specialties, unknown to American tourists. I'll take you there on condition you never tell any of your compatriots about it. Once the Americans discover a place it's finished."

"Sounds wonderful. But I'd rather go there tonight instead." She gave him what might have been a meaningful look. "Is it a date?"

"It's a date!"

"I'm looking forward to it," she smiled.

"I too."

He helped her on with her coat, sliding his hands down the sleeves once it was on. She cocked her head at him with a flirtatious smile.

He walked her out to the exit.

After she was gone he felt a twinge of guilt that he had made no attempt to arrange to include her fellow *pensionnaire* Miri Winter, and Pilieu, in their "date". It was selfish of him, but then, he was selfish. He knew that. Pilieu would have behaved differently, no doubt, because of his immensely charitable nature.

When Goulette returned to his office Dantan brought him the meeting write-up, and reported to him the visit of Mademoiselle Kugel and the information she had imparted. He did not mention that he was taking the young lady to dine that evening. He reminded the chief inspector that Madame Poivriere had said that her son departed from her apartment, and presumably from the building, around nine that Sunday night, and Pierre Poivriere himself had told them the same. Whereas Gabrielle now placed him on the sixth floor – alone – for a good hour from nine to ten, and then with her later.

"Clearly Monsieur Pierre Poivriere must be questioned again. He seems to have misrepresented, at the very least, his time of departure from 10 *bis* Rue des Ecoles on the fateful night. Perhaps there is more. On the other hand, does it not strike you as illogical that a man in the mood for lying with his *petite amie* would while away an hour by strangling another young woman nearby – and then showing no indication in his demeanor to his *petite amie*?"

"It certainly demands independent checking."

"I thought the point that Messieurs Giardini and Poivriere are of similar build was telling. In the dark they could have been confused."

"It is worth questioning Monsieur Poivriere. *Pierre* Poivriere."

18

Miri was still reading when Judy came bouncing in, slightly out of breath and pink in the face from the cold.

"I've been to the Police Judiciare," she panted, "and they took it all very seriously. I think they're going to question Pierre Poivriere because of what we found out! It ties in with something they found among Emilie Werner's effects, a *pneu* to her signed by someone named Pierre! No last name, but it's too much to think it's a coincidence, isn't it? They'll probably get to Gabrielle again too, I just hope she isn't so angry with me for telling them that she refuses to sell me her kimono. I made her an offer this morning and didn't give her a chance to reply because I was afraid on impulse she might refuse but I figured if she thought about it she would definitely agree. But now she might be too angry at me, for telling the police what she told us about Pierre Poivriere."

Miri had begun flinging things into her valise on the bed while Judy talked on and on. Judy now sat on it while Miri snapped it shut.

"I'll help you get your stuff over to Reid Hall. And the taxi will be my treat. I've been meaning to take a look at Reid Hall anyway."

Miri was horrified at the thought that she might not escape this timewasting featherhead even after she moved! Suppose Judy should decide to move in there too? But hopefully they would have no more vacant rooms, or if they did, Judy would discover that there weren't enough armoires in any one room to store her nineteen cashmere twin sets, dozens of pairs of shoes, innumerable boots, two fur coats, plus enough skirts, dresses, underwear and jewelry to persuade some hapless male that he should undertake to provide more of the same for the rest of their lives.

Judy opened the shutters and peered down into the cobblestone courtyard. "You could spy on everyone from up here," she remarked.

"Why would I want to?"

"I'm not saying *you* would want to, but one could. *On pouvait...* You can see right into people's windows if their shutters are open, and anyone leaving the building has to cross the courtyard. So even if they slipped past the concierge without her seeing them, they still could have been observed by someone at the window."

"If you're thinking of when Emilie was murdered, it was dark by seven or eight o'clock."

"But there would be reflected light from lower windows. Anyway, I'm sure the police will question everyone in the building, especially any little old ladies who like to sit by the window and spy on their neighbors. That's standard in mystery books."

That reminded Miri of the mystery she had been in the midst of reading when she fell asleep in her chair. She looked forward to soaking in a warm bath at Reid Hall that night with the water up to her chin and reading the mystery.

Judy turned from the window to the odds and ends still unpacked, among them the pile of yellow crumbling Livres de Demain on the commode beside the bed. "'Salammbo' by Gustave Flaubert. What a funny name. What's that about?"

"Oh I don't read those things, I bought them for the woodcuts. Take a look at the title-page of that one. It has a wonderful stylized lion with pincurls!"

Judy duly turned to the title-page and smiled over the "pin-curls". She turned over the pages one by one, looking at the occasional woodcuts, and at the back page she read aloud, "*Imprimé pour la collection 'le livre de demain'... septembre* 1933.' Wow! That's the year I was born. I wonder if any of these was published in April of 1933? My birthday is April thirteenth. If I find one can I have it? I'll trade you something for it, one of my cashmere sweaters or something."

"A cashmere sweater for a used book I paid thirty francs, or less than ten cents for? You're crazy. But go ahead and look."

"Cocteau, '*Les Enfants Terribles*'—no printing date, that page is missing, I know what that book's about, a brother and sister who go to bed together, Mauriac – no – some of these don't even have a date...' *La Petite Infante de Castille*' *decembre* 1935... Here's one! George Duhamel, '*Deux Hommes*' and it's published '*avril* 1933'! I never heard of this Duhamel but I don't care, I want it. Is it a deal?"

"No. I can't take an expensive sweater for a cheap used book. Just take the book."

"What's it about?"

"I don't know. I told you, I don't read them. I bought it for the woodcuts. That whole series is illustrated with woodcuts."

"And you have about a dozen of them."

"Just go down to the quais and browse the old books, and you can get that many yourself for about a dollar or two."

"But I want this one. I think you should take the cherry red turtleneck. It's a good color with your dark hair and it's big on me."

She left the room and returned a few minutes later with the sweater, a soft fuzzy thing of a beautiful deep cool red. Miri felt very guilty taking advantage of Judy this way and kept refusing, but she insisted so much Miri finally agreed, just to shut her up. She took off the navy pullover she had been wearing and put the cashmere sweater on. Although it weighed almost nothing it was incredibly warm! And not itchy. Miri planned on looking for more old books published in

April 1933 to give to her to make up for the sweater. The unevenness of the trade made her very uncomfortable. So did wearing red, as if she wanted all the world to stare at her. But it felt incredibly cozy. She could always keep her coat on all the time to conceal the red.

"I wonder why Jamie wouldn't stay around to help us work on this case?" Judy said. "After all he's the one under suspicion."

"I think I may have embarassed him last night. Not about the murder, about something else."

"What?"

"I don't think he would want me to say."

"You always do what other people want?"

"Oh all right." Miri told her that she had learned that Jamie was homosexual.

"You mean you didn't know that before last night?"

"You mean you did?"

"Of course!"

"He told you?"

"Of course not! It was obvious."

"It was?" Not to Miri. She felt like a fool, hoping for romance from a man who wasn't a real man and she didn't even know it while Judy said she had known it all along. "But if he didn't tell you how could you tell?"

"Lots of things. For one thing he was impervious to you getting up close to him, which you were always doing. For another – how you could not have guessed when we went to that *vernissage* with him back in November? Apart from the Fairy Queen who was sponsoring the thing we were the only females there! And the men, if you can call them that, all fairies. Don't you remember how furious I was at the time? I took one look around and realized that we had gotten all dressed up for nothing, they were all fairies! Don't you remember me saying it was a waste of time and I was leaving?"

"I remember you leaving in a hurry, and I remember I asked you, 'Don't you want to try to get to see the paintings?'

and you said, 'Of course not! I didn't come here to see any old paintings, I came here to meet men.' So I just thought you didn't see any you could get interested in." Miri didn't mention how crass of her she had thought this was. A typical pragmatist!

"But we were the only females there! Apart from our hostess, the Fairy Queen herself of course."

"We were not the only females. There was–" Then Miri remembered that the hefty woman who had come up to her while Jamie was fetching champagne had not really been a woman, she had only thought so at the time, but "she" was Tobey Peters, a young man who liked to dress up like a woman sometimes. How could she have missed seeing all that? She was an artist; she was supposed to see what others had missed.

"If I'd known you didn't know about Jamie I would have told you," Judy said, "to save you wasting your time. But I thought you knew, and didn't care, or maybe even liked it because he was 'safe'."

Miri was infuriated with herself that she had missed seeing facts that to this feather-brain had been obvious. Miri was supposed to be the intelligent one. It was intolerable. Maybe she was really stupid and didn't know it. They never did, did they? Stupid people never thought of themselves as stupid. People always seemed to be satisfied with their own intelligence, no matter how stupid they were. No matter how stupid they were, they didn't think they were. Maybe she was one of *them*! She couldn't stand this thought.

"Oh cheer up!" Judy laughed. "There's lots more fish in the sea. And some of them have much better prospects than Jamie! Isn't Seymour Levin still writing to you from Garmisch?"

"He's just a pen-pal. He's teaching me chess through the mail, using graph-paper and little chess-pieces I drew. He made up a bunch on the ditto machine in his office and cuts them out and pastes them on the graph-paper board. I redraw my own when I write back."

"He's a very smart fellow," Judy smirked.

Miri agreed that he didn't sound stupid; and his handwriting showed that he was intelligent.

Before they left Miri stopped to use the W.C. in the apartment. Judy waited in her room.

As Miri sat on the toilet, the notice which Madame Fleuris had placed over the torn-up pieces of telephone-book once again caught her eye. Usually it was the content of the note, arrogant and self-righteous, which irritated her. This time it was the elaborate script in violet ink, full of flourishes, rather than the message they conveyed that arrested her attention. The handwriting, she realized, was very similar to that of the *chambre* à *louer* notice which had tumbled out of Emilie's copy of "La Chatte" when she and Judy were questioning Gabrielle.

And then it struck her! As schoolgirls the two women must have gone to school together, must have learned penmanship from the same master, which was why the two handwritings, that of Madame Fleuris and of Madame Poivriere, were so similar. Then they must have moved as young marrieds to the house on Rue des Ecoles to be near each other. If they had had a lifelong friendship, it would explain why Madame Fleuris had lied about seeing Jamie the night of the murder, if in fact she had seen the son of her lifelong friend Madame Poivriere.

Miri had already suspected that Madame Fleuris was not merely mistaken but lying about seeing Jamie the night of the murder; this provided a powerful motive. The old women's friendship probably went back more than fifty years. Perhaps even to the nineteenth century.

Evidence pointing to Pierre Poivriere was multiplying.

One. He had been present on the sixth floor the night of the murder, and had tried to conceal the fact.

Two. The victim had been inhabiting a room owned by his own mother.

Three. The *pneu* the police had found among Emilie's things had been sent to her by someone named Pierre.

And now Four. Madame Fleuris must have seen *him* but had lied out of friendship for his mother when she told the inspector she had seen Jamie.

This was a discovery worth telling to the inspector! At first Miri thought she would go to the police, or rather, to Monsieur Dantan, herself. But then she thought that that would look stupid, especially since Judy had already brought them hard facts, while this discovery was only a theory. In fact she wasn't sure actually whether it was even worth repeating. She would have to think it over awhile.

The two girls got all Miri's stuff down by tumbling the valise down each flight of stairs. Miri carried her paintbox and easel and Judy carried a big shapeless bag she had around of the things that wouldn't fit into the valise. Miri ran to the taxi-stop while Judy waited on the sidewalk with the stuff, they piled it all in on the floor of the back seat and drove off to Reid Hall.

The henna-haired concierge remembered Miri and knew that she had become a resident at Reid Hall. She handed Miri a key, a long old-fashioned thing from which dangled a metal tag with the room-number, together with a note. The note was from Vanessa. "So glad you're going to be a neighbor. *Frappez forte* on my door when you arrive."

Miri wasn't enthusiastic about looking up Vanessa while Judy was around, because if Vanessa met Judy she might think Miri was just as superficial and as much of a husband-hunter as Judy was, but Judy wasn't about to leave, and after practically stealing her red cashmere sweater Miri felt bound to be civil. This made her furious with herself, that she was compromising herself for something material but by now she was unwilling to give up the sweater. She had never owned anything so soft and warm and comforting.

Vanessa was painting in her room when Miri and Judy pounded on her door. Something abstract and interesting was in progress on the easel.

Miri introduced the two, explaining to Vanessa that Judy had helped her move her stuff over to Reid Hall, and that they were collaborating on trying to solve the murder of Emilie Werner and had actually learned some new stuff that the police didn't know.

"Oh goodie!" Vanessa squealed. "I want to here all about it! Just let me clean my brushes..."

She stuck them in a small can of turpentine, and then wiped them with pieces of rag already well encrusted with paint. "There's a terrific shortage of rags," she said. "Haven't you found that, Miri? It's not like being at home, where you can always find something to rip up."

"I went up to the Marché aux Puces when I first got here and bought some old sheets. So far they've lasted me." Miri didn't want to admit that she hadn't done enough painting to run out of rags.

"What a great idea! I've just got to get up there, been meaning to, anyway. Want to come?"

Miri agreed, just to advance her friendship with Vanessa, and Judy invited herself along too, not to buy rags, of course, but to poke around for the real finds she had heard there were in jewelry and china and things like that.

"It's almost ten to twelve already!" Judy exclaimed, having consulted her gold wristwatch. "Miri and I have to be back to the pension for *déjeuner* at noon."

"We get *diner* here," Vanessa said, "at seven. Much more convenient. I usually pick up stuff for lunch at the *charcuterie*. They've got yummy patés. And I can make us some coffee if you don't mind lukewarm water from the tap? And milk from a tube?"

"How about coming back to the *pension* with us for *déjeuner?*" Judy said. "I'm sure Madame Fleuris won't mind as long as we pay for it. It will be my treat."

"That would be fun."

"I'll go call, to let her know," Judy said. "Where's the telephone?"

When she had left to find the telephone downstairs per Vanessa's directions Vanessa said, "She seems like a good sport."

Miri hadn't thought of Judy like that. "She's a feather-brain. Her goal in life is to get married. To a doctor or a law-yer or in a pinch a dentist or accountant. Preferably Jewish, preferably good-looking, preferably wealthy. Not that the Kugels don't have plenty of money already, but the guy has to have money to make sure Judy isn't being married for her money."

Vanessa sat down on the floor, cross-legged, and lit an American cigarette. "Somebody has to keep the human race going," she said with a little laugh. "It certainly won't be me! If she is willing to, I say good for her! And if she's going to have babies she may as well marry someone who can afford to support them and send them to good schools and all that. And I've always heard that Jewish men were the best in bed. Haven't tried that theory out for myself though yet!" she laughed. "What's happening with the murder?"

"The police *judiciare* had Jamie Giardini in for question-ing almost all day yesterday, and then they let him go, al-though Jamie thinks they still suspect him."

Vanessa hadn't seen the newspaper, so Miri told her that Inspector Goulette had been quoted in the newspaper as say-ing that they were close to solving the case.

"Oh they always say that so the public won't get ner-vous. Since they haven't arrested anyone, they haven't solved it. Whatever made them think of Jamie Giardini? The way you had described him to me he sounded rather a pet."

"Someone told the police that they saw Jamie leaving the victim's room at around the time of the murder. Judy and I questioned the *bonne* Gabrielle who lives up on the *sixième*, same as Jamie and I, she works for the widow who rented out the room to Emilie Werner, Madame Poivriere, and Gabrielle said that Germaine – that's Madame Fleuris' *bonne*, you know, at our *pension* – Germaine told her that Madame Fleuris is the one who told the police that she saw Jamie coming out of Emilie's room Sunday evening around the time of the murder. "

"How did this witness, whether it was Madame Fleuris or whoever – for after all you can't be sure that Gabrielle got the story straight, or that she was telling you what Germaine told her but that Germaine was mistaken – how did this person know that when he or she saw Jamie it was around the time of the murder?"

"I think she found out afterwards and that was when she realized the significance of seeing him – or someone. I don't believe it was Jamie she saw." She told Vanessa of the discreet little love visit which Pierre Poivriere had made to the sixth floor that night, and how he had waited alone in Gabrielle's room for at least an hour until she finished work. "He could have been doing anything he wanted up there, Jamie was out already, and so was I. And he's married. And Gabrielle said that Emilie had told her that her lover was a married man. And after all, Emilie was renting a room from his own mother, maybe because he had put her up to it."

"This is fascinating!" Vanessa breathed.

"Not only that! The police found a *pneu* in Emilie's pocketbook that was signed 'Pierre'."

"Wow!"

"Right." And then Miri thought she might as well tell her of her most recent discovery, that Madame Fleuris' handwriting looked a lot like the handwriting on Madame Poivriere's *chambre à louer* notice.

"That's fascinating! I'd love to see them."

"Well I have the *chambre à louer* notice in my room. Madame Fleuris' note is hanging in the W.C. over the erzatz toilet-paper.

"You didn't pinch it?"

Miri shook her head.

Vanessa looked thoughtful.

Judy bounced back in, announcing that Vanessa was indeed invited *chez* Fleuris for *déjeuner*, "My treat! Madame Fleuris said that although it was very short notice she would manage, provided that we pay a thousand francs for the guest, so I said I would." She giggled, "I hope you like horsemeat!"

"A thousand francs! That's highway robbery!" Miri said. "You could get the same kind of meal in an authentic restaurant for half that."

"Think of it as five hundred for the meal and five hundred for the entertainment! A kind of cover charge," Judy giggled.

"I'll pay for my meal myself," Vanessa said.

"No no, it's my treat. You can make us coffee from the tap sometime, with milk from a tube."

Judy really liked making unfavorable deals!

"Miri was telling me what you two found out from Gabrielle. What puzzles me though is if Madame Fleuris really was the witness who says she saw Jamie coming out of Emilie's room, and later realized it must have been around the time of the murder, how come if she thought Jamie was the killer she didn't ask him to leave the pension?"

"She was going to do that!" Miri explained. "When I told her I was moving out, she was angry because she had planned on kicking him out and didn't want two rooms vacant, but I talked her out of it."

"We don't know anything about Emilie's past," Vanessa mused. "That's where the answer lies. After all she's only been at your pension since New Year's or so. And she had been in a concentration-camp during the war. Maybe some deep conflict went back to that time."

Judy said, "I feel bad that I didn't know that about her until after she was dead. My daddy lost Polish cousins in the war, killed by the Nazis. There's a American girl we met who is doing her thesis on French Jews during the war. If only she had gotten to meet and question Emilie before all this happened."

"Well she didn't," Miri said flatly, feeling guilty in doing her part to keep Renee away. "Emilie had a lover, that we know. He picked her up while she was at work at Galeries Lafayette. Probably while he was buying a gift for another girlfriend or even a wife!"

"So that's a possible suspect!" Vanessa exclaimed. "The wife or girlfriend!"

"Who got into the building and out again without being seen by the concierge and knew which *chambre de bonne* was Emilie's and when she would be at home and nobody else would?" Miri hoped she didn't sound too sarcastic, after all, she wanted to become friends with Vanessa Tate. She wasn't as much of a mediocre snob as Miri had thought, she was more dedicated to art than Miri was, in fact, since she had made up her mind not to get married because of it, and her work looked interesting.

"Well who could have done all that?"

"Anyone who lives at Rue des Ecoles," Judy answered promptly. "Or was visiting. Like Pierre Poivriere."

The three of them walked back to Rue des Ecoles together to have *déjeuner chez* Fleuris. As they passed a café where a couple were kissing at one of the tables, and a circle of earnest students in black turtlenecks were all talking at once, and the elderly garçon in black with his white serviette over his arm was scampering from table to table, Vanessa looked around at it all, at the gray streaked stone of the buildings, and breathed, "I feel so lucky to be in Paris! I wish I never had to leave."

Miri wished she could feel that way, but she didn't. She saw Paris as cold and gray and mean.

19

From the moment the girls trooped into the dining-room *chez* Fleuris with their guest it was obvious Branford Duane Lee the Third was thunderstruck. He couldn't take his eyes off Vanessa, her hooded hazel eyes, her big rear-end, her long legs. He hung on her every word, actually traded seats with Jamie to sit beside her, and in general made an ass of himself. It was a pleasant change from his four months of silence broken only by occasional pedantry.

Vanessa didn't seem to mind, but she did treat him with humorous skepticism. When he told her, right in front of everyone, that she had bewitching eyes she immediately shut them tight and laughed, "What color are they?"

The two of them murmured together about horses and skiing with an engrossment that belied the trivial import of the conversation.

Monsieur Fleuris was in ecstasy over this open display of romance, even Madame Fleuris' face cracked into the ghost of a smile and Jamie and Miri exchanged smirks like old times. Only Judy seemed preoccupied, and uninterested in the new lovebirds.

When Germaine brought in a bowl of oranges and a plate of cheese, she murmured to Madame Fleuris that Gabrielle had stopped by to tell her that the Inspector Goulette was back at 10 *bis* Rue des Ecoles, on the fifth floor, questioning Madame Poivriere again.

Vanessa and Miri exchanged glances over this. Vanessa made as if to leave the table but it was clear that Branford was not going to let her slip away from him so easily. She reassured him that she would be right back, then signalled Miri to go upstairs.

"I'm just dying to see that *chambre à louer* notice," she breathed, as they climbed the stairs.

It was still between the pages of the book Miri had bought from Gabrielle. She handed it over.

"I'm a sort of amateur graphologist," Vanessa said with a little nervous laugh. "Do you suppose I could borrow this?"

"Okay." Miri wasn't wild about parting with what might turn out to be evidence, but she didn't like refusing, as she wanted a real artist as a friend. Furthermore, Miri was thrilled that they shared another interest: graphology. She rummaged through the books in the straw basket and pulled out "*La Graphologie*", the dog-eared book she had found along the quais. "I'm interested in graphology too. It really works." She explained briefly that she had analyzed some letters from a fellow who was writing to her from the army and it seemed very accurate.

"Oh? What's he like?"

Miri hesitated. She did not really want to talk about Seymour Levin. She did not want to think about what she thought of him. "He's a private in the army, and he works in the punch-card department of the Finance Office U.S.Army in Garmisch, where they keep track of expenditures for Germany."

"Accounting. Ugh." Vanessa gave an exaggerated shudder. Somehow this did not amuse Miri as much as she thought it should have. She decided not to mention that Seymour was teaching her how to play chess by mail.

"You think the inspector coming back to question the Poivrieres had to do with what you and Judy discovered about Pierre Poivriere?"

"Sounds like it."

"Gosh!"

"In fact, Vanessa, maybe you better give me back that room-for-rent notice. It could be a clue. I was thinking that I should tell the police my theory about it, you know, the handwriting on that, and on the W.C. notice."

To Miri's surprise Vanessa turned brick red. She then laughed nervously, "I had a theory too. But here." She held it forth, along with another piece of paper she had withdrawn from her sac. "I was going to call on your Monsieur Dantan, out of curiosity to see him, but it's only fair that you be the one to give him any clues."

The other piece of paper was Madame Fleuris' self-righteous notice not to take the last piece of paper.

"You stole this from the W.C.?"

Vanessa laughed. "In the interests of truth and justice."

Miri knew this would be a good opportunity to have Dantan to herself for awhile if she took these papers to him at the P.J. But something held her back. Suppose he thought her theory was ludicrous and useless? She would be humiliated forever. It might be better to bring Judy along. It never seemed to bother Judy whenever anyone laughed at her.

Vanessa, as she had promised him, returned to sit back down beside Branford. Madame Fleuris remained at table to chaperone them Miri went into the kitchen to kibbitz with Germaine. Germaine was seated at the wooden work-table, having her own *déjeuner*, the leftovers. Miri wondered what Germaine got to eat when there weren't any leftovers.

"Good day, Germaine."

"Good day, Mademoiselle Miri."

"I heard you tell Madame Fleuris that the Inspector Goulette is back."

"So Gabrielle said. The *pauvre petite* is very upset about it too. She seems to think it is her fault that the inspector is now inquiring into the affairs of the Poivrieres."

"I wonder why that is."

"I don't know, Mademoiselle."

Just then the telephone rang, and Germaine answered it. A moment later she signalled Miri to come to the phone and handed her the ear-piece.

"For me?" Miri was astounded. She never got phone-calls.

"Yes Mademoiselle."

"*Allo j'écoute!*" She had been longing to use this phrase.

"Miri, it's Renee Rubin. I just read about the murder in your building. It's terrible. I wonder if the police are looking into the concentration-camp angle. Do you know?"

"I have no idea."

"Maybe she was looking into what happened in 1942 when the Jewish family who lived there was denounced and dragged away by the police. We've got to get into that room where their things are stashed!!"

"I don't see any connection," Miri said coldly, "and as for getting into someone's padlocked room count me out. You could call Judy, she's usually game for harebrained schemes." Miri was astounded at her own bravura in standing up to Renee; she felt a rush of strength as if something important had just happened to her. "Got to go."

"Miri! Please put Judy on the phone. Please!"

"If she's around," Miri said coldly, placing the earpiece carelesssly on the marble counter.

Germaine was sitting at the long wooden work-table sopping up gravy with chunks of bread as Miri left the kitchen.

Vanessa and Bran had already left the dining-room as had Madame Fleuris. Judy was still at the table, waiting for Miri .

""Renee Rubin is on the phone and wants to talk to you. I'm going back to Reid Hall to do some painting."

"Please wait for me," Judy pleaded. "I need to talk to you about something."

"What's up?"

"Wait for me to talk to Renee."

Miri waited impatiently while Judy went to the phone.

Judy returned, said soberly, "Let's go to my room."

They settled in their usual places, but Judy did not bring out any Toblerone. "I'm upset," she said unhappily.

"What's up?"

"Renee wants us to break into the padlocked room on the *sixième*. She has the idea that Emilie's murder might be connected somehow to that, since she was in a concentraation camp. But even if there was no connection Renee wants to get a look at that stuff to help in her dissertation. That's what I think her real reason is. She said you didn't want to help break in, and she wants me to help her, and try to get Jamie to help too." Judy looked unhappy. "I told her I would talk to Jamie. But I'm scared. Not about the break-in part, that could be fun. But what scares me is if Renee is right about some connection with Emilie Werner. Then if we break in and find out something the killer might go after us! But that wasn't even what I wanted to talk to you about."

"If it wasn't, why did you?"

Judy tossed her curls at this barb at her logic. "Suppose we're getting Pierre Poivriere into trouble with the P.J. and he's innocent?"

"In the first place all we told the police, or you did, rather, was what we found out. We didn't make anything up. They're free to evaluate it and act as they think is proper, we're not telling them what to do. And in the second place, here is something else that might corroborate it. At least a possible indication that Madame Fleuris and Madame Poivriere go back a long ways, maybe eons to when they were schoolgirls."

Miri pulled out the two pieces of handwriting which looked so similar. "They could have actually learned penmanship in the same class. That could explain why Madame Fleuris would lie about seeing Jamie when it was Pierre she actually saw. Or it could have been a genuine mistake."

Judy was peering from one piece of paper to the other. "You're right. This could be something. I'm going to take it to the Police Judiciare and tell them your theory."

"Maybe since it's my theory I should tell them."

"I already have contacts there. I'll do it."
Miri didn't argue. She had been ambivalent anyway.

Now that Miri finally had a good place to paint, she felt like doing so! She was bursting with ideas. Her pocket sketch-book was full of nuns with top-heavy headdresses, priests on bicycles, children in the Luxembourg Gardens, a little girl rolling a hoop, a tot in a pony-cart led by a ragamuffin, little boys in short pants and sailor collars launching a toy boat on the pond, a nanny on a little folding chair watching them... these were all possibilities. And that dazzling dragon robe of Gabrielle's, which Miri wanted to paint draped on someone exotic but austere. She was excited over them all, and raced through the Luxembourg Gardens back to Reid Hall.

By the time she had made charcoal sketches and changed them over and over on the canvas, the light had changed. She was glad when Vanessa dropped in and she had to stop.

"He's really something!" she breathed, pulling off a green woolen cap and shaking her blond hair loose like a dog coming in out of the rain.

"Who?" For a moment Miri thought Vanessa might have gone to call on Dantan anyway, on some pretext other than the one Miri took from her.

"Bran of course."

"So you liked him? It was hard to tell."

"Mmmmm. He's really sexy!"

De gustibus non est disputandum! Or as the French say, each to his own goo. "Did he tell you what it is he's up to in Paris? Judy and Madame Fleuris have been trying to find out for four months."

"History or something," she said vaguely. "I'm hoping he's a writer!"

"If he is, why wouldn't he say so?"

"Maybe he's keeping it a secret until he gets published, or because he doesn't want to talk about his work to philis-tines."

Miri didn't bother to mention that neither she nor Jamie were philistines and Bran hadn't said a word about what he was doing to either of them in four months. "Well you're not a philistine," Miri said.

"But he doesn't know that yet. We're going skiing this weekend," Vanessa breathed happily. "Chamonix. We're leaving Thursday night."

"Tomorrow night? That was quick."

Vanessa laughed. "Why wait?"

"I guess you're not interested in helping solve Emilie Werner's murder now that you have this other interest."

"*Au contraire*, I'm as avid as ever. You'll see."

She left, saying she would save a seat for Miri at *diner*.

The seat Vanessa had saved was between herself and the Negro acting student, Bethel Washton. Bethel Washton wanted to be an actress, not on the American or English stage or in movies; she wanted to be an actress in France. And not just on any stage, but the Comedie Française. She was getting private tutoring to work on her accent. She went to the theatre every single night that there was a performance anywhere of anything, and had seen all the greats, Jean-Louis Barrault, Madeleine Renault and many others Miri had never heard of, over and over. She wanted to play *"Phedre"*. Miri admired her for setting her sights high.

Bethel had a regal bearing and a rather contemptuous way of looking at one from half-closed eyes, but when she heard that Miri had not only read *"Phedre"* but had seen it at the Comedie Française she became more friendly and even complimented her on being an oddball. That encouraged Miri to ask her to sit for a painting. She was the perfect subject to wear the Chinese silk robe. Now all Miri had to do was get her hands on it.

Bethel looked at Miri as if she were crazy.

"I saw this robe," Miri went on doggedly. "A Chinese silk robe, green and red and yellow dragons on a black background. I would have to borrow the robe. I would like to do a painting of you in the robe looking at the treetops from my balcony. When I saw that robe I felt I had to find the right person to wear it for my painting."

Bethel laughed a rich throaty laugh. "Well when you get that robe, let me know. Then we'll see." She was eating scrambled eggs and ham and had cut the ham into tiny little pieces, which she forked and chewed slowly, one by one. "What are you going to call it, 'Negro in Chinese Robe'? You know, like 'Uncle What's-His-Name As A Dominican Priest' or something?"

There was something derisive in the way she said this that made Miri uncomfortable. "I hadn't thought about naming it," Miri said. "I usually just number them, to keep track of the order in which I painted them so I can look at them as a progression. That is, I would if I were painting much these days, but I haven't been too productive lately. I have this murder on my mind, the one at 10 *bis* Rue des Ecoles. I was living there when it happened. And at first they suspected a friend of mine. Now I don't think they do. And also I don't think he's my friend anymore."

"Whew! No wonder you – "

"What?"

"Oh nothing. You go get that robe and I'll see if I can fit a sitting into my busy schedule." She reached into a leather sack on the floor by her feet, retrieving a black calf appointment-book with its own silver mechanical pencil. Bethel's time was scheduled in quarter-hour increments. She wrote in it everything she had to do on a given day, lessons in elocution or French or acting or classes in French literature at the Sorbonne, a ballet class in Montmartre with Madame Preobrajenska, who had actually danced with the Ballet Russe before the Revolution. "It would have to be Saturday morning. I usually going to a ballet work-out then, but there's another one in the afternoon."

"Great! Thanks!" Miri was tremendously impressed by Bethel's microscopic scheduling and resolved to muster the self-discipline to live like that.

20

Dantan was feeling better than he had since before going into the army. His job was becoming more interesting, holding out a faint promise of possible advancement. And he had a delightful new *amie*. He still liked the old one, like a reliably sound wine, but the carefree sexy American was like bubbly champagne. And she was rich! This opened up possibilities...

His daydreaming in his modest room was abruptly interrupted by his new love, who had arrived early. They peeled off their clothing quickly, and tumbled happily into the bouncing squeaky bed wrapped around each other and planting copious kisses on one another here, there and everywhere.

As they sat up in bed, perspiring after a joyful bout, Dantan told her he how happy he was that she had arrived early, but apologized for not having washed by the time she got here.

"Well we both need to now anyway. I sure wish there was a shower. I haven't gotten the hang of these sponge-baths. They don't make me feel clean."

"You Americans are obsessed with bathtubs. One can get clean with a sponge and pan of water just as well."

"Listen, Alphonse, I don't want to get into another debate about the French versus the American approach to cleanliness, I have another important clue in the murder case!"

"Really!"

She got out of the bed and rummaged in her large handbag for the two critical pieces of paper. She was completely naked and Dantan gazed at her curvaceous body, her ample breasts and behind, and considered whether... but no. She had retrieved two sheets of paper she was putting beneath his eyes.

"Miri Winter should get credit for this discovery, but she didn't want to go to the Police Judiciare with it as she was afraid she would look silly if it meant nothing. She doesn't know about us, though," Judy said with a sly smile.

He examined the first sheet of paper, cheap French stock, a printed form used by the student services bureau. It had been filled out by hand, a room-for-rent notice for a room at 10 *bis* Rue des Ecoles.

"Madame Poivriere's maid Gabrielle had been given a book by Emilie Werner and Miri bought it from Gabrielle. This notice was slipped into the book. Obviously the way that Emilie Werner had heard of the room in the first place.

"Then Miri made another discovery. That other piece of paper." That was also handwritten, also on cheap stock, and read "*Ici c'est un maison chrétien. Ne prenez pas le dernier morceau même si vous en avez besoin.*"

"This was pinned over the bits of paper for use in the W.C. at the *pension* Fleuris." Judy laughed. "The point is the similarity of the two handwritings. Miri's theory is that Madame Fleuris had lied about seeing Jamie coming out of Emilie Werner's room the night of the murder because she had actually seen Pierre Poivriere, Madame Poivriere's son, but because of the long friendship of the two women, dating back to grammar-school days when they learned penmanship and therefore wrote so similarly, was shielding her friend's son."

Dantan held the two pieces of paper side by side and looked back and forth from one to the other. The similarity of the two hands was certainly remarkable, but he was skeptical whether the inferences Mademoiselle Miri had made could be sustained by such slender evidence. Nevertheless, he would turn these over to the department graphologist.

"Very interesting, my sweet," he said diplomatically. "Thank you. Now where shall we dine? Our little aperitif has stimulated my appetite!"

21

The next morning, after eating two scrambled eggs at Reid Hall, Miri raced all the way through the Luxembourg Gardens so as not to miss breakfast *chez* Fleuris. It wasn't so much for the crusty baguette, although that was always delicious, as it was to see if she could borrow the Chinese robe now that she had the right model to sit for the painting. She was also eager to learn whether Pierre Poivriere had been arrested and what was happening with Jamie.

But Jamie didn't show up for breakfast. Neither did Judy. Jamie's absence was briefly noted by Madame Fleuris, who seemed relieved that the "murder suspect" was not contaminating her social ambiance. Judy's absence, however, evoked a quite different response. Madame Fleuris, with sniffs and self-righteous indignation at the flagrant disregard for the appearance of conventional morality, knew that Judy had not spent the night in her bed *chez* Fleuris. In fact she had not returned yet from wherever she had gone the previous evening, all tarted up.

The theme of Madame Fleuris' indignation was not that Judy was probably having sex outside of wedlock but that she was flaunting the fact, by staying out all night, instead of returning in the small hours so that the issue might remain in doubt.

As Judy had numerous acquaintances of both sexes it was not a big surprise that she might stay out all night once in awhile.

"Maybe she just missed the last metro," Miri said helpfully.

"What an innocent!" Madame said scornfully.

Branford Duane Lee the Third was not at all interested in Judy's whereabouts or even Jamie's guilt or innocence. All he wanted to talk about was Vanessa Tate. He plied Miri with inconsequential questions: what were her favorite foods, perfumes, treats, how many sisters and brothers did she have, did Miri know her birthday. When Miri said with a sarcasm he completely missed that she had no idea about any of these things as they only talked about important things such as Art and Philosophy, he urged her to guess.

Miri's silliest guesses were of momentous interest to him. This from a fellow who hardly ever said a word and had never taken an interest in anybody around him. After four months none of them still even knew what he was up to in Paris. According to Germaine his books were still locked up in a valise under his bed.

From the dining-room they could hear the telephone ringing in the kitchen. A moment later Germaine came scuttling in, her felt slippers flapping, to inform Madame Fleuris that there was someone calling on the telephone for Mademoiselle Miri. This formality struck Miri as ridiculous, that Germaine couldn't tell her directly that she had a phone-call but had to act as if Madame Fleuris' permission were necessary before she could take her own telephone call.

"You had better see who it is, Mademoiselle Miri," said Madame sourly. ""And since this is the second phone-call you have received in one week there will be a charge."

Miri rushed into the kitchen hoping it was not Renee Rubin again. Nobody else ever called her. Nobody she knew even knew the telephone-number chez Fleuris. (She didn't know it herself.) Maybe it was Dantan!

"*Allo j'écoute,*" she said.

"Is this Miriam Winter?" a man's voice asked softly in English.

"Yes."

"Can anyone hear you?"

"Who is this?"

"Oh sorry, so sorry. I'm a bit shaken up, you must excuse me. I'll explain later. My name is Tobey Peters. Don't say my name out loud. Just answer yes or no. Do you remember meeting someone last November at la belle Alexandra's *vernissage* who spoke to you about wanting the same thing from Jamie that you did? Someone you might have thought was a woman?"

"I remember," Miri said, feeling vaguely alarmed.

"I'm a man."

"So I've heard. I never would have guessed it then."

He tittered, "Jamie told you?"

"Yes."

"Good. That makes it so much simpler. I desperately need to speak with you – in absolute private."

"What on earth for?"

"I can't explain over the telephone. But it's desperately urgent."

"To whom?"

"Please don't be a naughty difficult little girl, just meet with me and the urgency will become clear."

Miri couldn't imagine what he could possibly have in mind, and she felt alarm at the thought of meeting with him especially in absolute private. "You'll have to tell me why before I agree."

"It has to do with the murder of that young woman in your building. Now mind what you say out loud... Will you for Godsake give me the opportunity to meet with you and tell you something very urgent?"

"Somewhere public."

"Of course somewhere public, you little idiot! I have no desire to cuddle up with you."

"You said 'absolute private'."

"You're so literal. What I meant was, away from the spying eyes of anyone who knows either of us."

"Okay. Café de la Paix." There would be Midwestern tourists around, the kind that would help you in a difficulty, not like Easterners who if you were having a problem would just stand around and watch, maybe even snap a few photos.

"How bourgeois! Very well. The Café de la Paix. Three o'clock tomorrow afternoon. Don't worry, I'll find you." He hung up.

She was rattled by this call; nervous. She wracked her mind to try to think of why he would want to meet with her. She couldn't imagine.

She could always stand him up, of course. She didn't have to show up at the Café de la Paix at three o'clock the next day, just because he said so. She would see what Vanessa thought of it.

Before she left she sought out Germaine to see if she had finished laundering Miri's handkerchiefs.

Germaine was kneading dough on the marble counter in the kitchen. Her big square hands covered in flour pushed and folded and slapped the dough on the marble to some internal rhythm. Impulsively Miri said she would like to try what Germaine was doing.

"Very well, Mademoiselle. Wash your hands, dry them well on the serviette, then plunge them into the flour and I'll show you what to do."

Miri did so, then followed Germaine's directions in kneading the dough. It felt alive! Like satiny human skin on a living being!

"You have a natural hand, Mademoiselle," said Germaine with respect.

Miri was immensely flattered. "How come you're making bread, Germaine?" What they bought at the *boulangerie* was always delicious.

"This is not to be bread. It is to be a *croûte* for *coq au vin en croûte* for *déjeuner*."

"Today?"

"Yes indeed, today."

That sounded delicious! Miri would definitely come back for *déjeuner* today. "Even though it's hard work there's something soothing about doing this," she said as she kneaded the satiny warm dough.

"Mademoiselle Miri, have you heard that Gabrielle is leaving?"

"No, I hadn't heard. That was rather sudden, wasn't it? Where is she going?"

"Madame Poivriere became extremely angry with Gabrielle when she learned that Gabrielle had informed the police that Monsieur Pierre Poivriere had not left as early as he had said and was on the sixth floor the evening that the poor Mademoiselle Emilie Werner was killed. Madame Poivriere is absolutely persuaded of the innocence of her son and is naturally angry that he should be imposed upon, questioned by the police like a common criminal. It was all so unnecessary, she said. If only Gabrielle had held her tongue."

"Poor Gabrielle!" Miri felt guilty that she might have contributed to her being fired, in a way, and yet in a murder investigation it was important that the relevant facts be brought to light. She didn't feel guilty about her part in that.

"Not at all, Mademoiselle." Germaine's leathery face cracked into a happy smile. "Gabrielle went right to Mademoiselle Judy for help, and Mademoiselle Judy called an American family of her acquaintance who are here in France to work for the NATO and who maintain a lavish household in Saint-Germaine-en-Laye and they were only too delighted to hire Gabrielle to assist the cook, the nanny and the housemaid. Gabrielle will have not only her own room but her own bathroom!"

Germaine's hushed awe seemed to imply that this private bathroom was the eighth wonder of the world. "And she is even permitted to bring her cat, Mitsou, providing that it will be able to coexist peacefully with the family's own two cats and a big dog.

Miri's first thought was for the robe! "When is Gabrielle leaving?"

"Oh Mademoiselle, she left last night. Madame Poivriere told her to get out immediately. It was very fortunate that Mademoiselle Judy who was about to go out for the evening when Gabrielle ran to her for help was able to arrange so quickly that Gabrielle had a place to go. The chauffeur of her new employers drove all the way from the banlieu to fetch her and her things."

Miri had really wanted to borrow that robe. "So now Madame Poivriere is without a *bonne.* That wasn't very smart of her, was it?"

"Oh she will have a new *bonne* very shortly," Germaine sighed. "My sister is coming up from Narbonne."

"Has Pierre Poivriere been arrested?"

Germained shrugged. "He has spent many hours assisting the police in their investigations."

All this time Germaine had been folding and kneading and folding and kneading the dough. She had now shaped it into a ball and placed it in a greased bowl with a damp tea-towel over it.

Miri listened carefully to her instructions on how the dough would have to rise, then be punched down, and let rise again before baking, in case she ever had her own kitchen and felt like making bread. It was a strange thought. She had never thought about having her own kitchen; her own home. She was a wanderer. She had no home. She thought of herself as *déracinée.*

She almost forgot to ask Germaine about her handkerchiefs. Germaine said that they would be ready when she returned for *déjeuner.*

She wandered over to the Beaux Arts, where she sketched all morning despite the attentions of the instructor, an old guy with a white Van Dyke moustache and beard who liked to be called "*maître*". The undraped model was as tired and bored and dirty and pathetic and shivering as usual, but somehow instead of being annoyed at this, Miri was able to put it into her drawings. Not consciously, though. She only noticed afterwards.

Vanessa had not turned up at the Beaux Arts and Miri didn't see her at Reid Hall before rushing off to the *pension* for *déjeuner*. She was supposed to be going skiing with Bran, maybe they had left already.

Jamie was in the Fleuris apartment when Miri showed up for *déjeuner*. He was like his old self, merry and mischievous. "Can't keep away from the gourmet cuisine?" he teased.

"I happen to know that the main dish is going to be delicious today, *coq au vin en croûte*. I even helped Germaine make the *croûte*."

"I am duly wowed."

"Have you heard about the new suspect?"

"I sure did. It's great! Now I don't have to worry about Madame Fleuris throwing me out. She was on the verge of it a couple of times." He took Miri aside into the front foyer and indicated a door which if she had thought about it all would have thought was a closet. He whispered that Judy had discovered that this was the room from which Monsieur Fleuris emerged before six in the morning with four metal boxes. The plan was that the three of them were going to try to break into it on Sunday morning, when Monsieur and Madame Fleuris were at church.

"And oh, Miri, by the way, thanks for your part in getting me off the hook." He grinned happily.

He looked so sweet she felt a pang of regret that nothing was going to come of all this.

Judy came rushing in while they were still in the foyer. Her face was radiant, she looked glamorous in her beaver coat, and her hair looked better than usual, as she had obviously neglected for once to set her hair in pin-curls. It looked windblown and natural.

"Have you heard about Pierre Poivriere?" she asked eagerly.

"Germaine told me that Madame Poivriere was upset because he was being questioned by the police. And fired Gabrielle over it."

"They really think he did it!" Judy gloated, dropping her coat to the floor. She gave Jamie a smug smile. "And you can thank Miri and me for that!"

"I do, I do," grinned Jamie.

When Jamie did not, as Judy seemed to expect he would, pick her fur coat up from the floor, she did so herself and sashayed into the apartment and to her rooms. Jamie and Miri went into the dining-room and slid into their seats. Judy appeared moments later, having combed her hair and powdered her nose.

As Madame ladled hot root soup into bowls and passed them along, Judy giggled, "I'm so hungry I could eat a horse."

"Well for once you won't have to," Jamie grinned. "My spies tell me we're getting *coq au vin en croûte*."

"Well I hope it isn't all *croûte!*"

Branford had not shown up, but as usual anyone absent was not awaited. The soup was duly ladled and passed along and slurped and cleared.

"I wonder where are our lovebirds today?" chortled Monsieur Fleuris. The twinkle in his eye implied that he had his own ideas about their location. He smiled benignly at Judy. "Did you pass a pleasant evening last night, Mademoiselle Judy?"

Judy broke into hysterical giggles, while Madame Fleuris glared from her husband to Judy and back with a murderous look.

"I'm very pleased that Jamie here," Miri said slowly and deliberately, "is no longer regarded as a suspect by the police in the murder of Emilie Werner. I hear that she was probably killed by the son of a neighbor in this building."

Madame Fleuris said stonily, "When the truth is at last determined, I am certain that Pierre Poivriere will be found to be innocent of any crime other than infidelity."

"Well if he didn't do it, who did?" Judy piped up.

Madame remained stonily silent. But she cast an angry glance at Jamie.

"Madame Poivriere is taking this hard," Judy remarked.

Madame Fleuris said grimly, "She has the money to buy the services of the best lawyers available for her son." She was certainly not stepping out of character to express any sympathy for her friend!

Jamie whispered to Miri, "To say nothing of the money to bribe anyone in sight that might help get him off."

Miri wanted to tell Jamie of the disturbing phone-call she had had from his acquaintance Tobey Peters. Tobey obviously didn't want anyone to know about it but she hadn't promised not to tell. She whispered to Jamie that she wanted to talk with him about something later, not at the table. He nodded. He did not seem curious.

The *coq au vin en croûte* was indeed delicious, and even adequate, for in the absence of Branford Duane Lee their portions were slightly larger.

Judy corraled her before she could corral Jamie. "You must come and see my latest clothing acquisition!"

Miri gave a pleading look to Jamie who pointed upstairs.

Miri sat on the edge of the chaise-longue while Judy dug out something from her clothing room. She came out carrying the Chinese robe!

"So you got it!"

"Naturally. I made a preemptive bid, much much more than Gabrielle ever dreamed she could get for it. If she lost her man for want of a thousand dollar *dot* then two hundred dollars for this robe must have seemed like a fortune to her."

"A fifth of a man."

Judy giggled. "Well it's a start. And besides, she was grateful to me for getting her a good job as soon as she got fired. She will be working half as hard and making twice as much money with an American family. You can bet she'll change her tune about *ces épouvantables americains-ça*!"

"Would you lend the robe to me for awhile? I want to do a painting of someone in it."

"How about doing a painting of me?"

"No. I'm going to paint Bethel Washton."

"Who's Bethel Washton?"

"A girl at Reid Hall who's studying acting."

"Why her? After all it's my robe now."

"It's the shape of her head, her long neck, Modigliani-ish. And the rich brown of her skin."

"Brown skin?" Judy shrieked. "Is she a Negro?"

"Yes."

"You want to put my robe on a Negro?" she shrieked. "Are you crazy?"

"Are you? What's the matter?"

"They smell, that's what's the matter. My beautiful new robe will – smell!"

"It probably stinks already," Miri pointed out, "since Gabrielle has been wearing that so-called new robe, and since Gabrielle probably never takes real baths the robe probably stinks already, of the perfume Gabrielle uses to cover up her B.O. Whereas Bethel lives at Reid Hall, where we get to bathe every day without extra charge. I'm sure she's immaculate."

"Well you can't have it."

"I was surmising that already." Miri got up.

"Wait!" Judy was holding out the Chinese robe. "I changed my mind. Take it. I can always get it dry-cleaned when I get back to the States. I want us to be friends."

But Miri didn't. However, she did want to use that robe in her painting, so she compromised her principles in the interests of art and reached out for it.

"I'll have to find something for you to carry it in. It's really a nuisance that they don't give you paper bags here for anything. Here, take my book-bag, you can return it tomorrow."

"I need the robe for the weekend. Bethel said she could sit for me on Saturday, and then I might still want to work from it on Sunday. Is that okay?"

"Sure. Why not? I'm not going to wear it until it's been drycleaned anyway. Listen, when the police actually put Pierre Poivriere in jail, let's throw a party and celebrate. You know, that Jamie is off the hook and we helped solve the case."

"Where would you have it?"

"Right here. In my rooms."

"Madame Fleuris will have a fit."

"She won't know. I'm going to treat her and Bushy-Beard to tickets to the opera for that night so they'll be out of the way."

It sounded boring to Miri, especially since she wouldn't have a date and Vanessa would, but there was always Gerhardt, he would probably be delighted, he loved Americans. He might even fall in love with Judy! He had said that his German guilt drew him to Jewish girls. Of course he was only going to be a pharmacist, and the Kugels were holding out for a doctor, but at least it was in the ballpark. They probably wouldn't be wild about his being German, in fact, they would hate it.

"Better wait until Pierre is behind bars before you celebrate and buy those theatre tickets for the Fleuris."

"You mean because Madame Poivriere might buy off the police or something? She is supposedly very well off."

Judy had pulled out a huge black patent-leather hatbox which was full of silk underwear and dumped the contents onto her bed. She began sorting them as she spoke. "I heard that Jean-Jacques Pilieu and Alphonse Dantan were both wounded severely in the French war in Indochina. In fact that's how they met, they were lying side by side in a military hospital for months."

"So?" What did this have to do with anything?

"Jean-Jacques is a very kind person. After he got out of the hospital and had gotten his job at the Police Judiciare once Alphonse was discharged Jean-Jacques worked on them until they hired Alphonse too."

"So?"

"Know how Alphonse learned such good English? He was a refugee child! His mother died when he was ten or eleven so the old aunt who was stuck with him bundled him off with a secret shipment of Jewish children to England!"

"Sounds unbelievable."

"It's true. That's why he's not antisemitic like a lot of Frenchmen. He grew up with a pack of Jewish kids from all over Europe and France itself, smuggled out because all the Jews were in danger."

Miri couldn't understand why she was saying all this, or where she had gotten it from, but she didn't want to ask, in case it opened a floodgate of more words.

Judy was still playing with the dainty slips and panties. She said thoughtfully, "You know, I can't think of a single time when Madame Poivriere visited Madame Fleuris."

"So?"

"Oh nothing. But doesn't it seem odd that if they aren't buddy-buddy now that Madame Fleuris would bother to protect the other old bat's son?"

Miri at last broke free and climbed upstairs to tell Jamie about Tobey Peters' phone-call. But Jamie had tired of waiting and left a note for Miri on his door. "Had to go, see you soon."

22

Back at Reid Hall Miri rapped on Vanessa's door. Sweaters and pants and thick socks were laid out all over her bed, and a small valise, empty, was open on the floor. A pair of tall skis, around seven feet long, stood against the wall. Heavy black boots were clamped onto a metal carrier also on the floor.

"Winter stuff is so bulky," Vanessa sighed. "And I don't want to be hampered by a lot of baggage."

Miri grunted unsympathetically. It seemed like a lot of heavy stuff to be lugging around just for a couple of days. Besides, she had something else on her mind. She wanted urgently to tell Vanessa about the strange phone-call she had received from Tobey Peters at the Fleuris apartment and how he had insisted that she meet him somewhere so that he could tell her something urgent that he couldn't say on the phone.

"How exciting!" Vanessa couldn't understand why Miri was so disturbed about it. "Aren't you bursting with curiosity? I would be."

"He gives me the creeps." Miri tried to explain that Tobey was weird. That he had been dressed like a woman at the prince's *vernissage*. That he had made out that "she" and Miri were rivals for Jamie. Miri had thought he was a woman until Jamie told her later he was a man.

"If you're worried about the meeting – and I can't see why you should be – I could spy on you two at your rendez-vous. Eavesdrop, which I would adore, and also keep an eye on you to make sure you're all right. But it would have to be Monday, after Bran and I get back from skiing."

"No, I'm sure that I would let on somehow, and then he would clam up before telling me what it's all about. And besides, I doubt if he would wait until Monday. He did sound frantic, although of course it could have been histrionics."

"Then you are going to go?"

Miri sighed. "I suppose so."

"Bran and I are catching a nine o'clock train for Chamonix tonight so I'll be gone before you've had your tryst. But first thing Monday morning I want to hear all about it!"

On Friday Miri showed up at the meeting-place hours early. She dreaded meeting with Tobey Peters. Was he going to threaten her to get her to leave Jamie alone? Was he going to tell her something sordid about Jamie that would spoil her pleasant thoughts about him?

She couldn't imagine anything good coming out of the meeting.

Some English people at the next table struck up a conversation with her. The stout gray-haired box-shaped woman started it. For a passing moment Miri wondered if she were a man in drag too. But then she was addressed as Lady Mary by the skinny blue-haired one whose name was Nonny. Lady Mary was obviously wearing a tight girdle under her tweed suit. Nonny could have used some padding under hers. Lady Mary was the mater of the dreamy-eyed man, whom they called Buffin, and the elderly gentleman with them, Henry-Dear, was somebody else's husband, the Honorable Patricia, who had gone for a fitting. Lady Mary kept trying to pair Miri off with her son Buffin, but only for an hour or two. Buffin was at least forty, and he seemed mentally able enough to have handled such matters for himself but he didn't try.

Lady Mary insisted that Miri go to lunch with them to Harry's Bar, a place she had been shunning as not only too

American but too touristy and expensive, but they all thought it would be jolly to get some American hamburgers.

At Harry's Bar, which was crowded with French, as well as Americans and English, they all wolfed down two delicious hamburgers each, dripping with real Heinz ketchup.

The English party were going to Spain next, where the money would last much much longer. They were only allowed to take out so many pounds at a time from England even though they might be very rich. Buffin explained to Miri that it was illegal in Great Britain to have the use of one's own money. The way they got around it was with the help of a few middle-European Jews in London who would make arrangements for one to deposit pounds for them in London and pick up francs or pesetas or whatever in the country they were visiting. Their rates were usurious, and it was illegal too, but they performed a real service. Lady Mary interrupted this conversation.

Miri took a matchbox marked "Harry's Bar" even though she no longer smoked, to display it ostentatiously if she should happen to need to hold her own against some snob. She thought of carrying it around with her and placing it on the table at *diners* at Reid Hall, so that any member of the snobby in-group who deigned to sit at her table would see that she and her twittery friends were not the only ones who got around.

Lady Mary wanted Miri to go on with them to some bar or other, but she explained that she had an appointment at three. She went back to the Café de la Paix, arriving slightly late. Buffin kissed her hand as Miri departed. Miri was annoyed with herself for having wasted a perfectly good two hours when she could have been doing something culturally enriching, but she had to admit that the hamburgers had been delicious.

Tobey Peters was sitting at a table out front in a cloud of smoke, his thick legs and heavy haunches, encased in tight black pants, crossed like a woman's. His elbow rested on the small café table as he held a long black cigarette-holder with its lit cigarette. In front of him was a fat glass a quarter full of cloudy greenish-yellow liquid, probably Pernod. He was gazing contemptuously at the passing crowd when he spotted Miri and waved her over with his cigarette-holder.

"I'm sorry I'm late."

He waved this away with his cigarette-holder, signalled an elderly garçon and without consulting Miri ordered a *té complet* for her and another Pernod for himself. He suddenly peered into her eyes as if to hypnotize her. "You *must* do something for me. This is serious. And you're the only one who can do it."

"What?"

"First promise you won't breathe a word of this to anyone. Not to Jamie, not to your dearest heart."

Without knowing what he was going to tell her she couldn't promise not to tell anyone. On the other hand if in conscience she felt she could not keep it a secret it wouldn't be so terrible to break a promise under those circumstances. Only priests had to keep their mouth shut if someone confessed murder to them. "Okay. I promise."

"You really promise?"

"Yes."

"Do you believe in God?"

"No. I'm an existentialist."

"Well what will you swear on?"

"How about '*L'Etre et le Néant*'?"

"Uch! I guess it will have to do."

"Why am I the only one who can do whatever it is I've sworn not to talk about?"

He grinned at Miri frighteningly. "Because you're a naive little ninny and my woman's intuition tells me I can trust you, and the police will believe you."

"Oh." She really didn't think she was naive, and she didn't believe in woman's intuition, especially in a man, but she was curious by now, so she didn't argue. "What about one of your real friends?"

"I can't ask any of my own friends. If one of them should approach the inspector in charge of the Werner case with what I am going to tell you, he would merely assume that it was a concocted tale to divert suspicion from Jamie Giardini."

"So it has to do with the murder."

"Yes, dear heart, didn't I already tell you that?"

"But Jamie isn't even their suspect anymore."

"Never mind that and pay attention. I shall begin with a little background. Last year I was a *pensionnaire chez* Fleuris."

She nodded. Jamie had already told her that.

"Do you know why?"

"The gourmet cuisine?"

"Cover."

"Cover?"

"My mother and my maternal grandmother send me generous allowances. My own money is in a trust and until I'm thirty years old it can only be used for university tuition and related university expenses. In order to keep the allowances coming I have to make my mother believe I'm living what she thinks is a normal life. So I moved into the *pension*, played up to the old lady who runs it, and by the time I had moved out she was willing to act as my mail-box."

"Madame Fleuris."

"That's right, Madame Fleuris."

"What do you mean, 'mail-box'? Couldn't you just get your mail at American Express?"

The waiter now placed before them a greenish-yellow Pernod for Tobey, and for Miri a delicate china cup and saucer, a pot of tea, a china pitcher of milk, a pretty little plate with lemon slices, and a plate of assorted rich-looking but tiny cookies, which Miri began munching immediately.

"It isn't so much for getting mail, although it is handy to have an address that reads 'c/o Fleuris' – sounds so bourgeois and respectable – it is to *send* mail. My mother is violently opposed to my affair with Pedro. I had to lie and cry and in general abase myself to persuade her that it was over. She had threatened to cut me off without a penny if I ever saw Pedrito again, so I simply told her I had given him up, was seeing a Freudian analyst in Paris, then I wrote letters of respectable content but total lies to my mother from Spain where I was cavorting with individuals of whom she would not have approved but sent them to Madame Fleuris who put French stamps on them and mailed them for me.

"The contents were pure fiction, depicting me as charmingly and heterosexually preoccupied with a young lady named Muriel who though deplorably unsuitable as a match was perfect for dalliance. Whenever I'm actually in Paris in the flesh I make sure to take Madame out for a treat. She favors Rumpelmayers. So far that has been enough to keep her happy. If she ever tried to blackmail me, I'd have to think of something else."

So he wasn't just being nice to an old lady.

"I still don't see what I have to do with all this."

"I'll get to that."

One day in early October Tobey had gone shopping with "one of the girls", he smirked, "up near Pig Alley where the hookers buy their hot rags. You know, black see-through lace tops, brassieres with the nipples cut out, panties with the crotch cut out...oh am I embarassing you? Sorry. In any case after shopping among the low-life we were titillated, famished and parched.

"We entered into the dingy depths of a local restaurant, seating ourselves at a table opposite a banquette where a man and a woman were cuddling and kissing oblivious to any audience. There was something familiar about his head... When he came up for air I recognized him. Philippe Jumelle. Madame Fleuris' son-in-law whom I had met on countless occasions at Madame's little Sunday coffees."

"Oh no I can't believe that. Philippe Jumelle is a stuffed shirt functionary, ultra-respectable. Ultra-ultra respectable! You must have mistaken someone else for him." If you saw anyone at all, you lying fake.

"You're quite right that it was a most unlikely neighborhood in which to find him, the proper bourgeois functionary, on a street of by-the-hour girls, by-the-hour hotels... But it was without a doubt Philippe Jumelle, I assure you. His little companion, to do her justice, did not seem quite that low, rather a little shopgirl, perhaps, making a little extra on the side, or perhaps even doing it for fun. I thought what fun it would be to confront him, how he would writhe! But I decided against it, thinking instead that the information might be more useful to me in some other way, to be determined."

Tobey took a slow sip of his Pernod.

"By the time of my next tete-a-tete with Madame Fleuris, about a month later, I had decided to use the information merely in the mildest way to amuse myself, namely, to make Madame Fleuris writhe, while seeming to do her the favor of informing her.

"Having heard her tale of woe many times of her husband's long-standing infidelity, as I'm sure you have also heard, I knew she would be utterly maddened to think that her one daughter was to endure the same fate.

""Madame thanked me bitterly for the information, agreeing as always to post my letters as I sent them. As torturous as it was for her to listen, she suffered through the details I could provide to lend credibility to my account of what I'd seen – the name and location of the restaurant, a description of the girl, the day of the week, the time of day... Each detail was another burr in her flesh, another scratch of the hairshirt, which she invited even as she suffered.

"I wondered if she were actually planning to put her daughter up to hiring a private eye and getting evidence for a divorce. I have no idea whether such a thing is even possible in Catholic France, and no interest either, for obvious reasons.

"Shortly thereafter I left for Spain, where I passed a delectable two months among my Spanish sweethearts, bull-fighters mostly.

"I returned to Paris on the tenth of January. About ten days after my return I read of a murder at 10 *bis* Rue des Ecoles. Naturally the address made me sit up and take notice. It was my old address. I perused the article, and looked at the photographs with more attention than I would normally give to such a lurid event.

"Imagine my shock when peering at the newspaper photograph of the victim to recognize her as the little shopgirl I had spotted necking with Philippe Jumelle in a little local restaurant near Place Pigalle. It was bizarre, to say the least! Naturally I considered the possibility that it was not the same young thing, merely a *doppelgänger*. But the resemblance was too perfect. It had to be she. Furthermore, the coincidence would have been too astounding, had someone who merely looked like an identical twin to the son-in-law's little toy been murdered in the mother-in-law's very apartment-building.

"I felt deadly certain that this was no coincidence. And equally certain I was that what I had told Madame Fleuris of seeing this girl with her son-in-law Philippe had somehow precipitated this horrifying event.

"I may be a naughty boy but I draw the line at murder.

"How and why the poor Emilie Werner had moved from Pigalle to her lover's mother-in-law's apartment-building I had no idea. But I was certain that the links existed."

As Tobey paused in his narrative to take several long sips of the greenish-yellow milky liquid in the fat glass, Miri almost burst out with total disbelief. "If this is all true, why don't you just tell Inspector Goulette yourself?"

"I gave you one good reason earlier, Miriam Winter. Here is my second reason. I want to continue using Madame Fleuris' services as a mail-drop, a pleasant situation which would of course cease were I to report my bizarre information to the police and she were to learn of it.

"On the other hand, I don't want to be considered an 'accomplice' to murder, in the sense that I would be withholding information that might be relevant to the case if I –

or someone – didn't report it. For I am sure that Madame Fleuris knows who committed the murder, and that it is someone in her own family, Philippe himself, or the much put-upon Lucille, or even Madame herself, as unlikely as that seems.

"But it is more unlikely to think of the incident as a coincidence. Therefore the police must be informed. But not by me. I do not wish the slightest contact with the police, nor is it necessary. That is where you come in, my dear girl. You are going to tell them everything I have just told you, without revealing my name or any information that could be traced back to me. I'm not going to ask you if you will do it. You *must* do it."

He signalled the waiter for the check, waving a five-thousand-franc note.

"Why should they believe me? If they would disbelieve you then they would disbelieve the person, me, carrying the story from people they would disbelieve."

"That's not your problem. Just tell them everything I've told you. Let them decide what if anything to make of it."

"Suppose they demand that I identify who told me."

"You simply refuse to tell them on the grounds that you promised not to, but you swear it's true."

"But I don't swear it's true. I have no idea if it's true or not. And I won't lie."

Tobey said in an exasperated tone, "You know that it's true that I made a statement to you and this is what it was, even if you don't know if the statement itself is true."

"You could almost pass for a logical positivist," Miri said admiringly.

"Good." He waved for the waiter, who gave Tobey his bill, made the change, smiled at his tip and rushed off at another customer's beckoning. Tobey got up, brushing non-existent crumbs from his lap. "Take your time, dear, finish your tea. And pocket any cookies that are left." He gave her a wave and sallied forth.

Miri was not at all sure that she was going to the police with Tobey's story. She was fearful that Tobey had made this all up in order to get her into trouble with the police, or to make a fool of her. After all, the one other time they had met he had told her point-blank that they were rivals. Hadn't he said aggressively, when she had barely met him, as soon as Jamie stepped away, "We both want the same thing from him, don't we, dear?"

But of course she hadn't made out with Jamie so she wasn't really Tobey Peters' rival. But maybe he didn't know that.

There were more reasons to suppose that Tobey was lying than there were to think that he was telling the truth. Apart from a desire to make a fool of her because she was his rival, he might be covering for someone who meant something to him. Suppose that Tobey *had* seen Emilie cuddling with someone, but the man was not Madame Fleuris' son-in-law, it was someone Tobey himself was interested in! It could even have been Jamie! Suppose Tobey realized that Jamie must have been the one who murdered Emilie, he wanted to save him, so he concocted the story about Madame Fleuris and her son-in-law for a gullible Miri to take to the police, so that they would "see" why Madame Fleuris said she saw Jamie coming out of Emilie's room to cover for her son-in-law Philippe, and realize it is a "lie". Tobey wouldn't mind framing Madame Fleuris – she was only a woman, therefore of no importance to him, or enmeshing Miri because she was not only a woman but his rival besides. And that would explain why he had not asked Jamie to go the police with this unlikely tale.

Furthermore, this interpretation of Tobey's story made it more plausible that Emilie got the room at Rue des Ecoles in the first place, since Jamie would have known about it and could have been the one to get it for her. If the story about Madame Fleuris' son-in-law were true then the whopping coincidence of Emilie just happening to rent a neighbor's room in his mother-in-law's building, by accident, would be too much to believe.

If Miri was right that Tobey was lying and his motive was to protect Jamie, then the last thing she wanted to do was carry his phoney tale to the police. But if his story was true then of course she should tell it. She would have to figure out how to figure out whether it was true or false. When Vanessa got back from Chamonix she would see what she thought.

Miri realized that in thinking that Tobey's story might be a lie she was willing to consider that Jamie might be the killer, as absurd as it seemed to her. Logically, though, it had to be admitted as a possibility, for completeness, and to be consistent with one possible motive for Tobey's lying.

If Tobey were telling the truth, however, then that would make it unlikely that Pierre Poivriere had had anything to do with the murder.

But if he hadn't, why had Emilie received a note asking her to a rendez-vous signed "Pierre"?

And why on earth would Philippe move his girlfriend into Rue des Ecoles right under the nose of his snooping mother-in-law? Did he think it was the safest place to "hide" her like the Purloined Letter, in plain sight, because the most unlikely? And then stop in upstairs on a Sunday between cups of coffee for a quickie?

And if Pierre Poivriere were not the murderer, then it wasn't fair to him not to be telling the police something that would cause them to cease suspecting him.

Miri didn't know what to believe. And she didn't know what to do.

She ate up the rest of the cookies and began walking toward l'Opera, thinking maybe she should get a ticket for something. The singing there was execrable but running up and down the enormously wide marble staircase had been fun. Of course that had been with Jamie. She wouldn't enjoy doing it by herself.

23

On Friday morning Miri arose early, opened the shutters and stepped onto the balcony in her nightgown to look out at a Magritte-like night of dark sky, houses sprinkled with tiny rectangles of light and curtained below by the gray stone wall on her left.

The air was cold and clammy and smelled damp. She watched her breath, puzzling over Tobey's story. Suppose it were actually true, that Tobey did see Emilie Werner in the Pigalle restaurant and that the man with was in fact Philippe Jumelle. Then either Philippe for some strange reason got her to rent a room in the same building as his parents'-in-law apartment, or it was sheer coincidence.

Miri couldn't believe that it was coincidence. But why on earth would Philippe want her living here, where they might more easily be found out?

It had to be that Tobey was lying, and had some reason for doing so. To cover for some other man? Perhaps he had seen Emilie with someone, but not Philippe Jumelle. To make a fool of Miri if she took the tale to the police? Although she felt he didn't like her this seemed too elaborate a hoax to be worth the bother.

She recalled that the police's first suspect was Jamie, because Madame Fleuris had said she saw him coming out of Monique's room that Sunday night, just at the time they later deduced the murder had occurred. When Miri first heard that

Madame Fleuris had placed Jamie at the scene she had assumed that either Madame Fleuris was mistaken as to the identity of the man, or was deliberately lying to cover for some other man. Pierre Poivriere, for instance.

But wasn't that too much of a coincidence too, to think that first Madame Fleuris lied to cover for, say, Pierre, then Tobey lied to cover someone else? Or maybe it wasn't too much to believe. Maybe people lied all the time. Even more than Miri thought they did.

As for the evidence against Pierre Poivriere. One. Fact. He had been on the sixth floor the night of the murder. But so had others, including herself. Including Jamie. Two. Pierre was married, and Gabrielle had said Emilie had said her lover was married. But so were a lot of other men! Three. It was a fact that Emilie had received a *pneu* signed "Pierre". The police had it.

None of this was sufficient, now that Miri thought about it, to send a man to the guillotine or even to suspect that he deserved to go to the guillotine. She didn't see how she could go to the police with such a flimsy unlikely story, especially since Tobey wouldn't allow her to reveal who had told it to her. If only Vanessa had been around they could have analyzed it together and maybe clarified what she should do.

Miri didn't go to Rue des Ecoles for *déjeuner* because she didn't want to see Jamie and find out that he didn't want to go with her to the American Club tea-dance the next day the way they always used to do on Saturdays. And she knew he wouldn't.

Bethel Washton was not at *diner* that evening, so Miri left her a note that she had obtained the Chinese robe and would be ready to start painting Saturday morning.

Saturday morning Bethel arrived right on time, wrapped herself in the Chinese robe and Miri began painting, conscious that she had to work quickly. Bethel sat for exactly one hour as promised, standing beside the dark green shutters to the balcony. In that time Miri got in the main lines, hit on the right palette, laid down some color and overall felt it was off to a good start. She pleaded with Bethel to sit on Sunday too but she refused. She did agree, however, to stay an extra hour that morning. Miri worked as in a trance. It was taking shape.

"You and I, we're kindred spirits," Miri remarked.

"Do tell."

Miri took this as an invitation to continue. "The little-white-gloved goodie-two-shoes who giggle in groups and take taxis to church, their fathers are in charge of companies and towns. They're the ones who own America. You and I, we just live there."

"You 'bout done with that picture?"

"You said you would sit for two hours."

"I'm standing, honey, in case you hadn't noticed."

"I mean 'pose'. If you're tired we can take a break, but I really need the two hours. More actually, if I could get it—"

"You can't. You know whom you remind me of? My dentist back home. He gets you in that chair leaning back with your mouth propped open so as you can only moan, and then he talks up a storm while he works and you can't say a thing." She laughed her throaty laugh.

"I'm not stopping you from talking. Only when I'm working on the face. I'll tell you when. Right now I'm doing an arm."

"*The* face? *An* arm? I'm a person, girl, not a collection of parts like a car. How 'bout saying *your* face and *your* arm?"

"Okay."

"You still don't get it."

"Bethel, I was wondering. Why do you want to do Racine, and in French? Why not Shakespeare, in English?"

"Maybe the grandeur and the power of Racine's women appeal to me, maybe it's something else. I don't know and I don't care about reasons. They're usually not real anyhow, just excuses or rationalizations. The real reasons are hidden. I just know I'm in my element. That's enough for me. When I play a character I try to get at her real reasons as well as her excuses, but my own? I could never. Do you get at your real reasons, not your excuses?"

Put that way Miri wasn't sure that she did. "Don't talk now, I'm working on the – your face."

By the time one of her frequent peeks at her wristwatch resulted in Bethel's announcement, "I've got to go," Miri had reached a point where she could work without her.

They looked at the painting together. It was far from finished, of course, but there was more to it than Miri would have expected for only two hours of work. She felt good.

Bethel laughed her throaty laugh. "Is my face really green and yellow?"

"Stand back. You're looking at it from too close. And besides, it's not finished. This is going to be one of my best paintings."

"Oh Gawd. Don't show me the others! Got to go."

She continued working on the painting after Bethel left, right through *dejéuner chez* Fleuris. She ate lunch while at work, munching on the remains of a baguette and several wedges of foil-wrapped cheese, *"la vâche qui rit"*.

Judy stopped by in the afternoon, uninvited. She was dressed up in heels and a tight-fitting black sheath, large glittery rhinestone earrings protruding from her pouffed pageboy. With her Persian lamb coat over her shoulders and a huge black alligator bag she looked like her own mother.

"I wanted to see how your painting was coming along," she said. "But I can't stay very long."

Miri was relieved to hear that.

"I have a date," Judy said smugly, frowning at the painting. "She doesn't look like a Negro. In fact," she giggled, "I've never seen anybody those shades of green and yellow. Is that a new race? The robe came out pretty good though. Are you done with it? The robe, I mean?"

"You can take it right now." Miri dug around the bottom of her armoire for the bookbag, stuffed the robe into it and handed it over.

Judy removed the robe from the bookbag, looked around for a hanger, and hung the robe in the armoire. "I don't want to drag this along on my date. Are you going out tonight?"

"No."

"Aren't you curious who my date is?" Judy grinned.

"No."

Miri attended the Sunday coffee-hour at the *pension* to see if Philippe Jumelle looked guilty to her. She studied his face but it looked as smug as ever. Lucille Jumelle simpered as usual, she didn't seem to suspect a thing. Philippe and Lucille Jumelle uttered their weekly inanities and alternately scolded and hugged their pale pimply son, while Monsieur Fleuris, his eyes twinkling, mumbled an ongoing commentary into his beard. Everything was as boring as usual.

Judy did not show up for the coffee *en famille.* Nor was Bran there, as he was still skiing with Vanessa. Jamie was in high spirits, now that it seemed he was no longer a murder suspect; he was secretly anticipating a job-interview at NATO.

He chattered a lot, even teasing Madame Fleuris that her "secret admirer" was back in town. Madame looked startled but didn't ask Jamie whom he meant.

The telephone rang in the kitchen. Madame scurried to answer it herself. A moment later, she fetched Miri from the salon. "It's the mother of Mademoiselle Judy, calling from America. She is worried because she hasn't had her usual letter from her daughter. Although I assured her that her daughter was well, she requested that if you – Mademoiselle Miri – were present she would like to speak with you."

Miri rushed into the kitchen to take the call.

"I've heard so much about you, dear, that I feel I know you," said Mrs Kugel over the crackles and sputtering of the transoceanic connection. "Tell me the truth, is my Judy feeling all right? Is she eating well? Is anything the matter?"

"She looks fine and she is certainly eating everything in sight as usual," Miri said. "And she is giggling her head off as usual as far as I can see."

"I was so worried when I didn't get my weekly letter," Mrs Kugel wailed. "Why isn't she there with all of you? Isn't it after-dinner coffee-time there? I always keep two clocks side-by-side," Mrs Kugel giggled, sounding uncannily like Judy, "one set with Paris time, one with home-time so that I'll always know what my baby is doing every minute."

"We don't always all come to Sunday coffee. Branford Duane Lee the Third isn't here either. Don't you usually call later in the evening on Sundays?"

"You're right, dear, but I just couldn't wait, I thought I would try sooner. Where is my baby right now?"

"I don't know where Judy is at this very moment but I can assure you she's just fine. The murder hasn't disrupted a thing, she's having fun and studying like mad."

"Murder?" Mrs Kugel screamed shrilly. "Did you say 'murder'? What are you talking about? Where's my baby?"

Her screams got shriller and shriller almost reaching ultrasonic levels and causing a ringing in Miri's ears.

"It's nothing, really, Mrs Kugel. There was a murder in the building a week ago, but it has nothing to do with us."

"Have the police arrested the murderer?"

"They're on to somebody that they're questioning. I'm sure it will all be wrapped up in no time at all." Miri didn't mention that she had moved out of the *pension* Fleuris to get away from the killer if he was still in the vicinity.

"She never said a word to me about it," Mrs Kugel wailed.

"Probably because there's nothing to say. It has nothing to do with us. I shouldn't have mentioned it." Just why had she mentioned it? It had just slipped out. Was her subconscious being malicious? Wanting to make Mrs Kugel writhe the way Tobey had wanted to make Lady Alexandra writhe? That wasn't nice. She didn't want to be like that.

"Now I am so worried..."

"Well call back later, I'm sure Judy will be here for your call, at the time she expects it, and you can hear for yourself that she's just fine."

Judy was going to have a fit when she found out that Miri had told her mother about the murder. Miri felt obliged to warn her before her mother's next phone-call. She left a note for Judy in her room before she left, confessing that a mention of the murder had slipped out, and in penance even suggested to Judy that if her mother insisted she come right home as Judy feared she would if she heard of the murder that Judy promise to move right in to Reid Hall, which was safe and secure. Miri could only pray that it wouldn't have room for her.

Late that evening, as Miri was reading herself to sleep with Delacroix' diaries, Vanessa rapped at her door, just back from Chamonix. She looked pink and healthy and happy. She and Branford Duane Lee the Third had had a marvelous time. For three days they had skiied all day and made love all night and drank hot wine in between.

"And I found out something strange about him," Vanessa breathed, as she sat crosslegged on the floor and smoked. "He's a Communist!"

"You mean he's really a Russian?"

"Of course not. He's from Kentucky all right. But he's a member of the Communist Party. That's why he's in France. Because some senator, McCarthy I think his name is, is making it too hot for Communists in the States. Bran belongs to some cell or other with a bunch of Frenchmen. By the way, he swore me to secrecy, so I hereby swear you to secrecy."

"How can you be sure I won't tell?" asked Miri, feeling guilty about letting slip to Judy's mother that a murder had occurred at 10 *bis* Rue des Ecoles.

Vanessa gave a breathy laugh. "You don't even tell your own secrets, so why would you tell mine?"

"I didn't know Communists liked to ski."

"I know, isn't it strange? He's so bourgeois in his tastes! More than me. Of course intellectually he condemns all that – for other people. I'll tell you a secret. He's even asked me to marry him!"

"I didn't know Communists got married. I thought they believed in free love. Did you say yes?"

"Of course not. I can't marry anyone who isn't an artist."

"Or who's a Communist."

"Oh I don't mind that so much, you can outgrow being a Communist. But if you don't have talent, you're never going to get it."

A sobering thought. Miri sure hoped she already had it.

"Did you know that your idol Sartre is a Communist?" Vanessa asked.

"What?"

"That's what Bran said."

"Oh well, I really don't care, I'm not interested in politics."

"Anyway you're still in one piece," Vanessa laughed, "So your tryst with Tobey Peters didn't prove fatal. Or did you stand him up?"

"Oh I went all right and he was perfectly civil, treated me to a *té complet* at the Cafe de la Paix. But he told me an unbelievable story."

"What was it?"

She repeated to Vanessa what Tobey Peters had told her.

"Gosh! That sure puts the murder smack in the middle of the Fleuris family and clears Jamie for good and all as well as clearing Pierre Poivriere too. I never did think either one of them were involved."

"Then you believe Tobey's story?"

"Well it doesn't sound implausible. After all he had gotten to know Philippe Jumelle when he was at the *pension*, so if he saw the man with Emilie Werner in the restaurant, he probably didn't mistake who it was, and why would he come forth with such a story if it weren't the truth?"

"I can think of several reasons. One, to throw the investigators off the scent of whoever it really was who killed Emilie if that person meant something to Tobey. Jamie Giardini for example!"

"Jamie! I thought you said you were positive that he couldn't possibly have done it."

"That was before I knew he was a fairy. If he could fool me about that, he could fool me about this."

Vanessa shook her head skeptically. "I don't know about that. It's not the same thing at all. What other reasons do you think could Tobey Peters have for making up this story?"

"To get me to go to the police and make a fool of myself. It would look to the police as if I were making it up to take any suspicion remaining off Jamie, and only said it was some anonymous third person who told it to me."

"Sounds kind of farfetched. No, I think it must be just what he says, otherwise why would he bother? It's an odd thing to have happened, but an even odder thing to make up."

"What really sounds odd, even unbelievable, is that if Emilie Werner really were having an affair with Philippe Jumelle, why would she move into his mother-in-law's building?"

"I know. That's really strange. But that's what makes it interesting. It could be true, and there could be some weird explanation."

"Do you think Philippe Jumelle killed Emilie Werner? When I think of that stuffed pompous functionary I just can't imagine him exerting himself to climb the two extra flights of stairs to the *sixième,* much less make the effort that murder requires. He looks as if he delegates everything."

"If it was her son-in-law Madame Fleuris saw on the sixth floor in or near Emilie's room that would certainly explain why she tried to place the blame on someone else! As she had already heard of their liaison from Tobey Peters. I think, why worry about what it all means, or whether it is even wholly or partly true? Just tell the police what Tobey told you and let them figure out whether it's true or not. You can tell them you don't know yourself if you believe it but you're telling them, just in case it has some truth to it. Better still, go look up your gorgeous Monsieur Dantan and tell him the story and let him translate it into French for the Inspector."

"I don't want to traipse in there with some farfetched tale that would only make me look like a fool."

"Well I think it's important enough to tell the police, so if you don't want to, I will." She smiled mischievously. "And I'm eager to get a look at *le beau* Dantan anyway."

"We could go together," Miri said tentatively. "That way you can get a look at him, and I won't feel as stupid if the story turns out to be a hoax."

"Terrific! Let's go first thing after breakfast!"

Miri hadn't thought much about Dantan in the past few days. She was wondering how she would feel about him when she saw him. She was still hopeful that once the case was solved he would ask her out, but she wasn't sure of how interested in him she might be once he did.

A young boy collected them in a dingy corridor of the P.J., ascertained their purpose, and led them into a dim windowless room that smelled of stale smoke. He said he would fetch Monsieur Dantan.

Some minutes later Dantan arrived, and the youth announced them, " *les demoiselles* Winter *et* Tate".

With Dantan was a tall homely grinning young man.

"This is Inspector Jean-Jacques Pilieu," Dantan said.

Dantan was cordial and attentive when Miri said that they had some possible information about the murder, but he was not flirtatious or even seemingly particularly interested in her, possibly because of the presence of Inspector Pilieu and Vanessa. His manner was very businesslike. Inspector Pilieu, though, kept smiling at her.

"I received a phone-call last week from a man who doesn't want his name revealed," Miri began. Dantan translated for the inspector. Miri resolved to continue her tale in French.

"Excuse me, Mademoiselle," Poilieu interrupted, "If what this anonymous gentleman told you is worthy of further investigation, we shall need his name."

"I promised him I wouldn't reveal it. He made me swear not to. He was afraid of getting into trouble with the police over something else. Before this phone-call, I had met him only once, very briefly, and at the time I had thought he was a woman. He was dressed up like a woman and made up heavily.

"I met her, only she was a him but I didn't know it then, at a *vernissage* for a prince who was an artist, or actually he really wasn't an artist, his paintings were terrible, but we didn't know that until we got there.

"This person phoned me and said that he had something urgent he had to see me about, and in order to explain who he was he reminded me of the *vernissage* and meeting someone I had thought was a woman. He was being really secretive and didn't want anyone at the *pension* to find out who had called me, but he insisted I meet him and even though I strongly didn't want to, I did. And he told me a story I just can't bring myself to believe because he is so weird, and might have some weird reason for making it up."

"I urged her to come and tell you all this," said Vanessa. "I believe his story. It's a very odd story, but wouldn't it be odder if he had made it up?"

"This man was a *pensionnaire* at the *pension* Fleuris in the past," Miri went on. "So he is familiar with members of the family, as we are. The Fleuris' daughter Lucille and her husband Philippe and their pimply-faced son have coffee every Sunday with the *pensionnaires*. This fellow says that last October he saw Philippe Jumelle with a young woman in a Pigalle restaurant, acting amorous. This fellow takes Madame Fleuris out to tea about once a month when he's in Paris, as a kindness, and when he took her to tea in October or November he told her about seeing her son-in-law with this girl acting lovey-dovey in this hideaway restaurant near Pigalle.

"Then this fellow goes off to Spain and stays through Christmas. Two months or so pass. He gets back from Spain and sees a newspaper article about the murder at 10 *bis* Rue des Ecoles. His old address! There was a photograph of the victim. He recognizes her! She's the girl he saw with Philippe Jumelle! He doesn't want to get involved with the police, but he thinks the police should hear about what he saw, so he calls me up and asks me to tell this to the police without bringing him into it. So there it is."

Dantan and Pilieu had listened attentively to all this. Pilieu mumbled to Dantan that this information might be helpful.

Dantan told them that the police already knew that Mademoiselle Werner had had a lover, but had not yet been able to learn his identity. This could be the break they needed! Now that they could show a photograph of a specific man to the concierge at Mademoiselle's former hotel and to waiters at the restaurant where she and her lover presumably had a rendez-vous..."

"You mean the one mentioned in the *pneu*?" Miri asked.

"Ah you have heard of the *pneu*?"

"Judy told me."

"May we see it?" Vanessa asked quickly. "The *pneu*, I mean?"

Pilieu gave her an indulgent smile. "But of course. Mademoiselle Tate. You deserve a little something. You have helped us already."

Dantan fetched the *pneu* from the evidence-room and handed it over to them. Vanessa and Miri peered at it together.

The handwriting was angular and orderly, possibly a man's. The name of the restaurant was "*Dans l'Ombre du Moulin*". No address. So they must have gone there before. It was signed by someone named Pierre.

"Look at that!" said Vanessa. "That's really peculiar!"

"What is?"

"The way it's signed. With quote marks around the name "Pierre".

Miri stared at it: What was written was "*ton* 'Pierre'". Vanessa was right.

"If I were writing a letter to someone I wouldn't sign it "Regards, quote Vanessa unquote," Vanessa said.

"But suppose," Miri said excitedly, "suppose for instance, Bethel Washton did get to play *'Phèdre'*, and wrote to someone and signed it *"Phèdre'*, she wouldn't sign it just 'Regards, *Phèdre'* she would sign it 'Regards, quote *'Phèdre'* unquote!'. She demanded of Dantan, "Don't you think it means his name is not really Pierre?"

The two men looked at each other and shrugged.

"I've just thought of a theory to explain it!" Miri said excitedly. "I happen to know that Emilie Werner was a big fan of Colette, Gabrielle told Judy Kugel and me that and in fact she had a book by Colette Emilie had given her, called *'La Chatte'* but I'm talking about another book by Colette, 'Mitsou'. And don't forget, Emilie had named her cat 'Mitsou'! Anyway in the book 'Mitsou' by Colette, one of the heroine's boyfriends, the one who seems to be older and have money and nicknamed her 'Mitsou' after the companies he's a director of, his name is Pierre. And here in the *pneu* he's actually written "my dear Mitsou..."

"Not in quotes," Dantan observed with a smile.

"But doesn't it seem like a reference to the book, using pet-names for each other from the book? He might have signed it that way deliberately, so that if anyone ever got their hands on it, it couldn't be traced back to him."

"Most astute," Dantan smiled. "I thank you, Mesdemoiselles Winter and Tate for a most interesting and enlightening interlude. First you tell us of evidence that provides one of our witnesses with a motive for disguising the fact that Pierre Poivriere was the culprit. Then you tell a tale that would implicate the son-in-law of that same witness. And finally you examine a piece of evidence garnered by the police and pronounce that it proves that the name signed was not the name of the person who wrote it. You have no doubt complicated our case, you have given us food for thought and perhaps a new angle on the crime, and for all that we thank you immensely! Furthermore," he added in French, obviously for Inspector Pilieu's benefit, "I suspect that my associate here would be enchanted to take you ladies to a café for coffee. But I have a report to write so for my part I'll say *Au revoir!*"

Miri had the uncomfortable feeling that he was laughing at her. He certainly hadn't made a pass at her! He didn't even offer to go with the three of them to the cafe. She didn't feel she had handled the interview very well. Of course having Vanessa tag along hadn't helped at all. He seemed less interested in her as a female than he had when they met before.

She wasn't sorry that they had gone, though. The great thing about having told the police Tobey's tale was that she didn't have to think about it any more. If she had realized what a relief that would be she would have told them sooner.

The three went to a café near police headquarters which Jean-Jacques, as he asked them to call him, was nicknamed "Café des Flics" in the neighborhood, because so many inspectors and police went there. There certainly were a lot of men there, mostly at the bar, and most of them smoking Gauloises Bleues. Vanessa lit up one of her American cigarettes.

Jean-Jacques asked them a lot of nosey questions about themselves, as if they were suspects, but when Vanessa and Miri talked it over afterwards Vanessa said she thought he was rather sweet and was not being a detective, just a guy who liked girls – and Miri in particular, she thought!

After the coffee with Jean-Jacques, Vanessa wanted to browse the bookstalls along the quais for secondhand books. Miri knew she should really go with her, as she felt she owed Judy some *livres jaunes* published on her birthday, for that expensive sweater she had insisted Miri take, but she was hungry so instead she raced back to the pension Fleuris for *déjeuner*. This was her last week of meals she had already paid for at the *pension*.

24

Dantan was more intrigued with the information Miri Winter had imparted than he had let on to her. It remained to be validated. But if it was, knowing who the victim's lover had been could be the break they needed.

As he pointed out to Inspector Goulette while relating it to the latter in a cloud of acrid smoke, it was peculiar, but not beyond the realm of the possible, that a man would want his *amie* to reside in the very building where his mother-in-law lived, and on the very floor where she had boarders.

Inspector Goulette wanted to interrogate Philippe Jumelle without further delay. He put aside his bias toward suspecting Pierre Poivriere for the moment, Poivriere wasn't running anywhere.

"You've been doing a good job, old man," Goulette told Dantan gruffly. "Beyond what we could have expected from you in the capacity of interpreter. If you would like to sit in on the interrogation of Philippe Jumelle, you are welcome."

Dantan was delighted. He knew he had to attribute his great luck in helping with the case to the meddling and gossiping of his charming girlfriend and her pals, but without his perception and agility in using what they brought him it would have been wasted. That Goulette invited him to sit in on an important interview was an auspicious sign.

As Inspector Goulette did not want to embarass Philippe Jumelle in the event the story about him was false and he had no involvement, Goulette wanted to go very softly in bringing him in for questioning, and attempted to do so by telephone.

Jumelle was reluctant to leave his office during working hours and resisted at first. Goulette regretted having to do it but he threatened to send members of the department to collect him if he continued to refuse to come in voluntarily. He then agreed to be there at noon, which gave them the two hours of the dinner hour before his absence would even be noted at his office. And a lateness of half an hour or so on top of that would not be particularly noticed either.

Philippe Jumelle was shown into Inspector Goulette's office about half an hour after the phone call. The chief inspector was seated behind his oak desk, Dantan on one oak armchair on the side, Vouray on another, equipped with a notebook to take down the statement. The inspector shook hands with his visitor and thanked him for coming in. He introduced Dantan, then invited Jumelle to take the other oak armchair before his desk.

"I know you are pressed for time, Monsieur Jumelle, so I'll come right to the point. We have the word of someone who says that he saw you in a restaurant in Pigalle back in October with a young woman he later realized, when her photograph appeared in the newspaper after her death, was Emilie Werner." The inspector paused expectantly. Would Jumelle deny it or admit it?

Philippe Jumelle turned very red, right to the tips of his ears. Tears welled up in his eyes. "It's true. I was seeing her. But I had nothing to do with her death. Nothing. I loved her. She was a person who had come through hell and was vulnerable and serene, not bitter."

"How do you explain where she was living? Right in the building where your mother-in-law lives? Wasn't that rather inconvenient for maintaining discretion in your trysts?"

"It was more than inconvenient, it was a disaster, inspector. Emilie had no idea when she moved into her little room at 10 *bis* Rue des Ecoles who else lived there. She found the room and moved in over the Christmas holidays. I was away with my wife and son in the Midi, visiting my parents. When I returned I was horrified to learn the new address to which Emilie had moved. She had written a *pneu* to me at my office. I contacted her in return by *pneu*, to meet me at our usual restaurant.

"Her explanation how the move had come about shocked me with its tragic irony She was at work at the Galeries Lafayette at the handbags counter. One day when she had helped all the customers on an especially busy day, she found a piece of paper on the counter, evidently left there by some customer. She had no idea which one. It proved to be a room-for-rent notice from the student housing bureau. As she had no idea to whom to return the notice, and as the rent listed was extremely cheap, she decided to apply for the room herself. Her hotel room in Pigalle was depressing. Not only did she think this room would be better, at an even cheaper rate, she had a very personal reason for reacting strongly to the opportunity. The address meant something personal to her and had a powerful emotional significance.

"She presented herself to the landlady, a Madame Poivriere, was shown the room, and the two came to a rapid agreement. She moved in the next day.

"When I returned from the Midi and received her *pneu* I was horrified, arranged a rendez-vous at our usual restaurant, and heard how it had come about. It was only then that Emilie learned that my in-laws were her neighbors. She was of course terribly upset but I reassured her that I was resolved to get her out of there, even if I had to pay part of her rent. I was in process of discreetly seeking another location for her when her tragic death occurred."

"And the very personal significance you alluded to, Monsieur Jumelle?"

"Emilie had lived there as a child. 'Emilie Werner' was not the name Emilie was born with. She was born in

Paris in 1930 as 'Berthe Maisel', the elder child of Daniel and Sophie Maisel, who also had a son three years younger than Berthe. Daniel had an optics workshop on the ground floor of the building where they lived on the first floor. Ten *bis* Rue des Ecoles. They lived an unexceptionable life until the difficulties began for the Jews in 1940, the necessity to wear a yellow star conspicuously, the banning from various places... In 1942 as you know there was a massive roundup of Jews in Paris, where thousands were taken to the winter stadium and then shipped, as we now know, to death camps in Germany and Poland.

"The Maisel family were seized that July morning in 1942. But Berthe, who was an assertive twelve year old, started screaming and flailing at the police who were hauling away her parents and brother, and the concierge at 10 *bis* who was apparently observing all this from her loge, offered to the police to take charge of the girl, calm her down and hand her over later. She took Berthe into her loge, gave her some hot chocolate, probably laced with a sedative, gave Berthe a stern talking-to with rules for her behavior, instructing her to pretend amnesia, and took her to the train for Dieppe, put Berthe in the care of a train conductor, telling him that the girl would be met in Dieppe, and prayed for the best.

"But the girl was captured by inquisitive police, shipped off to a French camp and then handed over to the Germans. She was tall for her age and treated like a young woman rather than a child, and put to work rather than to death. But a camp guard named Werner much older than Berthe fancied her, and took posession of her, ensuring her survival with extra rations and some other slight advantages. Berthe naturally had mixed feelings about the man, who had raped her and in effect enslaved her, but had without a doubt saved her life.

"When the war ended and the camp was liberated she tried to get mercy for Werner by marrying him, then for two years she tried through humanitarian organizations to locate her parents and brother, and she also worked for one of the organizations herself. The tensions between Berthe and her older German husband were great. After three years she divorced him.

"She had no papers. One of the agencies helping displaced persons created an identity for her. She chose the name 'Emilie' to replace her original name, to signify a new life, but kept the name Werner to honor the man who had saved her life, regardless of his motives.

"She worked her way back to France, and Paris. She went to her former home on Rue des Ecoles to see if she could learn anything about her parents or brother. The concierge, although it was Madame Poule, the very person who had tried to rescue her, did not recognize her. Emilie inquired about the Maisel family and was told that they had not lived there for over ten years. They had "gone away"' during the Occupation. The concierge did not know where. Nor did she admit to knowing what had become of the Maisels' belongings. No, nobody had come to claim them. But it was the war, you know...

"By the time I met her at the Galeries Lafayette she had given up trying to learn anything about her family. Then when Emilie saw the room-for-rent notice the chance to get a room at the very building where she used to live was like a summons from fate. She saw it as an opportunity to make some inquiries about her family.

"She had no idea that neighbors on her floor were *pensionnaires* of my very mother-in-law, and when she learned that fact, was anxious to get out of there as soon as possible.

"Alas, it was not soon enough."

Inspector Goulette although he may have found all this very touching, nevertheless pursued vigorously the subject of Philippe Jumelle's whereabouts at various times on the Sunday evening Emilie was killed. When he squeezed out whatever he thought he could on this subject, he thanked Monsieur Jumelle and asked him to wait until his statement was typed up and he could sign it.

After Philippe Jumelle had been allowed to return to his bureau, Inspector Goulette announced to Inspector Vouray and Alphonse Dantan that he was ready and eager to question Madame Fleuris. After all, there was the subject of the room-for-rent notice actually in their possession thanks to Monsieur Dantan here, and the proof that Madame Fleuris' handwriting resembled it greatly, according to a snide little notice from her W.C. presumably also in her handwriting, also, conveniently in their possession thanks again to Dantan's diligence.

The strong resemblance between the two handwritings was a fact, and a provocative one; the theory Dantan had reported that Mademoiselle Winter had advanced was just that, a theory. He was in mind to formulate his own.

25

Miri slid into her usual place next to Jamie. Branford pounced on her with enthusiasm to talk about Vanessa. What he had on his mind was, it was Vanessa's birthday on the coming Sunday, and Bran had arranged with Madame Fleuris to have a little surprise-party. He had ordered a special American-style birthday cake to be baked and decorated at the local patisserie and delivered to the Fleuris apartment in time for the Sunday coffee-hour. He was holding the party at the *pension* and inviting whomever of Vanessa's friends he knew about. He didn't think his own friends would be suitable. (Miri knew they were Communists, but he didn't know that she knew.) Miri wondered whether Branford Duane Lee believed that every single citizen under Communist rule should have a surprise party and a decorated cake on his or her birthday. She would ask him that as soon as she knew that he knew that she knew that he was a Communist.

Madame Fleuris acknowledged her complicity in this little surprise with a prim smile. She was dressed up, in a tight girdle and black dress, to go somewhere.

Judy was bubbling over something as usual, with Monsieur Fleuris' indulgent smile egging her on.

Madame Fleuris asked sourly, "Are you enjoying your new accommodations, Mademoiselle Miri?"

"Yes, thank you, Madame, I take a bath in hot water every night."

She rolled her eyes to the ceiling invoking the *bon dieu.* "What that must cost!"

"Maybe if more people did so," Jamie grinned, "they wouldn't have to spray the Paris Metro with perfume!"

"It's good for the perfume industry," Judy laughingly pointed out, "look how much perfume they can sell, and by the gallon, not just by the ounce."

"I think *le parfum* just makes the stink smell worse," Miri said.

Judy was quite taken with this quip, enough to repeat Miri's French in order to memorize it: "*Je crois que le parfum simplement fait pire la puanteur.*" Then in English, she asked Miri, "How's your cold?"

"Gone."

"Know what I think? I don't think you ever had a cold. I think it's an allergy. Look how you suddenly started sneezing when the cat came into Gabrielle's room."

"You said that at the time."

"Mesdemoiselles, you were in Gabrielle's room? For what purpose?" demanded Madame Fleuris.

"You could get a doctor to do something about it," said Judy, ignoring the old woman. "I'm sure that's what it was. I had the same problem once..."

"*En français, mesdemoiselles, en français s'il vous plaîtb!*"

Judy attempted to oblige. "Your eyes were all red and *comment se dit-il en français* 'puffy'. It reminded me of the garden of roses of my mother. She had around a hundred rosebushes *comment se dit-il en français* 'planted' all at once, in time for a big garden party, and as soon as I walked past it to get into the house I started sneezing and *comment se dit-il en français* 'choking' and I thought I would die."

Monsieur Fleuris had listened to this recital with his usual attentiveness to Judy. "And then?"

"*Et alors?*" Judy echoed. "And then she had it *comment se dit-il en français* 'dug up' and the roses thrown away. After the party, of course. It was that or I would have had to move out of our home, and my parents didn't trust me not to *baiser* around if I had my own place."

Madame Fleuris pursing her thin lips shook her head in intense disapproval, either at Judy's coarse sentiments and language, or at the extravagant waste the discarded roses represented. Madame was in a great hurry to get them through *déjeuner* as she was going out directly afterwards. Monsieur Fleuris teased her that she must be meeting her *amant.* This failed to amuse her. As soon as Germaine brought in the flan she excused herself, donned her black coat and the little black hat with veil and feather that she wore to church on Sundays, and which Miri had seen on her the day the three of them and had seen her strolling with Tobey Peters.

Tobey Peters! Miri felt she had to tell Jamie Tobey's story despite her promise to Tobey to say nothing. But Jamie was very tense and preoccupied with preparing for a job-interview a friend of his had set up for him at NATO or UNESCO or something like that. She decided to wait to talk to him about Tobey until after the interview.

"I'm glad you showed up here, Miri, saves me from having to track you down at Reid Hall. I have to ask a favor of you." The favor was this: if anyone happened to contact her about him he wanted her to tell them that she was his girlfriend. It had to do with his getting clearance for the job. Miri agreed even though she was still somewhat disappointed in the way things had worked out, or had not.

"I have something important to tell you," Miri said to him. She was nervous that Madame Fleuris was dressed up in her tea-at-Rumpelmayers-with-Tobey-Peters black dress.

"Some other time, Miri. I've got too much on my mind just now. The interview. It means a lot to me."

Miri went back to the pension for *déjeuner* again on Tuesday. Judy was absent, and Jamie was teary-eyed and looking very sad. Miri assumed that he had already had his job interview and had been turned down for the job. He asked her to come upstairs to his room to talk.

"You had your job interview?"

He shook his head. "Not yet. Thank God! I wouldn't be in any shape for it. I've had some terrible news. It's Tobey Peters. He's dead."

"What?"

"I got a phone-call late last night. Madame Fleuris was furious. Germaine had left already, so Madame Fleuris had to climb the stairs herself to get me because my friend absolutely insisted on talking to me threatening dire consequences if she didn't call me to the phone. He told me that he had been invited to Tobey's for dinner that evening, and had gone there to find the cook in hysterics. She had prepared the whole meal thinking Monsieur Peters was napping while she was working, and when she sent the *bonne* to rouse him from his nap she found him dead. The two women hadn't done a thing but wail and moan until Tobey's guest got there. They took him up to Tobey's room. He saw Tobey lying there, and called the American Hospital. A doctor came, said the patient was already dead and since the cause of death was not self-evident he called the police."

Miri was aghast, terrified that it was somehow connected with her having related Tobey's story to the police, even though he had asked her to. "What did he die of?"

"I don't know. There is going to be a post mortem."

She didn't know how to comfort him. She didn't know what to do. She hated seeing people unhappy or in pain. What could she do? She couldn't very well hug him, after what had happened between them, and she didn't know what to say. So she just sat there stupidly, inwardly frightened and also upset to see him so unhappy. "Do you want me to hang around?"

He shook his head. "It's okay. I'm going over to some friends."

She took a taxi back to Reid Hall, feeling too leaden to walk.

Vanessa was somber and reflective at supper when she heard of Tobey's death. "We should have thought of this," she murmured.

"What do you mean?"

"Tobey Peters was the one person who knew who Emilie Werner's lover was."

26

On Wednesday all the inspectors left the office early to continue the investigation in connection with the Werner murder and to embark on a new investigation into the suspicious death of Tobey Peters. Dantan, however, remained at his desk catching up on paperwork. Besides utilizing his services as an interpreter, the other inspectors had followed the chief inspector's lead in delegating much of their report-writing to Dantan. He didn't mind. Having access to their notes gave him a more comprehensive view of the case.

He had not yet been brought in on the Peters case. Although Peters was an American, the servants and friends the investigators had so far identified to question were French. If Peters' family should arrive in Paris, of course, Dantan would be brought in as an interpreter. Unless of course the case demanded the intervention of the Sixth Section, owing to the wealth of the persons involved.

Thus it was when one of the Americans from the Rue des Ecoles case turned up in the visitors area it was to Dantan whom the youth brought to meet with her. He recognized her as the blonde girl who had accompanied Miri with the handwritten documents. "Mademoiselle Tate. Charmed to see you again!"

"I'm glad I got you, rather than one of the inspectors," Vanessa said breathlessly, "my French isn't that great. The boy said I could wait if I wanted to see a *vrai* inspector but that it might be a long time. I actually prefer that I speak with you. Easier."

He led her into the smoky file-room.

"Tobey Peters," she said.

Dantan gave her his full attention. "You know something?"

"I don't know. Maybe. A guess, really. A guess where Madame Fleuris might have gone on Monday when she dashed out after the midday meal. Miri said she was all dressed up. It might tie in. Whenever he was in Paris, Tobey Peters would take Madame Fleuris to Rumpelmayer's for tea about once a month. She was mailing letters for him from Paris to his mother and grandmother, so that they wouldn't know of his peregrinations."

"How do you know that?"

"Miri Winter told me that Tobey told her that. That story Miri told you about the man who wished to remain anonymous but wanted the police to know that he had told Madame Fleuris that he had seen her son-in-law acting amorous with Emilie Werner in an little restaurant near the Moulin Rouge – that man was Tobey Peters. He didn't want the police to know who he was because he's a homosexual and didn't want to get in any trouble. And his two main sources of income, his mother and his grandmother, think he is a normal profligate heterosexual guy and they would have stopped his allowances if they had found out otherwise."

"It should be simple to check with Rumpelmayer's," mused Dantan, "to see if anyone there remembers seeing them. Suppose they *were* there together? They take refreshments together and then Monsieur Peters go home and dies – of poison."

Dantan got up hastily, knocking over his chair. "Please excuse me, Mademoiselle Tate, that was very helpful, but now I must go."

At this statement Vanessa got up quickly and left.

Her information, linking the two deaths to one person,

seemed critical. He had to track down the chief inspector to tell him, but no one in the office knew where Goulette had intended to go, or even on which case he was personally involving himself at the moment.

After the two American girls had come in on Monday and reported Philippe Jumelle's possible connection with Emilie Werner, and the chief inspector had intensively interrogated the hapless lover, Goulette seemed to be convinced that Jumelle had not killed her. But he might have decided to pursue him further anyway. Jumelle repeatedly and vehemently denied having seen his *amie* the Sunday of her death, and in fact had not been together with her since her incomprehensible move except for the brief meeting at their old restaurant at which they spoke of her move.

Jumelle had been horrified when, upon returning from Christmas vacation with his family he had learned that Emilie had not only moved but had moved into the very building where his in-laws resided! It had been incomprehensible to him how she could contemplate doing such a thing. Their *rendez-vous* would be far more difficult to arrange from then on, since he dared not send her any *pneus* to that building, and she would have to exercise the most extreme caution to call him at his bureau, and then on top of that they would have to take a hotel-room to be together, which created the risks inherent in registering and showing identity-cards.

It tortured him to know that Emilie was just upstairs on the Sundays when he visited his in-laws, but he had certainly not ventured up there even for a moment at any time.

Had Madame Fleuris planted the bait on Emilie Werner's counter so as to lure her to a place whence Madame Fleuris could remove her permanently from contaminating her family's life?

Or having been lured there unsuspectingly, Jumelle himself could have killed her. Maybe Emilie Werner did move in by chance, but once there might have attempted to blackmail him into a more overt stance viz-a-viz their relationship...

Dantan had to get to Goulette with the new fact which seemed to tie the two deaths together.

He pulled on his overcoat and rushed the short distance to Rue des Ecoles to see if the chief inspector, or indeed any of the inspectors, were there. The concierge informed him she had seen none of them that day. He went up to both the Pouvriere and Fleuris apartments anyway, but found none of them. Next he took the metro to Sablons, then walked briskly to the Peters house from there, but none of the inspectors were there either.

He could not find the chief inspector all that day, and was loathe to mention his discovery to the other inspectors as they started to come in later. He would catch Goulette first thing the next morning.

In the meantime he spent the night pleasurably with Judy in the charming little hotel not far from the Luxembourg Gardens where they had gone before. They were treated like pampered guests. Breakfast was always served to them in their room, and wine brought in the evening if their supply dwindled.

Judy was an amusing companion, full of droll stories, mostly about her fellow *pensionnaires*. She was especially amused by Miri Winter, who despite her high seriousness and appearance of being an intellectual, was so lacking in common sense. Judy never tired of the anecdote about the supposed cold which Miri thought she had had, and which she had thought she had cured herself with her Existentialist's Will. When it was plain that she was allergic to Gabrielle's cat. Whenever the cat was around she sneezed and sniffled, and whenever she went out, she stopped.

Dantan smiled indulgently, listening with only half an ear, waiting for himself to be ready to make love again, but a fleeting image did appear in his mind, from the morning he arrived with the inspectors to investigate the newly reported murder at 10 *bis* Raue des Ecoles. The American girl Miriam Winter was sneezing and sniffling with not a cat in sight. He filed this thought away for later consideration, as other more pressing matters were at hand.

As they were lingering over their breakfast coffee Dantan urged Judy to pack a small bag and move out of the *pension* and into the hotel just for a few days but she was congenitally unable to fit all her clothing needs into a *small* bag. She did agree to spend the night there every night that he wished!

"If you want me to move out of the *pension,*" she said teasingly, "you could invite me to move into your place."

He stiffened at that. His place was not the place for a rich American girl, nor did he want the public statement her moving in would make. "That would not be *propre.*"

"Well then," she giggled, "make it *propre.* Let's get engaged!"

"Are you serious?"

"Sure! Are you?"

"What about your *papa?*"

"What about him?"

"Will he agree to our marriage? What will he do for us?"

"He gives me everything I want. If you're what I want he'll give in."

"I can't support you as you're accustomed. Will he give you a *dot?*"

"He'll give us a whole house! He gave my brother Ellis a house in Great Neck just three blocks away from my parents' and paid for all the furniture too."

"But *chérie,* our home will be in Paris."

"I'll have to work on him for that."

Dantan was waiting for the chief inspector in his office before eight o'clock the next morning, and without preamble announced, "I've learned the identity of the man who told of seeing Philippe Jumelle and Emilie Werner acting like lovers, and it was – Tobey Peters!"

"Well!" Goulette pondered that for a moment. "How did you learn this?"

Dantan told him of Vanessa Tate's visit.

"If this is true then his life could have been spared had we known his identity when we first heard his story. But at least now we know clearly how to proceed – in both cases! The only caveat is that it is all hearsay, we have no proof that he was the one. It certainly would fit... We'll bring Jumelle in first for interrogation, before the old woman. You've done well, Dantan. Very well."

Dantan felt very good.

27

She was alone in a crowded *boite.* A Negro drummer was banging on a huge drum with his large fists when one of the fists suddenly became his penis! Miri sat up in bed startled, opened her eyes, shaking her head trying to dispel the gross image, but the pounding continued, augmented by a female voice saying over and over, "Mademoiselle Veentair there is someone below to see you!"

Miri ran barefoot to the door and opened it a crack. One of the maids in her black and white uniform, a little wizened thing named Bernadette, repeated her message in an awed voice. She had been sent to fetch Miri for this visitor, something Reid Hall usually did not do. You were not supposed to have unexpected visitors. And for expected visitors you waited downstairs. "He's from the police!" she breathed, handing Miri his card.

"Alphonse Dantan!" Miri's heart started thumping. She looked down at her pink flannel nightgown. "I'll be down as soon as I can dress."

It was eight minutes to nine. If she wasn't in the dining-room seated by nine sharp she would not get any eggs that morning, only bread and coffee, but if the case had now been solved and Dantan had come over to ask her for a date now that his professional duties were concluded it was worth skipping breakfast.

She pulled on the cerise cashmere sweater Judy had given her, her navy skirt and the black patent-leather pumps she had bought in Italy and hadn't worn since going to La Scala during the holidays, and raced downstairs to the concierge's loge.

"Your guests are in first salon," she said.

"'Guests' plural?" Miri hurried to the indicated salon.

Unfortunately yes. There on the stuffed flowered sofa sat Judy Kugel, grinning! Dantan leaped to his feet as Miri entered. He had been close beside Judy. Judy's beaver coat had been tossed on the stuffed chair beside the sofa. She was wearing an ultramarine cashmere twin set and a scottish plaid skirt of deep-hued reds and greens and blues, her legs crossed and the upper one swinging back and forth, on her feet saddle shoes and white socks. What was Judy doing there? And why was she grinning like that?

"Mademoiselle Miri! Thank you for seeing me!" Dantan effused. "I have come to put to you some questions that have arisen in my mind in connection with the Werner case." He turned to Judy. "Judy was telling me something last night–"

"While we were in bed!" said Judy smugly.

"She was telling me something that may be evidence in the case." He waved Miri onto the couch beside Judy. She looked at her watch. It was one minute to nine.

"Wait here for me," Miri said coolly, "I haven't had breakfast yet." And she made a dash out of there for the dining-room, determined to get her scrambled eggs before she bothered answering any functionary's official questions. If he had been interested in her personally, she would gladly have skipped breakfast, but since he had just been in bed with Judy and was here only in an official capacity, she wasn't going to forego her scrambled eggs.

Vanessa had just dashed in to the dining-room too, joining Miri at the otherwise vacated table. The third-year-abroad in-crowd from Scarsdale and Texas and places like that in their decorous hats and princess coats and little white gloves

were standing around *tutoyer*ing one another in their
épouvantable accents waiting for the taxis that would carry them
off to whatever group activity was on that morning.

"Dantan has showed up here," Miri told her. "He wants
to ask me some questions about something Judy Kugel told
him that may be evidence in the case. I told him I wanted to
have my breakfast first."

"Dantan! I saw him yesterday. He's quite a guy."

"You saw Dantan?"

"Don't you remember? I told you I had a hunch about
the murder."

"Well don't get too excited about him, he's sleeping with
Judy. In fact he brought her along now."

"I'm burning with curiosity. Come by my room when
you're done and tell me all about it."

Miri was humiliated that Dantan had preferred that *vâche
qui rit* to her. And that she had wasted a minute thinking
about him. All the time she thought he was interested in her
and had only been waiting until the case was solved to ask
her out he had been sleeping with Judy. The two of them had
been snuggling in bed and probably laughing at her. What a
fool she was!

She was sick of this whole case. She had a good mind to
sneak off to the Jeu de Paume and let them stew there in the
salon until they figured out that she wasn't coming back.

But after going back to her room to change into comfortable shoes, she did go down to the salon to see what Dantan
wanted. Judy was now sprawled on the sofa with her head in
Dantan's lap but straightened up – slowly, once she was sure
Miri had seen her recumbent – when Miri entered.

"First I want to explain about us," she beamed, "then
Alphie can ask all the questions he wants."

Alphie!

"We're engaged!" Judy thrust her left hand forward and
sure enough there on the third finger was an old-fashioned
ornate ring. "His grandmother's!" she crowed.

Miri was stunned. "When's the wedding?"

"Not for awhile," Judy said. "I have to break it to my parents gently. They don't even know I'm serious about anyone, much less engaged. And it will take awhile for them to get used to the fact that Alphie isn't Jewish or even American."

And had no money, Miri knew all about that criterion already. And wasn't a doctor or lawyer, or even a dentist or accountant.

Miri shoved the beaver coat aside and slumped into the armchair. "Well? What do you want to ask, Monsieur Dantan?"

"When I first interviewed you *chez* Fleuris the morning Mademoiselle Werner's body was discovered, you seemed *enrheumée*, Mademoiselle Miri. When did that condition begin?"

She certainly didn't expect to be asked about her cold. "What's that got to do with anything?"

"I'll explain later. Please respond, Mademoiselle Miri."

"Oh Alphie, drop the 'mademoiselle', call her 'Miri'," said Judy, "you'll have to start getting used to the way we Americans are."

"But why, cherie? We are living in France."

Judy smiled and for once said nothing.

"In any case – Miri – would you please recall for me when you first began sneezing?"

"I woke up with a cold the same morning we learned that Emilie had been murdered."

"That would be Monday, the eighteenth of January?"

"It was a Monday all right. I don't know the date offhand."

"But it was surely two weeks ago?"

"Yes."

"Then it was the eighteenth."

"If you say so."

"And then your cold disappeared when you left the house that morning?"

"Right. I was concentrating on it."

Judy giggled, "You thought that your existentialism and belief in your will made it go away."

"Then when you and Judy –" here he actually squeezed her hand! – "called on Gabrielle, Emilie's cat entered the room, prompting you to sneeze again."

"What is all this? And how come you have such a line on my cold?"

Judy bubbled, "I was just telling Alphie how funny you were, thinking you had gotten rid of your cold by willing it away, because you were an existentialist, when actually what seemed to be happening was that whenever you got away from the source of the thing you were allergic to, you stopped sneezing. And then started again when you were near it."

Just as Miri suspected, they had been lying in bed laughing at her! Her face burned with humiliation.

Dantan thanked Miri effusively for allowing them to trouble her. "Now I leave you two charming demoiselles to put your pretty heads together and confide things I know I will never get to hear. *Au revoir.*" He kissed Judy before departing from the salon, then put his head back in. "Mademoiselle Miri, would you be so kind as to step outside for a moment?"

She did so while Judy was gathering up her fur coat and handbag and satiny black leather Italian gloves.

"One more question, which I do not want Judy to hear. The person who told you he had seen Philippe Jumelle in a restaurant with Emilie Werner, was his name Tobey Peters?"

As Tobey was dead there was no reason to protect the anonymity he had requested. "Yes."

"Thank you, Mademoiselle Miri."

Miri went back into the salon mystified.

Judy was spinning herself around like a top, arms outstretched, before plopping on the stuffed sofa. "Isn't he wonderful?" she beamed. "Oh I must tell you, that sweater looks great on you!"

"That's irrelevant for goodness' sake, tell me what this is all about."

"Alphie is about to solve the murder of Emilie Werner and possibly another murder besides! Goulette had been off on another tangent, still thinking Pierre Poivriere did it but he gave Alphie full access to the files, and evidence and what-not and implied that if he solved it Goulette would help him get the post he wants. It's looking really good! As a bilingual detective he would get to investigate some of the most potentially sensitive cases."

"You mean like this one?"

"No, this is a purely personal tragedy. I mean cases with possible political ramifications. It couldn't come at a better time, just as we are planning to get married!"

Judy launched happily into a detailed account of the progress of their romance. It had started when she went to see him with the information they had drawn from Gabrielle about Pierre Poivriere. That's when it started. They went to bed at once. It was incredible. They kept seeing each other every day and it got more incredible. After a week they started talking about getting engaged, and last night they did.

"There's a few little things to iron out," Judy said, "but I'm not worried."

"Like what?"

"Well for one thing he expects my father to give us a *dot*; a dowry. Of course Daddy will give us a generous wedding-gift, once he agrees to the marriage at all, that is. But it's not the kind of money Alphie seems to have in mind. It's the French way, though, so he's pretty stubborn on the point."

"But it's not the American way."

"Exactly what I told him. He doesn't have a very high opinion of Americans and their ways, though."

"And the French are so terrific?"

"Exactly what I think. And I think Daddy will want to give us a house as a wedding-present, that's what he did for my brother Ellis, three blocks from my parents' house."

That took Miri's breath away, the idea of being given a whole house! "That's incredible!"

"Well it would be except that Alphie thinks we're going to live in France. He wouldn't dream of moving to the States. And I kind of like the idea of living here too. For awhile, anyway. Of course if I were going to have a baby I would go right back home to have it at Long Island Jewish Hospital, I wouldn't trust the doctors here."

"Why not? Lots of Frenchwomen seem to have babies."

"But they're all Catholic. If something goes wrong during delivery and they can't save both, they save the baby, and let the mother die."

"I didn't know that. Is Dantan – Alphie – Catholic?"

""Yes and no. That is, he was born a Catholic, baptised and all, but he doesn't practice any religion now. When he was ten his old auntie had the Resistance ship him out of France to England where they were taking in refugee children, mostly Jewish. He kind of lost his taste for any religion somewhere along the line. But my father will blow his stack when he finds out Alphie isn't Jewish. If he gets too upset I'm going to remind him, 'at least Alphie's white and heterosexual'. My brother Ellis had a Negro girlfriend once, long before he got married, and my parents really were out of their heads.

"I think they'll come around eventually. My mother won't care so much, she just wants me to get married, have babies and if possible be happy, but she won't dare contradict my father, she's going to go along with anything he says. What I'm hoping is that my father will be able to convince Alphie to go into the business with him and Ellis, that way we would have to live in Great Neck. And that way there would probably be less chance for him to find mistresses."

"You're worried that he'll be looking for a mistress? What's he getting married for? Is it for your Daddy's money?"

"Of course not! He doesn't even know how much they have, he's never asked me. And anyway, I don't know. But he told me that Frenchmen are such great lovers of women that they can't be expected to be faithful to just one for their whole life."

"And you're going along with that?"

Judy shrugged. "I'm not crazy about it, but at least he's honest."

"I've got a great idea!" Miri said. "Don't get married! Just have an affair with him. Then you don't have to tell your parents anything! And then when Alphie strays you can too!"

"But," she wailed, "I *want* to get married. More than anything in the world."

"Why?"

Judy stared at her. "I love him. And he loves me. I'm hungry, let's go get hot chocolate and croissants. My treat."

So Miri ran up to her room to get her coat, remembering when she got to the second floor that she had promised to look in on Vanessa, so she collected her and the three of them went to the Café Montparnasse for a mid-morning snack.

Vanessa was curious to hear what Dantan had wanted. At each of his questions she nodded as if that was no more than she expected but would say little more. She was, however, effusive in her congratulations to Judy on her engagement.

"What was it that Alphie asked you when he asked you to step outside the salon?" Judy wanted to know.

"Nothing much. How was London, by the way?"

"I wasn't in London, I was staying with Alphie. I'm going to stay with him tonight too. But tomorrow there's going to be a surprise-party...oops!" she clapped a hand over her mouth with a sidelong glance at Vanessa, who didn't seem to have heard.

"Are you coming for Sunday coffee *chez* Fleuris?" Judy asked with a straight face.

"Yes, Bran said he especially wanted me to come tomorrow. It's my birthday and I think he's going to surprise me with a cake. I pretended I didn't notice how anxious he was to get me over there tomorrow."

"Then I didn't give away the secret?" Judy asked.

Vanessa smiled, her eyes in a squint, and shook her head.

Miri had another surprise waiting for her when she returned from Café Montparnasse. Another unexpected visitor. Seymour Levin. He was grinning from ear to ear, and since his ears stuck out, it was a very wide grin.

"What are you doing here?"

"I've been transferred to FOUSAP!"

"To Paris? You never mentioned it in your last letter."

"I didn't want you to get your defenses up, and go hide out. So I decided I would just drop in after I got settled in my new office and new apartment."

"You already have an apartment?"

"Yep. They give us cost-of-living allowances. I got a great place from another fellow who was going stateside. You can see Notre Dame if you stand up in the bathtub. Want to come over and see it?"

"Now?"

"No time like the present."

Seymour's apartment was small and cozy. He was like a big bear in a small cave. It had a woodburning fireplace in the little living-room. And it was true that if you stood up in the bathtub you could see Notre Dame. The tub in the bathroom was a small sitting tub with a built-in seat and a hand-shower. There was a bidet, toilet and sink all crammed into a space the size of a closet. It had been some kind of pantry before, but the landlord knew that if he wanted to rent to Americans, for much more money than he could get from any French tenants, as the Americans who worked for the U.S. government in Paris got cost-of-living and hardship allowances, as well as much higher salaries than the French, he would have to install a bathroom.

The kitchen despite the loss of a pantry was a spacious room.

The bedroom would have seemed normal-sized but the bed was huge, much bigger than the usual French bed. It was a mattress and box-spring, no headboards, as French head-boards would have been too small. The previous American had ordered the mattress and box-spring from the States, and then sold it to the next American tenant: Seymour.

Miri and Seymour tried it out and found it acceptable. Miri had decided it was time anyway, and she remembered that Vanessa had said that Jewish men were the best in bed, so at least she was starting at the top.

Seymour made spaghetti and meatballs with canned spaghetti sauce from the PX for supper and Miri made scrambled eggs and toast for breakfast. They didn't bother to go out until it was time to go to the Fleuris' for the coffee-hour and Vanessa's birthday cake. By then Miri was in a stupor.

Seymour had bought her a present at the PX. "I didn't want to give it to you earlier," he grinned, "I didn't want you to think it was a bribe. But I was going to give it to you no matter what happened, or didn't."

He took a small black box from the top drawer of his chest of drawers and handed it to her.

She opened the box with trepidation. In it were a pair of pendant garnet earrings. A gleaming deep red.

"Real bohemian garnets," he said. "It's amazing what they have at the PX."

"But why?"

"Just because I like you. No ulterior motives, no strings attached. Hey, they'll go terrifically with that great sweater you have."

Miri felt nervous receiving this gift. But she didn't shove it back at him only because he seemed so pleased with himself at finding such a beautiful thing and giving it to her. She put on the earrings, feeling very strange. They finished dressing and went to the Fleuris' coffee hour.

They were greeted at the door by Germaine, who had been summoned to service although it was Sunday. She was wearing an old but well-pressed gray uniform and a white apron. On her big flat feet were the usual felt carpet-slippers.

As they were peeling off their coats, Judy Kugel arrived, alone. Germaine's face cracked in multiple places as it broke into an unaccustomed smile. "Mademoiselle Judy! A delightful surprise awaits you!"

"Alphie must be here!" Judy grinned at them, flinging her Persian lamb coat into Germaine's hands. "He said he would meet me here."

"In the salon," grinned Germaine.

The three of them hurried into the main salon. Alphonse Dantan was not there but on one of Madame Fleuris' fragile-looking settees a plump little middle-aged couple were sitting primly, and grinning from ear to ear.

"Mommy! Daddy!" Judy shrieked, flinging herself at them. The three of them embraced and kissed kissed kissed, then laughed laughed laughed, then babbled babbled babbled.

Monsieur Fleuris smiled indulgently at this display of American exuberance, while Madame Fleuris sitting as straight as a queen and presiding over the silver coffee-pot on a little table in front of her, stared straight ahead of her as if in a trance. Philippe and Lucille Jumelle, in armchairs near the window, watched the Kugel family reunion at a slight distance and smiled wanly at each other.

It seemed that after hearing from Miri on the phone the previous Sunday that their only daughter, the apple of their eye and their perfect little princess, was living in a building where a murder had occurred, Mr. and Mrs. Kugel had sailed on the very next ship out, First Class. They had rushed from their hotel directly to Rue des Ecoles. Before Judy got there they had been assured by Madame Fleuris that a mad killer was not on the rampage, and they had also been informed that their baby was having an affair with a penniless French cop, and that the affair had been quasi-legitimized by an actual engagement sealed with his grandmother's ring.

Judy introduced Miri to her parents, and Miri introduced Seymour Levin. Mrs. Kugel inspected each of them from top to toe, but both parents' interest was clearly in meeting Judy's "young man". That occurred soon. Alphonse Dantan arrived and now put in his appearance in the salon. The Kugels and their prospective son-in-law huddled happily until Bran and Vanessa arrived, were introduced to Judy's parents. Jamie was the last to arrive.

Somehow they all found themselves singing "Happy Birthday" to Vanessa, who looked embarassed and pleased as Germaine carried in the gooey pink and white birthday cake with candles on it and scrawled around the circumference on top in pink buttercream, "*joyeax anniversaire chère* Vanessa" which had been ordered by Branford Duane Lee the Third. Very strange doings for a Communist!

The cake was cut and eaten together with cups of coffee surpassing the weak brew of the mornings at the pension, the conversational din was rising, when several unexpected new arrivals walked in, led by Inspector Goulette.

Vanessa whispered to Miri, "This is it!"

"This is what?"

But Vanessa put a finger to her lips.

Judy introduced the chief inspector to her parents, and had the pleasure of once again announcing her engagement and showing her ring. Miri noticed that Bran looked from Judy's outstretched left hand to Vanessa, who turned her head away with a little smile.

Dantan and Goulette conferred briefly, then Inspector Goulette whispered a few words in Madame Fleuris' ear, at which she rose stiffly and accompanied him out of the salon through the double doors to the dining-room. Alphonse Dantan remained in the salon with Judy and his future parents-in-law. Judy had slipped her arm around his waist, he did the same with hers, and the two of them stood there entwined, Judy with a self-satisfied smile and Dantan looking slightly embarassed, as his future father-in-law asked him questions about his line of work.

One of the policemen came into the salon and exchanged a few words with Dantan, who followed him out of the room, returning moments later to speak softly with Monsieur Fleuris. The old man spoke briefly in muted tones with his daughter, then shuffled with the younger man back to the dining-room.

Lucille and Philippe exchanged whispered words, Lucille sobbing and rushing from the room immediately afterwards.

This was too much for Judy, who urged Vanessa and Miri to join her as she looked into what was going on.

The three of them started toward the dining-room but were diverted by the sight of Madame Fleuris, in her black coat and the hat with the feather and little veil, bearing herself with rigid dignity, and carrying a small valise, tears streaming down her expressionless face, accompanied by Inspector Goulette and followed by a sad Monsieur Fleuris, his eyes also tearing, emerging from the hallway to her private rooms toward the front hall.

At the door she whirled on her husband and told him not to follow, then left with the inspector.

Monsieur Fleuris rejoined his daughter and her husband in the salon, the three of them urging the others to enjoy their coffee, but they had to leave.

They looked utterly miserable. The twinkle had gone from old Bushy-Beard's eyes, he was crying, while Lucille cowered beside her husband, whose countenance had turned purplish-red. They hurried into the front hall, where they put on their coats and left.

Germaine immediately began bustling with more coffee and clean cups and saucers while keeping up a line of unintelligible patter unnatural to her dour taciturn nature. The Kugels looking baffled turned from one person to another with no explanation forthcoming.

Vanessa had sunk onto the floor cross-legged. Bran dropped down beside her, hugging his knees. Jamie was perched on one of the little carved chairs, sipping the fresh coffee Germaine had dispensed, patiently awaiting whatever was to be. Jamie was in a sad mood, he had attended the funeral of his friend Tobey Peters that morning.

Alphonse Dantan now rejoined the group. He explained to them the meaning of what they had witnessed, the arrest of Madame Fleuris. But when he began to explain how it had come about, his prospective father-in-law stopped him.

The Kugels had arrived only hours before on the boat train from LeHavre, taken a taxi from Gare du Nord to the Ritz hotel, remaining only long enough to oversee the satisfactory hauling of their trunks and valises and parcels up to their double suite before rushing in another taxi over to 10 *bis* Rue des Ecoles to check on their darling Judy's vital signs. They were now showing signs of wear.

Mr and Mrs Kugel wanted to go back to their hotel for a rest first, and Mr Kugel invited all present to be his guests at a sumptuous dinner that evening, at which all the talking could be done.

The Kugels would host a dinner for everyone in a private room at "some nice restaurant like Maxim's", to be selected with the aid of their prospective son-in-law, whose impeccable English and charming manners had impressed him enough to entrust the choice of restaurant to him, while at the same time arousing his suspicions that those very characteristics strongly suggested he was an "operator" and an unsatisfactory match for their darling daughter.

Murmurs of agreement were heard all around. Germaine, the remaining holdout at Fort Fleuris, was relieved to learn that they were all leaving the apartment. She could clean up and go home.

Everyone went off to unpack, make love, rest, bathe, dress, or whatever seemed the most appropriate use of the interval.

The elder Kugels insisted that Judy come straight to their hotel suite as soon as she had changed her clothes. They seemed particularly concerned that she not dawdle with Dantan. Judy asked Miri to come over early to her parents' suite to rescue her from what promised to be a continuous grilling about Alphie.

28

Inspector Goulette escorted Madame Fleuris into his office and ordered coffee. Vouray and Dantan did not partake of the coffee: they would be busy taking notes.

She was an old woman who should have lived out her remaining years calmly with her family around her, seeing her grandson grow up and marry and himself father a family. Instead she would be going to prison. Goulette often marveled at the stupidity of persons who committed serious crimes, persons who did not seem stupid but did the stupidest thing of all: destroy their own lives.

Goulette knew with almost absolute certainty that Madame Goulette had been present in Emilie Werner's room the fatal Sunday night. The cat Mitsou had betrayed her!

For Madame Fleuris by her own testimony had brought a blanket upstairs to put in Miriam Winter's room, more driven, he suspected, by Madame's need for an excuse to go upstairs than to make things more comfortable for her young *pensionnaire.*

Before placing the blanket in Miriam Winter's room she had stopped off to call on Emilie Werner. She had offered the young woman hot chocolate laced with paregoric. She said she had brought it for Mademoiselle Winter who, however, was not in her room (as Madame Fleuris well knew!). She waited patiently while Mademoiselle Werner sipped the chocolate, the blanket she had brought placed somewhere where Mitsou the cat had left her telltale hairs. Mitsou herself must have crept into the room, may have curled up on the blanket. For when Miriam Winter crawled under the blanket hours later, she began sneezing uncontrollably and continued to do so until some time after she had left the source of the irritation.

(Dantan was thrilled that his intuition had been correct, and that he had followed up with Judy's friend on the timing of her sneezing episodes. Dear Judy had in the first place called this to his attention with her ridicule of her friend Miri who had thought it was an "existentialist act of will" that had caused her sneezing to cease.)

As Goulette already knew that Emilie Werner was the little friend of Madame Fleuris' son-in-law, having heard this from the hapless man's own lips, he confronted Madame Fleuris with his theory that she had been the killer.

Tears welling up in her eyes, but her back as straight and stiff as a queen, she admitted to what she had done. And she explained how and why it had come about.

The occasional tea at Rumpelmayers which Tobey Peters offered her was the only treat Madame Fleuris enjoyed from one month to the next. It was paltry compared to what she would have liked, paltry in the extreme compared to what her rich neighbor Madame Poivriere could afford, but she made the most of it, dressing carefully and formally and trying to get herself iton a cheerful frame of mind. She enjoyed the interested glances she received in the company of the handsome prosperous-looking young man, who could easily have been assumed to be her son; a devoted son.

Their rendez-vous took place approximately monthly whenever Tobey Peters was in Paris. He frequently visited Spain, particularly Andalusia, where he had a lover, a would-be matador. It was for this reason that he needed Madame Fleuris' assistance in forwarding mail to his mother and his grandmother, each of whom provided him a generous allowance to live the kind of life in Paris they would approve of, namely, genteel playboy courting or at least flirting with suitably highborn females. So Monsieur Peters duly kept them informed of his frivolous but heterosexual life – a pure fiction which he embroidered convincingly in his letters.

Madame Fleuris knew this because she steamed open each of Monsieur Peters' letters and read them before stamping them with French stamps and mailing them.

Besides taking her to tea on the days when he handed over letters to mail, Tobey Peters paid Madame Fleuris a stipend for the service. But she truly enjoyed the thoughtfulness of his taking her out as much as the payment.

On the first Tuesday of December in 1953 the excursion became a nightmare.

They had finished two pots of fine tea, a plateful of delicate open sandwiches and anther of exquisite *galettes.* Monsieur Peters had then lit an English cigarette and was puffing it and looking at its ashy tip appreciatively when he said, "Oops, I almost forgot, Madame. I have something interesting to tell you. I was slumming with a friend in a small brasserie near Pigalle, where they have surprisingly irresistible cassoulet, when I was surprised to notice at a nearby table – all the tables in that tiny place are near one another! – your son-in-law! He was not alone. He was sitting side by side on a banquette with a very young lady and they were too amorously occupied to notice me gaping at them before I pulled myself together and urged my friend to leave with me at once. Fortunately we had already finished our marvelous cassoulet. We went elsewhere for dessert, coffee and brandies before Monsieur Jumelle could spot me. Assuming he would even remember me from more than a year ago on the occasional Sunday when I joined your family group for coffee."

"You must be be mistaken, Monsieur Peters," Madame Fleuris said coldly, even as an icicle of dread stabbed her in the heart. "My Lucille's Philippe would not betray her. You haven't seen Philippe in over a year, and you were not a steady guest at the Sunday coffees. You mistook someone else for Philippe."

"Madame Fleuris, I assure you it was he. I would not have imparted such information, sure to hurt you, if I were not certain of his identity. I thought you would want to know."

Madame Fleuris nodded brusquely and kept her head down. In her heart she believed him, but would not admit it.

She was devastated. She had always thanked *le bon dieu* that her daughter had married an upstanding righteous man, unlike herself, whose whole adult life had been poisoned by her husband's infidelity and fecklessness.

"What is the name of the restaurant?"

"Dans l'Ombre du Moulin. Rue Clauzel. Are you thinking of hiring an investigator? It was on Thursday evening last that I saw her."

"No no. Not at all. I don't believe it was Philippe."

But she did believe it had been Philippe, and she had every intention of finding out who the young woman was; what she was.

She wasn't sure just what she was going to do about it, but she was resolved to do something; something definitive that would save her daughter's marriage and, if possible, also spare her feelings. It infuriated Madame Fleuris to think that she herself had put up with a feckless unfaithful spouse all her long life and now her daughter, her only child, whom she had done all she could to help marry someone who wouldn't do that to her, was at risk.

Madame Fleuris began her quest that Thursday evening, rushing out immediately after her simple supper with her husband, and taking a taxi to Rue Clauzel. She had a secret store of money, not a fortune, but enough for such splurges. She didn't want to actually enter the restaurant if she could help it, and indeed with one glance from the doorway she could see that Philippe was not there. She was relieved, and yet disappointed. Because she believed what Monsieur Peters had told her, and she believed that Philippe would turn up again with his *amie,* but of course it was not certain that it would be to the same restaurant.

Rue Clauzel was not a locale where Madame Fleuris could stand around on a vigil. She entered a smoky bar across the street from the restaurant and sipped a cognac for an hour before giving up.

That Sunday when the Jumelles came for Sunday dinner *en famille*, no boarders until coffee, Madame Fleuris did all she could to turn the conversation to the general topic of off-the-beaten-path restaurants. But she was clumsy at this sort of indirection, where subtlety was required, and she learned nothing.

She repeated her vigil in Pigalle the following Tuesday and again on Wednesday and by Thursday was already being acknowledged with a nod by the bartender as a strange regular, an old lady in a thickly veiled black hat and black coat, amid workmen and suspect young females.

Then on Thursday she saw them! Philippe and a thin young woman half his age. He had his arm around her waist as the two entered the brasserie. Madame waited in the bar sipping cognacs for almost two hours, until the couple emerged from the brasserie. Madame Fleuris left payment and tip on the table and slipped outside. Fortunately for her the pair had separated, Philippe toward the Metro, the young woman in the opposite direction. Madame Fleuris followed behind her. There were others strolling on the street. It was easy to be anonymous.

She followed the young woman to a small seedy hotel, and was tempted to enter and ask the concierge who she was, proferring a generous tip of course, but decided that it was too risky to be seen by the concierge. She hadn't decided yet what she was going to do with any information she could gather. She wanted to know who the girl was, where she lived – was it at this dreary hotel? – where she worked, how often she met with Philippe, whether their rendez-vous had reached the bedroom yet.

Then what would she do about it? Try to buy off the girl? Confront her son-in-law? Or what?

Later that night Madame Fleuris took a taxi to the girl's hotel, having made an arrangement with the driver. He was to speak with the concierge of the hotel, offer a tip for the girl's name and any other information he could obtain.

The driver earned his tip.

He learned not only the girl's name – Emilie Werner – but the fact that she had lived in the hotel for over a year, worked in the Galeries Lafayette and did bring a man in from time to time, usually the same one. Madame Fleuris had the taxi drive her home, gratified to have accomplished this much and her mind spinning with possibilities of what to do next.

Once she knew something about the girl she ventured to take a closer look at her, and went to the Galeries Lafayette to browse among the handbags and covertly take in glimpses of Mademoiselle Werner. This was when she happened to see the concentration-camp tattoo on Emilie's arm. It infuriated Madame Fleuris. She gave not a single thought to what had happened to Emilie to cause that tattoo, all she thought of was that her son-in-law was betraying her daughter – with a Jewess! It was probably at that moment that Emilie's fate was decided, although Madame Fleuris only recalled that her first idea was to lure Emilie Werner to rent the room at 10 *bis* Rue des Ecoles so as to make it more difficult for Philippe to meet with her. But the thought that this girl was a Jew continued to rankle her.

Madame Fleuris was known at the student housing bureau. She had listed her own rooms frequently and had followed up with small tips to the clerks to ensure that they put her listings forward. So it was not noticed particularly when she examined the Poivriere listing, then took a blank listing form and later filled it in with Madame Poivriere's information.

Returning to the handbags counter at Galeries Lafayette at a moment when it was bustling with customers, Madame Fleuris merely left the listing on the counter, and prayed.

Her prayer was answered.

Emilie Werner did find the room-for-rent notice, she did apply for the room and rented it. The timing was felicitous. Emilie's move occurred during the Christmas holidays, while Philippe was in the Midi with his family.

Seeing that the new tenant quickly got acquainted with Gabrielle, and also with her own tenant Miriam Winter, Madame Fleuris realized that she had to act quickly. She wasn't able to accomplish her purpose before Philippe returned from visiting his family, but did so about two weeks later.

Madame Fleuris knew that Tobey Peters was the only person who could attribute a motive to her for the killing, but she was counting on his need for discretion about his own life to refrain from doing anything about this knowledge. She was however prepared to deal with him if the need and occasion arose. This occurred in late January when he contacted her and invited her to their usual rendez-vous for tea. He was prepared to toy with her! To hold over her his secret knowledge for the pleasure of torturing her from time to time. But she was prepared and it was an easy matter to deal with him by putting poison in his tea.

29

Miri left Seymour's apartment to take her bath at Reid Hall and change into her navy princess dress. The garnet earrings looked perfect with it. (She couldn't think of anything they wouldn't look perfect with.) Then she went over to the Ritz early, as Judy had requested. Seymour was to meet them there later. Miri was directed up to the Kugels' double suite. Outside the door she could hear Mrs Kugel within saying, "Now that fella your friend Miriam has, Seymour Levin, there's a *mensch*!"

So Miri didn't knock. She stood there listening.

"I'm very glad for Miri, she's a real wallflower, she was going around for four months with a fairy and didn't even know it! And she was so stuck on him she wouldn't go out on any blind dates or anything. I tried to fix her up with a buddy of Norman Barnett's when they came to Paris on leave..."

"Norman Barnett looked you up?"

"Yes."

"Now there's a *mensch*!"

"Oh Mommy, Norman Barnett was just out for a good time, which is fine, but that was all. You only like him because he's Jewish and he graduated from Columbia law school. He's a makeout artist."

"All men are, baby. Didn't I teach you how to handle them? You haven't known this Alphonse person very long, Judy baby."

"Mommy I know him long enough to know I love him."

"Well I don't think you could be happy in the long run with this – Alphonse. What kind of a name is Alphonse anyway? Reminds me of Alphonse and Gaston. 'After you, my dear Alphonse, no after you, my dear Gaston'. Or was it the other way around? Doesn't matter, they were both ridiculous. And meant to be. But this is your life, bubbala. You can't afford to mess it up. Well at least you'll have a chance to think it over once you're back home, which will be very soon. We've already booked our return passage – and yours. You'll realize what a fish out of water Alphonse would be in Great Neck."

"Then maybe we should live in France!"

"Your father would never allow that, you know that."

"I'm free, white and twenty-one, how could he stop me?"

"Don't be foolish, Judy, you don't want to break your father's heart, do you? Or your mother's for that matter? And believe me, if you ever did such a thing – God forbid! – he wouldn't give you one red cent!"

"I love Alphie and I'm going to marry him. I'll do what Miriam Winter did, she has been self-supporting ever since graduating high school, putting herself through school and working three jobs to do it. I'll get a job too."

"Miriam Winter is another bargain. She's not at all like your nice friends back home. She's... she's... bad news."

"That's why I like her, she's different. She's independent."

"Independent! God help me!"

Miri rapped heavily on the door.

Mrs. Kugel opened it a crack, then saw who it was and welcomed Miri warmly. "We were just talking about you, dear, were your ears burning? Judy was telling me what fun you girls have been having in Paris."

"I didn't come to Paris to have fun," Miri said coldly, angry at Mrs Kugel's cheery hypocrisy.

"No? Then what on earth did you come for?"

"To become a better artist."

"Oh. Artist. I see. And did you? Become a better artist?"

Although her painting of Bethel Washton in the Chinese robe was pretty good, it was only one painting, and the really big *magnum opus* she was working on with all the priests and nuns and kids she had no idea when she would finish it, and she hated all the previous ones and as Aristotle said, one swallow didn't make a summer so she answered "Not yet."

"Well at least you're honest."

"Oh Mommy, Miri's very honest!"

Miri grinned at Judy. "Just like Alphie!"

Mrs Kugel looked at Judy bewildered. "What does that mean, baby?"

"Oh nothing, just a private little joke. – I wonder what's taking Daddy so long?" To Miri Judy explained, "My father went with Alphie to make a reservation in person, to make sure he approved of the restaurant and to tip the *maître d'* to make sure we got a good table."

At six-thirty the others all began showing up at the Kugels' hotel and Mr Kugel led them to a restaurant near the Place de la Concorde which was decorated like a nineteenth century whorehouse, with plushy red velvet covering every inch of ceiling and those walls not of polished carved mahogany. The furnishings likewise were plushy red velvet with carved lionheads tipping the armrests, and little lamps with tan silk lampshades and beaded tassels were on each table. An immense elaborate crystal chandelier sparkled and clinked dangerously over their heads. The setting could have been out of Toulouse Lautrec except that his ineffably sad absinthe drinker was absent, as were the can-can dancers and the piggish men-about-town.

The *maître d'* and assistants, all in black and white evening dress, descended on the group like a flock of predatory penguins. There was not another soul in the restaurant at that early hour. Even if the Kugels had not engaged a private room they would have had total privacy in the main dining-room.

Coats were taken by a servile coat-taker in a tuxedo. Judy and her mother retained their furs which they had flung over their chairs. Introductions of those who hadn't met were made. Vanessa whispered to Miri that she thought Seymour Levin was much more sexy than Alphonse Dantan, who was good looking but in a somewhat frail Gerard Philippe kind of way. Seymour was big and robust. Miri was very gratified at Vanessa's approval, and also glad that Vanessa had Branford Duane Lee!

The first round of many bottles of wine was brought, tasted by Mister Kugel, accepted, and poured all around, a toast to everyone's health was proposed and drunk, and then Alphonse Dantan was urged by everyone to begin his explanation of how the murder case was solved.

He stood at his place at the large round table, calm at being the center of attention, not embarassed but not showing off either. Judy was on his right, Mrs Kugel on his left. Mister Kugel was between his wife and Seymour. Jamie sat between Judy and Branford, Miri sat between Seymour and Vanessa, who was on Branford's right. The *maître d'* had tried to arrange them male-female-male-female... but Vanessa and Miri wanted to talk, and Mister Kugel definitely favored having Seymour beside him, someone with at least a modicum of business sense with whom he could converse. He had already sized up his would-be son-in-law.

"Fortunately for my professional advancement as well as for my personal life," Dantan smiled at Judy, "Judy and I became close during this investigation. It was her delightful chatter, designed to amuse, which in fact was of critical utility in informing me of events whose comprehending led to the solution of the murder of Mademoiselle Werner."

Judy was smiling blissfully at her man.

"At the beginning of the case we knew little of the victim, Emilie Werner. Twenty-four years of age, employed as a salesclerk at the Galeries Lafayette, no known criminal connections although she had previously resided at a questionable hotel in Pigalle which catered to hourly guests. The more painful aspects of her life were learned later.

"Initially the investigations of the police were directed by a witness toward Monsieur James Giardini." Here a sympathetic nod toward Jamie. "I myself, I say truly, who participated in all the interviews engaging Monsieur Giardini, solely as an interpreter, mind you, not as an investigator, never for a moment believed that he had committed the crime."

Jamie and Miri exchanged smirks as of old. It was easy for him to say that now!

"Madame Fleuris told Inspector Goulette that she had seen Monsieur Giardini emerging from Mademoioselle Werner's room the night before, at approximately eight in the evening when she had mounted to the sixth floor to put an additional blanket on Mademoiselle Winter's bed. Mademoiselle Miri corroborated that she had in fact found an additional blanket on her bed when she returned to her room late that fateful Sunday night."

Jamie listened to all this with a cynical little smile.

"Intensive questioning of Monsieur Giardini did not result in any information which would have cleared him of suspicion. Although he might have been able to clear himself had he been willing to provide the names of individuals with whom he had been during the crucial period, he consistently refused to do so, for reasons about which we have no need at this time to speculate."

Here Jamie grinned at Miri and gave a thumbs up.

"His resistance to revealing the identity of individuals who might have cleared him in itself suggested his innocence.

"On the other hand, why should Madame Fleuris lie about having seen Monsieur Giardini at the scene of the crime at the crucial time? The explanation could only be, it seemed at the time, that she had been mistaken. That in the dark, with her failing aging eyes, she had mistaken the intruder for her own *pensionnaire*, a logical mistake since his room was right on the sixth floor where the crime took place. As for seeing the intruder entering another room right after emerging from Mademoiselle Werner's, Madame Fleuris could have mistaken which room he entered. Rather than Monsieur Giardini's he might have slipped into, for instance, the *bonne* Gabrielle's.

"Early interviews with another resident in the *immeuble*, namely the widow Poivriere," Dantan continued, sipping his wine with evident appreciation, "who after all had rented the room to the victim, revealed that her son who had moved to the provinces after his marriage had been in Paris and at his mother's apartment at the time of the murder. This seemed a richer vein to mine. An attractive scion who comes to town from time to time without his wife, a pretty young woman residing upstairs in privacy in a room owned by his mother, who perhaps had rented the room in the first place because of the young man of the family... How convenient it would be for him. He could visit his mother for dinner, then taste a little *amour* for dessert, his comings and goings unobserved by the concierge or anyone who might betray his clandestine affair to his wife... All very discreet.

"Several facts pointed to Pierre Poivriere's involvement in the crime. One. Monsieur Poivriere and his mother had told us that he departed before eight that Sunday evening. The concierge reported to the inspector that Pierre Poivriere left the building at least two hours later than that, around ten.

"Thanks to girlish gossip rather than professional inter-rogation, we were to learn that Monsieur Pierre Poivriere was indeed making a visit within the *immeuble* to someone on the *sixième*, but it was not to Emilie Werner as we had suspected, but to the *bonne* Gabrielle who worked for his mother. When it was put to him that his little *amie* had reported it he admit-ted it. He awaited Gabrielle alone in her room, placing him very near the scene of the crime during the critical period.

"A *pneumatique* found by the police among the victim's belongings addressed to Mademoiselle Werner at her previ-ous address was signed 'Pierre'.

"The police medical investigations revealed that she had indeed died of strangulation and that shortly before her death she had ingested a an opiate, not enough to cause death, but

sufficient to sedate her rather quickly, so that the act of strangulation, or to be more precise, garroting, took place calmly
with little or no resistance from the victim. The stomach contents of the victim suggested that the drug had been incorpo-
rated in a sizable drink of hot chocolate.

"The killer had offered the victim the drink of chocolate,
waiting until it had a soporific effect, then garroted her with a
thin strong cord, then once the girl was dead, wrapped the
silk scarf, the girl's own property, around her neck. No cup
with remains of chocolate was found in Mademoiselle Werner's
room. But this circumstance was corroborated in the even-
tual confession of the killer.

"This elaborate preparation and activity could only have
been performed by someone the victim was willing to admit
to her room, and from whom she trustingly would accept a
cup of chocolate.

"Pierre Poivriere certainly belonged to this subset of individuals. His unacknowledged presence on the sixth floor
the night of the crime, and the signature on the *pneu* certainly
pointed toward him, although not unequivocally.

"But then upon closer inspection of the *pneumatique* it
was noted that the name 'Pierre' was surrounded by quota-
tion marks. A subtle point but a telling one. For it seemed to
imply that the name 'Pierre' was not, literally, the writer's
name, but was a pet-name or an assumed name."

"Your discovery!" Miri whispered to Vanessa.

Vanessa shrugged.

"What was to be made of this, however, remained cloudy
until later information rearranged the focus of the investigation. At first the signature 'Pierre' on the *pneu* and the presence of Pierre Poivriere at the scene at the hour, together with
the ownership of the victim's room, Madame Poivriere,
seemed telling indications of possible guilt."

"A possible motive," Dantan went on, "apart from innocent error, for Madame Fleuris having identified the visitor to
Mademoiselle Werner's room as her lodger Monsieur Jamie

Giardini, when – or if – in fact it had been Monsieur Pierre Poivriere, was brought to my attention once more by the invaluable chatter of my now *fiancée*." Another squeeze, another soulful gaze into the eyes.

"She reported to me that her ever-observant friend Miri – "here a condescending smile at Miri – "had discovered the extreme similarity of two samples of handwriting, one that of Madame Fleuris – a little notice to her *pensionnaires*, and the other, that of Madame Poivriere, in the form of a room-referral from the student-housing bureau in the possession of Mademoiselle Werner, and accidentally acquired by Mademoiselle Miri in the pages of a book passed to her from Gabrielle, who had received it from the poor victim.

"From the similarity of the handwriting on these two documents, Mademoiselle Miri had inferred that the two ladies had learned penmanship together as girls, had been lifelong friends, and when Madame Fleuris saw her friend's son in a most compromising position, emerging from the room of the young woman found murdered the next morning, Madame Fleuris lied and placed the blame on someone who meant much less to her, her lodger Monsieur Giardini.

"At the time this seemed to be an interesting corroborating footnote to our suspicions of the guilt of Monsieur Pierre Poivriere. Much later this evidence proved to be extremely useful in solving the case, but not in the way in which Mademoiselle Miri had thought. I'll return to this point later.

"He gives me credit for that one," Miri whispered to Vanessa.

"Because it was erroneous," she smiled.

"Monsieur Pierre Poivriere consistently denied any acquaintance with Mademoiselle Werner. When confronted with the statement of the *bonne* that he had departed at a much later hour than he had originally stated, he readily admitted it, and furthermore admitted to his presence on the sixth floor on the fateful night. But he vehemently denied any contact with the victim or any knowledge of the tragic events.

"If it was not Monsieur Giardini whom Madame Fleuris had seen that evening and if it was not Monsieur Poivriere, then who was it whom Madame Fleuris had seen? Had she in fact seen anyone at all? I'll return to that intriguing question.

"If Monsieur Pierre Poivriere was not in a liaison with Mademoiselle Werner then who was the Pierre who had sent Mademoiselle Emilie Werner the *pneumatique* signed with the name Pierre?

"The salutation of the letter, 'my dear Mitsou' was clearly a pet-name. 'Mitsou', in fact, I might mention for the benefit of those of you possibly not as familiar with French literature as one might like, is the title of a splendid literary gem by our revered genius Colette. 'Mitsou' is the pet-name given a little dancer by her protector, a gentleman whose name in the novel is – Pierre!

"It was reported by the *bonne* Gabrielle, who had had conversations with the victim, that Colette was a favorite author. Indeed, the victim had even named her pet-cat 'Mitsou', so clearly the particular book was known to her."

Miri whispered to Seymour, "All that was from ideas Vanessa and I had..."

He squeezed her hand and said softly, "What's the difference? It's not important. Don't get upset over nothing. I love you. Now *that's* important."

Miri was stunned and missed some of what Dantan was saying. Seymour had said he loved her! In actual words! She had to figure out what she thought about that.

"If this inference was valid," Dantan went on, "it threw the identity of the lover back into the black pool. The identity of the lover, however, was only important if he were the killer!

"When my dear Judy – " here he looked soulfully into her eyes and gave her a squeeze – "was entertaining me with her chatter one recent evening, a little item designed to amuse me was that her intellectual philosopher artist friend here, Mademoiselle Miri Winter, had convinced herself that she had cured her nose-cold by willing it away. A humorous commentary on the young American girl's interpretation of existentialism.

"Judy observed that Miri had exhibited all the signs of someone with an allergy, probably to Gabrielle's cat 'Mitsou'. The cat, be it noted, that had been the property of the poor little Werner until she was killed. Madame Poivriere, who has a dog, did not wish to adopt the little creature, but allowed her *bonne* Gabrielle to keep the cat. When Judy and Miri called on Gabrielle in her room, and the cat entered, the previously 'cured' Miri began sneezing and choking again. Her symptoms disappeared miraculously when she and the cat parted.

"Thus Judy inferred that Miri was suffering from an allergy, rather than a cold. If this inference was correct, then what had provoked Miri's symptoms on the morning after the murder? I had assisted at the first interviews of the four Americans and had noticed Mademoiselle Miri at the time to be suffering greatly from a cold of the nose, sneezing and coughing. At the time this was of no significance relative to the case whatever.

"Now, however, that I already had reason to think that the theory of lover as killer was a false trail, Mademoiselle Winter's intermittent symptoms provoked me to wonder if Miriam Winter had herself entered the room of Emilie Werner and killed her?"

Miri was shocked to think that Dantan could have thought she was capable of such a thing!

"Mademoiselle Werner's cat might very well have been in her room at the time of the murder and could have caused Miri's allergic reaction.

"On the other hand, Mademoiselle Miri need not have been present in Emilie Werner's room to have suffered the effects of the presence of a cat in that room, if something had been introduced into her own room and left there, which bore enough of the cat hairs to cause the reaction.

"An item had been introduced into Mademoiselle Miri's room on the evening of Emilie Werner's murder. The blanket which Madame Fleuris placed on Miri's bed. If Madame Fleuris bearing the blanket had entered Emilie Werner's room first, and had remained there long enough for the blanket to have become contaminated by the cat's hairs, and had then transported the blanket to Miri's room, where she slept with it pulled up about her face all the night...

"As soon as this hypothesis occurred to me I verified with Mademoiselle Miri that her supposed cold had indeed only begun during the night when the blanket had first been placed on her bed, and then with Inspector Goulette's blessing to pursue my own line of investigation and to utilize the services of the crime laboratory, although the inspector was still pursuing the possibility that Pierre Poivriere was indeed the killer, I had the blanket removed from Mademoiselle Winter's room. It has been examined at the forensic laboratory for foreign substances including animal hairs. Hairs of a cat – the same cat, by the way, which had belonged to the victim, and which paid its fateful visit as Judy and Miri were in the room – were found in abundance on the blanket from Miri's room!

"Rather than seeing anyone else emerge from the victim's room that fateful night, Madame Fleuris herself had done so. She watched by the window overlooking the courtyard as first Mademoiselle Winter departed, then Monsieur Giardini, and knowing that Gabrielle was working in Madame Poivriere's apartment, she made her move. The timing of the murder would be so close to the time the concierge would see Monsieur Jamie leaving the building that he would have no alibi.

"A weak alibi might have been given by whomever he might be meeting, by confusing times. But Madame Fleuris was in luck, since Monsieur Giardini was unwilling to involve the person he had met upon leaving Rue des Ecoles.

"But what possible motive could Madame Fleuris have for killing that poor girl? The answer was in a report, unsubstantiated it is true, that an unidentified witness had observed Madame Fleuris' son-in-law in a restaurant behaving amorously with the victim some time before she moved to Rue des Ecoles. This unamed witness claimed to have informed Madame Fleuris back in November of what he saw, then two months later, upon his return to Paris, he learned of the girl's murder, and through an intermediary, to preserve his own anonymity, reported what he had seen, as possibly relevant to the murder.

"I made the supposition that this did occur. From my personal little informant – " a fatuous grin appeared on cue on Judy's round face – "I knew that Madame Fleuris viewed her forty-three years of marriage as unmitigated misery owing to the infidelity of her husband. Suppose that Madame Fleuris saw in her son-in-law's infidelity a forecast of the same lifelong misery for her daughter which she herself had been suffering, and decided to put an abrupt end to it?"

Dantan stopped to savor another long slow sip of wine. "When I began to formulate my new hypothesis with Madame Fleuris as its centerpiece, I obtained the two handwriting examples from which Mademoiselle Miri had drawn the inference that Madame Fleuris was protecting her friend Madame Poivriere because of their resemblance. One was a notice in the w.c. at the Fleuris apartment written in Madame Fleuris' hand.

"The other was a room-for-rent notice on the form used by the student housing bureau found among the possessions of the dead girl, which represented for rent the *chambre de bonne* owned by Madame Poivriere.

"The police graphology expert examined the two notes. He concluded not that the handwritings were similar but that they were *identical.* Both notes were produced by the same hand. Madame Fleuris'.

"If the handwritings were indeed identical then this was a good working hypothesis. But how had Madame Fleuris gotten the notice into the hands of her prospective victim and persuaded her to rent the room?

"Once Inspector Goulette gave heed to my discoveries and theory, he agreed to subject Monsieur Philippe Jumelle, among others, to more intensive questioning than had occurred in the early states of the investigation, before his acquaintance with the victim was even suspected.

"Philippe Jumelle had gone on holiday with his family over the Christmas and New Years period. When he returned and attempted to contact his little *amie* at the hotel in Pigalle where she was residing, he was horrified to learn that she had relocated to the very building where his in-laws had their apartment, where his own wife had been born and raised!

"He contacted Mademoiselle Werner by *pneumatique*, addressing her as 'Mitsou' and signing the *pneu* as 'Pierre', requesting that she meet him at their usual restaurant in Pigalle. At that time he learned from her that she had found the room-for-rent notice right on the counter where she worked at the Galeries Lafayette. The wording was enticing – the room was very private, and in a student neighborhood superior to where she was living. and it was priced extremely cheaply. Not only that, but she had a personal tie to the address. For it was the very building where she had lived as a child with her parents. Finding the notice right on her own counter, where she assumed some student had lost it, seemed like a message from heaven. She sought out the owner and rented the room.

"Madame Fleuris knew that Madame Poivriere earlier in the year had registered the room at the student housing bureau, but had been unsuccessful in letting it, perhaps because she was unwilling to provide bathing facilities or food. Madame Fleuris simply reproduced in her own hand a room-for-rent notice on a student housing bureau form, of which she was well supplied, and dropped it on the counter at Galeries Lafayette where Emilie Werner worked. If this had not lured the girl, no doubt she had other tricks to try.

"Emilie Werner was tempted by the terms. She applied to Madame Poivriere for the room and moved in during the Christmas holidays, while her lover was away with his family visiting his parents in the Midi. Madame Poivriere was indeed surprised that a potential tenant had appeared on her doorstep so many months after she had listed the room and had forgotten about it well after the school term had begun and no applicant for tenancy had appeared.

"Imagine Philippe Jumelle's consternation upon his return to learn that his lover had moved into his mother-in-law's building! Poor fellow. He didn't dare visit her there, he was too well known by all the servants and tenants and concierge to make one false move. So he sent his beloved a *pneu*, requesting a rendez-vous at their habitual restaurant in another quartier. Unfortunately he chose to sign this pneu with Emilie's pet-name for him, 'Pierre', after a character in a favorite book of hers, and this misled us temporarily into believing that someone named Pierre was implicated.

"In any case, at the rendez-vous he told her the immense *gaffe* she had made in moving into his mother-in-law's building. He insisted that she move out.

"Before she was able to do so, her life was brutally taken from her. This crime was planned carefully and efficiently executed.

"Philippe Jumelle, to be sure, might very well have suspected his mother-in-law of the murder from the moment he learned of it, and perhaps one of these days he would have assisted us in our investigations... But to this day he maintains he never suspected her of this heinous crime.

"There is one aspect to this case which I merely touched on without elaboration, and that relates to the anonymous informant whose information first led me to think of someone in the Fleuris household as the culprit. His story was brought to me by the person he contacted—"

Miri studiously put her head down and stared at the gilt-trimmed plate before her to avoid catching Jamie's eye, as she had never told him about Tobey Peters' call to summon her to a meeting at which he gave her what was to be information incriminating Madame Fleuris.

" – without telling me his name, at his urging. Therefore, days later when a young American named Tobey Peters, only twenty-three years old, was found dead in his rented house in Neuilly, neither I nor Chief Inspector Goulette had any reason to connect him with the crime on Rue des Ecoles. The doctor who was called to the scene by the friend who found him could not identify the cause of death, would not sign a certificate of death, and an autopsy was performed. The young man had been poisoned."

Jamie had put his elbows on the table, his face in his hands.

"This case might well have remained open in our files indefinitely, but when the informant who first brought me Tobey Peters' information, anonymously, learned of his death, and told a friend, this friend realized that there might be a connection between Tobey Peters' death and what he had seen. This individual came to me with the fact that the Tobey Peters who had died suspiciously was the same individual who had anonymously provided information leading to the solution of the Werner case."

Miri whispered to Seymour that she knew all about this and would tell him later. He nodded absently. She wasn't sure how much attention he was paying to Dantan's monologue. He looked more interested in getting some food, he kept looking around for a waiter, saying, "*manger, manger*," to the waiter who was continually refilling the wine glasses and responding to Seymour with nods and fatuous smiles.

"This same informant was able to tell me that Madame Fleuris and Tobey Peters always had a rendez-vous for tea at Rumpelmayers monthly when Monsieur Peters was in town. Tobey Peters had died the night of the twenty-sixth of January. Questioning of Rumpelmayers staff produced witnesses who had indeed observed the victim with Madame Fleuris, and one who remembered seeing them together – he had thought they were mother and son – on a previous occasion, perhaps two months before.

"The same opiate which had sedated Emilie Werner the night she was murdered by strangulation, was the one found to have been ingested in larger quantity, by Tobey Peters. Confronted with this Madame Fleuris confessed that she had placed it in his Pernod.

"By solving not only the murder case to which I had been assigned as a mere interpreter, but another which might have remained unsolved forever but for a combination of fortunate connections and my own logical analysis, I hope to be rewarded by the Police Judiciare with a post of my dreams!"

Alphonse Dantan received a round of applause from all for this recital, a kiss on the mouth from Judy, and a handshake from Mister Kugel.

As for Miri she felt like a fool. She had seen everything and understood nothing!

A waiter on the sidelines sensed his cue, and now flourished huge magenta menus with gold tassels at each of the men. (The women were supposed to eat what the men selected for them.) But Seymour and Miri put their heads together over one menu, so that she could make sure he did not inadvertently order snails, frogs legs, rabbit or anything whose identity wasn't clear to her. They ended up with the lowbrow choice, Chateaubriand and *pommes frites*, the one concession on the menu to culinarily illiterate Americans.

Many toasts were offered to the engaged couple, and the laughter rose higher to the crystal chandeliers as the quaffing continued.

Dantan and Judy fed each other, Bran could not persuade Vanessa to play with their food likewise, Jamie drank a large quantity of wine, the Kugels tried everything the waiter suggested even though Judy tried to tell them what each item was, while Seymour and Miri dug into their meat and potatoes like culinary philistines. They were the only ones not sick the next day.

30

The next morning when Miri went down to breakfast she found Seymour waiting in one of the guest salons. He gave her a big hug, then said he had bad news. He had to leave Paris with his captain on a special assignment in Washington. "I'll write as soon as I can. I don't know how long I'll be away."

""You're not in any trouble, are you?"

He laughed. "No. I'm going along to help solve somebody else's problem. I only hope they don't give me a promotion for it, they might try to keep me in the service longer! I'll write as soon as I can." Another hug, and he was gone.

Miri moped around Reid Hall all day, not even pretending to try to paint or read.

There would be no more *déjeuners* at *pension* Fleuris – there was in effect no more *pension* Fleuris – and everyone she knew was busy without her.

Judy and her mother were dashing from one boutique to another stocking up on the needs of a new bride. Vanessa was painting up a storm at the Beaux Arts. It was too much to expect Bethel Washton to spend any time talking to her as Bethel's time was fully booked, although she had said "Hi there!" in the dining-room at breakfast. Even Renee had ceased importuning her. And Jamie was buzzing around happily on interviews and apartment-hunting. But in the late afternoon he phoned Miri, inviting himself to tea at Reid Hall.

They were served in the same guest salon where Judy and Alphonse had announced their engagement to her the morning she had thought he wanted to ask her for a date.

Jamie was carrying a large parcel wrapped in newspapers, and tied up in string, which he placed beside his chair.

Although Jamie seemed genuinely glad to see her, and was prepared to spend a leisurely hour or two gossiping, he was principally there to remind her that she might be visited by military officers checking up on him for a potential position. She was to let on that she was his girlfriend.

"I've already agreed to do so, " Miri said impatiently. "As long as you don't expect me to say we're sleeping together or anything like that." She thought wryly of the night she had crawled into his bed thinking they would sleep together.

He assured her that would not be required. He just didn't want them to know that he preferred men. "They may not even bother you," he said. "In my latest interview what they seemed most worked up about was possible connections with Communism. One of the officers interviewing me was suspicious of the fact that I'm taking Russian lessons! I think I finally managed to convince them I don't have Communist sympathies, merely that I want to be a professional linguist. I pointed out that I'm already fluent in Italian, getting on in French, and Russian would be useful too. They also asked me if I knew any Communists, but of course I don't."

Miri was fervently thankful that neither she nor Vanessa had ever breathed a word about Branford Duane Lee the Third's "interests"! Ignorance was truly bliss.

Jamie then handed her the large parcel that he had brought. "For you, from Germaine."

Miri opened it with intense curiosity. Out tumbled out a large quantity of old sheets, including those that had gotten burned the night she had the fire in her room.

"Germaine remembered that you were always complaining about not having enough painting-rags!" Jamie grinned. "Besides your burned sheets she's included other old sheets with rips which Madame Fleuris had wanted mended."

There were so many old sheets Miri would be able to give Vanessa a pile of rags too. Vanessa had been doing a prodigious amount of painting, all of it great. She had always been productive but since beginning this affair with Branford Duane Lee the Third she was really going wild.

Jamie brought Miri up-to-date on Fleuris gossip.

Monsieur Fleuris had adjusted quickly to the absence of his wife. He had moved his mistress of a lifetime into the apartment. "She's a *modiste*, "Jamie reported, "and her cutting-table and head-dummies and felts and threads and scissors and feathers and veilings have been moved into the two rooms which Judy and her clothing had occupied."

Monsieur Fleuris was keeping as his bakery the room off the foyer which they had snuck into once, and he was planning to expand it into the regular kitchen besides.

Lucille Jumelle had told the remaining *pensionnaires*, Bran and Jamie, that they could stay on in their rooms, at no charge, until they could find other accommodations, up to a month, but no *déjeuners* would be served. Only *petit déjeuner* for which there would be a charge of two hundred francs. Germaine would prepare and serve it. So far Bran had not partaken once.

Madame Jumelle had wanted her father to come to live with her and her family. But he had set himself up well.

Jamie and Miri exclaimed yet again how incredible it was that Madame Fleuris could have done such a thing.

"I just thought she was a mean bitch because she complained about her husband to strangers and hated Americans and charged for extra baths. But she has killed two people! How could she be so evil?"

"And she'll have to live with that knowledge the rest of her days. She had acted so self-righteous, as if she believed herself more moral than anyone. Now she will have to face the fact that she is worse." And with that, Jamie was off.

Judy called her the following day. Miri was strangely happy to hear from her.

Judy invited her to lunch at a luxurious place near the Faubourg St Honoré where she had been shopping.

They ordered salads. Judy's digestive system was still recovering from the *haute cuisine* of a few evenings before. Her booty of that morning was strewn on the tile floor all around them, in gorgeous shopping-bags with thick rope handles.

Judy wanted to display her finds, but this was of no interest whatever to Miri, although she did covet a shopping-bag.

"I have something fo you," Judy said, rooting around in one of the bags, withdrawing from it another bag which she handed to Miri. In it was the Chinese robe. "I want you to have it. A farewell-gift. Not because that Negro wore it, I really don't care about that, they have good dry-cleaners back in the States, but because it was an inspiration to you."

"But now that I've painted it I'm through with it."

"Well anyway, Miri, I want to buy the painting!"

"I can't part with it yet. First I need to figure out what I did right."

"You didn't even ask how much I would pay for it."

"That's because the price is irrelevant. I'm not Gabrielle. I just don't want to sell it right now."

"No matter how much I offer?"

"No matter."

"Maybe later on?"

Miri shrugged. "Maybe."

"Miri, I have a favor to ask of you. Keep an eye on Alphie while I'm back in the States, to keep him from straying."

Miri broke out laughing. "That is beyond even my formidable abilities! Unless of course," she added sardonically, "you want me to have an affair with him myself!"

Judy was especially worried now that Alphonse was an even better catch than before. He was being promoted to inspector for having solved both the Werner and the Peters cases.

"You know, Miri, I wanted you to be one of my bridesmaids. But my mother said no. I hope you don't mind much."

"I don't mind at all," Miri said huffily. She knew very well from having overheard her in her hotel-room the other day what Mrs Kugel thought of her.

Judy went on to detail just who each of the seven bridesmaids and one matron of honor were to be. The matron of honor of course would be her brother Ellis' wife.

"Germaine is staying on with Monsieur Fleuris and his mistress for awhile, but she has promised me that once I become Madame Dantan and my household is set up she will come to work for me."

"Even if you move to Great Neck, Long Island?"

"I'm assuming my Daddy will give me and Alphie a house or an apartment in Paris. Listen, Miri, I told my parents about Seymour having to take off suddenly for Washington. My Daddy had some advice for him for you to pass along."

Miri listened glumly.

"My Daddy said that Seymour's captain is probably a WASP and not as smart as Seymour and must have taken him along to meetings in Washington to give the captain the answers to the questions they want to ask him that he doesn't know the answers to. He said to tell Seymour to be careful not to get into trouble for being so smart. After he helps them somebody might hate him for being smarter than they are."

Miri asked anxiously, "He really thinks that?"

Judy laughed. "Cheer up! If Seymour's so smart he'll think of all that himself!"

They doggedly picked at their salads supplementing it with ample hunks of crispy bread. "One more thing, then I've got to dash to meet my mother. I've arranged for some of us to have *petit déjeuner* together day after tomorrow at the Fleuris place. It's important. Please be there." She handed a wad of bills to a waiter who had been hovering, he made change on the spot from the front pocket of his apron, she scooped up her shopping-bags and dashed off.

Back in her room Miri wrote down what Judy had said her father had advised Seymour, in case she wanted to put it in a letter to him, in case he wrote to her from Washington.

Miri sat with Vanessa and Bethel at *diner* that evening. Vanessa was still having a great affair with Bran and dashed off immediately after eating. Bethel coolly announced a major move she was making.

Bethel Washton had suddenly given up her Comédie

Française aspirations and she would be leaving very soon for the States! She had met some bigshot from Hollywood at a drama social event and he wanted her to star in a movie. Bethel was skeptical at first tthat Americans would want to go to a movie with a Negro star, but he persuaded her that (1) Lena Horne is big box-office, (2) Bethel has class, like Lena Horne, and (3) there are plenty of Negros in the U.S.A. who would go to the movies in droves to see her who don't go now.

Miri was astounded that Bethel was able to forswear her life's goal so easily for what sounded suspiciously like money, but didn't like saying so, and merely wished Bethel all the best of luck, then hated herself for becoming more and more of a bourgeois hypocrite by the day. If she didn't watch out she would become "nice" enough to qualify as one of Judy Kugel's bridesmaids!

On the appointed morning Miri went over to Rue des Ecoles.

At Judy's invitation (she was paying the two hundred francs per person Madame Jumelle was charging per *petit déjeuner*) Jamie, Miri, Renee Rubin and Alphonse Dantan, in addition to Judy herself, were seated around the table. Absent were Madame Fleuris, who was in jail, and Monsieur Fleuris who had discreetly removed himself and his mistress for breakfast at a neighborhood café.

Germaine was clearly pleased to see them all; her crusty face crackled into smiles at each arrival.

There was a mood of high excitement; Jamie had been accepted to the post he had wanted, and Renee was bursting with anticipation because later that morning two police officers would be coming along to force open the padlocked room.

After inspecting the room's contents for any official documents that might be needed for government archives, the police officers would have disposed of the rest of the contents of the room. But Dantan, knowing that Judy and a couple of her friends were eager to see the stuff, made sure that the girls would be there when the room was opened. The girls would be allowed to rummage through things to keep what they wanted before the room was emptied out.

Judy had alerted Renee Rubin ahead of time. Renee had brought with her two large valises, in ecstasy at the prospect of getting what she referred to as "documentary evidence". In fact, once the police opened the room to the girls and she was allowed to rummage, she rapaciously grabbed all the papers and books in the room, which was a mess, letters, receipts, diaries, ledgers, children's school notebooks... When her valises were full but there was still booty to take, Renee moaned with frustration until Judy got the idea of persuading Germaine to provide pilllow-cases, so that Renee could take everything she wanted.

Miri had become mesmerized by the photographs; photographs in velvet-covered albums, photographs in silver frames, photographs in frayed envelopes... She had seized these while Renee was grabbing papers, put them in a pillow-case, and sat on it to prevent Renee from getting her hands on any.

There might have been a physical tussle, but Judy intervened. "I respect your project," she told Renee, "and I promise you you'lll get some of the photographs eventually, after Miri and I pick out what we want to keep." Since it was her fiancé who had gained them access, Judy firmly asserted the role of de facto boss.

Renee at last resigned herself to the overflowing valises and pillowcases, and accepted help from Jamie in taking them down the staircase to a taxi.

Judy was surprised that there had been no clothing at all in the room, as obviously the members of the family had not been permitted to take any with them.

Dantan, who had been silently and discreetly observing from the doorway, said quietly that clothing was a scarce commodity during the war; the women who had raided the Maisel apartment had either taken the clothing for their own use or had sold it to a second-hand dealer who would pay dearly for it and charge more dearly on the resale.

The thought that clothing could become scarce clearly seemed to startle Judy.

Judy and Miri decided to carry the photographs to Miri's room at Reid Hall to examine them more closely. Miri slung the pillowcase full of photographs over her shoulder, trudged down the five flights of stairs, and she and Judy clambered into a taxi to take them to Reid Hall.

They spread the photographs out all over the floor of Miri's large room, attempting to place the loose ones in chronological order along with the albums, whose pictures were titled with names, places and dates in white ink on the black paper.

Poring over the pictures, Miri suddenly began sobbing uncontrollably. Judy began sobbing too.

The members of the Maisel family looked so real, it was hard to believe they must all be dead. There were pictures from over the years, not only of the parents and the boy and Berthe, from infancy to ten or twelve, there were others, maybe cousins, on streets in Paris, in the country, and at a beach, the children squinking into the sun.

The Maisel parents would have been Judy's parents' age now if they had lived. In their wedding picture, framed in a silver frame, they looked young and happy.

What upset Miri most were pictures of Berthe Maisel. They began in infancy, in her mother's arms, and stopped at around eleven years old. Her resemblance to what Miri thought she herself had looked like as a child was eerie. They could have been pictures of Miri except that she never wore lace-trimmed dresses. She couldn't stop staring at them.

Berthe's parents were dead; murdered, just because they had been Jews; French Jews. It hadn't mattered that they might be good people, and loved their children. Nothing about them as people had mattered. Miri remembered what Renee had said to her on the *Liberté*, when they first met, and Miri had said she didn't believe in God or religion. "It doesn't matter whether or not you are a believer, if you're a Jew they don't care, they'll come for you anyway."

Renee had been right. That was what had happened to Monsieur and Madame Maisel. And their children.

Miri now understood that she herself was one of those

who might be come for, and always would be, no matter what she thought her philosophy was. It was as immutable as the color of her brown eyes.

Judy tried to hug her. Miri could not hug back. She was overwhelmed by how she felt, by allowing herself to cry.

A great angry resolve erupted from somewhere within her. She would paint these people, not tuck their pictures into some drawer, some oblivion. She starting sorting pictures all over her bed, thinking of them as elements in some painting.

And she would have to get the newspaper pictures of Emilie Werner. She asked Judy to ask Alphie for a print of Emilie's *carte d'identité*. She thanked Judy for all she had done.

Judy, subdued, tried again to hug her before going back to her mother's hotel.

Renee called Miri up the next day. Renee was highly excited. She was going to write a book about the Maisels! The papers she had collected from the storeroom documented their life as it had been in the everyday, while they were allowed to live it. Renee would write about that and to it she would add what she had learned had happened to them, and what she would learn as she did more research.

She reiterated a demand for the photographs. Miri reiterated a promise to let her have some soon.

The next day Miri received a letter from Seymour. His return address was an A.P.O.

Although she reassured herself that she did not miss him, after a long hot soak in the bath she sat up late the same night, composing her reply.

"Dear Seymour" (Miri wrote):

"Your airplane ride sounded funny, but I can't believe that it was, being jolted around and bounced up and down in the air like that for almost twenty-four hours. Whenever I have to cross the Atlantic I'll stick to the *Liberté* or some other ship, which only rocks from side to side and can be fun if you're on the dance-floor on one side and suddenly slide with your partner to the other. That's what happened when I came over. A lot of passengers were seasick most of the time and quite a few broke arms and legs and the food kept sliding off the tables into people's laps, but other than that it was an enjoyable passage. And there wasn't the threat that it might fall out of the sky."

She next passed along Mister Kugel's advice. "That's what Mr. Kugel said, anyway. I don't know, but I wouldn't want you to get into any trouble.

"Lots of things have happened since you left but the biggest is that the police opened up the padlocked room where Madame Fleuris and Madame Poule had stashed belongings of the Maisels after they were taken away in 1942, and Judy and Renee and I were allowed in to take what we wanted. Judy and I took the family photographs. Renee grabbed everything else. She is going to write a book. I can't describe it. It makes me too sad. A whole family is recorded there, wiped out only because they were Jewish. I knew about all that happening before, of course. But it's different when you see one specific little girl, one specific mother, one specific little boy, one specific father.

"My stepmother in a fit one day had thrown out all the old photographs of my mother, and of me as a kid. Keeping pictures of the Maisels was a kind of substitute. I can't explain how sad it all made me. Usually I don't let things get to me that much but this all did.

"Everything else I have to write about is pretty dumb stuff, but I'm going to write it to you anyway, because I can't think of anything intellectual to say."Monsieur Fleuris has moved his mistress into the apartment. She is a *modiste* and Judy is having her design and make her bridal head-dress, even though she is going to get her gown made in Brooklyn.

"Judy said she wanted me as one of her eight bridesmaids but her mother didn't want me, for which I was very grateful. I have no desire to participate in a major bourgeois event of conspicuous consumption. I know Mrs Kugel doesn't like me, I overheard her telling Judy I wasn't like her other friends. To me this seems like a compliment!

"I also overheard her say you were a real *mensch* so she isn't a complete idiot -- only partial.

"Judy's mother is torn between buying out all of Paris and yanking Judy back to Great Neck quickly to rush the wedding plans before Mister Kugel puts his foot down. He is not happy about Alphonse Dantan as a son-in-law but has not yet forbid it. Judy thinks he knows she'll have hysterics if he does, and her father will do almost anything to avoid listening to Judy have hysterics. She doesn't do it very often. Saves it for big occasions. This would a big occasion.

"Mister Kugel is leaving very soon by airplane as he misses his business. Judy and her mother are still shopping up a storm and then they're going back on the Normandie. Too much luggage to go by airplane.

"Branford is still hoping that Vanessa will marry him and is looking for a really charming apartment with north light to lure her. I doubt if she will, though. Not because he's a Communist (he could outgrow that) but because if you don't have talent, you are never going to get it. She likes having an affair with him, though.

"Jamie got the job he wanted at NATO or UNESCO or whatever it was, where his officer friend works, and now the lieutenant or colonel or whatever he is had the perfect excuse to invite Jamie to share the new place he had just rented, a luxuriously furnished house on a tree-lined street in Neuilly. It had been Tobey Peters' place.

"Bethel Washton, you know, the one Negro girl in Reid Hall, I did a painting of in Judy's Chinese robe? She dropped a bombshell at *diner* last night. She has suddenly given up her Comédie Française aspirations, and is leaving for the States. She met some bigshot from Hollywood and he wants her to star in a movie. So much for high ideals.

"And speaking of the Chinese robe, Judy wanted to give it to me after all that. But I didn't accept it. I don't need it anymore.

"Then Judy said she wanted to buy the painting! I was more thrilled than I would admit, as no one has ever offered to pay money for one of my works before, although I have traded paintings with other students on the rare occasions I've seen any talent. But I told her I couldn't sell it to her, that I didn't want to part with it until I could understand what I had done that had made it good. I knew it was good,but I didn't yet know why.

"Maybe by the time Judy gets married, if the wedding actually does take place, I won't need it anymore and will give it to her as a wedding gift. But I didn't tell her that. I didn't want to commit to it out loud, in case I change my mind later.

"I'm working on a painting now crowded with costumed religious figures you see around Paris, awkward outfits you wonder why anyone would want to wear, or why anyone would revere more those that wear them than those that don't. At least that's part of it.

"You asked me if I wanted you to bring me anything from Washington? Not really. I would like are a jar of peanut butter and a box of Kleenexes but you could just wait until you get back to Paris and buy them in the PX. Thank you very much. – Love, Miri."

She almost didn't sign it "Love" as that might be too much of a commitment, but did so because it might slip by as what everyone wrote anyway.

She was going to write, "I hope you get back soon," but did not. He couldn't choose when to come back, the Army would, so what was the use.

In fact, she almost ditched the entire letter. What did he really care about Judy and Germaine and Jamie and Bethel and all that? But she couldn't think of anything intellectual to say. She did, however, add a P.S. "I'll be glad when you're back in Paris."

GLOSSARY

amant - lover
amie - girlfriend lover
arrondissement - district
au contraire - on the contrary
baiser (noun) - a kiss
baiser (verb) - make love (impolite)
beau - handsome
bis - again; another
boîte - night-club
bon dieu - good God
bonne - maid
buvez - drink (it)
carte d'identité - identity card
cave - underground bar
chambre - room
chambre à louer - room for rent
chambre de bonne - maid's room
charcuterie - pork-butcher
chauffage centrale - central heating
chez vous - at home
choucroute - sauerkraut
chou-chou - darling pet
comment dit-on en français - how do you say in French
convenable - seemly
coq au vin - chicken in wine
coup de foudre - lightning-bolt; love at first sight
cours de la civilisation française pour les étrangers - course in French
        civilisation for foreigners
crime passionnelle - crime of passion
croûte - pastry-crust
curé - country priest
dégoutant - disgusting
déjeuner - midday meal (big)
diner - evening meal
dommage; quel dommage - too bad
dot - dowry
du (partitive - a grammatical construct) some of...
eau qui fait pshssst - water that goes pshssst (Perrier)
emigré - immigrant
en français - in French
enfants - children
enrheumé - having a cold

épouvantable - appalling; ghastly; horrible
esprit d'escalier - afterthought
fait pire la puanteur - make the stink worse
famille - family
flic - (slang) cop
fou - crazy
frappez fort - knock hard
gaffe - goof
galette - kind of cookie
immeuble - apartment-building
insouciance - carefreeness
j'écoute - I'm listening
jeton - telephone-token
joie de vivre - joy of living
juge d'instruction - examining magistrate
livre jaune - "yellow-book" edition of literature published
        with yellow covers in the 30's
manger - eat
minutière - button turns hall-light on for one minute
modiste- milliner
noblesse oblige - nobility obligates
paillaisse - straw mattress
pauvre petit - poor little one
pension - place for room and board
petit déjeuner - small meal, i.e. breakfast
pneu; pneumatique
pneumatique - same-day-delivery letter
pour vous - for you
propre - proper
qu'importe - what does it matter
té complet - tea with goodies
vâche qui rit - cow who laughs (brand of cheese)
vernissage - art-opening
voisine - neighbor
vrai - real; true

première - first
deuxième - second
troisième - third
quatrième - fourtth
cinquième - fifth
sixième - sixth